LADY ON THE LOCH

Recent Titles by Betty McInnes from Severn House

ALL THE DAYS OF THEIR LIVES
MacDOUGAL'S LUCK
COLLAR OF PEARLS
THE BALFOUR TWINS
THE LONGEST JOURNEY
LADY ON THE LOCH

One

Lachlan Gilmore slowed the piebald mare from fast canter to easy trot. The slower pace was less painful on the young man's aching jaw and would carry him gently home through Fife to his mother's cosseting. Marjorie Gilmore had been sorely vexed by her son's severe toothache and would be pleased to hear that Lachie's troublesome molar would throb no more. It had been extracted that Thursday morning at Falkirk Tryst, a renowned Scottish cattle and horse-trading market. A barber surgeon had left Lachie's jaw as bruised and sore as if he'd taken a bout with a bruiser in the wrestling ring.

Yet the barber's fairground reputation had been sound. Others in line outside the booth boasting the sign of blood-red pole striped with bandage were loud in the man's praises.

'A couthie surgeon this one!' said the countryman waiting his turn before Lachie. 'He'll draw your molar, shear your hair, shave your beard and let your blood, all in the blink o' an ee to the benefit o' your health.'

'Next!' A voice roared.

The countryman had turned sickly pale. 'I see by the cut o' your cloth you're a man o' substance, young sir; be pleased to step afore me—'

And he grabbed Lachie and struggled him into the booth, assisted by many willing hands.

It had rained a deluge the night before after a spell of scorching June sunshine and Lachie found the going treacherous on the road home. As he approached Kinross village the chill air increased his suffering and he shivered. Ahead of horse and rider hazy mist drifted across the cold black surface of Loch Leven, obscuring the high square tower of Sir William Douglas's castle built on an island one mile from shore. Patchy mist had crept inland hiding the road but this did not deter the weary traveller. His horse knew every twist and turn of the road home to the farmstead at Goudiebank.

Checking the mare's pace with a touch to the flank, Lachie turned

off the well-beaten track to Loch Leven pier and headed up the
farm wynd.

Behind him swathes of rush and sedge skirted the loch's banks.
On Lachie's right the Gelly burn wound sluggishly through peaty
marsh to empty into the loch, but to the left the ground rose higher
to Goudiebank Farm's infields, outfields and the heathery heights
of hillside grazing rising far beyond. Hard-working Gilmores had
farmed this land for generations as loyal tenants of hot-tempered
Douglas lairds.

Usually at this point in a long homeward journey the promise
of a warm stable and thoughts of his ma's supper would spur Lachie
and his steed to a mad gallop for home, but this evening his injured
jaw throbbed and the mare slowed as if in sympathy.

A remarkable bond did indeed exist between horse and man.
Lachie's piebald mare had been his staunch companion these past
nine years. As a ten-year-old laddie, Lachie had pestered his pa
endlessly for a horse of his own. His father Wil Gilmore loved horses
and had a notable reputation for breeding the best but Wil had
already discerned that the young piebald mare was gelt – barren,
that is – and would never bear a foal. He gave her willingly to his
younger son to stop the constant girning.

Besides, the 'piety' horse would be sweer to sell at market. There
were powerful superstitions attached to her black and white hide,
perhaps because a man on a showy horse is an eye-catching target
on the battlefield.

But the mare's mystery and danger had appealed to young
Lachie. He named her Kelpie after faerie water-horses that frequent
lappie pools and devour unwary strangers and she had served him
devotedly from mischievous boyhood to bonny manhood.

Now it was a sudden falter in the horse's stride that alerted Lachie
to trouble ahead.

He heard strange sounds and raised voices mingled with the flap
and squawk of startled ducks. He reined in and went cautiously,
peering through mist.

'Curses on this foul place! Who but daft moonstruck folk would
bide here?' a woman was complaining loudly.

Coming closer, Lachie could see the problem. A cumbersome cart
lay tipped into the marsh at a hopeless angle. A man knee-deep in
glaur had succeeded in unharnessing a struggling carthorse from the
traces and he and two bedraggled females were attempting to drag
the poor floundering horse to firmer ground.

'The coffer, Hector! Where's the coffer?' the same woman was demanding frantically.

'Coffer be damned!' Lachie heard the hard-pressed man mutter under his breath then raise the tone soothingly. 'The box is securely bound, my lady. No harm'll come tae it.'

The quivering carthorse scrabbled its way on to the track just as Lachie appeared out of the mist. The sudden arrival of the piebald mare was the final horror in the poor animal's nervous nightmare. It reared up with a terrified whinny flinging both women unceremoniously sideways to land squelching in mud. While the man Hector battled with the plunging horse Lachie hastily dismounted and ran towards the nearest tangled bundle of cloak and gown.

'Are ye hurt?'

The hood was flung back and the woman sat up. 'Of course I'm hurt, you gowk! I'm bruised black and blue and my gown's torn and filthy!'

It was a furious, mud-spattered young face. He could not tell the colour of the lady's eyes but assumed they were as dark as her scowling brows. Lachie could not stop staring. This was possibly the bonniest lassie he had ever seen.

'Stop gawping and set me on my feet!' she ordered.

He took her muddy hands and pulled her upright. He would have lingered longer holding hands, but she put her fists on his chest and pushed him away.

'Go and see to my maid!'

Nettled by her tone, he went. He hoped the servant proved gentler than the mistress. Lachie edged cautiously past Hector, who was stroking the wild-eyed carthorse and murmuring in its flattened ear. He found the lady's maid scrambling to her feet. She was a mature woman, a good deal older than her young mistress.

'How's my lady?' she asked anxiously.

'Fine. All that's suffered is her temper.'

'I heard that!' the young lady cried, rushing past Hector and seriously compromising his work with the nervous horse. Ignoring Lachie, she hugged the maid.

'Dear Dorcas, you're not hurt, are ye? Och, I could weep to think of the lady forced tae live in this dreich place—'

'Wheest!' the servant Dorcas said. 'Remember this gentleman may have some – *affection* – for the district.'

It sounded remarkably like a warning and the young lady eyed Lachie warily. She decided charm might serve better and smiled sweetly. 'Och, sir, you'll excuse ill humour and take pity when ye hear we sailed frae Leith across the Forth and travelled through Fife on atrocious roads unsuited tae the wheel. We're destined for Falkland, only pausing at the pier to offload goods for Lochleven Castle. In the mist we took a wrong turn on to this evil track and a wheel slipped sideways into marsh. Such a stramash! What are we to do?'

The dark eyes were tearful lustrous brown and Lachie's heart softened. 'A team of oxen from my father's farm could pull the cart free come morning,' he volunteered.

The three strangers considered the offer in silence. The man Hector had made remarkable progress calming the carthorse and studied Lachie narrowly.

The lady spoke up doubtfully. 'That's most obliging, sir, but we canna stand here till morning.'

'My mother will welcome ye gladly at the farmhouse for the night, lady,' Lachie offered boldly, praying his ma would not faint at the sight of them. They still seemed reluctant to accept hospitality and he added reassuringly, 'It's not far off and there's plenty room.'

It was no idle boast. Goudiebank farmhouse was more spacious than most dwellings in that district, a fine stone-built house hinting at the occupants' higher status and boasting Fife's crow-step gables. A red pantiled roof gave evidence of the healthy trade in tiles with the Low Countries.

The Gilmores enjoyed the favour and patronage of their landlord Sir William Douglas, laird of Lochleven and owner of the island fortress. Sir William's horses were stabled at the farm cared for by Wil Gilmore and the laird's larder on Castle Island was replenished with milk, grain, meat and fruit from the farm's fertile acres.

But Lachie's father Wil Gilmore was not strictly speaking a farmer. Having trained as a stonemason in his native France, Wil left his homeland more than thirty years ago as a young journeyman, joining the team of skilled French craftsmen hired to work upon additions to Falkland Palace in Fife, Scotland.

The palace was used as a favourite hunting lodge for generations of Stewart kings, and Mary Queen of Scots' father James V wanted a new facade built in French Renaissance style to impress his French bride, Marie de Guise.

Wil was known as Gillaume de Saint-Gilais in those early days but as building work was completed he had the good fortune to meet Marjorie Gilmore, sole survivor of a farming family wiped out in a diphtheria epidemic. Marjorie was a bonny young spinster cursed with a crippled foot that had made Scottish suitors wary of further misfortunes. She was struggling to retain the farm tenancy all on her own when Gillaume seized his chance to woo and win her.

To the delight of his adoring bride the Frenchman agreed to assume the name 'Wil Gilmore' when they married. Thus the Gilmore succession was secured and the former Gillaume de Saint-Gilais well pleased with his bargain.

The young lady ended an awkward pause with a gracious nod. 'This is kindness beyond the call o' duty, sir, and we are pleased to accept your family's help and hospitality.' She eyed the piebald mare. 'But I'm so jaded I could drop. May I ride your bonny horse?'

Lachie hesitated doubtfully. 'We–ell . . .'

The mare did not take kindly to strangers. Besides, although his father had made the fine saddle from leather instead of the more customary sackcloth padded with whatever came to hand, there was no footrest and it was unsuitable for a lady riding side-saddle.

She blithely ignored reluctance. 'Oh, bless ye, sir! You are gallant!' She began issuing brisk orders. 'Dorcas, you have a winning way wi' animals so you will lead the poor carthorse. Hector, untie the coffer frae the cart and bring it.'

The man gave his mistress a horrified look. 'But – Lady Annabel – it would take a packhorse tae shift it – and the glaur—'

She checked the protest with a withering stare. 'It canna be left i' the bog for any thieving country clod tae lift!' She turned to Lachie. 'You will help Hector carry my goods, won't ye? The weight will be as a feather to a gentleman sae big and strong.'

He felt the pressure of a small hand on his arm and was lost.

The effort of wresting the heavy box from the cart was the ruination of Lachie's best doublet, hose and riding boots of which he had been proud. The two men cursed, slipped and slithered ankle-deep in mud, but at last brought the oak coffer to firmer ground and dumped it at my lady's feet.

She studied the two muddy heroes with a gleam of mischief in her dark eyes and then held out a hand for Lachie to kiss. 'I am Annabel Erskine, sir. I'm sorry I dinna have the pleasure o' your name.'

'Lachie Gilmore.'

He kissed the hand – so white he doubted if it had ever done a hard day's work. He found the thought depressing. 'I'm greatly indebted to ye, Mister Gilmore. If ye would kindly help me mount the bonny steed, you and Hector will take the lead and show the way.'

Kelpie rolled the white of an eye when Lachie approached with
the stranger. Lachie's breathing constricted as he contemplated the
intimate task ahead, but before he could lift a hand to help, Lady
Annabel had swung a leg over the mare's back in a flurry of gown
and petticoat and was seated comfortably astride.

The lady's maid uttered a long-suffering sigh. 'Och, my lady, think
shame!'

'Necessity knows no law, Dorcas!' the lady retorted merrily. She
gathered the reins in a masterful grip that obliged Kelpie to abandon
thoughts of rebellion and stand passive. 'Onwards!' she ordered,
digging in her heels.

The lady's maid took charge of the carthorse, the men grasped
a handle each of the coffer and the little procession set off along
the wynd.

At that moment the interior of Goudiebank farmhouse presented
a peaceful scene. The large stone-flagged kitchen and living area
occupied most of the house below stairs and remained comfortably
cool despite several days of blistering heat.

Evening was drawing in, cruisie lamps were lit, hanging at inter-
vals from iron brackets around the large room, and rush lights burning
in pools of tallow cast flickering light on stone walls. The smell of
singed grass and hot oil mingled with the scent of pine logs smouldering on a bed of Fife coal in the huge arched fireplace.

This magnificent fireplace was Marjorie Gilmore's pride and joy.
It boasted bread ovens, roasting spit and swinging iron brackets or
'swees' to hold pots or cauldrons large enough to cook a goose or
bath a baby.

That evening Marjorie sat with her depleted family on a bench
in the pool of light cast by candelabra at one end of the long trestle
table. She was busy writing – a rare and unusual accomplishment
for a countrywoman, learned as a wee lass at her grandfather's knee.
The old man had been taught to read and write at the chapel school
in Lindores Abbey before followers of the Reformed Kirk, urged
on by the fiery Edinburgh preacher John Knox, sacked the abbey
and banished the monks. Marjorie had made sure to pass on her
grandpa's invaluable gift to her own three clever sons and two bonny
daughters.

She was busy adding a new receipt to a prized recipe book
containing instructions for nearly every dish cooked in the Howe
of Fife – not to mention cures for most ailments known to man

and helpful hints for the beautification of women. This evening, with her suffering son Lachie in mind, Marjorie penned a potion for easing toothache.

Boil a quantity of clean running water and add to it red sage . . .

She paused a moment to watch her daughter at work. Eighteen-year-old Christina Gilmore was embroidering a bridal nightgown, another exquisite garment to add to the dear lassie's wedding kist in preparation for her marriage to Hugh Ross, one of Loch Leven's boatmen, a steady lad with sound prospects.

Marjorie often wondered where the lass's exceptional talent for needlework came from. Not frae the Gilmore side, that's for sure! Gilmore hands were broad, with strong fingers suited to working the land. Christina's long-fingered, slender hands were Wil's – along with her father's artistic ability, vivid imagination and impulsive disposition. To Marjorie's way of thinking it was an awkward legacy to bestow upon any country lass.

She dipped the quill in ink with a sigh and went back to writing:

. . . twelve branches fresh-picked rosemary, daisies of feverfew, a pinch each of cloves, cinnamon and . . .

Only to be interrupted by Francis, her youngest son. The precocious ten-year-old read anything and everything that came his way and this evening Francis was poring over the farm accounts his father kept for Sir William's perusal.

'If Pa sells the stallion and brood mare at Falkirk Tryst for the pound o' silver he wants, Christina will have a handsome dowry, Ma,' the boy remarked.

Marjorie looked up, smiling. 'There's a gulf between will you sell and will you buy, dearie. Dinna raise your sister's hopes too high.'

The clever wee laddie was Marjorie's greatest joy, his delicate health her greatest sorrow. At birth Francis Gilmore suffered the same deformity that had marred Marjorie's existence and the lad would limp on one crippled foot for the rest of his days. Some evil humour of heredity had made his birth difficult and landed its curse upon Marjorie's brightest boy.

However, should wee Francis survive he looked set for a glowing future. When collecting farm tithes Sir William Douglas had been impressed by the lad's precocious grasp of counting on the tally stick. Jokingly their landlord had promised Francis the position of comptroller of the Douglas household if the weakling should reach manhood.

Though the promise was made in jest, it bolstered Marjorie

Gilmore's determination to stay in Sir William's favour. The laird was reputed to be a man o' his word.

Christina put finishing touches to the nightgown and held up the fine garment for inspection. 'Finished, Ma. What d'ye think?'

'Any lady would be proud tae wear it, love!'

Candles flickered in a draught at that moment and they glanced towards the door.

Jamie Gilmore came in, hung his bonnet on a hook and kicked off farmyard clogs. Jamie was Marjorie and Wil's eldest son and in his mother's opinion the most surprising of their five offspring.

Jamie was a man of twenty-four years, dark-eyed and dark-haired, the very image of his French father. Going by looks alone one would expect the lad to inherit Wil's Gallic charm and artistic skill, but Jamie was a Gilmore to the fingertips. He was dedicated to working the land and thankful to be first in line to claim tenancy of the farm when the time came. Farming was more than a livelihood to Jamie Gilmore, it was a passion pulsing through his veins with his Gilmore blood,

Which was all very fine, his mother thought, but Jamie's obsession left no time for courting. It was high time her eldest son looked around for a suitable wife to secure the succession. Jamie's two younger brothers Lachlan and Francis, though dearly loved, were hardly likely to make successful farmers.

'Any sign of Lachie and your pa yet, Jamie?' she called.

'I thought I heard voices a wee while back, Ma, but it wasna them.' He padded across the room on stocking soles and sat on the bench with a smile for his sister.

'More arrivals at the castle I expect, Chrissie. Sir William gives your lad hard work at the oars these days.'

She laughed. 'Every trip brings our wedding day nearer. The laird has generous guests, Hugh says.'

Her sweetheart's elderly uncle Ebenezer Ross owned the Loch Leven boatyard that supplied the Douglas family with sturdy craft necessary for an island existence. Orphaned at an early age, Hugh served an apprenticeship with his uncle the boatbuilder and was now employed as a boatman. His uncle offered Hugh a share in the business on the understanding that Christina's dowry would provide the means, but any stray coins the laird's guests tossed in the boatman's direction were welcome.

Jamie drummed his fingers thoughtfully on the tabletop. The family took no part in the tangled web of marriages, plots, feuds and intrigues woven by Scottish nobility. For generations, Gilmores had worked the farmland and left warring to the lords. However, one could hardly ignore unusual activity on the loch.

'Does Hugh talk to ye about his passengers, Chrissie?' he asked tentatively.

She hesitated. 'He keeps a curb on his tongue. Sir William demands discretion.'

Marjorie gave her son a warning glance. 'It's a wise man that courts Sir William's favour, Jamie. You'd do well tae mind it.'

There was a murmur of voices and the stamp of feet on flagstones outside.

'That'll be your father and Lachie now,' Marjorie said with relief. Her husband was ower fond o' a tipple when let off the leash. She began issuing orders. 'Pile logs on the fire, Christina. They'll be cold and tired and poor Lachie half-demented wi' the toothache.'

Jamie tightened his lips. He'd grudged his younger brother a trip to Falkirk Tryst. Lachie's interest would not be in cattle and horses; he would have more frivolous fish to fry. But a responsible person must be in charge of the farm and past experience had taught him that his bonny brother made a feckless custodian.

There was a scuffle and commotion outside and the door was flung wide. Lachie staggered into the room red-faced and sweating, sharing the weight of a large kist with a powerfully built stranger. The two men dumped their burden thankfully on the flags and rubbed aching muscles.

'What's in the accursed box that's so precious, Hector, crown jewels?' Lachie demanded testily.

The stranger shrugged. 'Nah, only woman's gear.'

There was a clatter of restless hooves in the yard and a woman's plaintive cry. 'Am I to be abandoned without assistance?'

The men exchanged a look and the man called Hector sighed. 'Dinna fash. I'll see to her.'

He went out, leaving Lachie to face questions.

'Where's your father?' his mother demanded.

'Still in Falkirk. He met some old billies frae Glasgow at the Tryst. I left them blethering at the inn and came home early. A demon barber drew my tooth and near broke my jaw.'

Marjorie's motherly concern took over. 'Christina, fetch a measure o' wine to cleanse the poor lad's mouth. Francis, bring a bowl from the press, add tepid water and a wee pinch o' salt to rinse the wound. Jamie, delve into the medicine poke and find poppy seed and henbane for a compress tae dull the pain.'

That done and his siblings sent scurrying, she turned to Lachie. 'Did your father drive a good bargain, son?'

'Aye, he did. Lord Livingston offered a high price for both stallion and mare. Pa's stock ranks high wi' the nobility – and speaking o' nobility, Ma—'

Lachie glanced towards the doorway where the Lady Annabel Erskine had appeared as if on cue. The young man was relieved to note she was in modest mode and very sweet and bonny with it.

She flew across the room to her hostess. 'Dear Mistress Gilmore! Please forgive the intrusion but we have had such mishap on our travels – losing the pathway, capsizing the cart, the poor horse sunk tae the belly in bog, my servants and I wallowing in glaur and my gown ripped and filthy.' She turned to Lachie. 'If this brave gentleman hadna happened to pass by and bring us to your care I swear I would have caught my death wi' cold.'

He was impressed. The dramatic account far surpassed his abilities and produced instant sympathy.

His mother rose all in a flutter clasping the lady's cold hands and drawing her close to the fire. 'Sit yourself down here, dear lady. Lachie'll fetch the bellows and rouse the flame tae warm ye.'

No mention of *my* affliction now! he thought wryly.

Dorcas and Hector remained in the background. The manservant stepped forward. 'I'll stable the horses, if it pleases ye.'

Jamie answered. 'Come, I'll show the way.' He was glad of an excuse to escape. As head of the household in his father's absence Jamie was mortified to be found sweaty, work-stained and in stocking soles in presence of a lady. He gave the lady's maid a cursory glance in passing. She was an older woman, tall, skinny and plain, a person of little substance.

Christina found the unexpected visitors tremendously exciting. She eyed the young lady's travelling cloak and gown, gold chains and lacy trimmings with envy. Most of all she envied the white hands with shapely fingernails held out to the fire.

Christina took good care of her own hands since sewing was her greatest pleasure, but cows must be milked, crops gathered, clothes washed and floors scrubbed and there would be even less hope of white hands and unbroken nails when she married. Her older sister Janet's daily round as wife and mother was typical of the life Christina could expect. Janet was a trachled mother of three young bairns with another on the way but seemed happy enough and contented with her lot as wife of a Falkland weaver.

Plainly, Janet had inherited their mother's homemaking talent whereas Christina was so much their father's daughter it was unsettling. Often as she sat quietly sewing she crafted dreams of a life full of freedom and adventure. Would she ever abandon such far-fetched notions and become a contented wife and mother?

Of course she would!

For Christina believed in the power of love to bring change. Hugh was a childhood sweetheart; they had grown up together and it seemed inevitable they would fall in love and marry. A bright future was assured. He would have a share in his uncle's business and they would start married life in a bonny cottage. Surely that was a prospect that promised a good measure of contentment, Christina thought as she hung the lady's damp cloak up to dry.

Marjorie and the young lady were getting along as famously as smouldering heather on a windy hillside.

Marjorie discovered to her delight that Annabel Erskine was a distant relative of Lady Margaret Douglas, Sir William's widowed mother, the formidable dowager known locally as 'the auld lady of Castle Island'. Apart from Sir William's mother, his wife and young family there was also a younger unmarried brother living on Castle Island. George Douglas was a young gallant whose handsome good looks had earned him the title of 'bonny Geordie'.

Aye, Marjorie thought contentedly, Lachie had done the Gilmores a good turn bringing Annabel Erskine to the house. This kind deed was bound to find favour with the laird and his illustrious kin. It was common knowledge that because of the tangled skeins of royal relationships James Stewart, powerful Earl of Moray, was Sir William's half-brother. This came about as a result of Lady Margaret's youthful fling with the late King James V, Mary Queen of Scots' father.

The Earl was reputed to be stern, pious and politically cunning as befitted a king's son, but he had no legitimate claim to the Scottish throne despite being twenty-four-year-old Queen Mary's half-brother and uncle of her thirteen-month-old son James, the one precious heir to the Scottish throne.

Aye, Marjorie thought smugly, Lady Annabel's kinship could hardly be bettered!

She ordered Christina to prepare supper of bannocks, bread, butter and Goudiebank's famed cheese with mulled wine to warm the lady and her servants.

The coffer was left where Lachie and Hector dumped it, a finely

carved clothes kist such as a lady of quality would take on a visit
to a noble house. Marjorie eyed it speculatively. 'They say Sir William
entertains many guests on the island these days, my lady. Will you
be visiting the laird?'

The young lady shuddered. 'Heaven forbid!'

To Marjorie's surprise the lady's maid nudged her mistress in the
ribs, whereupon Annabel added hastily, 'No, Mistress Gilmore, George
Douglas has arranged for us to bide in Falkland Palace, which he
assures me is near by.'

Marjorie was impressed. Could bonny Geordie be courting Lady
Annabel? 'You must be well thought of tae bide there!' she remarked.

The lady was giving nothing away. She shrugged. 'Och, it's a
matter o' convenience for the castle folk. The island ladies need new
gear and that is *my* responsibility.' She nodded towards the lady's
maid. 'Dorcas is a skilled dressmaker fortunately.'

Christina arrived at that moment to remove the precious bridal
nightgown out of harm's way before serving supper.

Annabel stopped her 'Wait! Let me see that.' She examined the
fine needlework closely. 'This is wonderful work, as good as any I've
seen!' She looked up, smiling. 'Could ye mend the serious damage
done to my gown, do you think?'

'I'd be honoured to try, my lady.'

She laughed. 'Dinna be so sure! I'm ill tae please!'

'Maybe you pass time wi' embroidery yourself?' Christina ventured.

'No. I've little patience for it, though I do admire the skill.'

Jamie and Hector returned as food arrived on the table. They had
struck up a good rapport and Jamie was loud in the man's praise.
'This lad's a wonder wi' horses, Ma. I wish Pa could see him work.'

Marjorie was too preoccupied with nobility to pay heed to
servants' accomplishments. She seated the new arrivals and began
serving her guests. What a blessing Maggie the washer-lassie visited
the farm on Monday past! she thought.

It had been a fine warm day and the women had a washday spree,
beds stripped and clothes washed in soap provided by Maggie's
father, the Kinross soap maker. What fun and laughter there was that
hot summer day! The lassies kilted their skirts above the knee, standing
in tubs of hot soapy water to tramp dirt out o' bed sheets, semits,
sarks and breeks prior to rinsing in the burn's sparkling rush o' water
and spreading to dry on the greensward.

Marjorie was confident the lady could find no faults wi' bedding.
Even so, sleeping arrangements took a fair amount of sorting. The

fire was stoked high and the room festooned with the travellers' damp gear. Lady Annabel and her maid retired to Marjorie and Wil's bed and the manservant made do with a straw mattress on the kitchen floor with instructions from his mistress to guard the precious kist.

Marjorie shared Christina's bed and was soon asleep, but Christina sat up late burning a fair supply of candles mending a long jagged tear in the lady's dress. She sighed. Such fine material! The gown was deep blue and made Christina's linsey-woolsey dress seem drab, yet she'd been pleased enough with it before. Blaeberry dye tinted the dress a pale blue that suited Christina's blue eyes, fair hair and sun-kissed skin. Embroidery on bodice and sleeve had given the workaday dress a superior look but nothing near as fine as this. She sighed and went on with the task.

Lady Annabel was amazed when the gown was returned next morning. 'The stitches are so fine I canna find where it was torn. Clever lass!'

Christina smiled at the compliment. 'There's dried mud on the cloak, lady. I'll brush it for ye if you'll wait.'

'No time for that, thank ye. We must be on our way. I've an errand to make.'

'You say the clothes kist is bound for the island. Do Sir William's ladies keep abreast o' fashion at Queen Mary's court?' she asked.

'That's their concern,' Annabel answered curtly.

Christina felt rebuffed. Another wi' a curb on her tongue! she thought resentfully.

Meanwhile Jamie had yoked a team of oxen and started the lumbering beasts along the track. The foundered cart was pulled out of the bog nae bother, but Lachie made sure the coffer went on a sled with the team to be loaded on the wagon. His muscles still ached from yesterday, but his jaw felt better.

Lady Annabel ate a hearty breakfast and was profuse in her thanks as she prepared to leave. She kissed Marjorie's cheek. 'I'll never forget your kindness, Mistress Gilmore, nor will I forget Lachie's gallantry and Christina's needlework. Should they ever seek work let them come to me at Falkland.'

She turned to the lady's maid. 'There's a gold piece in my pouch. Give it to our hostess, Dorcas.'

Marjorie drew herself up, insulted. 'You affront the laws o' hospitality, my lady!'

Annabel apologized hastily. Country folk were notoriously prideful. 'Of course, dear Mistress Gilmore. It shall be as you wish.'

Lachie selected a smart little filly from his father's stable for the lady's ride to Falkland and furnished the horse with the finest bridle and side-saddle in the tack room. Such items were reserved for sale to nobility and his father would not be pleased but Lachie was unrepentant.

When Annabel was comfortably seated in the saddle she glanced down at the family assembled in the doorway, a gleam of mischief in her eye. 'I'll mak' sure Master Jamie accepts gold for stalwart work done wi' the oxen. Now *that's* lawful payment for a service, Mistress Gilmore.'

She laughed, clicked her tongue to the filly and moved off with the lady's maid walking at the horse's head. Hector followed leading the carthorse.

'And that's the last we'll see of *her!*' Christina declared.

'You think so? I believe the offer of help was genuine,' Lachie said.

'Well, I don't.'

Christina left him and went into the kitchen. There were dirty bowls, cups and platters strewn across the trestle waiting to be washed and she was in an ill humour.

Lachie lingered in the doorway gazing after the lady. How unattainable she seemed and how he longed to see her again!

Wil Gilmore returned home next day. Marjorie greeted her husband with a kiss and seated him in the carved chair reserved for his use. He looked weary. 'Och, you're worn out, Wil. I told ye to send Jamie to the Tryst and save yourself the long ride,' she scolded.

He sighed. 'This sale was too important, *cherie.*'

Little Francis settled himself on his father's knee. 'Did you make a good trade, Pa?'

'Aye son, but – I . . . I should have fared better.'

He sounded so downcast Christina knelt by the chair and took her father's hand. It trembled and felt cold.

'Dinna fash, Pa! My dowry will be more than enough to set Hugh up in his uncle's yard. You'll soon be dancing at my wedding.'

He gripped her hand so hard it hurt. 'Christina, dear child – you make it hard for me!'

She laughed, hoping to tease a smile from him. 'I know ye grudge your favourite daughter tae another man, but Hugh and I will live close by. You'll no' be rid of me yet!'

Marjorie watched her husband and anxiety crept in. Had the journey overtaxed his strength? She spoke sharply. 'Stop pestering your father. He's tired.'

Francis tumbled off his father's knee and Christina stood up, indignant. 'I only sought tae cheer him!'

'The only cheer he needs is rest, not wedding blethers.'

Christina was furious. 'That's why he journeyed to the Tryst. He knows how important the dowry is tae us!'

The two angry women were prepared for a shouting match and Wil Gilmore leaped to his feet so suddenly the chair toppled. 'Stop it! Be quiet! I cannot suffer more of this!'

The outburst was so out of character the women stared in astonishment and the room fell uneasily quiet. All that could be heard was a trapped bluebottle buzzing frantically at a shutter.

Wil passed a hand across his eyes and groaned. 'There is no dowry, Christina,' he admitted heavily. 'For you, I play at cards with my Glasgow friends to double what I had earned from the sale of the horses. At first I won but then luck deserted me. I lost every penny of your dowry, child, and my heart it is broken.'

She stared in disbelief. Christina adored her father but this betrayal was too cruel. She doubted if she could ever forgive him for ruining all hope of a bright future for Hugh and herself. No share in the boatyard now, no bonny cottage waiting when they wed, only a heather-thatched hovel and a grim struggle for existence on a boatman's meagre earnings.

She could hardly contain her bitter anger. 'You promise me a dowry the equal o' Janet's and gamble it away boozing in a Falkirk alehouse. Well hear this, Pa. When you turned over losing cards on the gaming table you lost more than my dowry, you lost my respect. That's a credit you'll never retrieve!'

Francis cowered in a corner and Marjorie wailed. 'Dear lassie, dinna be so cruel!'

'Why no'? He deserves it!'

Her father was close to tears. 'Chrissie, have pity—'

'Never pity for you! I'll save pity for the lad I'm to marry.' Whirling round, Christina ran to the doorway and snatched her old plaid shawl off the hook.

Her mother called out to her piteously. 'Christina, wait! Dinna be so rash. Where are ye bound?'

'Out o' this house, Ma!' she answered bitterly. 'I'd rather bide in Falkland wi' Janet.'

She cast her father a contemptuous look before the door slammed shut behind her.

Christina ran to the stables along a pathway blurred with tears. She found Lachie mucking out the stalls. He looked up and frowned when she rushed in.

'What's ado?'

She told him in a few terse words and her brother sighed dolefully.

'I blame myself, Chrissie. I should never have left him open to temptation in Falkirk.'

'It's not your duty tae guard him. He's a man o' straw, Lachie!' she said angrily. 'I'll bide with Janet till the kirk banns are read, then make a new life with Hugh.'

He frowned uneasily. 'Aye well – if that's what you want.'

This quarrel gave Lachie a bad feeling. It was the first break in family ties that had been strong.

He helped his sister saddle Muckle Meg for the ride to Falkland village. Lachie chose the old mare deliberately. She was a steady horse, the two front hooves shod with scarce iron to give grip on slippery tracks. He knew it was not wise to ride when angry and feared for his sister's safety.

'Christina, if ye should see Lady Annabel—'

She looked down at him from the horse's back. 'What shall I tell her?'

'Say I'll gladly be of service should she need me.'

'More fool you!' she mocked and urged Muckle Meg into a trot.

Christina reined in the mare and waited when they reached Loch Leven pier. Hugh Ross's boat was close to shore ferrying a load of washerwomen back from the island. Hugh leaned on the oars and waved and Christina's heart lurched heavily. She dreaded telling him the awful news but better it was done now and make plans to face the future together.

She tethered the horse to the rail and walked along the pier to meet them.

The washerwomen were already disembarking, Maggie the washer-lassie among them. The women stood whispering in a huddle at the pier's end, their behaviour unusually subdued. Hugh was in high spirits, securing the ropes and shooing the women on their way. They scuttled past Christina with lowered eyes.

'What's put the fear o' death in your hardy crew?' she asked curiously.

'A warning frae the laird that was long overdue, promising dire penalties for gossip. You ken what blethers washerwomen are!'

He laughed and kissed her. 'So your father's back and the horses sold, my sweet! I saw him head home along the wynd a wee while back. We'll see the session clerk tomorrow. When the minister announces marriage banns on the Sabbath I'll arrange wi' my uncle to—'

She laid a hand on his arm in distress and interrupted hurriedly. 'Hugh – wait – please listen!'

Choked with tears, she blurted out the terrible news.

It was the worst moment of her life. His despair and disappointment were heartbreaking. She kissed him. 'Dinna despair, my dearest. I've left home and will bide wi' Janet in Falkland. We can be married from there.'

He sighed heavily. 'No, Christina! I'll not marry till my prospects improve!'

'But that could take time!' she said, dismayed. 'Why not make the best o' misfortune? I could make a living sewing for women and bairns.'

'I'll not have my wife working fingers tae the bone to keep thatch on a hovel,' he declared stubbornly.

She stepped back, bitterly hurt and angry. 'It's true what they say – a lassie lacking a dowry languishes long on the shelf! I thought it was me you wanted, Hugh Ross, but it's plain you only sought my dowry for your ain ends!'

'Dear lass, that's not true!'

He would have taken her in his arms but Christina was in no mood to listen to smooth talk. She was already running to loosen the horse's tether. Mounting quickly she dug a heel into Muckle Meg's flank and sent the startled mare off at a canter.

Out of his sight, Christina wept desolately, a fair measure of her humiliation for she was not a woman that wept easily. Two men she loved had failed her that day. No wonder Christina Gilmore wept alone in her misery on silent tracks through dark forests.

She would find it hard in the future to place trust in any man.

Janet Guthrie greeted her sister's arrival with surprised pleasure, hurrying from the weaver's cottage to hug her. Janet was expecting an addition to the family in about two months' time, praying for a laddie this time after their three lassies.

'Heaven preserve us, Christina! What brings ye here at this hour?'
she laughed. Examining her sister more closely, Janet grew alarmed.
'You've been greetin'! What's ado?'

It was some solace to sit on the bench outside the cottage and
tell Janet everything as evening shadows lengthened.

Two little girls played with pebbles in the dust at their mother's
feet, a toddler perched contentedly upon the swelling remainder of
her mother's lap, sucking goat's milk from the pierced tip of a cow's
horn. The steady clack-clack of Arthur Guthrie's loom within the
cottage accompanied Christina's account of events.

Janet's husband had not stopped work in order to greet his sister-
in-law but that caused no offence. She knew daylight is precious to
a weaver and the long summer evenings in June were an added
bonus.

'So what's to be done?' Janet asked.

'I had hoped to bide here wi' you.'

Janet smiled incredulously. 'Och, Chrissie, you're jesting! I'd love
to have ye but I'm duty bound to give Arthur's aunt Bertha a home.
The poor widow's put out o' her cottar house this week. She'll look
after the bairns while I'm lying-in wi' the next. If you bide you'll
make do wi' a pallet on the floor or a wee corner in the stable. I'm
sorry, love.'

She eyed her crestfallen young sister compassionately. Christina
had aye been quick to anger though bonny. She had a ladylike grace
Janet had often envied. 'Go home, Chrissie dear,' she advised kindly.
'When your temper's cool the morn, go home and make your peace
wi' Pa.'

After one night spent in her sister's hard-working household, Christina
was ready to accept the advice. The family roused at cockcrow with
the weaver, who was eager not to miss a moment of morning light
preparing loom and pirns. Christina carted night soil to the midden,
struggled to wash and clothe a baby and two lively wee lasses, while
Janet milked the cow and prepared porridge for their meal. By noon
Christina was exhausted, the bairns were settled for a welcome nap
and she was ready to creep miserably back home to Goudiebank.

Sadly, she kissed Janet and Arthur goodbye and walked to the
stables where she'd lodged Muckle Meg.

The clack of many looms followed Christina down the street.
She dodged pigs snuffling in the dirt and smiled at women spinning thread outside the doors. The village had become prosperous

under the patronage of Stewart kings. Queen Mary herself had visited the luxurious palace in happier times. It was a relaxed and tranquil spot to escape the trials and tribulations of her turbulent reign. Falkland village held the status of a Royal burgh and its weavers were renowned for excellence.

Arthur Guthrie was one of the best and Christina carried with her a length of fine linen that Janet had begged her sister to fashion into a christening robe, something the growing family did not possess. The Reformed Kirk tended to frown upon such luxuries, but who cared? Christina's spirits were low, but at least with no wedding to plan the christening robe would occupy her idle hands on dark days ahead.

'Christina Gilmore!'

She turned in surprise to find Lady Annabel Erskine, accompanied as usual by the watchful Dorcas. Annabel was smiling broadly.

'What luck, Christina! You were on my mind.'

'Honoured, I'm sure,' Christina said caustically, in no mood for courtesies.

The linen she carried caught the lady's eye. 'Where did you come by this? It's fairer than the finest Holland cloth.'

'My brother-in-law's a notable weaver, lady.'

'And your brother Lachie's a braw gallant! Is there no end to your family's talents?' Annabel laughed.

Christina brooded darkly upon her father's shortcomings and made no answer.

Annabel studied her pensively for a moment. 'If I were to ask ye to bide at Falkland Palace to sew garments for a lady on the loch, would you do it, Christina?'

The offer was so startling her heart pounded. To live in Falkland Palace! It was a dream beyond imagination, but . . . 'Sewing for nobility is a step above my station, lady,' she said awkwardly.

Annabel's smile was grim. 'This is a step higher still, my dear! This lady was brought from Edinburgh to Lochleven with no more than the clothes on her back. I am sworn to keep her supplied with garments fit for her high estate. My father is a Leith merchant trading with France and Flanders and I have a sound eye for cloth and cut. Dorcas sews well, but your embroidery skill would be invaluable! So what do you say?'

'First, I would know who Sir William's visitor is,' she answered cannily.

Annabel leaned close and whispered. 'She is Mary Stuart, rightful queen o' Scotland, Christina. Her lords claim she's kept guarded upon the island for her safety and protection but that's not our affair. We are only concerned wi' the Queen's clothing and comfort.'

The lady and her maid watched Christina closely as she hesitated but they could not guess the quandary she faced. It had been drummed into her that Gilmores did not meddle in state affairs for fear of Sir William's displeasure.

But this is not an invitation to meddle, Christina thought, only to sew.

Two

Christina's sudden departure from the farmstead had caused problems. She had been a valuable contributor to the unrelenting daily toil. Her mother was overwhelmed with household chores, her brothers grumbled at extra farm work and little Francis moped. A close-knit family had been ripped apart.

Wil Gilmore withdrew into himself, spending more time alone tending his beloved horses or working in the loft above the stables making leather harness and saddlery. Wil fashioned saddle and harness with craftsman's skill although most countrymen scorned refinement and made do with pads of wool and twists of rope. That was their choice but Wil's concern was the comfort of a hard-ridden horse and the ease of plodding packhorses.

Marjorie watched helplessly as her men sat in silence at the table with never a kind word for one another or appreciation of the tasty fare set before them.

She had little appetite herself. There was sickness in her stomach and growing dread in her breast. It had been ten years since she and Wil were blessed with wee Francis and Marjorie had believed she had done with childbearing. Recently, however, she'd started to wonder if she was wrong. Signs were that one last late bairn was on the way. She dreaded to think what Wil would say when he knew.

Weather in 1567 had proved unpredictable. A bitterly cold wet springtime killed calves and thinned flocks of sheep. This was followed by blistering drought at the beginning of June that withered burgeoning green shoots and ended with thunderous downpours to flood the remainder. If the trend continued and harvest was poor there would be a dearth of oats and barley. The additional burden of an infant in the house would not be welcome.

'Maybe we should ask Maggie the washer-lassie to help now that Christina's gone,' she suggested tentatively at the supper table.

Wil frowned. 'You think our daughter will not come home? Wait for time to heal the wound and then she will come, my dear.'

Marjorie sighed. 'She'll marry Hugh and leave us whatever the way o' it, Wil.'

'No, she'll no'!' Jamie declared suddenly. 'He'll not marry her without a dowry. They had a real tulzie on the pier, yelling at one another about the loss of her dowry and she was off to Falkland at the gallop afterwards. The washerwomen heard every word and you know what blethers they are. The row was the talk o' Kinross market last Thursday.'

Wil flung down the spoon and buried his head in his hands. He cursed his faith in the luck of the cards and the ale that made him gamble. His intentions were good but the damage was immense. A reckless gamble had cost him his family's respect and ruined his beloved daughter's marriage prospects. 'I had no word of this quarrel, Jamie,' he said miserably. 'One of us must go to Falkland and see how Christina is faring.'

It saddened Marjorie to see her husband so downcast. She had always known he could not resist a gamble if the stakes were high – after all, Wil's greatest gamble had been to marry a crippled wife to win a fine farm tithed to a hot-tempered Douglas landlord, she thought. She met her husband's despondent glance and smiled encouragement. 'Our Janet's a motherly soul, Wil love. She'll look after Chrissie and be glad of her sister's help when the new baby's born. I wouldna be surprised to see Christina back home soon after the birth if all goes well.'

Lachie seized his chance. 'In the meantime, I'll ride to Falkland and make sure she's settled, Pa,' he volunteered. He had been looking for an excuse to visit Falkland in the hope of meeting Lady Annabel. He dreamed about her constantly and sometimes felt quite sick with love, an exciting and disturbing state of affairs.

Christina Gilmore had accepted Annabel's offer and was installed in Falkland Palace, but sudden change from farm worker to seamstress had not been easy. Lack of suitable clothing had been the first hurdle.

She had felt honoured to help Dorcas sew garments for Queen Mary who was kept under Sir William Douglas's protection at Lochleven Castle, but excitement at the prospect faded the moment Christina stepped through the palace gatehouse following in Lady Annabel and Dorcas's footsteps. The manservant Hector brought up the rear leading Muckle Meg. Once inside the courtyard the sheer size and splendour of the palace was overwhelming and Christina stopped abruptly, panic-stricken.

This was a dwelling built for kings and she was wearing home-spun linen, coarse worsted plaid and clumsy leather clogs. The most menial palace servant would be better dressed and the other servants would be sure to despise her and poke sly fun at her expense.

Her Gilmore pride would not stand for that!

She felt a hand on her shoulder and Hector looked down at her sympathetically. 'Walk on, lassie. I promise they'll no' bite ye.'

She forced herself to go on, leaving him to stable Muckle Meg while Lady Annabel led the way through a doorway and climbed a narrow stairway to the upper floors. Christina kept close to her companions while passing through vast empty reception rooms hung with tapestries, but at last they came to a passageway lined with more intimate chambers. Annabel opened a door leading to a sunlit suite of rooms.

'These are our quarters, Christina,' she said. 'The palace can be freezing even in summer but these rooms are small and cosy and the windows well placed for good light. Dorcas has made a start to cut and sew a day dress fit for a queen to the pattern I designed.'

She gestured towards a trestle table strewn with a dazzling array of silks, satins, linens, woollens, velvets and furs.

Annabel turned to Christina, smiling. 'And you tell me you're at war wi' your pa. I find your spirit commendable! My own beloved papa is both father and mother to me and we have famous battles which I usually win, bless him. At the moment the dear old soul thinks I'm invited tae Falkland as George Douglas's guest. Papa considers George a famous catch as son-in-law and rates Dorcas and Hector suitable chaperones. The poor darling's mind rests easy at home in Leith and he has offered packhorses laden with anything I care to demand – if it will speed a love affair.' She chuckled wickedly. 'Heaven help us if Papa finds out my mission at Falkland is for Queen Mary's comfort!'

She took Christina's hand. 'But now let us see to your comfort, dear Chrissie, since like our beloved queen you left home wi' just the clothes on your back.'

Leading her towards a large oaken kist similar to one that caused problems for Lachie and Hector, Annabel raised the lid to reveal a rich store of dresses, detachable sleeves, stockings, shifts, chemises and nightgowns. 'Take your pick, my dear.'

'My lady, I canna!' she protested in dismay. 'They're too fine for the likes o' me!'

'Blethers!' snorted the lady. 'This is workaday gear not court finery.

John Knox preaches sobriety and thumps splinters frae the pulpit in St Giles thundering against the sin o' scarlet, purple and gold. He's in favour of dull black, miserable grey and sad brown but I'm told the rebel lords secretly plunder Queen Mary's court gowns and jewels at Holyrood Palace for themselves and their wives.'

Christina was shocked. 'Surely that's treason?'

Annabel shrugged. 'Who's to stop them? They hold the reins of state now. Their actions chill many stomachs – but that's not our concern.' She rummaged in the kist and produced an armful of garments. 'Here, these should do. Fortunately you're of the whippet breed like me and not much more in height so they should fit.'

Walking in a dream, Christina withdrew to the chamber allotted to her clutching a bundle of dresses and underclothes. It might not be court finery, she thought gleefully as she stepped into a deep-blue silk gown with fitted bodice and sleeves, small ruff to the chin, silk skirt draped to the floor, silk hose tied above the knee with embroidered garters and fine leather shoes – but this was gear that would not disgrace a substantial burgess's daughter!

Her companions fell silent as Christina stepped out shyly for their appraisal. She could not know that fine clothes had elevated the bonny country lass to a lovely lady of high estate.

'*Belle et plus que belle,*' Annabel murmured softly.

Christina blushed. Her father was French and his children were of course fluent in that language. Praise from a lady was praise indeed!

Dorcas too nodded approval. 'Any lord would be honoured wi' you on his arm, my dear,' she said.

Annabel shuddered. 'Heaven preserve this innocent frae lords, Dorcas! I'd rather she took her chance wi' wolves.'

The comparison amused Christina and she laughed. Wolves were relentless predators, dangerous to meet on lonely forest paths. 'Dinna fash, my lady,' she said merrily. 'I'll not abandon my homespun old plaidie yet. No lord will look my way wi' that auld shawl draped over head and shoulders.'

Annabel hugged her delightedly. 'Said wi' spirit, Chrissie! I pity any man or wolf that dares molest ye!'

The surface of Loch Leven was dotted with boats on a muggy, over-cast morning. Fish were rising to a hatch of flies and mosquitoes and fishermen were making the most of a bountiful catch. Hugh Ross rowed a leisurely path from the shore, ferrying washerwomen to the castle for their daily stint. Word of the queen's presence on Castle Island had spread throughout the district by now but his passengers remained subdued. All that could be heard in the boat was the creak of oars in rowlocks and muted whispering.

'Have ye seen the queen yet, Jessie?'

'Nah. She bides on the third floor, weel guarded. A chambermaid told me she's kept in no royal state and took to her bed after the lords brought her here in the dead o' night. The cooks say she didna eat or drink enough to nourish a mouse for two weeks. A'body was sure she'd dee.'

'But she didna dee!' Maggie the washer-lassie declared. 'I saw her walk in the garden hanging on to young Lady Douglas's arm, though later on I heard whispers that she'd lost the early wean she'd been carrying.'

There was much solemn wagging of heads.

'Aye, it's true, Maggie!' one woman agreed. 'She had a bad time o' it too, for I was given bed sheets to soak in the loch that turned Loch Leven red. The women tending her say it was early on but signs were the queen parted wi' twins.'

'Ah, the puir soul!' somebody sighed.

Sympathetic silence persisted for the remainder of the voyage. Mary Stuart was their sovereign but to these women she was also a young mother that had lost her babies. They could well understand the pain and distress she must suffer.

After the washerwomen had disembarked at the castle Hugh found a solitary passenger waiting for the return trip. This was wee Willy Douglas, an orphan cousin of the Douglas clan. The lad was not a great deal older than Christina's frail little brother Francis Gilmore but much more robust and cocky.

Once the boy was settled in the boat, Hugh turned back towards the shore. This was the drudgery of a boatman's work – to and fro across the water at the beck and call of the laird's servants and kin till the back ached and spirit rebelled. Hugh's work had seemed more tedious somehow since he and Christina parted and he longed for some diversion to relieve the tedium and ease the heartache.

'So where are you off to, Willy?' he asked idly.

'Falkland,' the lad answered promptly. 'Old Lady Douglas gave me leave. I've a list o' gear in my pouch to give to the seamstress at the palace. It's for warm sarks and woollens for Queen Mary. She finds the laird's castle a chilly prison.'

Hugh raised his eyebrows. 'Prison? Surely not!'

Willy nodded vigorously. 'Aye, it is! There are soldiers at the foot of the stairs and young Lady Douglas sleeps in the queen's room. Lord Lindsay and Lord Ruthven keep watch on her by day. Lord Ruthven treats her kindly but Lord Lindsay's cruel. When the queen was ill I heard the man yelling that he'd drag her frae the castle and slit her throat if she didna sign the papers.'

Hugh was shocked. 'What papers?'

Willy shrugged. 'I dinna ken, but George Douglas roused all the servants to stop Lord Lindsay's wicked game and now he darsent harm her.'

Hugh rowed on in silence, pondering the boy's startling account. It did seem to hold water. When the Queen of Scots returned to Scotland from widowhood in France six years ago the Scottish people fell in love with their beautiful eighteen-year-old queen. However, differences between her Catholic upbringing and the ways o' the Protestant Reformed Kirk caused serious problems. Subsequently, the murder of Darnley her young husband and an ill-advised and hasty marriage to the Earl of Bothwell had soured public opinion. A majority of crafty Scottish lords seized their chance to rebel against their queen and her consort.

Bothwell rode off in an attempt to raise royalist support and the Confederate Lords lost no time removing Mary and her baby son James from the Earl's influence – the queen to Loch Leven, the baby to Stirling Castle.

Hugh frowned, tugging on the oars. If the boy's account was to be believed there were darker plans afoot for Queen Mary that did not involve freedom and restoration. He dismissed speculation with a shiver. These were ruthless men and dangerous times!

Closer to shore Hugh observed that it was not only fish that rose early this morning. Two gentlemen awaited his arrival on the pier. A groom guarded fine horses hitched to the rail while a huge shaggy wolfhound took its ease, lounging in the sunlight. Wee Willy Douglas hopped ashore with the ropes and scampered off towards Goudiebank's stable to collect his pony for the Falkland ride. The strangers clambered aboard the boat and seated themselves in the bow, engrossed in conversation. For all the attention they paid Hugh as he cast off the ropes he might have been hewn from wood.

He soon discerned that one was an Englishman of substantial degree. The other he recognized as James Melville, Scottish envoy to the English court and a visitor to Sir William's castle in happier days.

The Englishman was a handsome fellow of perhaps five and twenty, travelling cloak edged with fur, black velvet doublet fitting a broad chest and white linen ruff outlining a strong chin. Gold chains glittering around his neck spoke of wealth and leather gauntlets rested upon a jewelled sword hilt. Polished riding boots reaching to the knee protected his feet from a swirl of muddy water sloshing in the scuppers and a flat black bonnet topped by curling black cock's feathers completed an impressive picture in contrast to the sober Scot James Melville. The older man wore sad grey set off with white linen in modest style, as approved by the Reformed Kirk.

As they headed out across the loch, Hugh's two passengers had adopted the style of English spoken in court circles. This differed so remarkably from Lowland Scots they would not expect a boatman to follow the conversation easily.

Hugh hid a grin. He had a keen ear for language and having transported so many of Sir William's English friends to and fro the English tongue presented no difficulty. An opportune breeze blew every whisper in Hugh's direction and he settled down to listen with interest.

'Do you think I'll be permitted to see the queen, James?' the Englishman asked.

His companion shook his head. 'No hope o' that, John. As you know, Queen Elizabeth's envoy Sir Nicholas Throckmorton hastened from London to Edinburgh when news came of the lords' uprising, but even he is refused access to the queen. It's unlikely any Englishman will be allowed near Her Grace – not even an Englishman with your impeccable credentials, John Haxton.'

The Englishman frowned. 'This is damned awkward. Sir Nicholas has sent me to lend weight to his advice to the queen. My mission is hardly worth the candle if I'm denied access to advise her.'

James Melville laughed grimly. 'Don't worry. Sir Nicholas knows advice must be smuggled in. Secrecy is the only way! I will be allowed to see the queen briefly, if only to assure the outside world that she is alive and digesting her captivity reasonably well.' He sighed sadly. 'Queen Mary's downfall saddens me, John. I knew Marie Stuart well at the French court when she was betrothed to the ill-fated young Dauphin. I found her an admirable princess.'

John Haxton nodded. 'Aye, she also impressed Sir Nicholas when she was briefly Queen of France and he was English envoy, but now he finds solving Mary's predicament the most delicate and dangerous task he has ever undertaken. He is convinced that the rebels mean to do away with her if she won't cooperate.'

At this, Hugh almost missed a stroke and the two men eyed him warily. He remained impassive however, muttering an apology and steadying the craft. The loch had obviously become choppy as a sudden squall struck the boat and his passengers relaxed, reassured.

'This dastardly treatment o' her cousin Mary must ruffle Queen Elizabeth's feathers,' the Scotsman remarked.

'Aye, Her Majesty's fury was fearsome when she heard of this arrogant treatment of queens. She knows rebellion spreads and there are Catholics in England eager to see the Queen of Scots set on the English throne. Elizabeth was all for declaring war on Scotland till wiser counsel prevailed and she considered the advantages to herself.'

Melville raised his eyebrows. 'You believe there are any?'

'Yes indeed. There is custody of Queen Mary's baby son. With his mother removed little Prince James's long minority is a valuable prize for any ward.'

'So it is,' John Haxton nodded thoughtfully. 'All Europe knows by now the child's father Henry Darnley was murdered in an Edinburgh gunpowder plot and there was universal outrage when the widowed queen married the Earl of Bothwell, chief suspect of the foul deed. Ill advised on Mary's part, don't you think?'

Melville looked away thoughtfully towards the castle. 'To be fair to her, John, I suspect Bothwell saw his chance and took steps to force her to marry him. The Earl has aye been loyal to the monarchy and has Scotland's best interests at heart. That would weigh heavily in his favour with the queen.'

John Haxton nodded agreement. 'It's true Bothwell persistently refuses to accept English bribes – unlike many other Scottish lords I could mention.'

His companion cleared his throat uneasily. 'Aye well, Bothwell's goose is cooked now. He's put to the horn and declared an outlaw with a huge price on his head. Rumour has it royalist support is fading and the Earl has fled the country. The confederate lords control Scotland while the queen is kept in protective custody.'

'Is that what they call it?' the Englishman remarked dryly. 'I'm told they threaten to arrange an unfortunate *accident* should she persist in her refusal to abdicate in favour of her thirteen-month-old son.'

'Exactly so!' Melville flung the boatman a quick glance and lowered his voice. Hugh angled the bow slightly into the wind to listen.

'Sir Nicholas slipped me a note advising the queen to sign the abdication documents in order to save her life since her signature given under duress would not be binding.' He patted his thigh. 'The note lies safely hidden in my sword's scabbard. I'll watch my chance and pass it to Her Majesty.'

The Englishman laughed delightedly. 'An excellent device, James; I pray she'll act upon it! In the meantime I have orders to remain close by to act as Sir Nicholas's eyes and ears.'

James Melville smiled. 'Well, well! Sir John Haxton is to be an English spy?'

He grinned wryly. 'I mislike that word, my friend! Should anyone ask, tell them I'm an English sportsman tracking wolves preying upon royal deer.'

And the two men chuckled at the joke.

Hugh Ross glanced idly over his shoulder as if his only concern was measuring distance to the castle. Could the Queen of Scots be freed from that grim fortress? he wondered. It was most unlikely but what an adventure it would be to try!

In a sunny sewing room at Falkland Palace the three occupants waited for the arrival of Edinburgh packhorses.

Lady Annabel had been pacing the floor. She was impatient to hear from Queen Mary's valet Robert Mackinson concerning the plundering of the royal wardrobe at Holyrood. Hopefully some items might yet be saved.

Meanwhile Christina had Annabel's permission to work on the baptismal gown for her sister's bairn due in two months, according to Janet's reckoning. Dorcas was mending a torn seam on a black day dress sent over from the island.

Lady Annabel was checking lists of material ordered but was in a restless mood, frowning, fretting and jumping up and down from her seat to look out the window. 'Not a packhorse for miles and Queen Mary in dire straits!' she grumbled. 'It was mean stuff they sent her in June: an old day gown furred with moth-eaten marten, red satin petticoat and a pair of red satin sleeves, linen cloak with muddy stains at the hem, single pair o' darned silk stockings, a box of sweetmeats and a box of pins.' She shrugged angrily. 'I ask you! What use to the queen's majesty was that load o' rubbish?'

Dorcas looked up. 'Remember our poor lady was in a state of collapse for days. She'd have no need of velvet.'

Annabel scowled. 'Maybe so, but Her Majesty's back on her feet now and very near naked.'

At that moment footsteps were heard on the stairs and voices echoed in the vast reception rooms. Annabel turned eagerly towards the doorway as a maid ushered in a small group headed by a freckle-faced youngster Christina recognized as wee Willy Douglas. He carried a scroll of parchment importantly in one hand. The boy doffed a blue bonnet to reveal a shock of gingery hair.

'I have a list frae Queen Mary writ in her own hand and authorized by old Lady Douglas. They wouldna trust anyone but me to bring it,' he ended smugly.

Lady Annabel snatched the parchment gleefully.

Christina eyed the lad's two companions. She was startled to find her small brother Francis cowering sheepishly behind Lachie. Lachie was no surprise considering the infatuation with Annabel but she pointed an accusing finger at their young brother. 'What's Francis doing here?'

Lachie looked shamefaced. 'Er – well – I was bound for Falkland and Francis went down on his knees begging tae come. Pa said he could since wee Willy was going.'

'Oh aye? And what did Ma say?'

That was met with silence and shuffling feet. They all knew their mother would put her foot down firmly on Francis's expedition had she been consulted.

'You're for it when you get home!' Christina said.

Lachie looked sulky. 'You're a fine one tae preach! What are *you* doing biding in the palace? Ma thinks you're with Janet.'

'There's no room for me at Janet's house. Lady Annabel offered work as a seamstress and I was glad to accept. But what are *you* doing here – as if I canna guess?'

'We – we were worried about ye, Chrissie, that – that's all!'

Christina met her brother's agonized gaze and her heart softened. Lachie was besotted with hopeless dreams of Lady Annabel, poor lad. She laid a hand on his arm. 'Och, I'm fine, Lachie!' she said. 'But take my advice and leave now. You could have Francis home before the kirk bell tolls for silence o' the night and Ma might be lenient.'

Francis turned eagerly to his brother. He too dreaded Marjorie's wrath. 'So we could, Lachie! I can ride faster than Willy.'

'I'm sure ye can, my lamb,' Christina said kindly. What delight it must be for a little lame lad to win that particular race!

Annabel had quickly scanned the letter and handed it to Dorcas. She had been following with interest the conversation between Christina and her brothers and now she decided to intervene. 'Och, don't heed your sister just yet, Mister Gilmore! I'd be a mean hostess to send you three off unfed. Come with me and we'll see what the cooks can do.'

She took Lachie's arm and led him into the passageway, the two boys following hungrily. Once outside, she spoke softly. 'I was hoping for a quiet word alone, Lachie. I have a favour to ask.'

Her perfume filled his senses, her touch made him weak. 'Anything!' he breathed.

'If Willy brings letters secretly from the island to Goudiebank, would you deliver them to me at Falkland? I could let it be known that you come to the palace only to visit your sister.'

Lachie frowned. He was not so lost in love as to abandon all caution. His mother's warnings rang in his ears and a troubling thought had also occurred. 'Who will send these letters – is it George Douglas?'

Her dark eyes danced. 'You guessed!'

'Love letters?' he demanded through clenched teeth.

'Perhaps!'

He wanted desperately to kiss the teasing smile on her lips but more urgently he longed to punch bonny Geordie Douglas's aristocratic nose.

Next day Lady Annabel set to work on Queen Mary's order. The list revealed a pathetic plea for warm undergarments. Annabel read it out:

> *Two velvet petticoats, four shifts of silk and wool mix, four wool chemises, as many pair of warm worsted stockings as may be found, two satin nightcaps, black satin dressing gown and four Falkland linen nightgowns, two pair leather shoes measured and fit to size, if they can be got from Holyrood, a pair black velvet sleeves, box of sweetmeats to sweeten weary hours and balls of scented white French soap, if it may be had.*

'And it is signed *Marie R*,' Annabel ended emotionally.

Christina swallowed the lump in her throat; Dorcas wiped away a tear; Lady Annabel squared her chin.

'It shall be done just as Her Majesty wishes.' She turned to Christina. 'Is your sister's christening gown finished?'

'Aye. It's made in plain stitch lest the preacher takes exception to
embroidery.'

'Deliver it to her quickly, my dear, and you'll be free to concentrate upon royal work. But mind to tell nobody we are sewing for
the queen,' she warned.

Christina gathered up the tiny gown and hurried to obey. Annabel
called after her. 'Wrap yourself in the old plaid, Chrissie. There may
be wolves about!'

Christina was smiling as she left the palace gatehouse and hurried
down the street making for the weaver's cottage. She was confident Janet would be delighted with the baby's robe. The bodice
was so exquisitely smocked its simplicity scarcely mattered. She
paused suddenly and her smile faded. Her brother-in-law Arthur
Guthrie was trudging despondently towards her with Janet's three
little girls.

'Janet was taken bad last night, Chrissie,' he told her sadly. 'The
baby was born just as dawn broke.'

She was horrified. 'Arthur, it's much too soon!'

'Aye, I know. Falkland matrons are with Janet now and the bairns
and I have been banished to find lodgings wi' my cousin. It's the
son we prayed for at last, Chrissie, but they say he'll not even live
to be baptized.'

There were tears on Arthur's cheeks as Christina hugged him
silently and left him to go on his way. She rushed into the cottage.

It was bedlam inside, a crush of women round the bed all talking,
wailing and lamenting at the same time. Somebody noticed Christina
and cried out, 'Wheest! Here's the sister!'

There was a hush as they turned to stare. A grey-haired matron
pointed a shaking finger at her. 'The wean's twice cursed! The sister
brings a christening robe for a weakling that'll no' live tae wear it!'

'Chrissie? Is that you?' Janet's voice was little more than a whisper
but Christina pushed past the women and fell on her knees at her
sister's bedside. Janet lay drained and pale but her eyes gleamed with
a feverish desperation. She clutched Christina's hands.

'Take my baby away, Chrissie! Arthur and I want him so much
and he might have a chance o' life at the palace. Please, Chrissie,
take him away from these women!'

'You ungrateful besom, Janet Guthrie!' one woman yelled angrily.
'We did all that should be done for a bairn born not much bigger
than a mewling kitten. We salted it, washed it in water purified wi'
burning coal, flung door and windows open tae drive oot evil spirits

and Jeanie ran thrice around your house wi' it. Syne we swaddled it in a woman's petticoat for luck since it's male. What more could ye ask?'

Christina stood up and faced them angrily. 'She could ask ye tae handle her frail son gently, not have him scalded and chilled by superstitious nonsense. Give him tae me!'

They thrust a tiny bundle truculently into her arms. The baby was so light it weighed scarcely more than thistledown and Christina's heart turned over. A wee red face with skin so fine you could trace the veins was all that could be seen. She cradled her precious nephew close to her breast and wrapped the plaid around him. 'Stand aside!' she ordered.

'No need tae sit upon a high horse because you work at the palace, lassie!' one woman cried.

'Aye,' yelled another spitefully. 'You're orra stock like the rest o' us. Cottar hoose or palace thon sickly infant will never wear its christening gown. Why bother?'

Christina turned to Janet, ignoring the taunts. 'What's your son's name?'

'Ninian! He's to be baptized Ninian!' Janet cried defiantly.

'Dinna worry, dear Sister, I'll see to it!'

Christina shoved her way past the women and took to her heels filled with a feverish sense of urgency. She had no idea how to care for the tiny mite, but she felt confident that Dorcas would know.

Yes! she thought. If he can be saved Dorcas will know how it can be done!

In her feverish haste to reach the palace she cannoned straight into a man strolling along the street in the opposite direction.

'Whoa there!'

He steadied her as she stumbled against him. Fearful lest the fragile baby was crushed she struggled wildly out of his grasp.

'Leave me be!' she cried.

The faded old plaid slipped from her head and shoulders to reveal the tiny newborn baby cradled in her arms and Christina and the stranger faced one another for a startled few seconds. A large wolfhound padding at the man's heels growled a warning deep in its throat and sent her fleeing in panic for the gatehouse.

'Hush, Boris!'

Sir John Haxton silenced the hound and stared after the young woman. His keen eye had noted that she was richly dressed in a silk gown hidden beneath the tattered old homespun plaid. He watched with surprise as the fair beauty and her newborn infant disappeared into Falkland Palace.

Who could this contrary lady be? John Haxton wondered, intrigued. What was she?

He had to know!

Three

Christina fled to the palace and brought Janet's tiny son to Dorcas. The lady's maid took the infant in her arms and touched his mouth with a fingertip. 'He can suckle. It's weeks before his time but there's hope for him yet. How fares the mother?'

'My sister is too ill to care for him, Dorcas, but her spirit was fierce to save him when others swore he'd die!' Christina was close to tears as she went on to relate events surrounding the baby's premature birth. 'But I fear Falkland goodwives weakened the wee mite wi' superstitious nonsense!' she ended sadly.

Dorcas smiled briefly. 'Don't dismiss ancient customs so lightly, my dear. Hot coals in the basin would warm water to wash the newborn. Fresh air might help a weakling's breathing – and surely there can be no swaddling more blessed than a mother's linen to wrap her baby boy?'

Lady Annabel listened with ill-concealed impatience. 'Dorcas, will you stop cackling like a broody hen and face facts? I've little to do with babies but I know the creatures need mother's milk. Where's that to be had if his mother can't give it?'

Dorcas turned to her young mistress. 'The chambermaid gave birth to a healthy wean and has milk enough to spare, my lady. Unlike you she dotes on babies. I'm sure the good woman will be glad to nurse this wee one.'

Annabel shrugged. 'See to it then!' she commanded. 'Tell her she shall have two gold pieces if it lives. But make sure that it's kept out o' the way till our work's done.'

Dorcas hurried off with her tiny burden and Christina faced her employer tearfully. 'I'm so sorry to bring my sister's misfortune upon ye, Lady Annabel.'

She smiled and patted her shoulder. 'Aye well, as it happens I *do* owe your family a favour. Your brother Lachie has agreed to act as courier to help our cause.'

Christina stared, horrified. 'No! He mustn't offend the laird. The Gilmores could lose everything.'

Annabel laughed. 'Dinna fash, my dear! Lachie will only carry
personal letters for me and George Douglas and bringing your ailing
sister's wee changeling here is a stroke of luck. Lachie and the piebald
mare will attract attention and if his visits to the palace reach the
laird's ears I'll let it be known that your brother's concern is for his
two sisters and the sickly infant.'

Christina could sympathize with Annabel's attempts to conduct a
secret love affair with George Douglas. Such matters must be
approached delicately and Her Ladyship had already indicated that
her father approved of the young man as prospective son-in-law. Poor
lovelorn Lachie would no doubt view the possibility with a jealously
sore heart, but all the same Christina's spirits lifted. Her brother's
visits would be a welcome link with home at this worrying time.

She sought Annabel's permission to ascertain that Janet's precious
son was safely settled with the motherly chambermaid and returned
to the sewing room with a lighter step.

The three women set about the task of selecting warm materials
suitable for Queen Mary's underclothes. Christina was intrigued to
discover that from an early age Annabel had the freedom of her
merchant father's tailoring workshops and, although she'd little
patience for sewing, displayed great skill in the design and cut of all
types of clothing. Her admiration for her young mistress grew as
warm undergarments and a simple but well designed velvet day
gown took shape, every one fit for a queen.

The demanding task was a welcome distraction for Christina who
worried constantly about her sister's health. She had good reason to
be fearful for Janet had developed a childbed fever and barely recognized Christina on her visits to the weaver's cottage. Fortunately
Bertha Guthrie, the widowed aunt Arthur and Janet had rescued
from an impoverished old age, nursed the invalid diligently and kept
the weaver's household running smoothly. Janet was now showing
some signs of recovery, helped by the news that her tiny infant
continued his stubborn battle for life.

Queen Mary's agent James Melville had arranged lodgings for Sir
John Haxton in the home of Joshua and Euphemia Sturrock on the
outskirts of Falkland village.

For many years, Joshua had been Falkland Palace's head huntsman
enjoying the freedom of a grace and favour dwelling on the edge
of Falkland forest. This fine house was well built of local stone and

sported distinctive crow-step gables and red pantiled roof instead of the more usual thatch.

Euphemia – or Phemie as she was affectionately known – was a compact wee matron with sharp eyes set in a deceptively mild rosy face. She and Joshua had produced a large family of seven healthy bairns who were now adults scattered widely throughout Fife, Perthshire and Midlothian. Gossip and shrewd observations delivered from a' the airts kept their adored mother's finger firmly upon Scotland's erratic pulse.

It was years since Phemie had had an Englishman to stay and though wary at first she was soon delighted with the young man. John Haxton was charming, appreciative and nae bother at a'. She very soon jaloused that he was not in Scotland for the given purpose of stalking deer and tracking wolves with Boris the big wolfhound. The real reason remained obscure but Phemie Sturrock was confident she would winkle the truth out of the man sooner rather than later.

Soon after her lodger's arrival he began receiving official-looking documents with red wax seals, brought by exhausted couriers on sweating horses.

Phemie handed these over with growing frustration. She had never mastered the art of reading and writing.

'Another letter from my father, Mistress Sturrock,' he would say casually.

'Your pa must be fond,' she'd remark sweetly, knowing fine he lied.

The documents had started arriving not long after the twenty-ninth of July, an auspicious date that Phemie recalled mainly because of a dinner of jugged hare for which she was famed. The Sturrocks and their lodger were seated round the table with bowed heads while Joshua said grace, when a thunderous cannonade split the air and made pewter platters rattle. John Haxton leapt to his feet, hand flying to his dagger hilt.

Phemie guessed at the cause of the din and restrained him. 'Calm yoursel', sir! My daughter's married to a Stirling packman and sent word of Queen Mary's abdication in favour o' her baby son. The lords decided to crown the wee mite King o' Scots without delay. That thunderous rummle will be the Douglas family celebrating the coronation wi' a blast of Lochleven artillery. It's whispered that the regent chosen for wee King James is to be the Earl o' Moray, old lady Douglas's son from a youthful romp with Queen Mary's father. That's more power to the Douglas elbows!'

John Haxton settled back on the bench with plenty to occupy

his mind while enjoying his landlady's excellent fare. So Melville's smuggled note had obviously reached the queen, who had wisely taken Throckmorton's advice and agreed to the rebels' demands, he thought with satisfaction. Since the abdication was made under duress it could easily be revoked should circumstances change and an opportunity arise.

Over the next few days frequent letters from Sir Nicholas Throckmorton kept John acquainted with events. Sir Nicholas wrote that he was convinced he had saved the unfortunate young queen's life for the present, but urged John to keep close watch upon developments at Lochleven.

He also described at length the baby king's coronation in Stirling, a ceremony performed under the rites of the Reformed Kirk led by the preacher John Knox. Mary's thirteen-month-old son was clad in cloth of gold, sacred vows taken on his behalf and crown of state held above his downy curls by the Earl of Morton, head of the house of Douglas.

Throckmorton added dryly that when Lochleven's artillery fired the coronation salute Sir William Douglas rejoiced with his wife and mother in the castle gardens while the deposed queen retired to her prison quarters and wept.

John Haxton settled down patiently to watch and wait as instructed, the tedious lot of the English spy.

Rumour of wolves lurking on passes in the Lomond uplands occupied him on several uneventful hunts with Boris the hound, but a day's stalking with Joshua near Falkland Palace proved more successful, providing a haunch of venison for Phemie's pot. Passing through palace grounds, John recalled the fair young lady he had encountered days ago in the street. He had hoped to meet her by chance walking in the gardens but the only sign of female occupation was ladies' garments and baby linen strewn across kitchen hedgerows to dry in the sun. The mysterious lady herself was nowhere to be seen.

That evening he decided to turn to Phemie for information.

It was two hours before Falkland's ten o'clock bell was due to announce the silence of the night – two leisurely hours in the Sturrock household as shadows lengthened. Lamps were lit and fading light slowly ended the long August day. Cats purred peacefully on the floor in the last slants of setting sun and Boris lay stretched at his master's feet like a shaggy grey hearthrug.

John flicked idly through pages of a small leather-bound tome on estate management his father had given him before John set off for Scotland. The gift hinted at his dear parents' desire for their restless only son and heir to settle down to help his father care for the Haxtons' North Yorkshire estate.

Joshua whittled a thick twig of mountain ash, carving a whistle to call staghounds to heel. Phemie was spinning wool, the distaff twirling in her skilled hands as fast as the bumblebee's flight.

John closed the book. 'Is the lady living in Falkland Palace one of the Douglas clan?' he asked his landlady.

She nodded. 'Aye. Lady Annabel's a distant relative o' auld Lady Douglas on the Erskine side.'

He looked thoughtful. 'Lady Annabel will be the golden-haired beauty I met in the street the other day.'

Phemie paused. 'Lady Annabel's bonny – but raven-haired.'

He frowned. 'But who is this other beauty? I noted that though she and her infant were wrapped in an old faded plaid she was richly dressed. I watched her hurry into Falkland Palace and it struck me as strange.'

Phemie rightly guessed the 'lady's' identity. This could only be Christina Gilmore, she thought grimly.

Falkland gossip had kept Phemie up to date with Christina's part in the dramatic birth of her sister's premature infant and unfortunately the bonny lassie must have caught this young man's roving eye while carrying Janet Guthrie's tiny wean across to the palace for better care.

Earlier on last month, Phemie's son the Kinross baker had brought his mother a white loaf and news that Christina Gilmore was left on the shelf after her father gambled away her dowry and her betrothed rejected her. Now word had spread that the ill-starred lassie had left home and been taken under Lady Annabel Erskine's dangerous wing at the palace.

In Phemie's opinion, that was quite enough misfortune for an innocent young maiden to have thrust upon her, Phemie did not have a high opinion of the morals of Englishmen and decided Christina Gilmore must be protected from this young nobleman's dubious advances at all cost.

She smiled pleasantly. 'Och, that'll be Christina Gilmore, sir. A bonny lassie, but they do say her pa's an awful jealous father, rash and hasty wi' the dagger to see off her admirers.'

John Haxton looked alarmed. 'I believe someone in Edinburgh

did mention a certain Sir Hamish Gilmore, a wild Highland laird credited with a fiendish temper and the suspected murder of his daughter's lover.'

'That'll be the very man!' Phemie nodded happily, twirling the distaff. 'You'd fare better facing a pack o' snarling wolves than that daughter's father.'

Christina had been sewing for many long hours. Her head ached and fingers threatened to blister with plying the needle but she loved every minute of the arduous work. Lady Annabel was a pernickety taskmistress but when every garment was finished to her satisfaction she smiled with delight, examining the embroidery adorning petticoats, chemises and nightgowns.

'Well done! The queen sews beautifully herself and will appreciate fine work.'

Christina had finished repairing gold thread and pearl beading on one of Queen Mary's gowns smuggled out of Holyrood Palace by devoted servants. The gown had arrived by packhorse along with a pair of the queen's leather shoes. Christina stood up, holding the gown above her head, the hem still trailing the ground.

'Is the queen really so tall?' she marvelled.

Annabel nodded. 'Aye, she's nearly six feet and taller than most men. Of course, folk living across the Forth will be unfamiliar with persons at Holyrood's royal court. Lord Henry Darnley was the only long lad Queen Mary could look up to. He was a fine figure of a tall man and perhaps that swayed her to fall in love and marry the ill-fated youth. I saw them dance together once at court and it was a vision to melt any woman's heart. Maybe she saw only a handsome face and figure and an acknowledged claim to the English throne and ignored his fatal flaws. Her advisers were set against the match, but alas, Her Grace would have her wilful way!'

Dorcas sighed. 'Aye, he was only eighteen when they married, three years younger than the queen herself. It was unwise infatuation on her part. Perhaps she hoped time would heal his faults but it was clear frae the start that power went tae the lad's head.'

Annabel snorted. 'He behaved like a dangerously arrogant spoiled brat, you mean! He was persuaded to join the rebel band that murdered the queen's secretary David Rizzio in the presence of the queen and her friends. She would discover then that her young husband was not to be trusted and realize how dangerous that could be for the future of the monarchy and their unborn child.'

'That's for sure,' Dorcas nodded. 'They do say David Rizzio was a strutting wee popinjay full o' his own importance but no man deserves such a vindictive end. It's fortunate the queen had the courage to slip out o' the clutches of the murderers and ride through the night to safety – and she was six months gone wi' child too!'

Annabel folded the velvet gown reverently and wrapped it tenderly in muslin. 'Aye,' she agreed. 'The queen's fortitude attracts many to her cause, myself included. It's tragic that Darnley had feet o' clay and made powerful enemies. I mind being wakened in Leith by the explosion that shook Edinburgh to the foundations and reduced the young king's lodging at Kirk o' Field to a heap o' rubble. He was recovering from smallpox there and was just twenty-one years old – a sad end to youthful folly and arrogance!'

Christina thought about her father's addiction to gambling and Hugh Ross's greed. 'Aye, a man's faults will never mend,' she said bitterly.

Annabel picked up the queen's list and studied it. She frowned. 'That's everything but white soap. Where's that luxury to be found in this back o' beyond?'

'Christina's mother had white soap as good as any frae Castile,' Dorcas reminded her.

Annabel brightened. 'So she did! I'd forgotten. Once more the Gilmores will save our skins! Where does your mother buy her soap, dear Chrissie?'

'Maggie the washer-lassie brings it in exchange for eggs, lady. Her father owns the Kinross soap-works but Ma believes Maggie does the favour hoping to catch my brother Jamie's eye.' Christina had to smile. The washer-lassie's attempts to flaunt her charms before Jamie Gilmore were a long-standing family joke.

'Perfect!' Annabel cried. 'You will ride back home at once and buy white soap. Tell this washer-lassie I'll pay her well for a supply and she can make herself a bonny gown to catch your brother's eye.'

Christina lifted her chin. 'No, my lady, I will not go; you forget I'm at war wi' my father.'

Annabel was accustomed to obedience from those of lower estate but this young woman acted more like an equal. She eyed Christina Gilmore with respect. Amazing what clothes can do! she thought. 'I'm sorry, Christina. I forgot your misfortune,' she said graciously and turned to the lady's maid. 'Dorcas, you will go to the farm in Christina's stead. Tell Hector to prepare her muckle horse for your ride.'

'Yes, my lady.' Dorcas said meekly, though her spirits soared. It would be grand to breathe fresh air after gruelling sewing sessions. For a few blessed hours she could be her own mistress and not at this beloved lassie's beck and call.

A blessed holy day indeed! Dorcas thought as she hurried to obey.

Jamie Gilmore had landed himself in serious trouble. He had taken a sickle to weeds encroaching upon ripening barley and in an abstracted moment had missed the stroke and the dagger-sharp curved blade had gashed his arm.

He cursed his luck. The wound was deep, bleeding copiously and he was on his own. His parents had ridden to Kinross fair early that morning with wee Francis to be sure of arriving when the peace of the fair was declared and buying, selling and fun began. Produce was at its freshest early on.

Jamie had hoped the excursion would lift his mother's spirits. Marjorie had been sickly and out of sorts recently. Lachie had left early that morning for Falkland to visit their sisters and inspect Janet's frail infant, barely clinging to life, and farm workers had a holiday to visit the fair.

Jamie was alone on the farm and must do what he could to help himself. He ripped the sleeve from his shirt, bound it tightly around the gash and staggered homewards.

He was in a pitiable state on reaching the farmhouse. He had no idea how to treat the painfully deep slash. At the back of his mind lurked tales of terrible ailments that could strike should an evil humour enter and mingle with his blood.

This was the situation Dorcas found when he answered the door to her knock. She took one look at the blood-soaked young man and ordered him to a chair. Hoisting her skirt, she ripped a wide strip off the underskirt, rolled white linen into a thick wad and applied it firmly to the wound. She used so much pressure he yelled, but she persisted.

'Dinna fash, Mister Gilmore. It's bled freely and that's good, but now it must stop.'

Jamie groaned. He remembered who the woman was, but had no idea what Lady Annabel's maid was doing here. He felt light-headed and strange and wondered if he was in the grip of a feverish nightmare. 'Am I dying?' he whispered.

She laughed. 'No' yet.'

But there was a worse fear. 'Will I lose my arm?'

'Not if I can help it.' She glanced around the big room. 'Where's the wine your mother served us when we came?'

'Wine?' he repeated stupidly. This had the strangeness of a weird dream. He gestured weakly. 'Over there. In the cask.'

She was back in an instant with a full stoup, the skirt hoisted and another wide strip ripped from the underskirt. She soaked the linen in wine and gently swabbed away the blood. The bleeding stopped and she seemed satisfied.

'Wine's better than water in this instance,' she announced cheerfully. 'Fortunately it's a clean cut. How came you by it?'

Jamie explained about tares in the crop and a moment's inattention with the sickle.

She nodded. 'Aye, that's a fearsome sharp blade. I've seen many similar injuries when reaping in the cornfields.'

'Are you frae farming stock?' he asked curiously.

'No, I'm not.'

She turned away, ripping a wide length from the ruined underskirt and bandaging the arm expertly. She borrowed Jamie's kerchief for a sling while he watched and wondered.

'You never learned these healing skills working for thon pampered wee besom, that's for sure!' he declared.

She glanced at him seriously. 'Dinna dismiss Lady Annabel so lightly! She adopts kittenish ways and keeps sharp claws but has wits to match any man and fearless courage.'

He laughed. 'Of course you must say that! Her Ladyship demands loyal servants.'

The bandaging completed, she gathered the soiled linen and flung it in the fire before facing him. 'Her dead mother was my dearest friend, Mister Gilmore. It's my duty and delight to care for my friend's beloved only child.'

He met the woman's cool blue eyes. She would be thirty if she were a day, he thought. Not at all bonny, though her appearance was wholesome, fine-skinned with high cheekbones and resolute chin. It was a face that might age well. 'I never asked how you come to be here. At first it seemed I was dreaming,' he said.

She laughed. 'I'm no sprite! Lady Annabel sent me on a mission to buy white soap from your sweetheart.'

'M–my sweetheart?'

'Aye, Maggie the washer-lassie. Your sister tells us that Maggie's father makes soap pure and white as Spanish Castile.'

'So – so he does,' Jamie agreed, badly shaken. 'The man uses white

oak ash and we supply the finest tallow. He swears it's the best and
will have none other. The washer-lassie brings white soap for my
mother when she comes, but – but Maggie is not—'

Jamie hesitated. He'd known Maggie from childhood and to him
she remained a child despite her flirtatious ways and the family's
teasing. But now he recalled that Maggie was seventeen and of a
sudden she did not seem so childlike to a bachelor of twenty-four
years. Maybe the time had come to pay Maggie more attention.

He glanced up to find the older woman watching him and grew
hot under the collar. 'I'll cut some soap off the bar for ye. Ma won't
mind,' he said gruffly.

'You'll do no more cutting today, my lad. I'll do it.'

At his prompting she cut four neat rectangles from the long bar.
These she wrapped in linen from the ill-used underskirt and stowed
carefully in her pouch before producing a handful of silver.

He objected strongly. 'Ma will be affronted if you offer siller.'

She laughed. 'I would not dare! This is for your sweetheart to
make a bonny gown. Tell her there will be regular orders for her
father's white soap and Lady Annabel Erskine will pay.' She put the
coins on the table and prepared to leave.

Jamie followed her outside. Muckle Meg was tethered in the yard
cropping grass. He watched the woman murmur a few words to the
horse then settle in the saddle and gather the reins. He stood like
a dummy nursing the injured arm, unable to help. Looking up at
her from the ground, he was very conscious of the debt he owed.
'I dinna ken how to thank ye,' he said lamely.

She guided the horse on to the track and looked down at him,
smiling. 'No need for thanks, Mister Gilmore. Next time you wield
the sickle dinna let your thoughts wander off to your sweetheart.'

He watched her trot away. Now that the older woman had put
the thought into his head Jamie saw that Maggie was the perfect
choice for a wife. She came regularly to Goudiebank to help his
mother now that Christina had gone and he would not even have
to leave the farm to go courting. Jamie stared after the lady's maid.
The sun on his back was warm as the gratitude he felt.

'Maggie – my dearest,' he muttered experimentally and went
indoors to plan a courtship.

Time had hung heavily on Christina's hands since Dorcas departed.
She helped Annabel package the queen's clothing in muslin. When
Dorcas returned with soap the completed order could be wrapped

in sailcloth ready for Hector's packhorse to transport to Lochleven. Meantime, there was nothing to do here and Aunt Bertha had decreed that Janet must rest and receive no visitors.

Annabel had found a lute in an unused closet and sat plucking the strings. She played well and the soft tinkling music echoed in the background as Christina stood by the window looking out. Sadly, she recalled a future that had once seemed full of promise and was now uncertain. She remembered hard-working days spent in the fields with her family in fresh cool air. This room's tapestries and painted ceiling spoke of luxury but it still felt like a stifling prison. Christina felt fit to weep.

Abruptly, Annabel jangled an angry chord and stopped playing. 'How can I concentrate while you mope? What ails ye?'

Guiltily, Christina turned her back on the view. 'I'm sorry, my lady. I was dreaming of working in the fields in clear air and sunshine. It – it saddened me.'

Annabel shuddered. 'No wonder. Such ugly freckled damage to fair skin!' She eyed Christina speculatively and sighed. 'Oh, very well! Go walk in the garden if you must.'

She returned to the lute while Christina escaped, the tinkling melody fading as she ran gleefully along corridors and down stairways.

The garden had once been a pleasant retreat but now the queen could no longer visit her favourite palace it was neglected and over-grown. Following a weedy path Christina came across Hector slashing moodily at thistles in an attempt to restore order to rose beds.

He straightened. 'So you escaped!'

She smiled. 'My lady wanted me out o' the way more like.'

'Aye. A palace can be a prison for both high and low. Lady Annabel grows thrawn and tetchy when the action slows.'

This was such an accurate assessment she was curious. 'How is it you know her so well?'

He shrugged. 'Years ago my parents challenged the Reformed Kirk. They were of the Catholic faith and died for their beliefs. Sir Allan Erskine rescued me as a wee lad and I rose to be his head groom. After Sir Allan's wife died he begged me on the quiet to curb his mettlesome wee lassie and keep her out o' mischief. A near impossible task!'

'Annabel's fortunate to have you as champion, Hector,' she said sincerely.

'You think so? That means so much!'

She noted warmth in his eyes and took a hesitant step along the path. 'I'm hindering you. I must go.'

He reached out and grasped her hand urgently. 'Christina, please – be very careful how ye tread! Take care!'

'Thank ye kindly, Hector, I will.'

She freed the hand with a shy smile and went on her way treading carefully. It did not occur to her that thistles on the slippery path might not be the dangerous hazard Hector had in mind.

The path ended in an open area of scattered trees and mossy grass. In the shelter of a ruined wall Christina came across an old plum tree laden with ripe fruit. She gave an exclamation of delight since fresh fruit had been sadly lacking in the diet. There were wasps buzzing around feeding upon fallen plums but she heeded Hector's warning and trod carefully amongst the hornets. She became so engrossed that she was not aware of John Haxton's presence till a shadow fell across the grass and she glanced over her shoulder. She saw a huntsman in leather jerkin with a large hound at his heels and assumed it was one of Falkland's staff. 'What a bounty this is!' She laughed happily. 'Would ye like some? But mind the wasps!'

John could hardly believe he'd found her. There had been word of a troublesome fox stalking Falkland's hens and he'd volunteered Boris to end the pest. However, as Joshua had remarked, foxes are as fly as Fifers. Even Boris had had no luck with the wily beast and John was making his way home when he spied the fair lady.

Christina Gilmore was even more beautiful than he had remembered. He took the fruit she offered and watched as she sank perfect white teeth into a juicy plum. A trickle of juice ran down her chin and she wiped it away with a hand, unconcerned.

John Haxton was enchanted. This lady was quite delightful.

The huntsman's silence had given Christina time to examine the man's attire and she paused doubtfully. She noted velvet bonnet, boots and jerkin of finest tooled leather, sleeves, breeches and hose of best quality. This was no common huntsman!

'Sir – I—' She began nervously, but at that moment a wasp landed on the plum she held. She cried out and flung it down, her feet slipping on the rotting fruit lying underfoot. John Haxton caught her or she would have fallen.

She looked up into his face. The hound let out a startled rumbling growl and Christina suddenly remembered. 'You!'

He released her and doffed the velvet bonnet. 'John Haxton at your service, Mistress Christina Gilmore.'

An Englishman! she thought in panic. An English wolf in fine clothing just as Annabel had warned! 'Why are ye here and how is it ye know me?' she demanded.

'I'm a sportsman stalking Scottish deer and hunting wolves and foxes. You may recall we met briefly in the street. Afterwards I was told who you were.'

He noted her ringless hands and was intrigued. So she was unmarried but who was the father of her child? Had her vicious father maybe murdered the man?

'Tell me, Mistress Christina, how is the infant?' he asked.

Christina felt reassured. He seemed genuinely concerned for Janet's frail baby. 'He's settled well with his wet nurse, I thank ye, sir, though it's early days yet.'

'Of course.' He nodded sympathetically, swiping at a wasp with the bonnet. He took her arm. 'We're on dangerous ground. Let's walk.'

He led her across the springy turf, away from prying eyes at the palace windows, the hound padding behind. Christina could think of nothing to say and neither could he but silence did not seem to matter. She was not even aware of silence in the sudden wonder of his nearness.

John Haxton had flirted outrageously and imagined himself in a fantasy of love with many lovely ladies at Elizabeth's court, but a chance meeting with a Scottish lady had surpassed mere flirtation. He was vibrantly aware of her touch, the rustle of her silk gown on the grass as she walked easily beside him, the sunlight shining on her hair. Her beauty took his breath away and banished superficial banter.

'You – you pass the time with Lady Annabel Erskine?' he asked.

'Aye, wi' embroidery,' she answered cannily – no word of sewing for the queen.

He was handsome and she warmed to him but she wouldna lose sight of the fact that he was an Englishman far from home! she thought. No doubt he looked for a casual affair with any willing country lass that took his fancy. He must know her humble origins from listening to village gossip and would not be deceived by borrowed gear. This huntsman would consider her easy prey. As he led her further from the palace she knew she must watch her step.

He stopped suddenly, took her hands and forced her to look at him. 'Christina, please consider me your loyal champion. I know your father's reputation but that will not deter me.'

She could not believe her ears. To flaunt her father's weakness in her face was the most abominable insolence. She would have slapped his cheek had she not been so humiliated. She stared at him with loathing. 'You can never be my champion, John Haxton! I love my father and will not have him despised by such as you!'

Gathering up her skirts, Christina ran back furiously to the palace.

John Haxton glared after her. He could not imagine what he had done to cause such offence. Her innocence and beauty had captivated him for a few unwary moments and he had only intended to assure her that he would remain steadfast – after all, she must know her jealous Highland father's murderous ways with her admirers yet seemed unmoved by his evil deeds.

What a vicious wolf's whelp! he thought, still smarting with indignation. This was a most remarkable example of like father, like daughter!

Calling Boris brusquely to heel he strode off angrily, vowing to be very wary of perfidious Scottish beauties in future.

Four

Annabel stopped playing when Christina rushed in.

'What's happened? You look as if the Devil's after you!'

'I was approached by an Englishman.' Christina collapsed on a chair.

Annabel was on her feet in an instant. 'An Englishman? Are you sure?'

'Aye. You can't mistake the tongue. He was glib and smooth and tried to lower my guard, but then he showed his true colours and insulted my father.'

Annabel frowned. 'Why would he do that?'

'A slip of the viper's tongue! He'd found out my history frae Falkland gossips.'

Christina still boiled with indignation after the encounter. It did not help to remember that at first she had warmed to the man.

Annabel paced the floor. 'This is serious, Christina. He could be an English agent sent to spy on our dealings with Her Grace. Why else would he take such an interest in you?'

'Why indeed?' Christina's thoughts were bitter. He would know she was a country maid easily swayed to fall in love with a nobleman. He would be confident that under the spell of his kisses she could be tricked into giving away vital information. What humiliation!

Annabel was quick to notice ruffled feathers. 'Och, Chrissie dear, don't be huffed! English wolves are all the more cunning when stalking bonny lassies. Did he question you?'

'Aye, but I let nothing slip. He knows I work at embroidery, that's all.'

'That's a blessing. The Keeper o' Falkland Palace is out of favour with the lords and left in haste to guard his own estates. I was sure we'd attract no attention working here. Seems I was wrong. Now we must decide what's to be done.'

A maidservant appeared in the doorway, bobbing a curtsey. 'Beg pardon, m'lady, there's a gentleman o' high degree come to visit.'

Annabel and Christina looked at one another. Could it be the

Englishman, heaven forbid? They froze as the maid stood aside to admit the visitor.

'Lachie!' Christina cried.

The servant's introduction had delighted Lachlan Gilmore who had taken trouble with his appearance before setting out that morning. He had cursed mud thrown up by Kelpie's flying hooves on the ride to Falkland but had dodged most of the divots. He bowed, sweeping off a feathered cap. 'At your service, ladies!'

His sister hugged him, laughing. 'Och, Lachie, we thought it was a gentleman but it's only you!'

He glowered moodily, taken down a peg. 'Aye, only Lachie Gilmore wi' clart on his boots.'

She kissed his cheek. 'Dinna take the tig; I was joking, dear Brother.'

'Aye, well—' Lachie had a clear view of his sister for the first time and the transformation was a shock. She wore silk and satin and her golden hair was combed and curled like a lady's. 'You're dressed very fine!' he remarked accusingly.

'You're a sight to soothe sore eyes yoursel', Lachie,' she teased, eyeing her brother's cloak, doublet and hose. Oh, it was so good to see him! she thought. He brought happy memories of home and she choked back tears.

Christina and Lachie were two of a kind and an affectionate bond existed. They shared their French father's adventurous spirit and Wil's taste for the finer aspects of life.

'What news of Janet and her wean?' he asked anxiously. 'Ma's been near out of her wits wi' worry about you two lassies but she's not fit to make the journey. Pa is taking her to Michaelmas Fair today as a diversion to cheer her.'

'Janet's too weak to care for a frail baby born weeks afore its time, Lachie. I brought him to the palace for better attention and you can tell Ma that Ninian may be tiny but the wee soul seems determined to survive. You'll meet him later.'

Lady Annabel came forward with a rustle of silk and a flutter of dark eyelashes to greet the visitor. 'I agree with your sister, Mister Gilmore, you do look braw!'

He grinned delightedly, quite overwhelmed.

'Did you bring a letter for me?' she demanded.

Lachie's grin faded. Dourly, he reached for his pouch. 'Aye, there's one for ye frae Master George. Hugh Ross rowed wee Willy Douglas over from the castle with it at first light.'

Annabel pounced on the document and held it close to her bosom. Lachie watched jealously.

'How is Hugh?' Christina asked. The encounter with the Englishman had left her shaken. Uncomplicated love for a childhood sweetheart served to remind her of the dangers of exciting encounters with men of substance.

'Hugh is fine and asks after you tenderly, but he could not tarry,' Lachie said. 'The washerwomen were girning because he'd made them late, ferrying a lady to the island.'

Annabel was interested. 'A lady? Who was she, Lachie?'

'Wee Willy told me it was Mary Seton, Lord George Seton's sister.'

She smiled radiantly. 'Och, that's grand news! Mary Seton is the queen's closest friend, one of the ladies-in-waiting known as the four Maries, and her brother George Seton was Master o' the Royal household at Holyrood. What comfort this will be for Her Grace! I wonder if the letter mentions it?'

Annabel turned eagerly to the window embrasure to read in brighter light.

Lachie whispered to Christina. 'I'm surprised the laird allows contact with the Setons if they're such strong royalists. Wee Willy Douglas should mind his step. That laddie kens too much and knowledge is a dangerous trade!'

She nodded agreement. 'Wise words, Lachie. Mind now – dinna you meddle in Douglas affairs!' she warned.

'Who's meddling?' He grinned. 'For all the laird kens I rode ten rough miles to visit my dear sisters and sickly wee nephew.'

'Aye! On purpose to deliver letters on the sly,' she said. 'Who kens the danger letters hold?'

Lachie scowled. 'Och, it's only a love letter frae Geordie Douglas, curse 'im! It took all my resolve no' to trample it in the glaur.'

Christina shook her head despairingly. Her brother adored Annabel with a passion that must end in heartbreak. She slipped an arm through his. 'Come away, Lachie dear. It's time to meet your new nephew. His good nurse dotes upon him and we begin to hope the wee lad may live.'

Euphemia Sturrock was baking barley bread when her noble lodger came storming in with an anxious hound bounding at his heels. There were thunderclouds gathering over the Lomonds and a sullen black sky matched John Haxton's mood.

He snatched off his bonnet and flung it in the general direction
of the peg. The velvet flopped on to dusty rushes softening flagstones to ease Phemie's feet.

'Good hunting, was it?' she said mildly as he kicked the door
shut.

'Plums!' he snarled. 'She had the impudence to offer plums with
smiles sweet as honey!'

Phemie thumped the dough with a fist. 'So the gift turned sour?'

'Aye, it did! She turned on me like a wolf's whelp when I
happened to mention her evil father.'

'This would be bonny Christina Gilmore?' she said.

'Bonny?' He snorted. 'A she-wolf in lambskins!'

He reached for the ladle and took a long draught of water from
the butt. It cooled him. He wiped his mouth reflectively.

'Mind you, Mistress Sturrock, her passion *was* magnificent.'

Phemie gave him a wary look, afraid that her careful plotting was
about to unravel. She checked the fire and slid dough into the oven.
'A wolf's whelp is ill to tame, Sir John.'

'So they say, but it would be exciting sport to tame this shrewish
whelp!'

'Oh aye, it'll be exciting if her jealous father gets wind o' it!'

He smiled grimly. 'He will! I told the lady her father's bad reputation will not deter me. You should have seen her face! She looked
fit to claw my eyes out!'

'I can imagine,' Phemie remarked with feeling.

She eyed the young man and prayed Heaven to forgive her for
a scheme that had started with good intentions and could have
unseen complications. She could not imagine mild-mannered Wil
Gilmore reaching for sword and buckler if confronted by the fierce
young Englishman's dagger, but Wil *was* French by birth and you
never could tell wi' foreigners, she thought.

Eager to change the subject, Phemie remembered the courier
that had come hammering on the door earlier that day. 'By the by,
Sir John, there's another letter frae your fond pa.'

She could hardly stop her lip from curling. The missive awaiting
him on the settle was heavy with official seals. Tantalizing snippets
of writing could be viewed and the frustration of illiteracy had been
hard for Phemie to swallow.

John Haxton moved to the farthest corner of the room to read
his master's latest bulletin:

John, I am returning to London forthwith, Sir Nicholas Throckmorton wrote.

Queen Elizabeth is greatly perturbed by recent events concerning the Scottish Queen and demands reassurance. Her greatest fear is that the French may send a large force to Scotland to free Queen Mary and the invasion may not halt at the Scottish border. Some argue, the French included, that Mary Stuart's claim to the English throne has more legitimacy than Elizabeth's, daughter of Anne Boleyn and Henry Tudor.

Strange times in which we live, John – two realms in one small island seething with intrigue and rebellion and both ruled by contrary young women. We have a Scottish queen too willing to wed and secure the succession and our own queen Elizabeth, who coyly will not. Who is to say which woman is the wiser?

I have spoken with the Earl of Moray, Queen Mary's half-brother, recently returned from exile. He visited her at Loch Leven and harangued her for her faults, namely choosing husbands unwisely, favouring the advice of base-born favourites and scorning the counsel of lords. He swears she repented and wept, begging him to act as regent on her son's behalf.

The man seems upright and pious, though I believe cunning in his ambition to rule, denied him by birth. He certainly rants and thunders like the prophets of old, enough to alarm one of weaker disposition. I am not surprised that Mary Stuart trembled and wept.

Keep vigilant, my good friend: when I have news you need to know, I will send an agent to you secretly . . .

John Haxton read the document through again carefully, then rose and committed it to the flames. Phemie watched sulkily as the corners curled and blackened, wax seals flamed and unknown writings were totally consumed.

'Your pa would be saddened to see it burn,' she remarked.

His expression hardened. 'My father knows I carry no burdens, Mistress Sturrock.'

But she noticed he sat a long time musing by the window, a hand absently caressing the faithful hound and gaze fixed upon the palace grounds. Did he dream about ripe plums and bonny Christina Gilmore? Phemie wondered. And were the dreams that burdened his thoughts sweet or sour?

Lachie Gilmore was shocked at first sight of his new nephew. He had never seen such a tiny scrap of humanity but Lachie was encouraged

to note that Janet's frail infant had the best of care. A fire heaped high
with Fife coal warmed the east-facing chamber in the chilly palace.
Wee Ninian was warmly wrapped in woollens and slept in a carved
cradle. A small girl sat patiently rocking the crib.

Impulsively, Lachie searched in his pouch and handed the little
rocker a penny while her mother the chambermaid looked on beaming.
The woman held her own plump infant in her arms, a tragic contrast
between two newborn weans. She smiled sympathetically. 'He may
be uncommon wee, sir, but I never met a bairn wi' such will to live.
God willing, he might.'

Lachie doled out silver from the pouch and left the room with
tears in his eyes.

Outside, he turned to his sister. 'I'm sorry, Chrissie, but I must
away to see Janet immediately. Ma will demand a speedy report.'

She was disappointed. 'I thought you might bide here tonight.'

He glanced towards Annabel's apartment. 'So did I, but I'll not
risk her refusal.'

'At least bid her goodbye, Lachie,' Christina urged.

He obeyed hesitantly and Annabel frowned. 'Must you leave so
soon?'

'I've a long ride ahead afore dark, lady.'

She pouted. 'How tiresome! I hoped tae walk and talk wi' you.'

Lachie was rendered speechless.

She noted his discomfiture with a smile. 'Och well, it can't be
helped! Perhaps it will serve if we walk to the stables together. I've
a mind to view again thon magical piebald beast o' yours.'

She led the way from the room, Lachie following dazedly. Christina
watched them go with an uneasy mind but knew better than to follow.

Lachie fell into step beside the lady as they walked along corridors and through echoing halls. Glancing around cautiously, Annabel
spoke in low tones unlikely to be overheard. 'Lachie, the letter
brought word of decisions to be made at Lochleven Castle. I would
be failing a duty if I didna warn ye of an event that will enrage the
laird and bring vengeance down upon all our heads.'

He met her eyes, darkly serious for once. He could well imagine
the event that would infuriate the laird. Geordie Douglas planned
to marry Annabel Erskine and she intended to accept him. Both
must know that Sir William would aim higher than a merchant's
daughter as wife for his young brother. The laird's anger and the
wrath of old Lady Douglas their mother at such a mean match
would be fierce and vengeful.

At that moment Lachie's heart broke. He had always known that loving Annabel was hopeless fantasy on his part. Her future lay with a man of substance more suited to be a husband than an orra farmhand. He stopped and held her arm, forcing her to face him. 'What do you want me to do?'

'Nothing! I'll bear ye no grudge if you decide to serve me no more as courier for your family's safety.'

'My lady, I would serve ye with my life, if need be.'

'Ah, Lachie—!'

The light was poor in the dark corridor but she leaned so close that for a moment he imagined she might not object if he kissed her. He struggled against the temptation and the intimate moment passed.

'So be it, Lachie!' she said briskly. 'Henceforth we are conspirators and I pray with all my heart you'll not regret the alliance.'

Marjorie Gilmore still concealed the secret of her pregnancy and was reluctant to accompany her husband to Kinross Fair. In the end she yielded to her youngest son's pleading. Francis had saved some pennies and was desperate to spend them. Wil Gilmore seemed eager to have her company. 'If you will not go, my sweeting, then I will not go!' he'd declared with a loving kiss that melted the last shreds of resistance.

After a cold murky ride to the fairground Marjorie began to enjoy herself. The sun struggled through after the peace of the fair was proclaimed and revealed colourful stalls and festive crowds spread across the fairground. This gathering was known locally as Michaelmas Fair, the last to be held before the Michaelmas Day feast on the twenty-ninth of September that marked the official start to autumn. The troubled state of Scotland in 1567 made this year's event even more significant than usual.

Despite kirk Reformers' disapproval, every child at its mother's knee heard the story of Archangel Michael's struggle to cast the devil out of Heaven. Lucifer the defeated fallen angel fell from the sky just as summer ended and landed in a bramble bush roundly cursing the thorny fruit. That is why nobody dared pick tainted blackberries after St Michaelmas Day. The brave Archangel Michael also protects soldiers from harm, an attribute to be secretly encouraged these days when a man could be roused by the wake-staff with an urgent call to arms.

The Kirk session frowned severely upon festive gatherings and had banned dancing as sinfully carnal, but pipes and tambours played merrily today nonetheless. Lads and lassies danced together in the sunlight on the green beside the loch.

Watching their capers, Marjorie smiled. She had never danced herself – a twisted foot saw to that – but she saw no harm in it. Winters are long and happy memories of frolics in the sun warm the heart when icy draughts whistle round the lugs.

Francis watched the scene in open-mouthed wonder. Marjorie smiled and sent the boy off to sample the fair's delights on his own. Wil was drawn to a sale of horses and left Marjorie to sit on a bench with other mature wives enjoying a chance to gossip.

Francis jingled pennies in his pouch as he made his way across the fairground. What to buy made a difficult decision. The air was rich with the succulent aroma of hog roast turning on the spit, but that was a treat reserved for later in the day, to be sampled with Ma and Pa before a cold ride home.

In the meantime there were jugglers and play-actors, peddlers and chapmen selling ribbons, laces and all manner of fancy gear. A small group of wandering Egyptians performed gypsy dances to the beat of a drum while their womenfolk offered a halfpenny glimpse into a future writ on the palm of a hand. A Fife fishwife pushed past the boy yelling her fishy wares, creel packed with smoked herring, cockles, mussels and fresh boiled shrimps.

Francis limped on past stalls manned by bonnet makers, fleshers, cobblers and carpenters. He paused at one to buy a carved spoon for brother Jamie, sadly left behind to mind the farm, and headed straight as an arrow for a crowd of bairns clustered around the candy stall. He wriggled his way to the front.

Children drooled over dishes of caramels, candied fruits, small cakes and sweetmeats crowned with sugar and spice. Recklessly, Francis handed over the remaining pennies and was rewarded with a random selection of sweeties tipped into a paper poke.

Fortunately there was still plenty entertainment to be had although every penny was spent as Francis idled along contentedly past the stalls. In the fisticuffs ring he watched two stalwarts squaring up to the scratch with knuckles raised, but lost interest when one lad soon hit the ground. He wandered off to watch old and young throwing stones to knock down tenpins and others racing hounds, ending more often than not in a snarling dog fight.

At the far end of the field foot races and a rowdy game of football were in progress. Mighty hammer men, muscular blacksmiths and brawny porters, pitted their massive strength against one another, hurtling huge boulders towards a mark.

Tiring of viewing strenuous activity, Francis found a quiet spot beside a clump of whins and settled down to eat sweets. A shadow fell across his refuge and wee Willy Douglas stood grinning down at him.

'Weel met, Francis! I was lookin' for a friend!' He planted himself cheerfully on the grass and eyed the poke. 'What's that ye bought?'

'It's sweeties.' Francis swallowed reluctance heroically. 'Help yoursel'.'

'Thank ye, but no. The pieman's going the rounds and I'm starving. Let's have pies first and sweeties after.'

A bowl of early morning porridge had long since ceased to satisfy and Francis's stomach grumbled. He would dearly love to sink his teeth into a meat pie. But alas, the pennies were spent!

'I've nae money, but dinna let that stop ye, Willy. I'll eat later wi' my ma and pa.'

Willy Douglas laughed, scrambling to his feet. 'Och away! I've more than enough to pay for two.' He detached a leather pouch from his belt and spilled a heap of silver into his palm that made Francis gape.

'It's a ransom! How came ye by that?'

'Geordie Douglas pays me tae carry letters across the loch. I'd to hand a letter to your brother Lachie early this morning for the lady at Falkland Palace.'

This was news to Francis. 'Lachie never said anything about a letter for the lady. He was off tae Falkland to see my sisters and the new baby.'

Willy looked worried. 'It's a secret. You're no' tae breathe a word tae a living soul, cut your throat an' hope tae die!'

'Not even tell Ma and Pa?'

'Heaven forbid! If George Douglas learns I've been blethering I'll have my head in my hands and my lugs tae play wi'!'

With this ominous prediction, the boy darted off to waylay the pieman.

A few bare-legged Wild Scots had come down from the Highlands to attend the fair, bringing with them the skirl of pipes. Lowland folk had good reason to be wary of upland men but Highland melodies are hard to resist and soon groups of Fifers were dancing and hooching merrily on the green. Marjorie sat watching with a smile, foot tapping in time to the music.

Wil appeared at her side. He'd been to the horse sale, visited an ale seller with some farmer cronies and was in sparkling good humour. He took off his bonnet and bowed.

'Will you dance, *ma belle?*'

She laughed, delighted. 'Och, Wil love, dinna jest, you know I canna!'

'My sweeting, with me you can. To me you are perfection!' He put an arm round her waist and lifted her from the bench before she could protest.

It was strange, but Marjorie felt steadier held in his arms. She discovered a natural rhythm and lightness of foot she hadn't known she possessed. Her face glowed with happiness.

Wil looked down at his bonny wife with a smile. The wild tempo of the music had changed to a plaintive pipe tune, surprisingly lilting and tender coming from such a fierce clannish source. He had something to say and what better time to say it than this? He bent closer and whispered in her ear. 'My love, I believe there is a secret we must share!'

Shocked, Marjorie almost missed her step. He knows about the baby! she thought incredulously – although upon reflection it was not so surprising. Her husband was a perceptive man and she had been sick in the mornings and acting strangely for weeks. She eyed him nervously but he seemed relaxed and happy. Marjorie felt ready to cry with relief.

'Och, Wil, I've been meaning to tell ye for weeks I was with child, but I thought it wise to keep news o' the baby to mysel' till I was sure. I had a word wi' the howdie that brought Francis into the world and the woman says the signs are our baby will be born by Easter, God willing.'

He stopped so suddenly she stumbled.

'What ails ye, Wil?' she cried, alarmed.

He groaned deeply. 'This bad news you tell me about a baby! Ah, Marjorie, Marjorie – this is not the secret I had hoped to share!'

Marjorie listened to every word but could not believe what she had heard. She shoved her husband away and stepped back.

The Highland pipes had quickened to a wilder tempo and dancers flung themselves screeching into a reel. Marjorie and her man stood on the outside staring at one another.

'What are ye saying, husband?' she said.

'Dearest – this harvest is poor, sheep and cattle have not fattened as they should on parched grassland and yet the laird will still demand the greater part. We could starve this long, hard winter. How can a tender baby thrive, my dear?' He took a step closer and took her limp hand. 'Soon we will be too old to give the growing child the care it needs and what if it's born a crippled weakling like Francis?'

She stiffened. 'What if it is?'

She faced him with eyes blazing. At that moment she felt no warmth for the man she had loved without question.

Wil Gilmore was suddenly afraid. News of this baby's coming was a devastating blow on top of his other problems and he had spoken with the desperation of a man at the end of his tether. His response to the news was heartfelt but now he regretted it.

'Marjorie – sweeting, I'm sorry—'

'Keep remorse for your unborn bairn, Wil!' she told him tight-lipped and turned to leave.

He caught her arm. 'Wait, dear wife! You do not know a more profitable secret we can share. This morning I bought a colt from a poor widow woman. The moment I set eyes upon the stallion I knew it was a remarkable find. I offered the poor widow a generous price and she went away blessing the day. Now I can groom and train the colt to its full potential. There could be a fine young stallion to trade at Falkirk Tryst next year to redeem Christina's dowry. I'll not fail ye this time!'

'Aye that's as may be, if you can steer clear of an alehouse!' his wife declared bitterly. For the first time in their marriage Marjorie faced what she had long suspected was the truth. 'You aye loved the farm and fine horses more than you ever loved me, Wil,' she said sadly. 'From the start I was just part o' a profitable deal. I made allowances because I loved ye, but no more, Wil, no more!'

'Dearest—!'

He paused, deeply shocked. Accustomed to kissing and cajoling his wife into loving compliance, this time the look in her eye told Wil that he had gone far beyond hope of forgiveness. Dismayed, he watched Marjorie turn her back on him and limp slowly away from the howls and capers of fast and furious jiggers.

Annabel Erskine remained quiet and thoughtful for a good while after Lachie Gilmore's brief visit. She returned to the apartment and picked up the lute. Tactfully Christina left her mistress to the comfort of music and busied herself folding material on the tabletop and retrieving precious scraps of fur, Flanders silk and cloth of gold from the floor.

Dorcas returned from Goudiebank that evening after candles were lit and maids had set supper on the table. Her riding kirtle was mud spattered and she complained of cold but otherwise was in good spirits and bursting with news.

Christina was alarmed to hear of Jamie's accident. 'Will he be all right? Was he well when you left?'

'Aye, quite recovered.' Dorcas warmed her hands at the fire. 'I believe he might even hae plans to woo Maggie the washer-lassie.'

Christina laughed. 'Jamie and Maggie? You're joking!'

'I am not. Your brother's a worthy man, Chrissie − if a wee bit wild wi' the sickle. The lassie's a lucky woman.'

Annabel seemed unusually quiet and Dorcas eyed her speculatively. 'You seem troubled, lady?'

'So I am and with good reason!' Annabel frowned. 'I had a letter frae George and with it a list from the queen. She begs for sweets, more boxes of pins and lengths of fine Holland material to make clothes for the demoiselle Marie Courcelles, a devoted chamber-maid that came with her to Lochleven. Her Grace pleads for Spanish silk and writes that a silk dressing gown and handkerchiefs will suffice if they may be had. She implores Pierre Veray, her embroi-derer at Holyrood Palace, to send patterns to sew and more skeins of red, blue, green, gold and silver embroidery thread.'

Annabel's expression grew dark. 'The queen is forced to beg even for so much as a pin. It's shameful!' she declared. 'Fortunately I had sent Hector to Leith last month with an order to my father for more fabric and some small luxuries that will comfort her, but I swear to ye I'll use every ounce o' strength and cunning to have her set free.' She eyed her two companions defiantly. 'And if ye find that prospect daunting, the pair o' ye better leave my service!'

Dorcas and Christina exchanged a glance that showed them to be of the same mind.

Dorcas sighed patiently. 'Afore you banish us, lady, will you tell us which Falkland gossips ye have in mind as replacements to sew fit for the queen and be sure to keep tight-lipped?'

Annabel hesitated. 'You make a point, dear Dorcas! I'm a butter-fingers at the mercy o' skilled needlewomen I must trust implicitly. I beg you both most humbly, please dinna desert me now!'

'As if we would!' the two assured their little mistress, laughing.

So the pact was sealed, even though Christina knew that her

commitment added to the danger. She had wilfully ignored her own wise advice and become entangled in Lady Annabel's dangerous net.

Och well! What's done is done, she thought resignedly. I'll sew a straight seam and keep a tight lip. Where's the harm in that?

Next day, Christina sought permission to visit Janet. She went boldly into the street with head and shoulders shrouded in the concealing folds of the old plaid.

Falkland was busy that day. A convoy of packhorses and chapmen had arrived in the village to carry wool and woven webs to the coast prior to transport across the Forth to Leith. Men and women were noisily disputing prices with traders, bairns were getting in everyone's path and the usual aimless hordes of pigs and poultry rooted and scratched around household middens. Above all sounded the relentless clacking of busy looms.

Christina picked her way with fastidious care, lifting high her silken skirts. Eyes on uneven ground, she did not notice the horseman till he was nearly upon her. He reined in the startled horse and dismounted,

'I knew it was you,' John Haxton said, the wolfhound Boris snuffling at his feet. He lifted the coarse plaid distastefully away from her face between finger and thumb.

'Why in Heaven's name must you wear this ugly old rag?'

'To protect me from Englishmen like you, sir.'

'Why bother? I recognized you despite the beggar's gear.'

'They say a wolf aye recognizes its prey!' she said, hurt and humiliated.

'How odd you should say that!' he remarked in genuine surprise.

Last night he had dreamed of hunting this wild she-wolf, in the dream taunting his quarry to drive her into a corner and rouse her passion. But now that they stood face to face his mood changed. He had hurt her and was sorry.

'Forgive me. I didn't mean to offend,' he said awkwardly.

But Christina had found the insult unforgivable. Admittedly the old plaid had seen better days, but it was all she had to remind her of home and this man's disgust was a cruel reminder of a humble background and cheap worsted masquerading in silk. She stubbornly refused to look at him.

If only she would say something! John Haxton thought, exasperated as an unforgiving silence stretched between them. He intended to warn her about rumours a Scottish agent had passed on to him in confidence.

The spy whispered that rebel lords had set about catching and convicting minor suspects in the gunpowder plot that killed the unpopular young king. Unfortunately for the lords, men with nothing to lose and an attentive audience gathered at the scaffold steps denounced those in power in government as the true culprits. This had a sobering ring of truth and support for the queen was growing apace, which left her captors in a quandary.

They had stated at the outset that the reason for Mary Stuart's incarceration was to preserve her from the Earl of Bothwell's evil influence. The man was now safely out of the way in captivity in Norway and it was rumoured that the queen was prepared to annul a Protestant marriage the Earl had forced upon her.

In other words, the spy whispered, Mary had complied with every demand the rebels asked of her and they had no valid reason to keep her imprisoned – unless more damning evidence of guilt could be found.

Restoration was not an option since the rebels feared the deposed queen's vengeance. Besides, the authority to govern Scotland during the baby king's long minority was a prize too valuable to relinquish. It was obvious to devious men that a way must be found to destroy the queen and ruthlessly nip i' the bud a growing number of her loyal supporters. The spy warned John that the Confederate Lords already had plans afoot to that end.

The news had alarmed John Haxton. He was now convinced that Annabel Erskine and Christina Gilmore were heavily involved in the queen's affairs and he had kept a covert watch upon all comings and goings at Falkland Palace.

'Who is the man on the piebald horse?' he demanded.

Christina was caught off guard. She turned cold, fearing for Lachie's safety. 'That's none o' your business.'

'I believe it is. You could be in danger.'

'As if you care!'

He loomed over her, hot with anger. 'I do care, Heaven alone knows why! Go home to your disreputable father for God's sake. You'll be safe there.'

Tears threatened, but she was too furiously angry to weep. 'I hate you,' she cried. 'I never hated anyone in all my life as I hate you!'

He stepped back as if she'd slapped him, then turned swiftly and mounted the horse, galloping off madly towards the Edinburgh road, scattering pigs, poultry and packhorses in his path, the wolfhound bounding behind.

Christina tugged the despised plaid closer, covering rich clothing and fair hair curled and crimped by Dorcas's skilled hand. She was proud of her honest farming background but at that moment her pride was in tatters. Rich trappings could not disguise humble origins and John Haxton's contempt of her father's behaviour was the final humiliation. She scurried across the cobbles to the cottage with head bowed, no longer bothered that the gown's hem trailed in the glaur.

'Is that you, Chrissie?' her sister called as she lifted the latch.

'Aye, only me!' Christina replied.

Janet lay in the box bed in an alcove close by the fire. An iron cauldron of mutton stew simmered gently, hanging by a swee-chain in the wide fireplace. The appetizing aroma was reminiscent of home as Christina sat on the stool by the bedside. She was relieved to find no trace of the childbed fever that had nearly cost her sister's life. 'You look better the day, Janet love,' she remarked.

'Lachie's visit cheered me. He told me my dear wee one is thriving at the palace.'

'Aye. Ninian's doing fine; his nurse dotes upon him.'

Janet frowned. 'I dare say she does, but she's no' his mother! I want him brought home.'

'Janet dear, is that wise?' Christina glanced around the draughty living quarters in dismay. Bring the frail baby home – to this?

Agitated, her sister struggled to sit up. 'Of course it's wise! My baby should be where he belongs with his own mother and loving family. I want Ninian brought home. You must see to it at once, Christina!'

Five

Janet broke down in tears as Christina hesitated.

'How can I get well when my baby is taken from me and my arms are empty, Chrissie? I need my son!'

Christina comforted her sister as best she could, but Janet was a motherly soul devoted to her children. Pining for the tiny baby must hinder her recovery.

Christina could see clearly that this decision might end in disaster whichever path she chose. She must weigh the health of her sister, with three young bairns dependent upon her, against the precarious survival of one sickly baby.

A tragic choice!

Ninian was making slow but steady progress in the Falkland chambermaid's care, but bringing the delicate wee soul from palace luxury to workman's cottage was taking an enormous risk.

It was true Falkland weavers were better housed than their cottar neighbours working on the land. The Guthries' thatched cottage was stoutly built, with a floor of flagstones warmly strewn with clean straw. Janet was an efficient housewife and exemplary mother but even so the cottage was not palatial and Christina eyed the interior dubiously.

Wooden shutters shielded small windows from autumn gales and winter storms and a fire burning in the wide hearth was well equipped to heat the room and cook meals. A massive stone chimney stretched upwards through attic and roof space to a circle of daylight glimpsed in the turf. Even so, occasional smoky down draughts escaped into the room.

Arthur Guthrie's workroom occupied the opposite end of the living space behind a wooden partition. As usual, Arthur was working at his loom, barely taking time to shout a greeting to his sister-in-law. Every moment of daylight was precious to the family's livelihood and the flying shuttle sent motes of lint and fluff drifting in shafts of autumn sunlight and the dust settled everywhere. No wonder Janet's bairns were forever sneezing and snuffling!

A barred door beside the fireplace led to stable, byre and pigsty. Pigs grunted, a cow lowed mournfully to be milked and a restless horse kicked moodily against the stall.

Christina sighed. Conditions were certainly not ideal.

Janet had stopped crying. She clutched Christina's hand. 'Please, Chrissie! Bring him home!' she pleaded.

'You've barely recovered from the birth, dear! Are you sure you're strong enough to care for a baby born afore its time? It's a demanding task.'

'I ken it'll be a struggle but I'm his ma and I love him. I'll manage somehow!' she said. 'Arthur's Aunt Bertha will help, bless her. She's grateful for a lodging and has done all the cooking and cleaning while I'm laid low. She took the bairns to play in the woods today to let me rest.' She eased herself up on the pillows. 'My mind's made up, Chrissie. I'll aye be grateful to the palace for saving Ninian but it's time my wee laddie was home.'

Christina could see that further argument was useless. 'Very well, dear, I'll bring him.'

Janet Guthrie smiled for the first time. 'Tomorrow?'

'Aye, tomorrow,' Christina promised dutifully.

Lachie Gilmore returned to Goudiebank after visiting Falkland, arriving home just before bells tolled for the silence of the night. He reassured his anxious parents concerning the health and welfare of his sisters and the new baby but took care to leave the way open for future visits. Once his mother's mind was set at rest on that score, Marjorie's scolding and lamentation over Jamie's injured arm continued and Lachie slipped quietly off to bed unnoticed.

The fuss surrounding Jamie's mishap with the sickle was resumed at breakfast next morning. Marjorie found no sign of infection in the wound by morning light and was forced to admit that Dorcas's treatment had been adequate. She bound up the wound with clean linen and added a few words of medical wisdom. 'Lifeblood ebbs and flows like the tide, ye ken, Jamie! It's a mercy thon woman happened along when the tide was flowing or you'd no' be so chirpy today.'

Jamie nodded agreement. 'Aye whoever taught Dorcas taught her well, Ma. You should trade secrets with her next time she comes to buy Maggie's soap.'

'Humph!' Marjorie responded with a jealous glare and began ladling porridge into bowls.

Jamie judged this an opportune moment to break the news of
his intended courtship. He took a steadying breath. 'By the by, I've
decided to try my luck courting Maggie. Dorcas put the thought
into my mind and it seems a good idea.'

His father and brothers sat up.

Marjorie was taken by surprise, spilling the brose. 'Maggie?' she
said weakly. Despite light-hearted family banter Marjorie had never
considered the washer-lassie a serious match for her eldest son but
now she wondered – why not?

The girl was a wee bit on the young side but none the worse
for that. Her father the soap-man was a substantial tradesman
employing two soap boilers and an apprentice in his strong-smelling
establishment. No doubt his only daughter could look forward to a
handsome dowry.

It went against the grain to agree with the lady's maid but Marjorie
had to admit the plan had merit. She made a token show of mild
indignation. 'That woman has the devil's cheek! Who you fancy is
none o' her business, Jamie.' She set a flagon of buttermilk on the
trestle top with a thud and added, 'Though come to think on it, I
dare say wee Maggie might suit ye well.'

Jamie finished an awkward breakfast squirming under his family's
intense scrutiny. He tested the injured arm gingerly, found it trouble
free and stood up thankfully. Muttering a plausible excuse about
mildew in barley, he escaped. He felt a need for solitude.

Extensive ploughed infields were at the prosperous heart of
Goudiebank Farm. The land's ancient boundaries, marked by Douglas
march stones, stretched from marshlands at the loch's edges across
orchards and well-tended fields sown with oats, barley, peas and
beans. Then the land rose steeply to outfields stocked with hardy
sheep and goats. Herds of hill cattle and wild deer grazed the rough
heathery uplands.

Jamie's remarkable grasp of husbandry ensured that broom planted
on the loch side stabilized marshland and banished mosquitoes.
Forbidden marigolds were not found in Goudiebank's crops or crows'
nests in the farm's treetops. The soil's fertility was preserved with
peat ash and stable manure, cattle grazed on fields left fallow, but
not one beast was seen straying amongst growing crops after June
twenty-fourth, the feast of John the Baptist.

Of course neighbouring tenants cast envious eyes upon fruitful
Gilmore land. They grumbled that fine sheep and cattle, horses and

orchards laden with apples, pears and plums curried unfair favour with the laird – not to mention honey from a line of bee skips and acres of choice malting barley reserved for Sir William's favourite tipple.

Jamie Gilmore was aware of jealousy but lost no sleep over it. He had a clearer understanding of his family's strengths.

The secret of their prosperity – apart from relentless back-breaking toil that coarsened hands and strained every muscle – was down to passion.

Passion for the land was bred in the blood of former Gilmore generations and they had benefited from knowledge gleaned from methods used by the old farmer monks. Jamie's talented French father was not a farmer but Wil's passion for breeding fine horses filled the laird's stable with excellent bloodstock, enriched the soil and contributed vastly to the Gilmores' success.

This morning Jamie climbed hilly ground on his quest for peace of mind. Facing into a keen wind whipping across the loch he stopped to shade his eyes against the morning sun reflected rosily upon Loch Leven – the ancient Scottish name meant wide-open space between trees and it was well named, he thought.

The beauty of the open view brought moisture to his eyes but even so the laird's tenants were not encouraged to forget Douglas dominance. Lochleven Castle was a powerful man-made intrusion upon tranquil Nature.

The Douglases' ancient stone keep rose five storeys high on one of the loch's four islands. Gardens, a smaller round tower, outbuildings and a high forbidding apron wall spanning the island's whole perimeter, surrounded the square keep.

Smoke from castle fires drifted in the wind. Jamie could make out two arquebusiers guarding the gateway, muskets in hand. Servants were grouped at the waterside washing garments, filling buckets or maybe just blethering. Two or three boats bobbed at the castle moorings, several fishermen were out trying their luck on the loch and a Loch Leven boatman was rowing his leisurely way from mainland pier towards the castle jetty with another load of servants.

The soldiers' presence reminded Jamie that Sir William's stronghold was in reality a state prison and the prisoner was the highest in the land – Mary Queen of Scots.

Nobody in the farming community had set eyes on the queen since she was brought secretly to Loch Leven in June at the dead of night, but her presence had unsettled the whole district. Four years ago, in summer 1563 at the height of the young queen's popularity, hundreds of farming folk had flocked to see her on a progress through Fife. Despite a few demonstrators in Kinross against her Catholic leanings, cheering crowds greeted her entourage, Jamie among them. He flung his bonnet in the air with the rest, swearing loyalty and love for the bonny young queen.

Now tragic events had soured public opinion. Scandalous rumours circulated about the young woman once reputed to be as virtuous as she was beautiful and nobody knew what to believe.

Jamie wisely followed his mother's advice and kept in favour with their landlord. As a result he'd heard it whispered contemptuously at market that he was 'Sir William's creature'. He had ignored the jibe, but it rankled.

'You're no' really serious about wee Maggie, are you?' Lachie said, coming up behind him and breaking the chain of thought.

Jamie turned to face his brother. 'Why not? I could do worse.'

'Aye, you could,' Lachie agreed. 'It's just – we've joked about you and her for months and you laughed. That's all the lassie was to you. A joke.'

'She's a wee bit more than a joke now.'

'You mean this time it's serious?'

'Maggie's a hard-working lassie. She'd make a grand farmer's wife.'

'But do you love her?' Lachie knew the cruel pangs of love and hoped to spare his brother the agony.

Jamie hesitated. He wanted to give an honest answer but found love difficult to define. He loved parents, sisters and brothers but passion for the land was entwined with the need to marry and secure this beloved place for future generations. Was that enough to satisfy Maggie? 'It is more a question of does Maggie fancy me?' he said.

Lachie laughed and clapped him on the shoulder. 'Dinna fash, Brother. She fancies you. That's the joke!'

A movement on the hill caught Jamie's eye, startling him. 'Michty! Here she comes!'

The washer-lassie was heading purposefully for them. She halted before Jamie and held out a leather jerkin and blue woollen bonnet. 'Your ma says there's a snell wind and you're to put these on. She says to tell ye to stay out o' the fields till your arm mends.'

'Och away, Maggie!' he protested. 'Ma kens I can't ignore my work. The last downpour laid the barley flat on the ground and scythes won't cut it. I'll rouse the men to make a start wi' the sickle today.'

'You'll no' be joining them if Mistress Gilmore gets wind o' it!'

Maggie spoke with new authority and the two men studied her with surprise.

The washer-lassie had sensed a change in status the moment she set foot in the Gilmores' doorway that morning. Maggie had been welcomed with beaming smiles, excused scrubbing dirty gear on a chilly morning that would rip the skin off your knuckles and served wi' a bowl o' steaming porridge and top o' the milk, to warm her.

Afterwards she'd been despatched to find Jamie Gilmore on an errand that Maggie guessed was contrived. She smiled sweetly. 'The horses need fresh bedding, Jamie. Your ma says could you see to it for your pa? And she says I've to help in the stables to save your sore arm.'

Lachie grinned widely. 'Good idea, Maggie. It'll be cosy in there for the invalid and I dare say the men in the barley field will manage fine without him,' he said, blithely ignoring his brother's scowl.

Francis sat finishing breakfast thoughtfully after his brothers left. The boy's kindly nature made him sensitive to others' moods and he found his parents' unusual silence disturbing. They did not exchange a single word on the journey home from the fair last night but Francis had blamed that on exhaustion. However, a cold silence persisted that morning and became even more pointed after his brothers had gone.

Francis dredged his conscience for any of his own misdemeanours worthy of this level of displeasure but could find none. He searched for an innocent topic to end the deathly hush. 'I met wee Willy Douglas at the fair,' he volunteered.

His mother looked up. 'Did ye, sonny? You never said.'

'You never asked, Ma. Willy bought us pies.'

That caught Marjorie's attention. She was curious. 'Where did the orphan laddie find the siller tae buy pies?'

Francis realized his mistake with sinking heart. Ma would not rest till she'd ferreted out the truth. 'Willy's paid to carry letters across the loch,' he admitted weakly.

'Letters?' Marjorie was alarmed. She was wary of letters. A perfectly innocent letter could be waved in your face to condemn ye to the Tolbooth – or worse. She had no worries about Francis's future prospects, apart from the health issues. He was her brightest boy and despite a crippled foot Francis was in high favour with the laird. Now it was as if danger had reached out a tentative finger and touched this precious bairn.

'To whom does Willy Douglas deliver these letters?' she demanded sternly.

Francis squirmed. He dare not implicate Lachie. 'To – to a messenger waiting on the pier.'

Marjorie relaxed. No doubt the messenger carried Sir William's official letters onwards to Edinburgh. The orphan's part in the exchange seemed innocent but she had already marked wee Willy Douglas as a potential troublemaker and Marjorie doubted if her opinion would change. She wagged a finger at Francis. 'It was wrong tae take charity frae a Douglas. No more free pies for you, my lad!'

'It wasna charity, Ma. Willy Douglas ate all my sweeties,' he said gloomily.

When the hour arrived for Christina to remove Janet's baby from the chambermaid's tender care, Lady Annabel was reluctant to let him go. 'It will weaken your brother's excuse to visit the palace, Christina. What ails Mistress Janet anyway?'

'She feels stronger now and wants her baby brought home.'

'I can't imagine why. He thrives well here.'

'It's a mother's love, my lady.'

She shrugged indifferently. 'Och that! Well, take him to her if ye must but—' She stopped suddenly as a loud commotion broke out in the corridor.

A breathless maidservant rushed in. 'My lady – oh, my lady – the soldiers!'

Three arquebusiers followed hard on the girl's heels. The men brought with them a smell of sweat and hard-ridden horses. The officer sported a sword but the others were unarmed save for a dagger in the belt.

'What's the meaning o' this outrage?' Annabel demanded angrily.

Their leader sketched a scant bow. 'Orders frae Lord Douglas, lady. You three women are tae be brought to the castle.'

'This is beyond reason! What if we refuse tae go?' she stormed.

He shrugged. 'I'll see to it that the laird's orders are carried oot, along wi' the three o' you! I suggest that you come down frae your high horse, lady, dress in travelling gear and prepare to ride. We leave at once.'

Christina faced the officer. 'I canna leave, I've a promise to keep.'

'Do ye indeed?' he said coldly. 'Aye well, ye can keep it – for later.'

'No – please, you don't understand, I cannot!' she cried in panic, picturing her poor sister waiting in vain for her baby's arrival.

But he turned his back and began issuing orders to his men. 'Bide in the room and stand no nonsense frae this lot. I'll send word to bring the women down when the groom has the horses made ready.'

'Aye, aye, Mr Drysdale sir.'

The soldiers grinned, delighted with the licence given and allowed the women no privacy. It was shameful treatment and for the first time Christina was afraid.

Had Sir William found out that Lachie carried secret letters to Falkland? she wondered. Or was the laird suspicious of Annabel's loyalty to the queen and her association with Bonny Geordie?

Either way, they were in grave danger.

When the three women arrived in the stable yard they found Hector waiting with the horses. The groom was fuming with helpless anger but Drysdale's unsheathed sword made Hector powerless to resist.

Lady Annabel indulged in one last defiant outburst. 'My father will be told about this! He's sheriff o' the Leith burgh court and will have ye thrown in the Tolbooth to rot.'

The officer laughed dryly. 'Och, your pa's miles away across the Forth, my dear. You'll be locked awa' in Sir William's castle long afore news spreads tae Leith. I'd keep a civil tongue in my heid if I was you.'

Once they were mounted and out in the street, Christina begged permission to stop for a moment to tell Janet what was happening but Drysdale slapped Muckle Meg's rump and urged the startled mare past the weaver's cottage. The little cavalcade thundered through Falkland village without pausing and Christina could hardly see the way for tears.

Sir John Haxton and Boris the wolfhound arrived in Leith to meet with Throckmorton's special Scottish agent after a day's hard riding and a choppy sea crossing by pinnace. He located the Leith lodging house recommended by the Scottish spy and after a hearty supper fell exhausted into bed – only to toss and turn dreaming of a wild she-wolf snarling viciously just out of reach.

Next morning he hired a horse and with Boris loping at his side headed inland for the arranged meeting in secret in Edinburgh city.

For the mile and a half journey from Leith he chose the busy Easter road rather than the longer Wester route by Broughton and Bonnington. It was a pleasant morning and John rode in leisurely fashion up the hilly track where teams of barrel rollers had transported casks of French wine from Leith vaults to Holyrood Palace in happier times.

He had hours to spare. His meeting with the unknown Scottish agent would not take place till much later that day. In the meantime he intended exploring the city more thoroughly than on previous visits.

Reining in at a viewpoint overlooking the man-made North loch, Scotland's capital appeared to John confined to high buildings perched upon an ancient crag. An uneven spine of tall tenements connected a royal palace at the lower end to a formidable castle crowning impregnable cliffs at the top. He recognized the high wall that encircled most of the city, reinforced after an English army defeated the Scots at Flodden Field near Berwick. The wall was known as the Flodden wall, a name that still held bitter memories.

Approaching one of the eight gates, John could see why citizens preferred to build upwards on a cramped site rather than outwards in open ground. The wall's massive stonework, ruinous in places, still offered protection from attack. He passed through the Netherbow Port straddling the High Street and found himself in the hustle and bustle of a typical market town.

High Street ran almost straight as an arrow from Holyrood Palace just outside the city wall to the castle at the top of the hill. It was a wide, well-paved street lined with fine buildings but John knew from past experience that foul wynds and vile stinking closes led from the main thoroughfare on either side.

Nobility frequented purer air in the Canongate area closer to Holyrood, or favoured the select small burgh of Cowgate set at a lower level to the south. John turned the horse's head southwards. He wanted to see for himself the scene of a recent baffling and horrendous crime.

Just within the city wall he located the ruined kirk that had given its name to a group of former monastic buildings and dwellings known as Kirk o' Field. These stood for the most part around a courtyard in the shadow of the Flodden wall. A postern gate in the wall led to gardens, orchards and the open fields beyond.

The dog at his heel, John dismounted and examined a tumbled mass of stone, charred timbers and shattered debris piled high, blocking the path. This ruin had once been the young King of Scots' lodging for a short time while recovering from smallpox. John marvelled at the destruction, hardly one stone was left on top of another. The amount of gunpowder required to reduce the house's stout walls to this state was almost beyond belief.

Yet John knew that the King and his valet had somehow escaped the blast only to be found murdered by persons unknown in an orchard garden beyond the Flodden wall.

John frowned as he surveyed the desolate scene. It would take more than one man to plan and execute destruction on such massive scale, yet the outlawed James Hepburn, the fourth Earl of Bothwell, remained the only official suspect charged with the unpopular young king's murder. Much plotting would have taken place behind closed doors before this deed was done! John thought grimly. So how many more of Scotland's noblest were involved in this gunpowder plot?

The horse and hound grew increasingly restive, as if the wise animals sensed evil humours still lurking in this silent, abandoned place. John rode away from the melancholy scene with a cold shiver running down his spine.

A tavern in Ainslie's close had been chosen for the meeting. Evening was drawing in as John approached the tavern, which he found discreetly situated in a dark narrow wynd. He tethered the horse at the rail by the horse trough and left Boris on guard. Seating himself in a quiet corner of the hostelry he ordered a tankard of Scottish beer. He sipped the strong brew with caution, determined to keep a clear head.

The agent was an older man soberly dressed in black. He noted John's black velvet bonnet with the modest white cockade, a prearranged signal, and came across, seating himself at the small table. The two men took stock of one another and the Scotsman smiled. 'You are English?'

'And you are Scots!'

The older man laughed. 'Aye, that's the password and a' we need to know!'

'I'm told you have news for me?' John said.

'Aye, concerning the Queen o' Scots.' He glanced around and leaned closer. 'There's nae doubt that Nicholas Throckmorton saved the queen's life this summer but I've news of a new move to destroy her.'

'The Queen of England won't stand for that! Queen Elizabeth disapproves of the assassination of monarchs, especially female monarchs,' John remarked.

'Ah, but there are mair cunning ways to destroy a queen, there are letters!'

'Letters? Surely not!' John was startled. His thoughts flew to a man on a piebald horse, often seen in Falkland.

'Think on it, man!' the Scotsman said, leaning forward. 'Letters can be forged, words altered, genuine phrases taken out o' context to make darker meanings. Honour can be tainted, virtue defiled, reputations ruined. All it takes is the written word. Never underestimate the power o' the pen!'

John met the older man's eyes. 'And you think letters could be used to incriminate the queen?'

'Aye well, think on it – the rebel Lords cannot let her walk free now they have control of the wee baby King James. They must find good reason to condemn, imprison or execute her and must convince Queen Elizabeth of Mary's guilt. It's well known that our young queen was forever writing letters when she came from France to her Scottish kingdom, even using code for secrecy sometimes. I'm told her enemies have gained access to her private correspondence and that is where the danger will come – but I'll send word to Falkland when I have more definite details.'

John Haxton took a sip of warm beer and frowned. 'What part would ladies living in Falkland Palace play in this tragedy, sir? My guess is they are somehow involved with the queen. Why else would young women leave city comforts with winter on the way?'

The older man shrugged. 'Och, I'm told they pass time with harmless sewing and embroidery. Outspoken young women are no' backward in airing dangerous loyal opinions and the queen's supporters are safer kept off Edinburgh streets wi' rebel mobs running riot.' He smiled, eyes twinkling in the candlelight. 'Besides, there is the attraction of a union wi' the powerful Douglas clan. Young George Douglas is a grand catch for any ambitious lady willing to endure a dreich Falkland winter!'

The Scotsman glanced around the shadowy taproom and stood up. The meeting was at an end. He smiled. 'I'm sorry that English doesna trip too lightly from my Scottish tongue.'

John laughed ruefully. 'My command of Scottish dialect is worse!'

'Even so, I think we both understand the dangers,' the older man said gravely.

John Haxton nodded. 'Aye, sir, I think we do.'

Their eyes met briefly, hands clasped in a quick handshake before the stranger disappeared into the dark wynd as silently as he had come.

* * *

Drysdale and his men set a gruelling pace, pausing only once on the ten-mile ride to rest the horses. At last, weary and mud stained, the three women dismounted on Loch Leven pier at twilight and watched the two arquebusiers lead the horses away to Sir William's stables at Goudiebank.

Christina wondered what her family would make of Muckle Meg's return. No doubt they would be concerned but too scared to question.

The officer was impatient to finish his assignment. He hustled the women towards a boat waiting at the pier's end, its boatman huddled in the folds of his cloak to combat chill mists drifting on the loch.

Christina's apprehension eased a little when she saw that the boatman was Hugh. There was nothing he could do to help her but at least she could be sure of his support.

Drysdale ordered the women aboard and Hugh gave a start of surprise as he recognized Christina. He seated her on the thwart facing him. The officer took up a position in the bow where he could keep a strict eye upon Lady Annabel, whose murderous stare would kill him stone dead if it had the power.

Hugh cast off and headed out across the loch into a damp chill that struck Christina like an icy blow. She drew the riding cape closer, shivering uncontrollably.

He gave her a scathing glance. 'So – fine feathers are colder than wool worsted!'

She flushed. 'That's uncalled for, Hugh!'

'You deserve it. Not so much as a kind word from you for months.'

'Dinna expect kind words. You made it very clear it was my dowry you wanted, no' me!'

'And you swore you'd settle for a boatman's bothy! What blethers! Just look at ye now, living in a palace and too soft-skinned to stand the night air.'

He gave an angry tug at the oar and the boat lurched. Drysdale growled a warning oath.

Christina's spirits sank lower. If her childhood sweetheart scorned her what mercy could she expect from an enemy?

Through drifts of mist she saw the dark mass of the castle with glints of yellow light shining from narrow windows less than a mile away. Light meant warmth and a welcome, but these lights were anything but welcoming. To her frightened imagination they were malevolent, evil eyes watching their approach.

Hugh's own heartbeat had quickened anxiously as he observed

her terror. What did the laird want with the women? What crime
had they committed? he wondered.

He felt powerless to help Christina and was heartbroken. She had
caused him such grief that his feelings for her remained confused.
Did he love her still or did he only love Christina, the carefree lassie
walking barefoot in the cornfields with sunlight in her hair? Christina
acting the lady only roused rage and resentment. He pulled angrily
on the oars.

'What have ye done to offend the laird?' he demanded.

'Nothing, I swear!'

'Were you three plotting to rescue the queen?' he whispered,
bending forward.

She stared incredulously. 'Weak women? Och, Hugh, dinna be daft!'

'Crafty vixens, mair like,' he growled.

'You have a cruel opinion o' me now, Hugh,' she remarked sadly.

A marshy smell of withered sedge drifted in the night air as they
approached the island and Christina's eyes were wet with tears. She
had never been so scared and lonely.

Hugh was sorry but they had reached the jetty and there was no
time to make amends. He clambered ashore with the ropes. Drysdale
was next, tersely shepherding Annabel and Dorcas.

Hugh held Christina's hands and whispered as he helped her from
the boat. 'Dinna be afraid, Chrissie; I'll be on the loch, coming and
going every day, I'll aye be here for you!' he whispered.

A light in his eyes suddenly brought back memories of happy
days when they were not much more than bairns. She clung to him,
unwilling to see him go.

Drysdale gave an angry bellow. 'None o' that! Follow me!'

Christina let go reluctantly and followed the others. She did not
look back as they silently crossed a narrow strip of grass and passed
through a gateway guarded by the night watch and leading into a
large dim outer courtyard, shadowy dwellings, smoky fires and dim
lights. Drysdale unlocked an iron-studded doorway close by the
looming castle tower and brusquely ordered the women to enter.

They found themselves in a dimly lit inner courtyard enclosed
by high walls and surrounded by more dark buildings. Holding
hands, Christina and her companions huddled together as the heavy
door clanged shut behind them and a key grated in the lock.

Six

In the month of November 1567

In the gloom of a winter evening Lochleven Castle's inner courtyard was not a cheerful sight, although lanterns shone here and there
on the walls and glimmers of light came from shaded windows in
shadowy buildings. These houses were of a domestic nature and
serving women were busy with evening chores, scuttling to and fro
carrying buckets and bundles. All were shrouded in shawls against
the cold and paid no attention to three strangers.

Christina shivered and huddled deeper in her cloak. She could
hear the restless lapping of the loch not much more than an oar's
length from the base of the outer wall. It was a chilling sound.

The towering face of the laird's ancient keep dominated the courtyard. Looking around curiously she could detect recent additions to
the original that would be of interest to her stonemason father.
These consisted of a large imposing building close by the main tower
and a small round tower built into a corner of the wall-walk encircling the courtyard. Lamplight glowed behind the small tower's glazed
windows and a halberdier guarding the doorway with a formidable
spear shouted a greeting to Drysdale, who growled a response.

One of the servants pushed open a nearby door and an appetizing
smell of cooking drifted out, reminding Christina and her companions that they had not eaten since breakfast. Annabel held Drysdale
personally responsible for this sorry state of affairs and looked daggers
at the officer. 'We're parched and faint wi' hunger. Dogs are better
tended than this!'

He shrugged indifferently. 'That's no' my concern. Follow me if
you please.'

He led the way to a narrow wooden staircase at the side of the
main tower. The steps disappeared steeply upwards into darkness.
'Pick up your skirts and climb,' he ordered.

Annabel protested vigorously but he cut the protest short.

'Haud your tongue, woman! I'm pledged to bring ye to the castle
hale and hearty. Lift up your skirt when you're told – I'll have no
broken bones at this stage.'

Annabel sulkily bowed to the inevitable and the women climbed gingerly.

They reached the top without incident and Drysdale seemed satisfied. The stairway ended abruptly on the second floor of the five-storey tower and the women were faced with an arched doorway in the forbidding expanse of wall towering upwards through the remaining three storeys to the battlements. Below them the feebly lit outer courtyard and castle gardens lay in the darkness of a moonless night. A sour wind whistling around their ears on this unprotected spot brought damp earthy scents across the water from the shore.

Drysdale's mood mellowed slightly. He indicated the massive iron-studded door with a proud jerk of the thumb.

'Behold the only entrance to my lord Douglas's stronghold! Storerooms and kitchens occupy ground and first floors wi' no access frae the outside. Cooks, scullions, sides o' beef, royalty, lords and ladies must a' tread the path we've trod to enter – a braw defence against unwelcome visitors and a secure ward for traitors!'

His captives' spirits sank. Narrow stairs, locked doors, well-guarded inner and outer courtyards and a mile of open water made escape or rescue well-nigh impossible.

Annabel broke a heavy silence. 'Aye well, I'm thankful we'll no' be imprisoned underground at this height; I've never fancied dungeons.'

Dorcas summoned a weak smile. Christina took a deep breath of cold air. It could be the last breath of freedom for a while.

Once inside, Drysdale guided them through a dark hallway before stopping at a door and rapping perfunctorily on the panel. Without more ado he ushered his charges into a small high-ceilinged apartment.

This room was cosy and brightly lit, walls covered with luxurious tapestries. Candles flickered in wall sconces and branched candlesticks lighted a supper table. A richly decorated painted ceiling glowed in shadow above their heads and a coal fire blazed in a fireplace embla-zoned with Douglas crests. Christina longed to stretch out freezing hands to its warmth, but did not dare.

The room's four lady occupants seated at supper turned in surprise at their entrance. Several serving women standing by with napkins and bowls to wash the gentle ladies' greasy fingers eyed the strangers speculatively.

A white-haired dowager sat in state at the head of the table.

'The Falkland women, m'lady,' Drysdale announced.

She nodded graciously. 'Thank ye, Drysdale, that's a duty well done. You'll find a bite to eat downstairs in the kitchen for you and your lads.'

The three captives watched the door close behind their abductor with relief.

What now? Christina wondered.

The elderly lady was studying Annabel Erskine with interest. 'Michty me, Annabel, you were but a wee lassie when last we met! I mind that even at the tender age o' three you found fault wi' my dress – and your fond pa encouraged you with laughter to tell it to my face.'

This was an unfortunate start. Annabel eyed her distant relative warily. 'I apologize for a wee lassie's indiscretion, Lady Margaret. I promise to keep opinion to myself and my tongue on the leash.'

'I'm glad to hear it,' old Lady Douglas said dryly. She turned to the fascinated servants and shooed them out of the room with a wave of the hand. 'Stop gawping, you lassies – away to the kitchen and bring supper for Lady Annabel and her women. They've had a long ride frae Falkland and small consideration for their frailties from our officer of the guard, I'll warrant.' The old lady eyed the muddy and dishevelled travellers with ill-concealed amusement.

'That hard-hearted devil deserves tae be douked i' the loch,' Annabel said venomously, aching in every limb from unaccustomed exercise.

Lady Douglas laughed. 'Och, that's Mister Drysdale's way whether one is lady or fishwife! Take off your wet cloaks and come sit by me at table. You've yet to meet the family.'

Christina hung the cloaks beside the fire and joined the others at the supper table. Seated shyly with nobility she felt as out of place as a common brown trout dished up on a silver platter.

The old lady was busily making introductions. They learned that those also present were Sir William's wife Agnes, a matron in her early thirties, their eldest daughter Elizabeth, aged about thirteen and another young lass seated opposite, introduced as Agnes's niece Jean Leslie, whom Christina judged to be a year or two older than Elizabeth.

Old Lady Douglas was enjoying the novelty of entertaining visitors. 'Of course my younger grandchildren bide with Agnes's relatives in Rothes Castle at the moment,' she went on. 'Agnes will be brought to bed wi' her next baby in the spring, God willing, but Lochleven Castle is not a safe haven for young bairns running loose at present.

The garrison would find them an unwelcome distraction to essential guard duties.'

Agnes Douglas sighed. 'Aye, Sir William and I miss our wee ones sorely, but at least my mind's at rest knowing the bairns are safe from harm.'

The atmosphere round the table was relaxed, even friendly, but Annabel was fidgeting. Dorcas and Christina exchanged an anxious glance. They knew an impulsive outburst from their mistress was imminent.

'That's all very well for *your* bairns, Lady Agnes, but will *we* be safe from harm in Sir William's care?' Annabel demanded. 'Could it be that our attention to Queen Mary's cause has singled us out?'

The two Douglas ladies exchanged a startled glance and the young girls sat open-mouthed staring at fiery Annabel.

'Well, well!' the old lady remarked dryly. 'So prattling wee lassies grow to be outspoken maidens! Her Grace's well-being has aye been this family's concern and you are quite correct, Annabel – your diligent attention to the queen's affairs *has* been noted. That's why you and your women were brought.'

Christina clutched Dorcas's hand. This was confirmation of all their fears.

Annabel had turned pale. 'What – what's to become of us?'

But before the question was resolved footsteps and voices echoed in the hallway. Maidservants had toiled up inner stairs from kitchen quarters bearing steaming platters of meat, gravy and hunks of bread. They crowded into the room and placed the meal before the three women, providing each with a meat knife before stepping back to wait, napkins and bowls in readiness.

With so many listening ears grouped around the table all hope of privacy had gone. The old lady settled back comfortably in the chair. 'Och well, time enough to worry about tomorrow – when tomorrow comes.'

Christina had endured such distress that day she hardly dared to contemplate the morrow. Janet must be distraught, waiting in vain for her beloved baby. Christina's promise was broken through no fault of her own but Janet could not know that. What must she think?

Christina cut a tender morsel of meat and found her throat so choked with grief she could barely swallow.

There was consternation at Goudiebank when soldiers returned the Douglas horses to Wil Gilmore's stables along with Christina's mare,

Muckle Meg. The men could supply the anxious family with little information apart from the fact that Christina, Lady Annabel and the lady's maid had been brought to the castle under escort. The soldiers did not know what the crime was but jaloused it could be serious.

After they'd gone, Marjorie Gilmore sat in the kitchen and wailed. 'This is what comes of meddling wi' nobility! I've warned ye till I'm tired to keep in Sir William's favour and now Christina's folly has brought about the ruin o' this family! The Gilmores will be cast out o' the tenancy for sure this coming winter and me wi' another wee baby on its way, God willing.'

Her three sons had been kept in the dark about their mother's pregnancy and this was a severe shock. Jamie and Lachie exchanged a stunned look and young Francis sat down abruptly on the settle.

It would be disaster beyond imagination to be turned out of their home! Francis thought. His conscience was not altogether clear on that score either. He knew that Lachie was delivering Lady Annabel's letters in secret and out of misguided loyalty to his brother Francis had not informed his parents, who could have put a stop to Lachie's misdeeds before any damage was done. Now it was too late.

As for Ma having a baby . . .

Francis realized that he would be a whole eleven years older than this baby when it came. When it was old enough he would tell it rhymes he had enjoyed when wee and how to name birds in the trees and wild flowers in the pastures.

His spirits rose. He would teach it to read, write and count and show it which nuts and berries were good to eat and which it must not. He'd be its big brother, strong and perfect in the baby's admiring eyes – even though he limped. Francis did not care a button whether it was a laddie or lassie because its birth would free him forever from a role he hated.

I'll never be the youngest o' this family again! he thought gleefully.

Then the rosy dream suddenly faded. Francis had noticed that his mother seemed tired, sick and somehow older and heavier lately. Although her changed appearance had caused surprise it had not worried Francis unduly. He had accepted that forty-five *was* quite aged, but now that he knew about the baby he recalled with panic that childbirth was an extremely dangerous experience even for fit young women and many died. His own dear Ma must face that ordeal before the baby could be born and he could not bear it if Ma or the baby were to die!

Francis bit his lip hard but a few stray tears escaped and slid
furtively down his cheek.

Wil Gilmore noticed and glowered at his wife. 'Now see what
you've done – distressed the poor boy with dismal talk!'

Marjorie flushed with indignation. 'If my talk's dismal it's your
fault!'

'My fault?' Wil yelled, waving his arms. 'Everything is my fault
with you these days! Is it my fault rain ruins crops? Did I ask summer
sun to scorch pastures and cattle to die? Is it my fault Christina
offends the landlord?'

'Aye, it is, Wil!' Marjorie screamed back at him. 'You drove our
daughter out of this house wi' your weak drunken ways, straight
into the clutches o' Lady Annabel. Now Chrissie could pay a cruel
price for reaching above her station – and you canna deny that
you're tae blame!'

Wil had no answer to give, because it was true. The shame of
gambling away his daughter's precious dowry preyed upon his mind
and the threat of the laird's displeasure only added to the heavy
sense of guilt. His wife's savage attack was the last straw that toppled
Wil Gilmore's tottering stack of self-esteem.

He turned on his heel and left the house without a word.

Night was drawing in and the wind felt icy on his tear-stained
cheek. He was thankful the family had not seen the tears, a further
evidence of weakness. He stumbled towards the stables and the un-
demanding comfort of his beloved horses.

Wil made straight for the young colt's stall and leaned his arms
upon the rail. His daughter's future and his own redemption centred
upon this fine young stallion. The bonny beast gently nuzzled the
man's sorrowful face.

Wil Gilmore laid his head on his folded arms and let his heart
break.

'Will Pa be all right, shall I go after him?' Jamie asked, unnerved by
the bitter quarrel. He had never seen the like before. His parents
sometimes had lively arguments but this had been impassioned and
frightening.

Marjorie was slumped in the chair. 'No, Son. Let him be,' she said
wearily. She knew her man was tender hearted and once upon a
time she'd seen that as a virtue. In her present desperate state of
mind it seemed further evidence of weakness when she needed
strength.

Lachie bent over her anxiously. 'You should rest upstairs for a wee while, Ma. We didna ken about the baby or we would have spared ye the work when Chrissie went.'

'Aye,' Jamie nodded. 'It's lucky I'm courting Maggie. She'll help ye in the house.'

'God bless you both. You're good lads.'

Marjorie did not want to shatter illusions but had little faith in the quantity and quality of wee Maggie's help. The lassie's demeanour had undergone a drastic haughty change for the worse since Jamie had shown an interest.

With their mother settled in bed, her sons retired to the kitchen to discuss the evening's momentous happenings. Jamie was deeply concerned about the three women held in Lochleven Castle. He visited the laird's stronghold with farm produce and had viewed the strength of its defences. Jamie accepted that the place was impregnable and its prisoners could not be freed by force. More worryingly, he also knew noble lords could wriggle free of blame while less substantial innocent victims suffered to satisfy public opinion. It was a sad fact of life, unjust but well proven.

Diplomacy is their only hope, Jamie thought.

Lachie was in a fine state of restless agitation, pacing the floor and grating upon Jamie's nerves.

'Och, sit ye down, Lachie! You make my head spin.'

Lachie paused. 'You could clear your heid if you stand up like a man and help me free those lassies tonight!'

'Dinna be daft, Brother. It's pit-dark outside!'

'All the better! We could have a quiet word wi' Hugh!' Lachie suggested. 'He'd row us across while the garrison's asleep. We can scale the wall and hide inside till we see our chance.'

Jamie sighed. Lachie always rushed in where it was wiser to wait.

'We wouldna get past the night watch on the wall-walk, Lachie. It makes mair sense tae wait till Maggie goes over to wash. She can find out quietly where the lassies are kept and how they've offended the laird. We can maybe help them when we know the facts.'

Lachie agreed that exercising a little patience could prove more fruitful, but it was not an easy option. He was sure the women were in trouble because word of George Douglas's billets-doux had reached Sir William's ears. It might only be a matter of time before Lachie himself landed in the Tolbooth. It would ease his conscience to confess his folly to his older brother but pride forbade it.

Lachie's eye fell upon wee Francis sitting quiet as a mouse, all ears. What bairns hear in the house will be blabbed in the fields! he thought grimly. 'Get away to bed, you sly wee whelp!'

The boy lifted his chin. This was just the sort of treatment he resented. 'No, I will not! I'll wait till Pa's safe home.'

'You'll wait a good while! It was your snivelling that started the row that sent Pa out. You're just a soft wee peepie-weepie!'

Accused unjustly of fretful whining, Francis was beside himself with fury. 'A peepie-weepie, am I? That's the last time I hold my tongue on your behalf, Lachie Gilmore! When I'm asked who delivers George Douglas's letters to Lady Annabel I'll tell everyone it's you!'

Lachie was horror-struck. 'Francis, don't – please don't!'

Jamie leapt wrathfully to his feet. 'So you're at the root o' the whole sorry mess, Lachie! How could ye be so daft?'

Miserably, Lachie hung his head. 'I love the lady,' he admitted. 'I love her so much I'll do anything she asks of me whatever the cost. I – I canna help myself.'

Jamie was at a loss for words. He found his brother's obsession pathetic and yet conversely, he envied him.

Could I ever muster the same passion for Maggie? he wondered. Even after stealing a few furtive kisses in the warmth of the stables, he was not so besotted as Lachie. Jamie's duty as eldest son always lay heavy as a yoke upon his shoulders. Still, it was early days yet and it was said love grew strong, given time, he thought more hopefully.

He sighed and shook his head. 'Aye well, Lachie, that's enough misfortune for this family tae stomach for one day!' Lifting the lantern from the shelf he reached for his bonnet.

'Where are you going?' his brother demanded nervously.

'To fetch our father home. He'll be in the stable – the only room where he can be sure o' peace and quiet.'

With that Jamie went out into the night, the door swinging shut behind him, guttering candles flickering blue in the draught.

John Haxton did not spend time in Edinburgh once the meeting with the Scottish agent was done with. However, next morning he did pause to go shopping in the port of Leith while waiting for the pinnace. He noticed a haberdashery offering woollen goods and was reminded of the fair Mistress Gilmore – though why the trouble-some she-wolf should leap to mind he could not imagine. Perhaps because he remembered an ugly tattered plaid worn to hide love-liness from the eyes of English wolves.

He smiled to himself. As if it could!

The haberdasher recognized a substantial customer the moment John walked in. Upon demand the woman hastened to display a lady's shawl of the finest quality. John remarked upon a blend of colours exceptionally pleasing to the eye and the shopkeeper beamed.

'Aye, such is the skill o' our northern dyers and weavers, sir! Being o' the English persuasion you'll maybe no' ken that Highland ladies are renowned for their graceful beauty and becoming Highland dress. As you can see, this fine garment is made loose and flowing in a pattern o' gentle colours. When the fullness is gathered in graceful folds over the bosom the effect is exceeding bonny!'

He could imagine – and the image was exciting. 'I'll take it!' he said.

His pleasure in the perfect purchase speeded John Haxton's journey to Falkland. The waters of the firth had never seemed so blue and the rowers so willing, nor the ride through Fife so exhilarating and resonant with robin redbreasts' sweet winter song. He galloped through the royal burgh of Falkland at a speed that turned heads and dismounted in the Sturrocks' stable yard with a song on his lips and Boris panting beside a sweating horse.

Phemie came hurrying outdoors to see what the stir was. 'Och, it's only you – I thought it was the guard mustering the lieges to war. You weren't looked for quite so soon, Sir John.'

'I didn't linger in the city's stink, I longed to breathe fresh air.' He smiled, removing the precious gift from the saddlebag before handing the horse to the stable lad.

He had also bought small gifts for his hosts while in the haberdasher's, a red girdle with silver pomander for Phemie and a decorated leather pouch to hang from Joshua's belt.

In the kitchen Phemie was deeply affected by the thoughtful offerings, weeping copious tears of gratitude. She mopped streaming eyes on a corner of her apron. 'I swear it's the bonniest girdle that ever spanned an auld wifie's waist, Sir John. My man will be fair awa' wi' himsel' when he comes down frae the hill and sees his grand pouch!'

Diffidently, John unwrapped the colourful shawl and spread its folds upon the trestle for Phemie's inspection. 'Do you think this fit for a lady to wear, Mistress Sturrock?' he asked.

Phemie fingered the fine warm wool and recognized the close weave of skilled Highland weavers. Fierce clansmen slept warm at night on frozen hillsides wrapped in plaids like this but she had never seen a bonnier weave. The colours were as soft as heather hills, grey skies, blue lochs and the green shadowy glens of the wild northern uplands.

Was this wonderful garment a measure o' the depth of the young man's fancy for Christina Gilmore? she wondered anxiously. If so, far from scaring the nobleman off, she had succeeded in whetting his appetite.

Phemie found herself struggling in murky waters. What would the Englishman do when he heard the lassie was imprisoned in Lochleven Castle?

He was watching her eagerly. He frowned. 'What's wrong? Don't you like it?'

'It's fit for the queen, let alone a lady.'

He relaxed, smiling. 'That's what I thought. Woven in the Highlands, which makes it ideal for my purpose.'

'Er – that will be to cover bonny Christina Gilmore's shoulders?' Phemie ventured cannily.

He laughed in high good humour. 'Ah, you detect a scheme to tame a wolf's whelp, Mistress Sturrock!'

She swallowed her apprehension nervously. 'So I do, sir, only – you've missed the chance, so tae speak. Some other body cornered and trapped the lassie while you were away. Christina, Lady Annabel and the lady's maid were taken under guard tae Lochleven prison.'

'Wha–at?'

The enraged bellow made Phemie cower.

He took a step forward, towering over her. 'For what reason?'

'Support for the Queen is growing in the district, sir. Folk are whispering the Lords themselves are no' free of blame for the poor young king's murder and were behind the events that drove poor distracted Queen Mary tae marry the Earl o' Bothwell. Maybe the Douglases won't tolerate royal support frae Falkland Palace.'

He clenched his fists. 'I'm told the ladies pass time with embroidery. That is not a crime!'

Phemie eyed him nervously. She had never seen the mild man so roused. 'What – what will ye do?' she asked.

He was silent for a full minute. 'There's nothing I can do,' he said wearily at last. He must remember instructions to remain unobtrusive, anonymous and only observe and report. He was poised for action but forced to remain passive. He had never known such frustrated anguish.

Phemie was relieved but could not help pitying him. He looked sae cast doon, she thought, taking his arm in motherly fashion. 'Come awa' ben the hoose and rest till supper's ready, Sir John.'

He followed obediently, leaving the beautiful shawl lying abandoned on the trestle along with the dreams he'd pinned upon it.

John's strength revived with rest and a generous platter of Mistress Sturrock's excellent pigeon pie. That night he lay in bed contemplating the day's events and assembling his thoughts more rationally. He remembered the man on the piebald horse seen in Falkland and was sure that the rider had visited the ladies in Falkland Palace. Now why would he do that? he wondered.

A man who rode an outstanding mystical beast must surely attract attention and should be easily traced. Once located, John had confidence in his own ability to worm information from the man without arousing suspicion.

His mission for the days ahead now clear, he settled down more composedly to sleep.

Janet Guthrie persisted in restlessly pacing the floor and rushing frantically to stare up and down the street, long after Christina had failed to arrive with the baby and night had fallen on the appointed day.

Arthur and his aunt Bertha were seriously concerned.

'You hardly ate enough to nourish a sparrow, my dearie. I'm making a pot o' porridge for ye to sup,' Bertha said kindly. 'It'll help ye rest.'

But it was as if Janet had not heard. 'Why doesn't Christina come? I can't understand why she doesna come!' she kept repeating, over and over.

Aunt and nephew exchanged a worried look. Arthur took his wife's hand. 'Janet dear, Bertha went down the street earlier on this evening to find out why Christina had been hindered at the palace. The neighbours told her your sister and Lady Annabel went storming through Falkland at full gallop. The lady's maid and an escort of Sir William's men were with them.'

Janet had been clinging to a desperate hope that Christina would still come. She let out a low despairing wail. 'So she broke a solemn promise tae me and rode off wi' fine friends on some frivolous ploy! I could tell she despised my house and was sweer tae bring Ninian home frae a grand palace but like a fool I trusted her. I can never forgive Chrissie for this!' She sank down on the settle and buried her face in her hands.

But after several moments of blackest despair Janet discovered that cruel betrayal could spark an unexpected surge of feverish energy. This was no time for weeping and wailing, she thought and raised her head – what was needed was strength o' purpose! 'Bring me a bowl o' porridge, Bertha love. I'll eat it now,' Janet said calmly.

Janet slept soundly that night and wakened at daybreak. She ignored a debilitating fatigue and rose at once. Arthur was surprised to see her up and dressed and kissed her delightedly.

'Dearest, it's grand to see you back in command o' this family.' He laughed.

Janet found the fire already blazing, a large pot of porridge simmering and Bertha stirring the brose with the spirtle while keeping an eye on the huddle of sleeping bairns on a mattress in a warm corner. She glanced at Janet. 'Aye, we'll need tae mind wir step the day, mistress, by the resolute look o' ye!'

Janet finished a large bowl of porridge cooled with buttermilk. She helped Bertha dress and feed the three little lasses when they wakened and waited till the reassuring clatter of her husband's loom saw him settled to work. She wrapped a shawl around her head and shoulders. 'Mind the bairns for me, Bertha. I fancy a breath o' fresh air.'

'Aye, a wee dander down the street will do ye good, lovie.' The old dear beamed.

Bertha took full credit for Janet's transformation. She had implicit faith in the curative power of oatmeal. The diet had sustained Bertha's sturdy little frame for many years when she worked as ferry woman on the river Eden. At the height of her powers Bertha carried men, women, bairns and merchandise on her back across the ford, fortified daily by a dish of porridge and bowls of kail and shin skink.

Janet walked tentatively along the street, testing her strength. She felt feeble but forced herself to go on till she reached the palace gatehouse. She stood resting in the shadow of the impressive edifice before unobtrusively joining the tail end of a group of domestics hurrying inside.

Janet had no clear idea of what she planned to do apart from a desperate need to see her baby. Fortunately, she was no stranger to the interior of Falkland Palace. In the early days of Queen Mary's seven-year reign, Janet had been one of a number of local women recruited to serve at the Keeper's banquets. Now she crept cautiously upstairs towards reception rooms and family apartments before pausing uncertainly at the top.

Fighting exhaustion, she made her way along a corridor and was confronted by a baffling array of closed doors. Her strength was ebbing and she despaired. How could she be sure which room held her baby?

Then she heard an infant crying. The strong, healthy wail issued from the nearest doorway and without more ado Janet rushed in with a joyful cry, pausing in the middle of the room, swaying a little and breathing hard.

A buxom woman sat nursing a tiny infant.

The crying came not from this tiny mite, however, but from a rosy-cheeked infant protesting loudly in a nearby cradle. The wails died to startled whimpers as Janet burst in and the woman glared angrily.

'What a start to give us! How dare ye come rushing in without so much as by your leave? I dinna ken who ye are but you've no right to be here.'

'I've every right! I'm Ninian Guthrie's mother,' Janet cried.

She could see his wee face against the woman's breast. He had grown, though still smaller than he should be. The sight of her son overwhelmed Janet with love and longing. Involuntarily, she moved closer.

The other woman grew alarmed, clutching the baby to her bosom. 'Go away! You canna be his mother, I never set eyes on ye before!'

Janet reached out wildly to snatch Ninian from her. 'Give him to me!'

'I will not!' the chambermaid cried lifting the baby against her shoulder. 'Your manner's uncouth and ye act like a mad woman. I'll call the guard tae ye!'

Janet lost all reason. Diving forward, she attempted to wrestle Ninian from the woman's grasp. The chambermaid retaliated with a hefty kick to Janet's shins.

Dizzy with pain Janet staggered backwards, caught her heel on the hem of her gown and fell, hitting her head on the floor with a resounding crack.

She heard the chambermaid scream and Ninian wail – then those sounds faded from Janet's consciousness and she slipped into darkness.

Seven

In the month of December 1567

That night Christina and her two companions were offered straw mattresses and coarse blankets on the floor of a small chilly room not much larger than a pantry.

Lady Agnes Douglas came with them to apologize for the poor accommodation. 'The occupants o' this house are crowded like peas in a pod. Queen Mary's attendants and guards occupy the third floor and battlements above. I sleep in the queen's apartment under the silence o' the night to be sure all is well. My mother-in-law and I accompany Her Grace during the day for walks in the garden if the weather is fair – and often if it's not. Queen Mary is unco partial to fresh air and exercise!' the young Lady Douglas explained ruefully.

Already quite well advanced in her latest pregnancy, Agnes was finding embroidery sessions and freezing cold walks with their energetic royal prisoner an onerous burden.

Annabel appeared resigned to a mattress on the floor. 'Dinna fash, Agnes, this'll do fine. We've a horror o' dungeons.'

It was disconcerting all the same to bid their hostess goodnight and listen to the key turn in the lock. Nightly prayers were more heartfelt than usual before the three women settled uneasily to sleep.

Christina wakened at daybreak to find the others already stirring. Their fate was still in the balance but Annabel put a brave face upon it.

'Geordie Douglas will speak up for us, my dears. Geordie's leal and true.'

Secretly, Christina could not share her optimism. She knew one possible reason for the laird's displeasure could be his fierce disapproval of Annabel's love affair with his younger brother. If so, bonny Geordie's loyalty was not worth a candle. To make matters worse Lachie's role as the lovebirds' courier had placed Christina in a dangerous position as an accomplice.

The door was unlocked shortly after and bustling servant lasses arrived with ewers of hot water, basins and towels, cheerfully removing pots of night soil for disposal in the loch.

Dorcas produced a comb from the pouch she carried, filled with necessities for her lady's toilet, and skilfully combed and braided her companions' hair. When that was accomplished Christina ordered Dorcas to sit patiently while she performed the same service for the lady's maid. Washed and tidy, they sat waiting apprehensively for the day's events to unfold.

Presently the servants returned and led them from the overnight prison to the room where they dined the night before. The apartment was unoccupied but a fire burned brightly, heaped with fresh coal and logs. Maidservants set three bowls of porridge, a jug of goat's milk and platters of freshly cooked trout on the table. A basin and napkins were left nearby and the servants withdrew. Annabel rubbed her hands together gleefully. 'Bedding may not come up to the scratch, but we canna fault the fare!'

Christina was not inclined to feel grateful. 'Fish are easy come by frae the loch, my lady, but my brothers slaved for long hours in the fields to put these oats on Sir William's table.'

Her Ladyship blithely topped the porridge with a liberal dash of milk. 'I must say the work makes bonny men o' them, Chrissie dear!'

'Amen to that!' Dorcas added, smiling.

The bowls were emptied, fish bones picked clean and the table cleared before the Old Lady and Agnes put in an appearance. The Old Lady explained that it was their custom to breakfast upstairs with the queen in her apartment.

'That must be reassuring for Her Grace. The threat of poison will be always uppermost in her mind,' Annabel remarked sweetly.

'Well, really!' The dowager glared resentfully but chose to ignore the jibe. 'Are your hands washed and fingernails clean?' she demanded coldly.

Annabel took the remark as a personal insult. 'We have not brought the plague wi' us, Lady Margaret, if that's what you fear!'

The Old Lady raised her eyes to heaven. 'Grant me patience wi' the lassie! Did I not tell you that we noted your diligent attention to the queen?'

'Aye, and I tell *you* we're unrepentant and prepared to suffer for it!'

Lady Margaret gave a long-suffering sigh. 'Och, Annabel! We're not asking ye to suffer, only to sew!'

'Sew?' she repeated blankly.

Lady Margaret seated herself, neatly arranging folds of a black velvet gown. 'Aye. That's what your women do, is it not? You were brought to the castle to sew material much too precious to entrust to packhorses. If footpads and wild Highland thieves learn such a prize is travelling on country tracks to Falkland they'd be drawn to it like wasps to a honey pot.'

'Is it cloth o' gold, my lady?' Dorcas asked curiously.

'Och, hardly! The kirk would demand public Sabbath repentance barefoot in sackcloth for such showy excess. No, no. Lady Sempill brought this valuable pack to Leven personally frae Holyrood under heavy guard – you'll maybe recall that before her marriage the lady was Marie Livingston, one o' the Queen's four Maries.'

But Annabel's small store of patience was already exhausted. 'Oh, please spare us the history and tell us what it is we're summoned to sew!' she begged.

'Sables!' the dowager declared triumphantly. 'The finest fur frae the farthest reaches o' distant Russia! Her Grace is aye thoughtful for the comfort of those that serve her – and so, mindfu' of Agnes's condition and knowing my poor old bones ache and I dread winter walking, the queen orders that our cloaks be warmly lined and trimmed wi' sables.'

'Black Siberian mink!' Annabel declared in hushed tones. She had often heard her merchant father mention this rare and hugely expensive commodity with awe. A consignment of pelts could arrive in Leith brought in by Russian fur traders, but that was a very rare occurrence, he said. Only those of the very highest degree wore sables! 'Will we be trimming Her Grace's cloak too?' she asked hopefully.

'That won't be necessary. Queen Mary's cloak is lined wi' black civet which only royalty may wear.' She fixed Annabel with a meaningful stare. 'You have no call to meet the queen and Sir William expressly forbids it. My son is aye mindfu' of her safety and will allow no outsiders into the queen's presence. You three are to bide and work in the Glassin tower at the far end o' the courtyard and will be well watched tae be sure ye observe the rules. Cloaks, furs and sewing materials await ye there. The rooms are small but the light is better for sewing.'

'How long do you intend to keep us?' Annabel demanded.

She shrugged. 'Till ye make a satisfactory finish. Off ye go now! Mr Drysdale waits below to guide ye to your place.'

Christina could hardly suppress a groan. Janet and the baby were never far from her thoughts and every passing day made the worrying situation worse. She knew her sister's health was fragile, her state of mind disturbed and Christina was trapped, powerless to help her.

At that moment Janet was drifting on the fringe of consciousness after her disastrous fall in Falkland Palace.

'Janet! Janet dearie, can ye hear me?' Aunt Bertha's voice sounded faint and far away.

Janet became mistily aware of a sensation of unusual comfort. She tried to open her eyes but the lids felt heavy. The little light that filtered through her lashes brought awareness of pain.

'She's waking, thanks be to God!' Aunt Bertha's voice seemed stronger and closer. A warm rough-skinned hand stroked Janet's brow.

Falkland! Janet thought hazily and then – Ninian! Her eyes jerked painfully open and she struggled to sit up. 'My baby!'

'Hush, hush!' Voices soothed her panic and hands pressed her down.

'He's fine, hen. Sound asleep i' the crib,' a stranger assured her.

Subsiding, Janet discovered to her astonishment that she lay in a fine carved bed hung with embroidered drapes. Pillowcases and sheets were of white linen topped by warm coverlets. Blissful comfort beneath her body suggested the presence of a goose-feather mattress.

Two concerned faces hovered within Janet's swimming vision and she recognized dear Aunt Bertha and the plump red cheeks of her former adversary the Falkland chambermaid. The whole situation became dreamlike and confusing.

'Where am I?' she murmured.

The chambermaid answered. 'In Falkland Palace, dearie. When ye fell down in a swoon I cried out for help and one o' the maids recognized ye, so your auntie was sent for.'

The chambermaid looked shamefaced. 'Och, Mistress Guthrie, I'm sorry I doubted your word and treated you so harsh but you looked so wild I was scared oot o' my wits. I'd no idea you were truthfully wee Ninian's mother and Chrissie Gilmore's sister.'

Mention of Christina aroused bitter grief and painful tears. 'Chrissie promised tae bring Ninian home. But she didna come!' Janet wept.

The chambermaid and Bertha exchanged a worried look.

'She couldna come, my dear,' Bertha explained gently. 'Sir William's soldiers arrested Christina, Lady Annabel and the lady's maid and carried them off as prisoners tae the castle. It's the talk o' the town!'

Janet felt as if she had suddenly wandered from dream into nightmare. 'I dinna understand. What have they done?'

The chambermaid shrugged. 'Nobody kens. You hae tae mind your step wi' the laird these days or the only step you'll take is into a dungeon.'

Janet groaned. 'My mother warned her tae watch out! Now the whole family will suffer!'

'Och, maybe it's only Lady Annabel that's sinned. A'body kens she's hot-heided,' Bertha said comfortingly.

'But why take Chrissie and the lady's maid?' Janet cried.

'Och, a lady canna comb her hair or don her gear withoot a maid will do it for her,' the chambermaid declared wisely.

Janet closed her eyes wearily, utterly heartbroken. In the heat of the moment she had cursed her sister and sworn never to forgive her. She should have known that loyal Christina would not willingly break a solemn promise.

Aunt Bertha and the chambermaid eyed the grieving invalid with concern and exchanged a conspiratorial look. The woman nodded and quietly left the room.

Janet had drifted into an uneasy doze when Bertha roused her several minutes later.

'Someone here to see ye, lovie.'

Janet opened heavy eyes and stared in disbelief at the precious bundle they placed in her arms. 'Ninian!' she cried joyfully. 'Oh, it is Ninian, my ain wee laddie!'

And Janet Guthrie welcomed her tiny son with a kiss and gathered Ninian safely to her breast.

Maggie the washer-lassie came swinging along the path leading to Loch Leven pier. She was so pleased with life she could have whistled a tune. She never would, of course, being mindful of the old rhyme:

'Whistling lassies and crowing hens, both be sure tae make bad ends!'

And Maggie had no intention of making bad ends. She was hopeful of a very good end indeed, as Jamie Gilmore's wife.

Did she love him? Well, he prattled on about farming till she could scream and his ma was a bossy old scold, but she could put up wi' that if she must. He was a handsome man, kind and respectful of Maggie's person – a wee bittie too respectful to make a satisfactory lover, she sometimes thought.

By now news of the courtship had spread to Kinross and beyond. Washerwomen piling into Hugh Ross's boat greeted Maggie's arrival with hoots, sniggers and snide remarks quite unsuited to the modest ears of a maiden.

She seated herself demurely facing the boatman with eyes cast down.

'So you're to be off wi' Jamie Gilmore one o' these days,' Hugh said, leaning on the oars.

Maggie gave him a speculative glance. 'Mr Gilmore's been – attentive,' she admitted.

'Aye well, I wish ye mair luck wi' the Gilmores than I had!' He pulled savagely on an oar, whirling the boat away from the jetty and calling down a string of curses upon his head from his shaken passengers.

'Och, it was only Christina's dowry you were after, Hugh,' Maggie said. 'When her pa gambled it away you disappeared like a puff o' smoke in the wind.'

He scowled. 'Gilmores are chancy folk. You'd better mind how you tread,' he warned.

She sniffed. 'At least I'm assured o' a dowry when I wed. I'm my pa's only wee ewe lamb and he's much too fly to gamble away good siller.'

He made no answer. The loch was teeming with traffic that required his full attention. Boatloads of fishermen were out in strength and a small pinnace loaded to the gunwales was storming up the loch under full sail from Levenmouth.

'Anyway,' Maggie went on. 'The Gilmores are in a right stew the now, not knowing what Christina's fate will be.'

Jamie had urged her to find out what had become of Sir William's captives and she was sure this boatload of accomplished gossips would know.

She was not disappointed.

'My cousin in the castle kitchen says the three women are lodged in the Glassin tower under guard,' one woman said.

Hugh frowned. 'Why there?'

'It's round the back o' the island in a corner o' the inner court-yard behind locked doors. From there ye canna signal tae the shore for help,' someone else volunteered.

He gave a frustrated tug at the oars. 'That's a' very well, but what's the crime?'

'There isn't one. They're sewing fine cloaks for the Douglas women,' another said.

'Aye, but that'll be frowned on by the kirk!' an older woman remarked. 'Ministers will not tolerate fancy sewing. A wee peep o' embroidered petticoat below your Sunday sad brown and you're off tae the stool o' repentance.'

'Aye well, there was fine embroidery aplenty in Christina Gilmore's marriage kist. I saw it wi' my own eyes before the poor lassie was jilted,' Maggie said innocently.

A battery of accusing glares immediately fastened upon the boatman, speeding Hugh hastily towards the island.

Maggie's report caused anger and distress when it reached Marjorie's ears.

'How can embroidery be a crime if it is a God-given gift?'

'It's so unjust!' Lachie agreed staunchly. These were anxious days for Lachie, with the fate of Sir William's three hapless captives preying upon his mind – one very dear lady in particular.

It was lowsing time after morning work was done on the farm and the family sat at table enjoying a midday break of bread and cheese. Jamie drummed fingertips thoughtfully upon the trestle top. He was not convinced that Maggie had grasped the right end o' the stick. His intended delighted in drama and could be guilty of embroidery – of the truth, that is.

'Annabel Erskine's a distant relative of old Lady Douglas and the Douglas clan stick together like fleas in a blanket,' he said. 'We dinna ken for certain if the women were called upon to perform a service or apprehended for some other crime.'

'You could be right,' Lachie nodded more hopefully. 'But how to find out?'

Wil Gilmore cut a slice of full-bodied cheese and nibbled it pensively. 'Hostelries are few and far on the Cupar road but the Kinross Inn is a famous rendezvous for peddlers and packmen. These men will know the true facts of this matter if anyone does,' he said.

'I'll go, Pa!' Lachie offered instantly.

Wil shook his head. 'No, my son, you are too young and beau. They will be more likely to trade ale and secrets with me, an old farmer.'

'Aye! Secrets and ale!' Marjorie taunted. She turned to her sons. 'You'll note your father never misses his chance!'

'That is unfair, wife,' Wil said quietly. He rose without a word, leaving his family sitting in an awkward silence.

Wisely, John Haxton did not involve Euphemia Sturrock in the search for the man on the piebald horse. Well trained in the nuances of human behaviour, John had long ago detected Phemie's

disapproval of his pursuit of the fair Christina Gilmore. He knew
the landlady would not hesitate to foil his plans.

Falkland was too close at hand to risk questions about the young
man he sought. That would attract unwelcome attention and John
decided to search for information farther afield.

He worried that there was not a moment to be lost securing the
women's release. He knew from his Scottish contact that the lords
were scheming to rid themselves of the Queen of Scots and her
supporters. The queen's existence as a prisoner on the loch was an
inconvenient embarrassment to those now in power.

'I have business to attend to and will be travelling for a few days,'
he announced at breakfast that morning.

Phemie gave him a quick glance. She longed to speir what business and whereabouts? The information given was much too vague
to alert any of her widespread offspring – as the cunning man well
knew! she thought with annoyance.

'What'll I do if a letter comes for ye frae your loving pa?' she
demanded dourly.

He met her eyes and smiled. 'Same as always, Mistress Sturrock.
Set it aside and keep it safe.'

'Aye, so ye can feed your father's fair words to the flames,' she
muttered viciously, swinging a broth pot on its swee over the glowing
embers.

Her husband Joshua wiped bacon grease from beard and fingers.
'The deer are down frae the Lomond heights and ye'll miss the
hunt, Sir John. Pity!' the huntsman remarked laconically.

After breakfast, John set off at the canter in cold winter sunshine
and great good humour with Boris bounding at his side. He skirted
Falkland and headed for the Kinross road, a well-travelled route to
Edinburgh and beyond, where a stray Englishman in sober black
gear would not attract too much attention. The hills were pure white
and there was a dusting of snow on lower ground but the frozen
track was clear and the going good. He chuckled recalling Phemie's
sulky visage. What frustration it must be for the old gossip to be
unable to read and what a blessing she could not! He expected a
communication from the Scottish agent any day now keeping him
abreast of events.

December is a fickle month and the morning's fair weather did
not last. As John's journey progressed the sun disappeared, the sky
turned leaden and a snell wind rose blowing icy particles of snow
in his face. Cold soon penetrated the travelling cloak and leather

gauntlets holding the reins. Fortunately before the short afternoon
ended and daylight faded altogether John arrived at the roadside
hostelry where he planned to spend the night.

The inn's taproom was packed and he surveyed the noisy scene
with satisfaction, one hand resting reassuringly on Boris's faithful
head. Someone here could know the man on the distinctive piebald
horse – but whom to choose?

A lone man sat quietly on a bench in a far corner. John's attention
was drawn to him because this man studied the room's occupants
as intently as John did. Their eyes met speculatively for a fleeting
instant before the older man looked away quickly. John ordered a
tassie of ale and made his way casually towards the bench. 'May I
sit here?'

The man nodded, shifting to leave more room. John judged him
to be in the late forties or early fifties of his age, with dark intelligent
eyes and black hair dusted with grey at the temples – an interesting
face, John thought. He wore sheepskin boots, a countryman's grey
garb of sound quality and was possibly a local tenant farmer.

The man leaned forward to pet Boris and John noted strong
shapely hands, the nails clean and well kept. He was surprised. This
indicated a man of unusual refinement despite outward appearance.

'It is a handsome hound,' the stranger remarked.

'More than handsome. Boris is lion-hearted when facing a wolf!'
John smiled. His keen ear had detected a slight foreign inflection in
the Scottish tongue. He took a casual sip of ale. 'Wolves have menaced
the Lomonds recently and Boris and I volunteered our services to
rid Falkland of the nuisance this winter as the brutes grow hungry.
Perhaps you know the district?'

'Yes, I know Falkland.' Wil Gilmore could hardly suppress a smile.
If the Englishman only knew it, he spoke to one of a team of French
stonemasons responsible for the magnificent facade of Falkland
Palace's south range.

John let a moment or two pass. 'I wonder,' he continued tentatively. 'Do you happen to know where a young man seen recently
in Falkland may be found? He was riding a distinctive piebald horse
and I'm told he came this way.'

Wil was badly shaken but gave no sign. The Englishman's dangerous
interest in his son was alarming but he shrugged nonchalantly. 'I am
thinking that a man daring to ride such an outstanding steed must
ply an innocent trade wi' a clear conscience for he must attract
attention.'

'True!' John nodded, noting with interest the skill with which his query was parried. He took another sip of ale and continued. 'But this man visited young women living in Falkland Palace and now they are taken to Lochleven Castle under guard. I wonder if he knows why that should be?'

'Your concern for these women does ye credit, sir,' Wil remarked mildly.

John leaned forward confidentially. 'Well, you see – there are those in Falkland that fear for their safety in these troubled times. If I knew the true facts of the case I have friends who might use diplomacy to have them set free. I'm told Christina Gilmore's father has an unreliable reputation and my fear is that this man will attempt to storm the island and free his daughter.'

'I can assure ye there will be no need for violence!' Wil declared grimly. 'Sir William's servants are saying that the women were brought to the island to sew warm winter gear for the queen and the Douglas ladies.'

'Yes, it makes sense to sew,' John nodded, feeling as if a weight had been lifted from him. 'I did hear that the queen came to Lochleven Castle with little more than the clothes she stood in and the gowns left behind in Holyrood were stolen by others.'

'Between us, good sir, I think we hae established the truth,' Wil said jovially raising a tassie to the man. Now all that remains is to put a stop to this Englishman's dangerous interest in Lachie's doings! he thought. Wil lowered the tassie and wiped his mouth. 'As for the lad on the colourful horse, I'll suggest to ye that he is a chapman come to Falkland with saddlebags packed with fine linens, ribbons, sewing threads and patterns for women's gear to tempt the ladies. What could be mair eye-catching for the man's fancy trade than a fancy piebald?'

'I'll drink to that!' John smiled, raising the tassie once more, unsteadily. Strong Scottish ale on an empty stomach was beginning to take adverse effect.

Wil drained the cup and stood up. 'It's been a real pleasure meeting wi' you, sir!'

He patted Boris kindly and was out the door and disappearing into the December night before John's fuddled brain registered that he had omitted to ascertain the stranger's identity.

Christina and Dorcas enjoyed working in the tiny Glassin tower, but Annabel baulked at the restrictions, staring pensively through glazed oriels at an unchanging scene of water and bleak, far-off shores.

'I'm not even allowed tae walk in the garden with the queen and the ladies. What joy that would give me!' she grumbled wistfully.

'I saw Queen Mary yesterday,' Christina said, looking up from the hard graft of sewing sable pelts to thick woollen nap. 'The guard let me stand on the wall-walk for a breath o' fresh air and I saw her leave the castle to walk with her ladies in the outer garden. I've never seen a lady so tall and stately. She was smiling too and looked so bonny – but so pale!'

'Aye, she would.' Annabel nodded. 'The queen's milk-white beauty is the envy of every princess in Europe. She had smallpox as a child but was not marked, thanks to her French physician.'

'Queen Elizabeth caught the disease and nearly died a few years bygone,' Dorcas added, thankfully snipping off a final thread. 'They say she covers pock marks wi' paste.'

'My mother thinks milk and the grace o' God saved us in the last smallpox epidemic tae scourge Fife,' Christina said. 'Ma swears milk will stop the evil humours o' the pox and made the whole family work tae milk the herd dry and drink the milk. Sure enough, we all escaped wi' just a wee fever and were spared the worst.'

Annabel turned impatiently from contemplation of the loch. 'Aye well, I'll bear your ma's magic potion in mind, Chrissie. Are we not done yet wi' this poxy sable?'

The sables had tried their patience to the limit. The small mink pelts must be matched and joined before lining and trimming the cloaks and Annabel, Christina and Dorcas were not expert furriers. Annabel had struggled to match and cut pelts that the other two laboured to sew. Despite precautions with extra-stout needles and strong thread, hands and fingers were left blistered and bleeding by the end.

'Both cloaks are finished, my lady,' Dorcas announced, easing an aching back. 'I'll wear fustian wi' pleasure for the rest o' my days after enduring such torture!'

Annabel picked up a cloak and snuggled into the furry folds. 'It's wonderfully soft and warm. What a thoughtful gesture by the queen!'

'It is indeed!' Lady Agnes Douglas agreed with a smile, arriving in the doorway at that moment. She examined the finished articles with delight. 'Och, you've performed miracles! Winter walks will be a pleasure now.'

'So we're free to go!' Annabel demanded eagerly.

She hesitated a moment. 'There have been – certain disturbing developments concerning the queen. His Grace the Earl o' Moray will decide whether you return to Falkland to sew or not.'

'His Grace?' Annabel queried, frowning indignantly. She knew the title was reserved for the monarch alone. It would seem Queen Mary's bastard half-brother had achieved the highest accolade in the land.

Agnes Douglas lifted her chin. 'Aye! My brother-in-law has earned the right as regent for our infant king. Scotland is peaceful under his guidance since Queen Mary's supporters vanished like the mist.'

A warning nudge from Dorcas silenced Annabel's boiling outrage. She contented herself with a sulky glower as Agnes tried on the refurbished cloak.

'Queen Mary will be pleased. No more red noses and chattering teeth when the north wind doth blow!' Agnes laughed. 'The queen's in better spirits since Lady Sempill arrived with wigs, hair pieces and other accessories for Mary Seton to dress Her Grace's hair. My young daughter and niece were permitted to join the queen's two Maries to share the pinning, combing and crimping. Afterwards George arrived and then they all danced so merrily to the lute!'

Agnes paused guiltily, suddenly remembering the kirk forbade such sinful goings on. 'It – it was a joy to hear laughter after so much sorrow, you – you understand?'

'Of course, my lady,' Dorcas replied. 'Queen Mary is a young woman celebrating a twenty-fifth birthday – the official coming of age of a Scottish monarch. Who would deny Her Grace joy on such a significant occasion?'

Agnes was much affected by the kind words. She laid the cloak on the trestle and looked earnestly at the three women. 'You've worked well and willingly, my dears. I promise to do everything within my power to send you safely home.'

Marjorie Gilmore had been driven nearly frantic by young Francis's demands for a Christmas jollification. 'For Heaven's sake, child, how many mair times do I have tae tell it's forbidden? If John Knox got wind o' it we'd end up barefoot in the kirk or worse!'

'Och, Ma, the man's far away in Edinburgh! Who's to ken if we roast a goose to celebrate Christ's birthday?'

'Half the district would sniff us out. They've noses keener than a tinker's cur,' she growled grumpily.

Truth to tell Marjorie would have enjoyed a Christmas celebration.

It went against the grain to treat such a joyous event as the Saviour's birthday as an ordinary working day. But that was the Kirk's rule and with the Gilmores' fate in the balance, she dare not take risks.

Francis was desperate. There was an air of gloom hanging over the house and he longed for a small celebration, be it never so humble. He understood that it was a shame to harass his mother when the evidence of her pregnancy was beginning to show despite the folds of the flocket she'd started to wear. This was a loose, wide-sleeved garment usually worn by old women and his beloved ma's aged appearance almost broke Francis's sensitive heart. If only he could make her smile again!

'We could have a Yule log, Ma!' he suggested with sudden inspiration. 'Jamie could cut the tree stump that fell in the gale and decorate it wi' holly and ivy. We could drag it into the house and burn it on the fire wi' a grand blaze and roast chestnuts and have mulled wine and bannocks. Nobody would be any the wiser, Ma!'

Poor bairn! Marjorie thought compassionately. There was precious little joy to be had in this divided house at the moment. She ruffled his hair fondly. 'Aye well – burning a Yule log, eh? I can see no sin in that, sonny!' she agreed.

Marjorie should perhaps have remembered that sin, like beauty, is in the eye of the beholder.

The outer door burst open at that crucial moment and in rushed wee Willy Douglas, scarlet-cheeked and breathing heavily. 'Mistress Gilmore, the women are free!' he panted. 'Hugh's tae row them over frae the castle and Jamie says to tell ye we're taking horses to the pier head to meet them.' Marjorie sat down heavily. She felt such an overwhelming relief she could have hugged the wee troublemaker – but resisted the temptation.

It had all happened so quickly that Christina could hardly believe they were released. Seated in the boat with Hugh smiling at her and the island rapidly receding into the distance she shared Annabel and Dorcas's heartfelt relief. Freedom had taken the women completely by surprise. Drysdale arrived at the tower and in his usual surly manner hustled them out past guards and locked doors. He left them shivering outside the wall close to boats bobbing at the jetty. Hugh arrived soon after and Maggie seized the chance to leave work and appeared from the outer courtyard at the last moment to join them.

The washer-lassie draped a shawl over head and shoulders against the bitter cold and sat on the thwart beside Christina, casting jealous glances at her warm cloak and hood of thick Bristol nap.

Hugh was exultant, laughing and pulling strongly on the oars. 'So they only wanted ye to sew! I knew it frae the start, Chrissie. How could a lass sae sweet and bonny be guilty o' crime?'

Maggie snorted. 'Och, Hugh, tak' off the blinkers! The cruel lassie abandoned her poor mother in her hour o' need.'

Christina rounded on her angrily. 'That's a lie!'

'It is not! Your mother's old, sick and more than four months gone wi' child.'

Chrissie grabbed the gunwale or she might have toppled with shock. 'Ma's with child? I was not told. I – I didna know!'

'Well, you ken noo!' Maggie said. 'If you've any decency left you'll come home and support your ma through the ordeal.'

Hugh nodded seriously. 'She's right, Christina. You should come home.'

The boat seemed to rock dizzily and Christina gripped the gunwale tightly. If her mother needed her of course she must go home, but Christina's loyalties were mixed. Falkland was calling her back.

Janet and the frail baby weighed heavily upon her conscience and how could she desert Lady Annabel and Dorcas in their attempt to support the queen? Christina had experienced imprisonment. She knew it meant constant fear, danger and uncertainty and pitied the royal prisoner on the island with all her heart.

She noticed her brothers waiting on the far shore to greet them and her heart sank. She must very soon make a choice and Christina knew that no matter which path she chose, the course of her life was about to change.

Eight

In the Christmas season 1567

Christina's brothers raised a cheer as Hugh brought the boat to the moorings and helped the women clamber ashore. Christina picked up her skirts and ran to hug them. Decisions about her future could wait.

Wee Willy Douglas was also present, hanging back from the family group, and Christina hugged him too, much to the orphan lad's embarrassment.

Lady Annabel merely embraced freedom and laughed. A playful wind tugged at her hood and tangled curling locks of raven-black hair. Entranced, Lachie watched the adored one's pleasure and his heart ached. He wondered if her happiness stemmed from meeting with her lover George Douglas at the castle. What had passed secretly between them there?

Dorcas paused to study the weather. It did not look promising. The sky was leaden grey and more snow was on the way. She noticed Jamie Gilmore standing a little apart from the group. 'Mr Gilmore, we should leave at once if my lady is to ride to Falkland before the weather worsens.'

He frowned. 'I wouldna advise riding tae Falkland today. I had hoped you'd bide at the farmhouse till conditions improve.'

She smiled and leaned close to whisper. 'I thank ye kindly for the offer but the decision doesna rest wi' me, alas. My lady can be contrary but I'll see what I can do to persuade her. This would be a grand chance to patch your sister's quarrel with her father.'

'Healer, matchmaker and peacemaker! Is there no end to your talents?' he teased.

She laughed. 'I only pray for health, happiness and peace for all. How is your arm, by the by?'

'Good as new, as you can see.' Smiling, he flexed the muscle of one brawny arm for her inspection.

The washer-lassie watched them narrowly. Maggie was fiercely jealous of her relationship with Jamie Gilmore and the heightened status it brought. No fortune-seeking jade dare venture into Maggie's territory!

She judged this woman to be on the wrong side of thirty but predatory old spinsters could be a serious threat to guileless young bachelors. They were whispering and laughing together and Jamie Gilmore was as close to flirting as she'd seen him. This must be nipped i' the bud! Maggie thought.

She rubbed her nose to redden it, pulled the shawl close round her head to hide the glow of rosy cheeks and made her way towards the pair. She touched Jamie's arm and he turned in surprise. She put on a show of shivers.

'What is it, Maggie? You look cold.'

'If it please ye, Jamie,' she said meekly, 'the wind's freezing and my plaid doesna keep out the chill, so I'll be on my way walking tae Goudiebank. Your dear ma will need help wi' the work if she's to find time for rest.'

He frowned. 'Och, Maggie – you'll catch your death walking. No, no, you'll ride wi' me!'

So saying, Jamie unhitched the horse from the rail and helped her up into the saddle behind him. He gathered the reins and smiled down at Dorcas. 'I wish you success wi' Lady Annabel and hope to meet later!'

Maggie fastened her arms around his waist and laid her cheek against his back.

Dorcas stepped hastily aside and watched them ride off. She was pleased for him. He was a fine man and deserved to be happy. His young sweetheart was modest, pretty and caring, everything that Dorcas could wish for Jamie Gilmore.

Sighing, she turned away to attend to her capricious mistress – thereby missing the triumphant warning glare cast in her direction as Maggie was carried off, arms clamped possessively around her catch.

A flurry of snow borne on a bitter wind finally settled Christina's dilemma. It would be folly to set out for Falkland with a snowstorm imminent. She would go home and try to be at peace with her father.

Annabel graciously accepted an invitation to shelter with the Gilmores and Lachie Gilmore could hardly believe his luck. In recent years winters had begun early and been more severe than usual and he knew the threatened storm might make travel impossible for days to come. Snowflakes fine as white mist were already sweeping down from the Lomonds and the horses were restive, eager to head home to a warm stable.

Although packages and passengers for Castle Island waited on the jetty, Hugh seized a chance to have a quiet word with Christina. Snow settled on her cloak and stung her cheek as they stood together.

'Could we maybe forget the past and start afresh, Chrissie?' Hugh begged quietly. He held her hands and she did not resist. How strange if a quirk o' weather should decide their destiny, she thought.

'I don't know, Hugh. Perhaps.'

He appeared satisfied with the canny answer. 'Think on it, my dear. Send word wi' Maggie if you want me.'

He kissed her cheek and turned away.

Willy Douglas would return to the island with Hugh but first Annabel exchanged a few whispered words with the lad. Willy nodded and grinned before scrambling into the boat. Lachie watched the secretive pair with an expression black as thunder.

If he guessed correctly, Annabel was making certain that Bonny Geordie's love letters would reach her – at Goudiebank.

Marjorie Gilmore would not admit to panic but it was not far off. Jamie had arrived at the gallop with Maggie a wee while ago to announce that the women were on their way and aiming to bide in the house. Marjorie longed to see Christina but joy was tempered with apprehension. When father and daughter met, sparks would be sure tae fly.

Jamie returned to the stables to help Wil with the rest of the cavalcade but Maggie remained and seemed unusually eager to assist with frantic preparations for the guests' comfort.

'I canna stand thon lady's maid!' she confided as she helped Marjorie prepare the best bedchamber. 'Dorcas is a spiteful jade, aye lookin' down her nose at honest folk.'

Marjorie was surprised. 'Jamie speaks highly o' the woman.'

Maggie thumped the bolster with a fist. 'Aye well, he would wouldn't he? She's all over him like a poultice. An old spinster like her will be on the lookout for a gormless young bachelor wi' a fine farm at his back.'

'Aye well, maybe so,' Marjorie nodded. True also of an adventurer like Wil on the lookout for easy pickings! she thought grimly.

Years ago a dashing French stonemason swept a young crippled lass off her feet and secured custody o' a fine farm, but since she and Wil were estranged Marjorie often wondered if her husband had ever truly loved her. The similarity wi' this predatory spinster was unnerving. She wouldna wish that sorrow upon her son!

Reluctantly, she laid the last piece of precious white soap beside the basin, ready for my lady's toilet. Maggie struck a hard bargain for white soap but Marjorie craved its gentle lather and felt bereft without it.

'I'd be grateful if ye could bring more white soap, Maggie,' she said.

'You're in luck. Pa made a large batch for the Queen and the Douglas ladies. He tempered it wi' rose water and scented it wi' musk and it smells just lovely. I could beg some for ye but it doesna come cheap, mind.'

Marjorie could not resist the tempting offer. She hated wearing a shapeless old wives' flocket to hide her increasing girth and a little fragrance would help to boost her self-esteem.

'Beg as much as ye can, lassie!' she declared eagerly.

Christina had dreaded meeting her father, but a reunion in the stables surrounded by cold and hungry travellers was easily accomplished. Wil was in full command of any situation that involved horses.

He steadied Muckle Meg while his daughter dismounted. 'You look well, Daughter. It gladdens my heart to see ye.'

'Thank ye, Father.' She swallowed a catch in the throat and longed to hug him, but it seemed too soon for forgiveness. News of his reckless gambling had spread. Even the Englishman John Haxton had heard about her father's bad reputation and taunted her with it. The humiliation still hurt.

There were no reservations when Christina was reunited with her mother. Marjorie gave a glad cry and limped across the room to gather her daughter in her arms.

'Oh, Chrissie dearie, I've prayed for this day every night on my knees since ye left!'

Christina laid her head against her mother's shoulder and shed a tear or two. She felt safe at last after the troubles in Falkland and the fear in Sir William's custody. She knew the feeling could not last but it was a relief to give way to a weak moment.

Marjorie did her best to comfort her daughter. 'Och, dinna greet, lovie! It must be God's will to send ye to Falkland to help Janet and the wee baby. The Almighty works in ways ye canna fathom.'

Although Christina had been prepared for her mother's pregnancy it was a shock now that the evidence confronted her. She decided tactfully to make no mention of the promise she had broken and her fears for Janet's seriously disturbed state of mind.

★ ★ ★

Annabel watched the joyous meeting of mother and daughter with an odd ache in her breast. She retained only a few hazy memories of her own dead mother – a hint of perfume, a fond smile, the touch of a hand and the silken rustle of a gown. Annabel wore a gold locket and chain her father had given her on her sixteenth birthday. It contained a miniature of her mother and she valued it highly. She knew her father must have loved her mother dearly for he had never remarried, keeping always faithful to the memory of his lost love.

Dorcas had nursed her mother in her last illness and Dorcas would insist upon calling herself lady's maid when in truth she was so much more. She was the only true friend, companion and loving guide that Annabel had ever known.

Lachie had noted his lady-love's melancholy and appeared anxiously by her side. 'What's wrong?'

She sighed pensively. 'My father indulges my every whim and spoils me outrageously, Lachie, and dear Dorcas tolerates my bad temper and contrary ways. I would be a better lass today if only my mother had lived.'

He laughed. 'Och, I've felt the whiplash o' your tongue and had experience o' the contrary ways, but I wouldna want ye changed for a' that.'

For once, Annabel found herself at a loss for words.

Dorcas did not feel welcome in the Gilmores' home.

The sojourn had begun well enough. Dorcas was pleased that the first meeting between father and daughter had passed without incident. Wil Gilmore had shown tactful patience with his feuding daughter and kindness and consideration for his unexpected guests. Dorcas was a fair judge of character and decided that Christina's father was a good man. No doubt he had weaknesses, but who doesna? she thought.

Which made the mother's behaviour all the more baffling.

Dorcas detected Marjorie Gilmore's antagonism soon after crossing the threshold.

The reunion between mother and daughter was heart-warming and afterwards Marjorie greeted Annabel warmly. 'It's grand to have ye bide wi' us once more, my lady!'

Annabel laughed. 'Och, be it cart stuck i' the mire or the threat o' snowdrifts, Gilmores aye come to my rescue, Mistress Gilmore!'

Marjorie flushed with pleasure and issued orders. 'Lachie, take my lady's cloak, her hands are like ice and your sister's no' much better. Seat the lassies near the fire to thaw.'

Lachie leapt to obey and Dorcas and Marjorie were left alone in the doorway. The hostess's welcome was cold. She greeted the lady's maid with a frosty nod and bustled off to attend to pots and cauldrons simmering on the fire.

Dorcas was perplexed. What way had she offended Mistress Gilmore, who had been kindness itself after the incident with the cart? What had changed in the interim?

Jamie saw the cool confrontation and his mother's rudeness astonished him but unlike Dorcas he could imagine a plausible explanation. This was a case of professional jealousy!

His mother took immense pride in her healing skills and boasted wide knowledge of helpful herbs and potions to rival any apothecary. She kept a well-stocked store of remedies in the press and noted information and receipts in the pages of a book she kept up to date in her beautiful, careful script. She obviously considered Dorcas a serious rival and could not hide her jealousy.

Jamie blamed his own lack of tact for the unfortunate state of affairs. He had praised Dorcas's skill as a healer enthusiastically and the lavish praise had doubtless offended his mother, whose pregnant moods had been much in evidence in his parents' bitter quarrel. Poor Dorcas was left standing awkwardly in the doorway looking pitifully confused and forlorn.

He crossed the floor and took her cold hand with a smile. 'Come away into the warm, Dorcas. Let me take your cloak.' In a deliberately intimate gesture he undid the fastening at the neck and put an arm across her shoulders to remove the garment.

Quite shaken by powerful emotions aroused by his bravado Jamie hung the cloak on the pegs. He was pleased to note a hint of laughter in her eyes.

'Thank ye, Mister Gilmore, that was gallantly done,' she told him.

Holding her hand, he led her towards the group by the fireside and seated himself beside her on the settle.

Marjorie watched every move with growing alarm. It was true what Maggie said, she thought. The lady's maid was stalking her son and to make matters worse the gullible lad was obviously fair game. Marjorie searched desperately for a way to break up the cosy partnership around the fire.

As usual, Wil was no use. The danger would not even occur to him. He was busy charming the visitors and making them laugh. Even Christina was smiling, her hands held out to the flames – pale hands with pink, perfect nails.

Hands that would grace any lady! Marjorie noted with a little stab of unease.

Maggie had tried without success to wriggle between Jamie and the conniving spinster, but to Maggie's annoyance Francis, the little imp from Hell, had thwarted every move. The boy sat on the floor at the lady's maid's feet like a sentinel and the washer-lassie could cheerfully have throttled him. Finally she decided upon a more direct approach. She fetched her shawl, draped it round head and shoulders and stood before Marjorie with a respectful wee bob.

'If you've nae mair need o' me the day, Mistress Gilmore, I should be off home afore the weather worsens. I'm late already and my faither will be at the soap-house door looking out. Pa's awfy protective o' his only wee ewe lamb!'

No harm dangling the prospect of a handsome dowry before a prospective mother-in-law's eyes! she thought.

Marjorie gratefully seized her chance, as Maggie knew she would.

'You've been a grand help, Maggie, but ye canna walk tae Lochleven in this foul weather.' She summoned Jamie with a shout. 'Maggie's leaving and the snow's falling faster, Jamie lad. Ride out wi' your wee sweetheart and make sure she reaches home safe; her pa will be anxious.'

Jamie rose obligingly and Christina spluttered with laughter at the mention o' the wee sweetheart. Maggie's pursuit of Jamie had been a family joke for months and it was difficult to adjust to changed circumstances.

Jamie glowered at his sister as he passed, shrugged on a riding cloak and ushered Maggie out. She clung to his arm, well pleased.

In Falkland at that moment the first serious snowfall of winter mantled the middens and formed drifts along streets and wynds but Janet Guthrie left Falkland Palace with a brisk step and a happy smile that would have amazed her younger sister. The wind was bitter, but Janet lifted her face to its icy bluster and laughed.

Wee Ninian was doing well.

She and her good friend the chambermaid had come to an amicable agreement that suited both parties. Janet spent the afternoons feeding and caring for her baby. Today she had rocked Ninian to sleep in her arms and laid him sleeping in the cosy crib before leaving him in the chambermaid's care in the palace warmth.

Nothing the elements could throw at Janet could daunt her now. She could visit the palace daily to feed and look after her son and the kindly chambermaid cared for him at night. The regime suited Ninian and he had thrived and grown in the weeks since Christina's departure.

Janet's mind was at rest concerning her absent sister. Word had leaked out that Lady Annabel and her seamstress companions had been summoned by the queen to sew cloaks for the Douglas ladies – and not many would dare refuse that command! She should have known Chrissie would never willingly break a promise.

She tugged the plaid closer and carefully negotiated slippery cobbles. To her surprise she noticed a wooden sled such as farmers use standing outside the weaver's door. Sleds were a common sight all year round since wheeled carts were worse than useless on atrocious roads, but sleds were a positive blessing in winter with snow lying on frozen ground. Janet studied the vehicle curiously as she approached. It was sturdily built with rare features consisting of metal runners and a wooden cab with dashboard to save driver and passengers from weather and flying divots.

A patient Highland garron stood between the shafts, warmed by a sackcloth horse rug padded with straw. The whole contraption revealed unusual ingenuity and attention to the comfort of man and beast.

Janet could not imagine what it was doing outside her door.

'Here she comes now!' her husband announced as she entered. She detected vast relief in Arthur's voice as she shook snow off the plaid.

'We have company, my dear,' he announced.

Janet recognized Euphemia and Joshua Sturrock, a couple with considerable stature in the community because of a long association with Falkland Palace.

She noted that everyone was on best behaviour. The three little girls sat motionless on the box bed, quelled by Aunt Bertha's eagle eye.

'How fares the poor wee baby, Mistress Guthrie?' Phemie asked sympathetically when the formalities were over and done with.

'He feeds and grows well, thank ye. The palace folk have been more than kind.'

'Aye, Falkland's fortunate to have the royal connection.'

Which brought Phemie neatly to the reason for the visit. She produced a folded sheet of parchment from the sailcloth bag she carried. It was a letter – unsealed for once – covered with writing on one side only. It had appeared mysteriously last night, slipped anonymously under the Sturrocks' door.

The curious document had been driving Phemie nearly daft with nervous anxiety, since Sir John Haxton had not returned and she did not know what to make of it.

'We never learned tae read, Mistress Guthrie, more's the pity, but you and Christina are lassies o' learning. She's awa' tae Lochleven so we'd be indebted if you'd scan this letter for us. It may be intended for ourselves or the English gentleman biding wi' us. Since the man's gone off gallivanting, I canna tell which.'

Janet glanced at the document. The urgent heading caught her attention:

Englishman—

She hesitated uncertainly, but curiosity won and she read on:

> *You should know that there is significant danger threatened to the life of Queen Mary wrought by a recent Act of the rebel Parliament. As you already know Her Grace agreed under duress to abdicate and seems agreeable to renounce her union with the Earl of Bothwell now held hostage in Denmark. All the rebel lords' conditions have been met and they are left without good reason to hold the queen in captivity. It is of course to their advantage to keep her confined.*
>
> *Therefore, by Act of Parliament passed lately in this month of December 1567 they claim her abdication perfect on the grounds that the Queen was privy, art and part of the murder of the King her husband, formerly Lord Henry Darnley. They claim sundry writings in her own hand as proof of conspiracy and plotting with Bothwell, chief suspect of the foul crime. This development bodes ill for the queen. Believe what you will, my friend, but many who know and revere her remain totally unconvinced.*

The letter was unsigned.

The parchment shook in Janet's hand. She wished curiosity had not overcome her scruples. She was in possession of information that could lead straight to the Tolbooth should Sir William Douglas or his half-brother the Regent Moray learn of her unwitting involvement.

Phemie leaned forward eagerly. 'What does it say, Mistress Guthrie? Is it frae the Englishman's fond faither?'

Janet grabbed gratefully at the straw. 'Aye, so it would seem. It – it is of a personal nature and I feel shamed to read a letter intended for another.' She folded the parchment hastily and handed it back. 'Please dinna tell the gentleman I scanned it, Mistress Sturrock, I beg ye.'

'You have my solemn word!' Phemie declared emphatically. The man would be blazing if he knew!

Phemie heaved a regretful sigh. Personal or no, she would love to know who had delivered the message and what the father had written – before John Haxton returned and committed the letter to the flames.

A brisk wind whistling across Loch Leven had whipped fresh snow into deep knife-edged drifts and it was decided that the Gilmores' guests would remain till it was safe to travel. Marjorie's work as hostess had trebled, but Christina helped and the lady's maid worked unobtrusively in the background, keeping well out of Marjorie's way. As for Christina's brothers, they seemed remarkably unperturbed by weather conditions that hindered farm work as the idle days slipped by.

Jamie eyed falling snow cheerfully. 'It's grand to see a white Yule. Keen frost kills disease and pestilence while a green winter means a full kirk yard, as they say.'

'No fear o' that!' Lachie said. 'Lady Annabel tells me ice forms so thick on London's river they hold fairs and merriment on the ice.'

Marjorie frowned. She was busy making another batch of bannocks and wondering if stocks of meal would last. 'Well, I wouldna fancy a fair on Loch Leven, that's for sure!' She flattened the dough with a thump of the fist, ready for the hot greased girdle on the fire. If she made the bannocks thinner maybe they'd go farther.

Francis appeared by his mother's side, glowering. 'You promised, Ma!' the boy said accusingly.

'What's that, lovie?'

'The Yule log, Ma! Tomorrow's the day.'

'Oh aye. I'd forgot – but—' She hesitated. She hated disappointing the laddie but it was deliberately flouting the Kirk's decree. She'd agreed to celebrate Christmas in a weak moment but on mature reflection Marjorie was not sure it was wise.

Francis was swift to seize the initiative. 'It's only a log, Ma. You said yoursel' there's no harm burning a log. The ladies would love it!' he added cunningly.

As he'd hoped, his brothers joined in enthusiastically.

'I can see no harm, Ma!' Jamie said. 'There's little to do round the farm in this weather and there's a big log i' the wood store that's dry as tinder and perfect for the purpose.'

Lachie laughed. 'What a lark! I'll help bring it in tomorrow morn.'

Francis clapped his hands. 'And I'll see it looks braw wi' holly and ivy!'

'It'll make a rare blaze i' the hearth!' Jamie grinned.

'My lady will love it,' Lachie added gleefully.

'And we could hae a feast after!' his young brother cheered.

Marjorie flattened bannock dough to an even more economical thickness. She could see that protest would be a waste of her energy.

'Ye may curse snow for hindering us but it's bonny when the sun shines,' Jamie said cheerfully at breakfast next morning. His father had just delivered the Gilmores' special grace for Christmas Day, an annual event spoken in French.

Marjorie glanced around assembled family and guests with a lighter heart. Everyone was in high spirits and laughter filled the room as they supped the porridge. The bonny, bright young faces of her bairns shone with happiness. Wil sent her a secret smile that even now could make Marjorie's heart race. She turned hastily aside to study the fireplace. Would the festive log fit the hearth?

Marjorie normally held the Kirk in high esteem but could not understand why the birth of Christ must not be celebrated. To her way of thinking it was a sin to treat the anniversary of that wondrous event as an ordinary working day.

'It's a grand log,' Lachie was saying. 'We'll hae to put it on a sled to haul it in.'

Lady Annabel chuckled. 'Chrissie and I volunteer to sit on the sled to hold it steady. You'll no' need decorations wi' two bonny lassies aboard, Lachie.'

'Mind and hop off afore you meet the flames!' Francis warned earnestly.

They roared with laughter and Jamie ruffled his wee brother's hair fondly.

Marjorie bustled around in the kitchen preparing a feast after the young ones had donned cloaks and mufflers and departed noisily outside. Wee Willy Douglas had joined the party, claiming that the queen was refused a hearing to plead her case in Parliament and was woeful and sad. Lochleven Castle did not promise much in the way of Christmas entertainment.

Marjorie glanced out the window to watch horseplay in the snow. They romped like bairns in the drifts and snowballs flew. Even the spinsterish lady's maid joined in, pelting the lads with accurate aim. Dogs barked, lassies shrieked and the hillside rang with laughter. It was all as it should be on this joyful day, she thought.

'I believe Christina will stay home with us,' Wil announced now they were alone.

Marjorie jumped. He'd been sitting so quiet in the corner she'd almost forgotten he was there. 'What makes ye say that?'

'I have seen how she looks. She knows her duty is with you.'

'I dinna want our daughter home frae duty, I want her home frae love!' she cried.

He sighed, recalling his conversation with an Englishman at Kinross Inn. 'Her mother she loves, my dear, but her father she can never love! Christina embroiders the truth to blacken my name. My infamy spreads and even strangers believe the worst of me.'

Marjorie glanced at him. Christina took bitter revenge and he took it hard! He had ruined their daughter's life and was paying a heavy price. Soberly, she continued to prepare the festive table, determined to give family and guests a feast to remember.

Jamie had judged the Yule log to a nicety. It was large but not too large to overwhelm the hearth. Eyes shining and cheeks glowing, the young men and women came crowding into the kitchen dragging log and sled behind them. They brought cold clean air and gales of laughter with them. The log was heaped with holly and ivy and sparkling with snow. Marjorie clasped her hands and held her breath. She had never seen anything so beautiful.

The lasses removed the greenery to decorate the fireside while the lads tipped the log on to glowing embers. The dry wood caught almost immediately lighting the room with flickering firelight.

United, they raised hands and voices to shout 'Hallelujah!'

It was a spontaneous moment of joy and praise none in the room would ever forget.

But then—

'Stop!' a voice thundered.

The parson stood in the doorway, black robed and forbidding. A petrified silence fell. Nobody moved.

The log burned brighter, crackling and sparking merrily.

The clergyman kicked the door shut and stalked into the room. He paused, taking in the scene. The table stood laden with a cauldron of sheep's head broth, Marjorie's famed haggis on a platter, haunches of mutton from hill sheep famed for tenderness and sweetness, flagons of elderberry wine, apple pies bursting with apples from the store sweetened with heather honey—

His arm shot out, a quivering finger pointed accusingly at the log blazing in the decorated hearth. 'What is that?'

'It is only a log, Minister,' Wil said.

'Hah!' the parson scoffed. 'Much more than that I think, Mister Gilmore! I see hellfire burning in your hearth, a pagan abomination! A feast laid upon your table in open defiance o' the Kirk.' He cast a withering glance over the womenfolk. 'And shrieking and devilish levity was heard; I was told of evil on-goings in the snow!'

'If you please, sir,' Marjorie ventured, 'it was but a snowball fight, a wee bit o' harmless fun.'

'Fun?' he roared. 'On a day demanding sober temperance an' hard work! Nah, nah, Mistress Gilmore! The behaviour was unchaste and you ken what that merits!' He turned and pointed the finger at Wil Gilmore. 'When Sir William Douglas hears o' this conduct i' the parish, I wouldna be surprised if you and your heirs forfeit the lease.'

Marjorie broke the shocked silence with a despairing groan. She couldna blame her husband for this disaster; she had permitted the Yule log to burn in the grate and prepared the Christmas feast that was chilling on the table. Her actions had brought public shame and punishment down upon innocent heads – and the fault was hers!

Nine

The Yule log, dry as tinder, was now aflame from end to end. Marjorie had never seen such a blaze. Troubled, she stared at the leaping flames but all she saw was glorious light. Try as she might, she could not see the hellfire the parson saw. Fire was a familiar friend Marjorie fed daily, tended and coaxed back to life if the spark faded. In return the family was blessed with warmth, hot meals, bread and bannocks.

But the minister said the log was an abomination and the feast she had lovingly prepared was sinful. He was a man of God. He should know.

Marjorie straightened her back and stood before him. 'If the Kirk seeks repentance ye shall have it in full, Minister, but my husband, family and friends shouldna be asked to suffer. A word frae me at the start could have put a stop to celebration but I held my tongue. I admit their conduct i' the snow was misguided, but it's natural for young lads and lasses tae revel in its purity. I'll wager we've a' thrown snowballs wi' no evil intent in the light-hearted innocence o' youth – even yoursel'!'

She could hardly believe she'd spoken so boldly but the stakes were high.

The man had listened with an expression that would freeze blood – but at least he listened. Marjorie held her breath in terror, but an unexpected champion was at hand.

Wee Francis stepped forward. 'Please, sir, it was me that wanted tae celebrate Christ's birth. My mither was sweer tae break the rule but I took advantage o' her condition and wore her down. I begged tae burn a Yule log and she saw no harm in it. It's only a log, sir; we never knew it was heathen hellfire. It was too cold tae work outside today onywey – and if the fare seems a wee bit beyond ordinary, hospitality demands we feed the women that brought my sister safely home.'

Willy Douglas ranged himself beside the younger boy. 'Sir, you'll never persuade the laird tae end Wil Gilmore's tenancy o' Goudiebank!

I serve at Sir William's table and hear him praise the farm produce. He swears it's the finest in Fife and there's none can beat Jamie Gilmore's husbandry and Mister Gilmore's horses. It would take more than a wee snowball fight to change the laird's tune. He's sworn tae fall upon his dagger, should Queen Mary escape.'

'And rightly so!' the parson declared. 'Lords o' the Congregation swear they have proof the woman plotted her husband's murder wi' her lover the Earl of Bothwell.'

That was more than Lady Annabel could stand. 'The Queen makes an easy target for guilty men's arrows!'

The minister chose to ignore the remark and turned to Marjorie. 'Your laddie laid his finger on the truth when he spoke o' weakness, Mistress Gilmore. You let your bairns rule your roost!' He sighed and shook his head. 'To my way o' thinking you're a poor weak wandered woman that's lost control o' family discipline and your spouse is no' much better. The elders are beyond redemption but the two young loons may yet be saved.'

He contemplated the boys in frowning silence for a full minute. There was hope of reprieve in the air. Nobody dare move a muscle.

'I'll no' demand public repentance frae the mother in her weak state,' he decided. 'The twa laddies will attend kirk after noon for catechism on Mondays, Wednesdays and Fridays and twice on Sundays – till I'm satisfied.'

The boys were dumbfounded. This was a serious curtailment of liberty.

'But sir, what'll I tell the laird?' Wee Willy wailed.

'The truth will serve,' the minister answered dryly, gathering his cloak and preparing to leave. He paused in the doorway. 'I've been lenient – God forgive me for it! See that you douse that pagan flame, Mister Gilmore.' He eyed the adult sinners dourly. 'Pray thon feast does not stick in your thrapples tae choke ye. Gird your hurdies against the cold and go about your work like godly folk.'

That said, the parson stepped out into the snowy yard and rode off towards the village, black vestments flapping in the wind.

John Haxton had taken an hour or two to recover from strong Scottish ale drunk with a wily Fife farmer. As his head cleared he remembered too late the warning he received at the start of his Scottish mission. Be wary of 'fly' Fifers! They were reputed to be devious, sly and cunning as the tod and he suspected this man was one of that ilk. The farmer had supplied plausible answers to questions yet left

John vaguely dissatisfied. After a restless night spent at the crowded inn John wakened next day unconvinced.

It could be – he mused as he lay on his back drowsily scanning the ceiling – he had lived too long in the company of wary men at Queen Elizabeth's court who used words as shields, but in the sober light of day he was uneasy. Undue concern for a certain young lady urged John to treat the wily countryman's information with caution.

It did appear that Christina Gilmore and her companions had been summoned to Castle Island to sew for the queen's retinue, but Lochleven Castle had an ominous reputation as secure confinement for high-ranking prisoners of State and their supporters before summary trial and execution. He considered the unfortunate Queen of Scots a dangerous mistress to serve.

Christina's vivid presence drifted dreamily across his mind. He saw her in a garden with sunlight in her hair, a smile on her lips and ripe fruit in her hands. In sharp contrast, he pictured a cold street in Falkland, a worn plaid and angry eyes sparkling like diamonds as she screamed how much she loathed him. Angel woman or vicious vixen, the fair lady's behaviour was unpredictable like her wild Highland father. John knew Highland chieftains were notoriously clannish and vengeful. How could a Lowland farmer be so confident Sir Hamish Gilmore would not storm Sir William's castle to avenge his daughter's abduction?

It made no sense but Scottish clan allegiances were beyond his comprehension, John decided. He threw the covers impatiently aside and rose, shivering in the morning air.

New Year 1568 passed soberly at Goudiebank. The Gilmores' guests had not yet braved the return journey to Falkland although there was no more snow and skies remained hazy blue. Marjorie was in the late stages of pregnancy and the extra work was an added burden she tholed patiently. She knew that when the visitors went Christina could go with them.

Sitting peacefully by the fireside, just the two of them alone for once, she stole a glance at her bonny daughter, who was sewing a patch on Francis's breeches. Christina's face was shadowed as she plied the needle. She had not yet made her intentions clear and Marjorie's pride would not let her ask.

Christina snipped the thread. 'There, that's done. I dinna ken how he managed to rip his best breeks.'

'Better no' ask!' Marjorie said. 'He and Willy Douglas are up to all sort o' devilment after attending kirk for catechism.'

Christina laughed and stood up, folding the mended breeches. 'The minister wastes his time on those two scamps. It'll take more than catechism tae mend their ways, bless them.' She headed for the doorway, pausing only to don a cloak and shove her feet into deerskin buskins.

'Where are ye off to?' Marjorie called in surprise. She had hoped to have her daughter to herself for an hour or two. The others were out with a sled gathering wood for the hungry fire. The lady and her maid seemed as keen to sample cold fresh air and exercise as the two lads.

Christina hesitated momentarily. 'I want a word wi' my father.'

'Not afore time,' Marjorie muttered as the door closed behind her. Father and daughter circled one another warily, barely exchanging a word. It had been painful to watch.

Christina had only been gone minutes before Francis rushed in. Punitive excursions with Willy Douglas had benefited Francis. His cheeks had a healthy glow these days, his halting gait much more assured.

Marjorie sighed as the door crashed open and he charged into the room. 'Where's the fire, Son?'

He kicked the door shut gleefully. 'There's to be a Twelfth Night celebration down by the loch side, Ma, and a big bonfire!'

'Well, it'll no' be the minister that blesses it!' his mother declared.

'Och, he'll turn a blind ee!' Francis said confidently. 'Kinross baxters and fleshers are to celebrate the twelfth night of Christmas. Their trade suffers frae the weather and they plan a bonfire, play-acting and market stalls tae draw the crowds. Willy Douglas says the trade guilds are powerfully strong in the district and the minister darsna say a word for fear o' a riot. He calls it Epiphany in honour o' the three Kings o' Orient and puts a dour religious face on it for the Kirk's sake.'

Marjorie smiled reminiscently. 'I mind my grandmother aye baked a big cake for Twelfth Night in the auld days when I was just a wee lassie. There was a dried bean, a pea and a clove baked in it and the lad who picked a slice wi' the bean was king for the night. The lassie who found the pea was his queen and the knave had the clove and played the daft fool. It was the grandest fun.'

Francis hopped excitedly from foot to foot. 'The baxters have baked a cake, Ma. Willy says it's huge and it's to be ha'penny the piece. Will there be a bean, a pea and a clove in it, do ye suppose?'

It was a delight to see the laddie so happy in these difficult days. His news took Marjorie back to her girlhood and she laughed. 'Och, it wouldna be Twelfth Night without it, lovie!'

Wil Gilmore was alone in the stables grooming the young stallion, the focus of all his hopes. He paused warily with brush in hand as his daughter approached the stall. He had no idea what to expect.

She examined the colt admiringly. 'This fine lad is new, Pa.'

'Aye.' He smoothed the stallion's glossy hide. One false move might send his daughter off in the quick fiery temper he had bequeathed to her. 'I was lucky to find him at Kinross fair and I call him Lochinvar after a notable horseman. He'll fetch a fine price at Falkirk Tryst this summer and bring redemption should ye choose to forgive.'

Wil met his daughter's eye and held his breath. This was a daring gamble. How would she take it?

Christina's expression darkened. 'No need for a dowry now, Pa. You can sell your fine colt and drink your fill at Falkland.'

She regretted the cruel dig the moment it was said. She had come with a genuine desire to make amends. No hope of that now. Her father was furious.

Of all his bairns Christina was perhaps Wil's best beloved. He saw in her his own creative ability and delighted in the refining influence of her artistic talents. Unfortunately this talented lassie had inherited the curse of his acid tongue. Wil found her scorn particularly hurtful.

'Aye, no dowry and no charity in your cold heart either, Daughter!' he cried furiously, startling the horse. He soothed its restless prancing and turned back to face her. 'I can stomach your contempt, Christina, but I will not stand to have my reputation blackened by your evil lies!'

The accusation took her by surprise. 'Pa – I never did!'

'Aye, ye did so! I spoke to an Englishman at the Kinross Inn who believes your father to be the devil incarnate. Where would a Falkland stranger hear such slander if not from you?'

'An – an Englishman?' she faltered.

'A man of more substantial quality than his wolf hunting trade suggested. All his concern was for you.'

'He – was concerned?'

'I reassured him, but did not show my hand. I played the simple farmer and never let on you were my daughter. He took unhealthy interest in a man on a piebald horse seen in Falkland, but I steered him from our Lachie with a load o' nonsense. I admired the fine wolfhound at his heel but did not trust your English friend one bit.'

'No friend o' mine!' she said hastily. 'He would hear about your folly at Falkirk Tryst from Falkland gossips, never from me!'

Wil shrugged non-committally. The stallion gently nuzzled his neck and he stroked the bonny beast. The quick heat of his anger had cooled. 'So what brought you to me – did you come with the intention of trading insults?'

'Of course not. I came to say when Lady Annabel rides for Falkland I'll stay home and care for Ma.'

'You bow to duty?' he said flatly.

'Aye, Father, I do,' she answered quietly and walked away.

Wil stared after her. So the decision was made and one might say it was the right decision, but he was not convinced. The craftsman in him raged against it. Her gifted hands would soon be swollen and painful with chilblains, shapely nails broken and ragged, delicate white skin split with painful hacks and coarsened by harsh winter weather.

Wil's sight blurred with sudden tears. It was a sinful waste of God-given talent and the fault was doubly his. There would be no call for duty had there been no baby.

John Haxton left Kinross and made a detour to Melville lands in the Bow of Fife hoping to meet with James Melville, only to find his friend had been called away urgently to Edinburgh. The Melville family made him very welcome over New Year but John was glad to be back in Falkland two days later as the horse clattered into the Sturrocks' stable yard, Boris panting at its tail. An early gloaming cast purple haze over snow-clad hills as he dismounted and tossed the reins to the stable lad. There was a savoury aroma of cooking in the frosty air. Phemie was tending a pot of rabbit stew simmering on the fire as he pushed open the kitchen door. She glanced up. 'So you're back. It's about time!'

He grinned. 'Did you miss me?'

'Och, we gave up hope o' ye days ago. Joshua says wolves are a menace on the Lomonds for want o' a good hound.'

All the same she was pleased to see him safe and sound. The letter was waiting on the shelf. She blew the dust off and handed it to him. 'It's come frae your pa and is of a personal nature.'

'How do you know?' he demanded quickly.

Phemie froze. Be sure your sins will find ye oot! she thought. With his eyes boring into her like gimlets there was nothing for it but the truth.

'It was slipped secretly under the door and we didna ken if it was for you or us. It seemed urgent so I – I had it read.'

He scanned the letter briefly and took a menacing step towards her. 'Who read it?'

Now Phemie faced a dilemma. If she told him the reader was Christina Gilmore's sister the innocent lassie was easy prey for the predatory Englishman. Phemie had lived through incursions by an English army and had scant respect for English morals. She dithered, but her lodger looked so fearsome she was scared out of her wits.

'It was scanned by Mistress Guthrie the Falkland weaver's wife, Sir John,' she babbled.

He looked blank. The name meant nothing to him and Phemie gained courage. 'The woman was sweer to read a privy letter but she took a wee look and confirmed it was frae your pa. She told us it was of a personal nature, but wouldna say what.'

'That was – commendable of Mistress Guthrie,' he remarked dryly. He read the incriminating document grimly through more carefully. He guessed it had been delivered by one of the Scottish agent's men to alert him to the Queen of Scots' precarious situation. Crossing to the fire, he reduced the letter to ashes.

So that's that! Phemie thought thankfully.

Sir John Haxton watched the document blacken and burn. He resolved to seek out Mistress Guthrie the weaver's wife at the first opportunity. He had to know where this cunning woman's loyalties lay.

Janet Guthrie was preparing to leave for the Palace next morning when a knock came at the door. She opened it with a smile expecting to find a gossiping neighbour and saw a man standing on the step. She noted his cloak was sober but of fine quality.

'Mistress Guthrie?' He lowered his voice when she nodded. 'I believe you scanned a letter intended for me?'

Janet almost fainted with shock. 'Sir – I'm heartfelt sorry – I didna mean to pry – but I couldna help but read—'

She was sure her heart stopped beating for several terrified seconds.

John Haxton studied her keenly. He saw a woman with pleasing features and matronly figure. Something about her made him pause. Where had he seen her before – walking in Falkland, maybe? Blue eyes that seemed familiar puzzled him momentarily but at least they held no guile.

He smiled to set her at ease. 'To be sure, Mistress Guthrie, the content is of little consequence since it must be public knowledge by now. What concerns me is what it revealed about my presence here in Scotland. You'll have guessed I did not come to Falkland to rid the Lomonds of wolves – though Boris and I will play our part.' He patted the wolfhound waiting patiently by his side.

Janet lost her fear. After all, what had she to lose? The moment she'd read the letter she had known it was intended for an English spy and it was only a matter of time before Euphemia Sturrock confessed what she'd done and the man tracked her down. 'I know what you are, sir,' she said.

He met her eyes. 'I mean no harm to your queen and country, Mistress Guthrie. I only observe. All I ask is your discretion – and your silence.'

'You shall have it.'

He smiled. 'Good! I already have proof o' the discretion. Phemie Sturrock remains in ignorance. That's no mean feat!'

Within the house the loom had never ceased its monotonous clacking as they spoke. He could hear children's voices raised and an older woman calming them. Janet glanced towards the sound nervously but John had one more question to ask.

'Has Falkland had news of Lady Annabel's ladies?'

Her smile was radiant. 'Oh aye! We had word they're freed and biding at a farm nearby Lochleven till the track to Falkland is clear.'

He bade Mistress Guthrie good day and came away from the door with lightsome step. The good mood encouraged Boris to frolic in a heap of snow.

Christina Gilmore is safe! John Haxton thought.

In an excess of high spirits, he gathered an icy snowball from the heap and threw it far down the street for the dog to chase.

Wil Gilmore and his sons had adapted a farm sled to convey family and guests to the Twelfth Night celebrations. It boasted wooden seats and a canvas awning when finished and was light enough for Muckle Meg to pull fully laden. The mare had the added advantage of two iron-shod front hooves for extra grip on icy tracks.

Marjorie refused to join the party despite Wil's pleading.

'I'd dearly love to go for auld times' sake, but I'll no' risk the unborn wean's safety,' she declared stubbornly. 'I'll stay and mind the house.'

Her husband was bitterly disappointed. He had hoped for reconciliation in more joyful surroundings.

Wil's spirits lifted once the party set off just before dusk. The sled ran easily on hard-packed snow and Muckle Meg took kindly to finding herself between the shafts. With Wil's expert hands on the reins the mare appeared to enjoy the experience as she trotted, snorting breath blowing like steam in ice cold air.

The young men and women seated behind huddled together for warmth on the makeshift bench. Christina sat in the middle with Annabel and Dorcas to right and left. Her two brothers were seated either side in case the sled's jolting threw the lady passengers off balance. This meant Lachie's steadying arm was around Annabel while Jamie tenderly supported the lady's maid. Christina could imagine Maggie's wild outrage and smiled complacently.

Christina herself was the gooseberry in the middle, a lassie lacking a lad. It was a lonely feeling.

'The bonfire's lit!' Francis yelled. He was sitting up front beside his father with a good view ahead when the evening sky suddenly lit with an orange glow, sparks rising into clear air. The night promised to be clear and beautiful.

Wil left Muckle Meg and the sled in the shelter of trees, a horse rug on her back for warmth and nosebag of oats to keep the patient mare content.

Festivities were already under way by the loch, the scene dominated by a huge bonfire. A large proportion of the able-bodied population for miles around had crowded on to the snowy field.

Baxters and fleshers united to produce trays of hot meat pies laid on trestles surrounding a large octagonal Twelfth Night cake, already cut in slices. As they approached, the Gilmore party heard the merry jingle of silver dropping steadily into guild pouches. The usual complement of Highland musicians, Egyptian dancers and performing vagabonds enlivened the scene, along with a motley collection of stall holders selling tawdry Twelfth Night paper crowns, cheap baubles, ribbons and sweets. Roast chestnut sellers ladled piping hot chestnuts from glowing braziers dotted around the field into bonnets and leather pouches, a grand way to warm frozen head and hands.

Francis soon found wee Willy Douglas and the two disappeared into the crowd with the pennies Wil had generously donated.

Hugh Ross appeared out of the crowd and strode purposefully towards Christina. He took her aside. 'Would ye try your luck wi' the cake, Chrissie? The king and queen are not yet found.'

'To win would be a waste of good siller,' she said, smiling. 'I'm just a poor lassie lacking a dowry at the end o' the night.'

He drew her close and whispered, 'I'll not deny a dowry's essential, Christina. But that's because I hold ye in high regard. I wouldna ask ye to bide in a boatman's bothy.'

'And I told you I would! I'd work right willingly to buy a share in your uncle's yard if I loved ye.'

He sighed quizzically. 'Aye – if? That's the question.'

The light-hearted mood of the festival lifted Christina's spirits. There were happy couples arm in arm all around and there was no need to play gooseberry now. Here was a handsome lad offering to be her escort and it was a pity to miss the chance. A Highlander piped merrily nearby, the bonfire blazed and shouts and laughter echoed across the frozen reaches of the loch. Christina linked Hugh's arm laughingly.

'Och, Hugh, let's forget the past and try our luck wi' the cake.'

In this happy mood he would follow her to the ends of the earth, he thought, reminded wistfully of youthful Christina, a young lassie revelling in the heady delight of innocent calf love.

The remainder of the small group wandered on without them. Lady Annabel looked forward to play-acting, scheduled for later that evening with the bonfire as backdrop. She hoped the play would be *Robin Hood and Little John,* which was both exciting and amusing. She had attended a performance once with her father in Edinburgh. The play was a favourite with the city crowd and regarded favourably by Edinburgh bailies since it encouraged the practise of archery. Scots were not famed for skill with bow and arrow, preferring the more precise broadsword and Lochaber axe in battle.

Hanging on to Lachie's arm with the field slippery underfoot, Annabel shivered. 'It's so cold, Lachie! My hands are freezing.'

He was immediately concerned. 'What ye need is a pouchful o' roast chestnuts to hold. Wait here wi' my father, I'll fetch some.'

'Well said!' Jamie smiled. He turned to Dorcas and took her hands. 'As I suspected, cold as ice! Come along, let's follow Lachie tae the chestnut stand.'

Laughing, stumbling and slithering in melting snow they set off past the bonfire and were fast swallowed in a capering crowd.

Wil and Annabel Erskine were left in one another's company, a rare occurrence. Wil offered the lady his arm. She accepted gracefully and they walked a little distance together.

'*C'est bon!* Now I can air my French!' she said in that language.

Wil was surprised and delighted. 'I did not realize you spoke so fluently.'

'I am not just a pretty face, *Monsieur*,' she said with a twinkle in her eye. 'You might say I am a businesswoman. My father is a Leith merchant and has no son so I work with him arranging shipments of fine materials, furs and luxury goods from France and other foreign parts. We speak French and a few other tongues so that we can bargain freely with traders and customers.'

'I am impressed!' Wil said.

Shared language formed a bond and they exchanged a smile as they stood in a quiet haven of peace by the loch side looking across frozen water to the darkened castle. Laughter and merriment must seem part of another world to those marooned upon that far island, Annabel thought sadly. By the light of the rising moon she could see that the loch's surface was frozen in places, open water in others.

'Mr Gilmore, could the queen escape by walking across the ice?' she asked curiously. She took a risk, for she did not know where his loyalties lay.

Wil shook his head. 'It is not possible. Ice is too thin and dangerous in parts, even after many days of frost.'

Annabel turned her head to meet his eyes. 'Perhaps you hope Marie Stuart may never go free?'

Wil remained silent for a moment or two. 'My lady, I worked as stonemason for her father King James and his queen Marie de Guise at Falkland Palace and was honoured to do so,' he said at last. 'It troubles me greatly to see their daughter cruelly maligned and falsely imprisoned.'

'It troubles many folk and the numbers grow day by day,' Annabel said grimly. She looked out thoughtfully across the dark loch. 'Should the queen escape, she will need good horses waiting on the shore to carry her swiftly to safety.'

He responded softly. 'Mine are the best and swiftest in the land, *Mam'selle*.'

'I know it, *Monsieur*.'

And Annabel Erskine and Wil Gilmore shared a dark, secretive smile of complete understanding.

Christina and Hugh were consumed with laughter when slices of Twelfth Night cake contained only almond, ginger, cinnamon and little else.

Word was already going the rounds that the blacksmith was King
o' the bean, the bellman's buxom daughter was his queen and the
knave was a wee shilpit tannery apprentice who was already larking
around swiping at ankles with a leather belt and making a perfect
nuisance o' himself.

Hugh was offered sips of mulled wine from the ladle at the guilds'
table. The generous offer was made on the strength of his abilities
as boatman and he had made full use of liberal ladlefuls. The potent
brew simmering in the pot cheered him and made him bold. In
this festive mood Hugh could conquer the world – or a reluctant
lassie for that matter. Amorously, he enfolded Christina in his arms.
'How about a kiss for auld times' sake, eh, lass?'

Christina smiled uncertainly. 'Auld times are past, Hugh. One kiss
solves nothing.'

'You're right!' he declared boisterously. 'Two or three will do it!'

Too late, she realized her merry mood had encouraged him to want
more than she was willing to give. All she asked was companionship
not kisses. 'No, Hugh. No! Please dinna—' She struggled wildly, but
he was too strong.

He forced a bruising kiss on her mouth and laughed. 'That's one!
Now for the rest.'

She pounded fists on his chest and cried out for help to no avail.
Such squabbles were all too frequent at the height of festivities and
often as not lassies made a modest show of shrieking reluctance. It
was all part of the fun and games. Passers-by walked on smiling broadly.

But a heavy hand fell on Hugh's shoulder, hauling him away. 'I
believe the lady does not welcome your attentions, my friend!'

It was pleasantly said but Hugh was held in an iron grip. He
birled round indignantly. 'Mind your ain affairs, stranger!'

With a shock of surprise John Haxton recognized the lady in
distress. At once he tossed Hugh unceremoniously aside to sprawl
drunkenly in trampled slush.

John Haxton turned anxiously to Christina. 'Did that oaf harm
you, lady?' he asked, taking her hand. 'I had hoped to find you here
but never thought to save you from drunken assault,' he said, prod-
ding Hugh contemptuously with the toe of his boot.

Hugh scrambled to his feet, sobered and furious. 'Is this a sample
o' your fine English friend's harsh treatment, Chrissie?' he demanded
scathingly.

'English or no', it seems I'm in safer hands wi' him than you!'
she answered coldly.

'More fool you to trust the likes o' him!' Hugh growled. He turned and pushed his way roughly through the group of disappointed onlookers that had gathered, hopeful of a fight.

By now Christina had recovered from the shock of the encounter.

Her champion smiled down at her. 'Now that I've found you again, will you walk with me?'

There was no need for a reply. Her hand rested in his and there was warmth between them. The night was dark but the bonfire cast strange, flickering shadows on the snowy ground as they walked.

'I can't understand how you come to be here,' she said.

'Simple! Mistress Sturrock boasted about a grand Twelfth Night cake baked by her son the Kinross baker for festivities planned this evening by the loch side. I was told you were free and sheltering near Loch Leven so I lodged at Kinross Inn and prayed you would attend the celebrations.'

'Why you should favour me wi' prayer I canna imagine! I offered ye nothing but hatred,' she marvelled.

He laughed. 'I do not believe you capable of hatred. A shrewish temper perhaps but a loving heart.'

His words ruffled a few feathers but she had to smile. 'Should I be flattered or affronted?'

'I care not which, Christina. Just be yourself.'

But who am I? she wondered. She was a trespasser in both stations of life. At least her fine clothes did not deceive this fine gentleman. He had her full history from Falkland gossips.

'Falkland lost its charm when you were taken. I missed you,' he said.

Inside her head an alarm bell rang – beware of predatory noblemen whose intentions are to seduce vulnerable country maidens! She had hidden under the old plaidie when venturing out in Falkland but the Englishman had easily penetrated her disguise. The shame was that in doing so he had somehow found a pathway to her heart.

'I canna understand why you should care; I give ye nothing but grief,' she retorted sharply.

'But at first you smiled. Don't you remember a meeting in a garden?'

'Aye, of course I do! You insulted my father and roused the shrewish temper.'

'Not before I glimpsed the gentle heart beyond the wolfish snarl.'

'Now I am affronted!'

'And your eyes sparkle. The finest diamonds cannot compete—'

In suspicious mood she cut him short. 'I'll not be buttered wi' flattery! What do you hope to gain?'

He looked shamefaced. 'I'm sorry. I have spent too many hours at court in the company of vain women with vacant minds. I promise I will never again insult your sturdy Scottish intelligence with idle compliments – but in a rage your eyes *do* sparkle like diamonds.'

She hid a smile. 'Och, sir, you tease me. You are hopeless!'

'No, dear lady, I do not tease and my hopes are high, for I am deep in love with you.' He stopped and looked down at her seriously in the flaring light of windswept torches set around the field.

Christina panicked then. All this time they had walked hand in hand warmly and naturally. She had not even been aware their fingers were intertwined but she knew the significance all too well. Since ancient times lovers had linked hands across a rushing burn to pledge a betrothal. Now she could appreciate the powerful force behind the act. She dragged her hand free. 'It cannot be, Sir John. It's fantasy!'

'What passed as love for me before was fantasy. This is reality, sweetheart.'

She shook her head in distress. 'No, no! You despise me busked in old tattered plaid!'

'Only because it hides your beauty!'

'How can ye say that?' she cried tearfully with a vision of herself toiling with her brothers in muddy fields. 'You have not seen me at my lowest ebb, Sir John!'

He met her eyes soberly. 'Aye, Christina, I assure ye I have faced the facts. I have thought of little else since I first saw you in the street cradling your newborn baby.'

'My baby—?' Christina's thoughts went spinning. What lies had Falkland gossips fed him? she wondered. She had offended the matrons attending Ninian's birth and some might take delight in cunningly blackening her reputation under his questioning. Did he believe she was a wanton woman easily seduced by talk of love? Of course he did, and had enjoyed the thrill o' the chase like the sportsman he was.

The humiliation was complete and cruel, because she had been drawn to him so strangely.

He noted her expression and frowned. 'What is it – what's wrong, dear love—?'

'Never talk to me of love!' she cried. 'Ye dinna ken the meaning of the word!'

She whirled and ran from him in a haze of humiliated tears and barged straight into her father's arms.

'My dear!' Wil hugged her anxiously. 'Hugh told us he was manhandled and you were in danger. He's gone to fetch help but I came at once and I find you distressed and in tears. What has this scoundrel done—?'

Wil Gilmore stopped short in astonishment as he recognized the Englishman. The meeting was a staggering shock to both men.

Wil scowled ferociously. 'Sir, how dare you harm her!'

'I did not! I foiled a drunken clodhopper's unwelcome amorous advances.'

'Take care!' Wil warned dangerously. 'You insult the man who may be my son-in-law one day.'

'You have my sympathy on that score,' John said. 'And I suggest you have no right to embrace the lady so intimately.'

'Damn your impudence!' Wil yelled hotly. 'I have every right. I am Christina's father!'

John Haxton stepped back in stunned disbelief for a moment.

So *this* was Sir Hamish Gilmore, the murderous Highlander! he thought. No wonder he had felt uneasy after their meeting at the inn; the man could assume the guise of farmer when it suited him and was obviously as cunning as the Devil.

'My sons are on their way,' Wil said doubling his fists. 'When they find their sister in such distress it'll be the worse for you!'

'Then I will leave now,' John Haxton told him coldly. 'Not for want of courage, you understand, but for your daughter's sake there must be no bloodshed.'

He gave a stiff little bow in Christina's direction and stalked off. With oddly mixed feelings she watched him walk away out of her life till all sight of him had faded into darkness at the edge of the field.

Ten

After the Twelfth Night festivities a lull in winter weather forced Annabel's decision to return to Falkland within the week. She seemed reluctant to leave which caused lovelorn Lachie some heart searching. Could it be because Goudiebank was conveniently close to George Douglas or did she enjoy a cosy family atmosphere within the farmstead and his mother's devoted attention?

He wished he knew for sure.

Wee Willy Douglas was a constant visitor to Goudiebank these days. He and Francis were always mumbling together in some corner or another, ostensibly learning catechism to the preacher's satisfaction. Lachie had grave doubts. He suspected wee Willy acted as Annabel's courier, carrying love letters to and fro in secret.

Passing by the pair in a secluded corner a whisper caught Lachie's ear and stopped him in his tracks.

'Is Bonny George really in love wi' her?' Francis queried.

Willy nodded. 'Aye, he asked the laird's permission again tae marry her but the family's against it. They say it's ower mean a match—'

The boys caught Lachie's jaundiced eye and began gabbling in panic:

'*Wh–what is sin?*'

'*Disobedience tae God's law!*'

'*What is the penalty for sin?*'

'*D–d–death!*'

Lachie glowered down upon them.

'Aye, and you'd do weel to mind it!'

Under the circumstances Lachie was pleased to start departure preparations to distance his lady from her handsome suitor.

All the same, George Douglas's behaviour puzzled Lachie. Had Lachie considered himself a more considerable match for the lady he would have courted her diligently. It seemed strange that the young nobleman had not taken full advantage of Annabel's proximity to visit

her. It was rumoured that George Douglas had been seen twice or
thrice in the district, but if so the man had made no attempt to
contact Lady Annabel.

Unless by letter of course!

Lachie continued to watch wee Willy Douglas like a hawk.

Annabel and Dorcas were dismayed to discover Christina could
not be persuaded to return to Falkland with them. Marjorie's pregnancy was far advanced and the reason for the decision was evident,
but Annabel found the loss of a gifted needlewoman and valued
friend hard to stomach.

'Och, you'll come back to us in Falkland once the baby's born
safe and sound, God willing,' she said confidently, hugging her.

Christina shook her head. The parting distressed her but she would
not change her mind. 'No, my lady. That's when my help will be
most sairly needed.'

Annabel raised her eyes heavenwards. 'Puking babies and girning
bairns – what a scunner for the Almighty tae inflict upon us
females!'

The travelling cloaks were warming in the ingle and the women's
few possessions stowed in saddlebags. Wil had gone to the stables to
prepare horses for the journey, mindful that conditions were still
treacherous and slippery.

Lachie volunteered to act as the women's escort, a mission that
had put him in the highest good spirits. His lady-love looked upon
the arrangement with approval and so did the family, anxious for
news of Janet and her sickly son.

Wee Willy Douglas appeared in the midst of final departure preparations, tugging at Lachie's sleeve.

Lachie glowered. The laddie was persistent as a flea and just about
as irritating. 'What do *you* want, you wee scunner?'

'I canna bide or I'll be missed, Lachie. I heard word the women
were leaving and guessed ye'd go wi' them.' He gave Lachie a knowing
grin and wink. Not much escaped wee Willy's notice.

Lachie's scowl deepened. 'Get on wi' it! Is it a letter frae braw
Geordie, curse 'im?'

The boy leaned closer, whispering. 'Nah, it's frae the queen herself
tae Lord Seton, Mary Seton's brother. She wrote it in secret while
her guards were at supper and sneaked it tae George. He says Lady
Annabel will ken what tae do when she reads it.'

Lachie froze. Secret love letters were a dangerous enough cargo,
but this was sailing into deep and perilous waters. His fears were

not only for himself and his family but also for Annabel. It would go badly for her should she be stopped and searched and the queen's letter discovered by the laird's men on the way to Falkland.

'I'll see to it. Give it tae me,' he demanded quietly.

Willy looked shiftily right and left and slid the letter from under his bonnet. Lachie tucked it swiftly into his pouch. There it would remain till they reached the safety of Falkland Palace.

When he glanced up again the young messenger had vanished as silently as he had come.

Jamie helped assemble the visitors' belongings in saddlebags then drew Dorcas aside into a quiet corner.

'I want tae thank ye for the tolerant kindness you've shown my mother in return for nothing but cauld ingratitude. I dinna ken what's got intae her!'

She smiled. 'Och, in her condition it's a trachle caring for visitors. She'll be glad tae see the back o' me.'

'I won't. I'll miss ye, Dorcas,' he said.

She met his eyes. Truth to tell, she would miss him too. She prayed that he would enjoy a long and happy life wi' his bonny wee sweetheart.

She smiled to lighten a parting that threatened to become emotional. 'You'll miss skylarking in the snow, you mean! I'm sorry I sent a snowball down your neck.'

He laughed merrily. 'You have a powerfully straight aim for a lassie, Dorcas, but I forgive ye. Our frolic i' the snow is a memory I will hold dear – even though the minister condemned us tae hellfire.'

She shook her head. 'The man was wrong, Jamie lad. It was only harmless fun.'

The cosy conversation had not escaped Marjorie, who was forever on guard to foil the predatory spinster's advances. Her heart nearly failed her when she heard her son laughing. He never laughed wi' Maggie! What vile spell had the lady's maid put upon poor guileless Jamie? Marjorie wondered. Thank Heaven the woman would leave today and that would put an end to her cunning devices. The sooner her son was safely married to Maggie, the better.

Maggie had got wind of the departure from one of the farmhands and turned up in their midst. She carried a sailcloth bag under winter cloak and shawl and looked pale and wan.

Marjorie greeted her kindly. 'Come awa' in tae the warm, lass. We were concerned when ye didna attend the Twelfth Night feast.'

'My ma and I ate rotten meat and took tae bed but Pa didna suffer. Ma swears Pa can swallow leather and never blink an ee,' the washer-lassie said.

'Aye weel, I'm glad ye recovered in time tae speed our visitors on their way.'

Marjorie cast a significant glance towards the couple in the corner and Maggie needed no second bidding.

She nipped across the kitchen and confronted Dorcas with a sweet smile. 'So you're off at last! You must be sweer tae return tae Falkland duties o' course, after a leisurely time wi' poor Mistress Gilmore running at your beck and call.'

Dorcas raised her brows slightly. She had worked hard and unobtrusively to keep Marjorie's work to a minimum, but she answered pleasantly. 'Yes indeed, Mistress Gilmore is the very soul o' kindness and hospitality.'

Maggie gazed up at Jamie, giving him full advantage of the unusual pallor. 'Did ye miss me on Twelfth Night, Jamie? I've been awfy no' weel!'

He was concerned. 'I did wonder where ye were. What ails ye, Maggie?'

'A bit o' badly salted beef. I'm all the better for seeing you though.'

He was touched. 'Here, give me your cloak. Leave on your shawl and sit by the fire.'

He seated her on the settle while Dorcas quietly withdrew and left them together. She would always cherish memories of happy hours spent with Jamie Gilmore and his family but the time had come to leave him to woo his young love.

Christina watched dejectedly as her two dearest friends rode off with Lachie along the farm wynd. Jamie stood by her side waving till the little cavalcade was out of sight. He was saddened to see them go. They had brought light and laughter into his hard-working life and now his heartbeat felt slow and heavy. He could sympathize with Christina's obvious distress as a tear slid down her cheek. Impulsively, Jamie hugged his sister. 'Dinna greet, Chrissie. They'll be back again one day. I know they will!'

'I wish I could be sure!' she said sadly.

'Come away tae the stables with me,' he suggested kindly. 'The walk will do ye good and Pa and Francis will be feeding the horses. You can admire the fine young stallion Pa swears will be your salvation.'

He was pleased to note the remark raised a smile and the suggestion met with favour. Brother and sister set off arm in arm, picking their way along the slippery frozen path and laughing when they stumbled.

Marjorie and Maggie were left alone in the house. She smiled kindly at the lassie seated by the fire. 'Feeling better?'

'Fine and warm, thank ye.' She glanced towards the doorway. They had heard the visitors ride off a while ago with shouted farewells but there was no sign of Christina or Jamie. Maggie was leaving nothing to chance where the lady's maid was concerned. 'Where's Jamie gone to?' she wondered suspiciously.

'He said he'd help his father i' the stables then feed sheep in the fold and draught oxen and beasts i' the byre. I expect he took Christina wi' him to divert her. The poor lassie's fair upset at losing her friends.'

Maggie nodded. 'Aye, she's grown so ladylike and soft it'll be hard tae settle tae honest labour.'

Marjorie sat at the table trying to summon enough energy to prepare the midday meal. She suddenly noticed a sailcloth bag lying at the washer-lassie's feet. 'What's in the poke?' she asked curiously.

'Och, I near forgot in a' the stir, Mistress Gilmore! I brought ye white soap.'

Maggie rose and brought the bag to the table. She loosened the drawstrings and tipped three long bars of pure white soap on the tabletop.

A heady perfume of roses, lavender and musk filled Marjorie's nostrils.

Ah, the luxury! She breathed ecstatically imagining the pleasure of soft perfumed lather on the skin! Even the ugly shapeless old wife's flocket whose folds disguised the girth of her ungainly body would seem more bearable. However, Marjorie paused a moment. She must not appear too keen. Maggie drove hard bargains!

'Your Pa's made the bars thinner this time, lassie. It'll no' last long once it's cut into pieces, so I expect it'll be a good bit cheaper?' she ventured cunningly.

Maggie shrugged. 'Pa says it's made the way the queen and Douglas ladies demand. I couldna tak' less than ten silver shillings. Tak' it or leave it.'

Marjorie nearly choked. That was an exorbitant price that would take a terrible toll of Wil's hard-earned savings kept hidden in the iron-bound casket under the bed. It was out o' the question and couldna be done. 'I'll leave it, Maggie,' she said sadly.

'Och, that's a pity,' Maggie said. She had purposely quoted an impossible price and the outcome was expected, but she had a better plan in mind. She began stowing the soap back in the bag before Marjorie's longing eyes and suddenly paused in the act.

'Mind you, Mistress Gilmore, I've aye admired the garments in Christina's marriage kist; mine are no near so fine. It's a crying shame the poor lassie has no dowry and no hope o' marrying now. So I'll tell ye what I'll do. Ye can have the soap in exchange for my pick o' Christina's kist. That's fair exchange and a favour tae the lass, since we'll be kin when I marry Jamie.'

Maggie's bargain stunned Marjorie. The heady perfume of white soap was powerful temptation but the violation of her daughter's precious kist smacked of selfish greed.

The silence stretched awkwardly and Maggie looked sulky. 'Of course, if you're no' keen for me tae marry Jamie, Mistress Gilmore, there's nae more to be said.' Huffily, she went on stuffing the soap into the poke.

'Och, no, Maggie, wait!' Marjorie cried in desperation. 'Of course I'm keen to see Jamie settled, it's just—'

She paused unhappily unable to find words to describe the pleasure she'd taken watching her talented daughter sewing garments a lady would be proud to own and the aching sorrow she felt when it all came to naught. She often shed a tear when she came across the abandoned kist gathering dust at the back of the press.

'—I keep hoping Hugh Ross will change his mind and marry Chrissie,' she ended lamely.

Maggie was not without sympathy. 'Aye, it was a cruel blow when he rejected her. Lochleven was looking forward tae the wedding feast. But the man needs a dowry, Mistress Gilmore. Without it there's cauld porridge in a bothy for Christina – and her so ladylike.'

Marjorie dabbed her eyes. 'She's so talented. She takes after her father's foreign French folk.'

'Och, it's a mortal sin tae see the result o' Christina's talent go tae waste in moth and dust!' Maggie declared indignantly. 'And it would be such a comfort to ye tae ken that your braw son will wed a weel busked bride!'

Marjorie sighed. 'Truth to tell, Maggie, it's breaking my heart tae see Christina's bonny garments mouldering away unworn.'

'A mortal sin!' The washer-lassie nodded eagerly.

Coming to a sudden decision Marjorie heaved herself to her feet and limped across to the press. Maggie followed with alacrity and helped to drag the kist out into the daylight. She knelt and opened the lid with shaking hands, then sat staring with dazzled eyes at the scented finery lovingly folded within.

Christina's visit to the stable did help to raise her spirits. She left her father and brothers and wandered pensively to the far end of the stable block to view the colt Lochinvar. He was certainly a beauty; black as coal with a white blaze on the forehead and powerful lines that promised he would fly like the wind at the gallop.

The colt raised its head and looked at her with intelligent brown eyes, ears pricked questioningly. She reached out and fondled him.

Like her father in so many ways, Christina loved horses and had ridden many favourites over the years, but even she could tell this colt was special. Wil's unerring instinct had not failed him. She felt her heart beat faster as the horse gently nuzzled her outstretched hand.

'Will ye be *my* salvation, Lochinvar?' she murmured sighing.

'You may be sure he'll do his very best for you at Falkirk Tryst,' her father said, taking her by surprise. She turned to him, smiling.

'I have fallen in love with him, Papa. See, I make him mine!' She leaned forward and kissed the white blaze on the forehead.

They had slipped naturally into the French she and her father had spoken since her early childhood when alone together. The colt meant reconciliation and redemption and must be sold, but she knew it would break her heart to see him sold.

'How could I bear to let him go?' she said quietly.

Wil watched his daughter. He had lived long enough to discover that in every life there might be a special animal that steals the heart. To lose that one precious companion can rip a heart to shreds.

He patted the young stallion thoughtfully. 'I've ridden him often and found him full of spirit yet eager to please,' he told her. 'He has a gallant heart and gentle nature and I promise I will make very sure the next owner is worthy.'

'I would like to ride him till that time comes, Papa.'

'So you shall!' Wil promised. 'But first I will make you a saddle with pommel, footrest and cantle of fine leather, a beautiful saddle fit for a lady – fit for my daughter!'

Christina kissed him laughingly. 'I'll never be a lady, Papa, but I'm right glad to be your daughter!'

Did this mean he was forgiven? Wil wondered – but did not dare to ask.

Christina returned home alone along the icy path. She needed time to think. Sadly, her attachment to the bonny colt must be short-lived and Lochinvar would be sold at Falkirk Tryst. She sensed that her father would not fail this time and soon she would have a substantial dowry to offer Hugh.

Christina was confident Hugh would ask her to marry him and if she agreed her life could go ahead as planned in a comfortable cottage. Disturbing memories that plagued her of a very different outcome would disappear in the humdrum routine of daily chores. Soon she would forget summer fruit shared with an Englishman in a sunlit garden and the magical enchantment of walking warmly hand in hand with a nobleman in a frozen fire-lit field.

She had unconsciously quickened the pace to escape the thoughts and was almost running as she reached the farmhouse.

Maggie had just selected a bonny embroidered nightgown from the kist and was testing it for length, when Christina burst in and stopped abruptly, breathing hard.

It was an incredible scene of wanton pillage and Christina stared in disbelief at the open marriage kist with her most precious possessions spilling out untidily upon the floor. Her mother and Maggie looked the picture of guilt.

'What are ye doing?' she demanded wildly.

The enormity of the deed suddenly struck Marjorie like a fist and she collapsed heavily on to the bench and wailed miserably. 'Chrissie love, I'm heartfelt sorry! It was an exchange for white soap Maggie brought – I wanted it so much—'

Maggie lifted her chin defiantly. 'It's a fair bargain, Christina. Your ma canna pay for soap so I'm taking my pick o' the marriage kist instead. It's no' as if any lad will take ye now ye're on the shelf.'

Christina sprang forward. 'How dare ye condemn me tae an auld maid!'

'Och, face facts, Christina. Who would marry ye lacking a dowry? Poverty's an evil trade!'

'I'll marry a man who can love me for mysel' alone. A man I will love till the end o' my days.'

Maggie laughed in her face. 'Aye weel, it'll no' be Hugh Ross. That man needs siller.'

'Who are you to ken what he needs, you puffed up wee jade?'
Christina grabbed handfuls of garments from the kist and thrust
them furiously at Maggie. 'Here's ample payment for your pa's
accursed white soap. Now get out o' my sight.'

The flustered washer-lassie scrabbled on the floor gathering fallen
finery and stuffed the plunder into the sailcloth bag. She fastened
on her cloak and glared at Christina. 'I'll tell ye this for nothing,
Christina Gilmore, you and I will never bide at peace when I marry
your brother and become mistress o' this house!'

There was deathly silence in the room after Maggie had stormed
out. Christina folded the kist's remaining contents carefully and
closed the lid.

A soft sob broke the silence and Marjorie wept. 'Chrissie dearie,
I'm so ashamed!'

Christina put her arms around her mother and kissed her cheek.
'Dinna be shamed, Ma dear, this is thon cunning wee hussy's doing.
I wouldn't put it past Maggie to set the price beyond your reach
to get her fingers in my kist.'

'But she's away wi' your bonny gear!' her mother sobbed.

Christina laughed and hugged her. 'For all I care she can take
the lot now her greedy wee fingers have defiled them. You shall
have as much white scented soap as ye want without any blame
frae me.' She sighed ruefully. 'After all, Ma, I understand better than
anybody the powerful temptation to sample just a wee taste o' life's
luxury!'

And Christina and her mother shared a sad wee smile.

John Haxton strode angrily into Phemie Sturrock's kitchen with an
anxious Boris slinking at his heels. He aimed bonnet and cloak at
the pegs and flung himself into Joshua's favourite chair. 'Damnation!'
he growled.

'And a good morning tae ye too, Sir John,' Phemie said dourly.
She placed her fists on her hips and studied him. 'Ye look as if ye
glowered at the moon and fell in the midden. Where have ye been
these two days past?'

'At the Twelfth Night feast. I heard Christina Gilmore was free
and hoped to find her there.'

'And did ye?' asked Phemie, startled. She wished she had not
mentioned the festivities to him in an unguarded moment but her son
had a hand in the Twelfth Night cake and that had made her proud.
A'body kens pride goes afore a fall! she thought despairingly.

'Oh yes, I found her!' he answered grimly. 'We walked and talked together most pleasantly – till I met her father.'

'You didna!' Phemie flopped on to the settle. The truth was out! she thought.

'So now ye ken Christina Gilmore's no' a fine lady at a',' she said. 'She's just a bonny country lassie mair cultured than most – and her father is not the wild Highland laird ye took him for, but a hard-working wee tenant farmer beholden these many years tae the laird o' Lochleven.'

He sat up slowly and stared in utter astonishment. 'What are you saying? You told me that her father was Sir Hamish Gilmore, a murderous Highland chieftain and Lady Christina his untamed whelp!'

Horrified, Phemie realized she'd unwittingly let the truth out of the bag. 'Nay, sir, I did not,' she protested desperately. 'It was yoursel' suggested the vicious Highland nobleman and put the idea intae my heid.'

He sprang to his feet and began pacing the floor. 'Why would you do such a terrible thing? Why create such cruel fantasy?'

Phemie summoned courage to face him. 'Why not? I lived through an English invasion as a wee lass and watched my bonny sister shamed and killed by English gentlemen!' she told him.

His expression was fearsome but Phemie was past caring. She continued coldly. 'Ye'll maybe remember that the English King Henry planned the betrothal o' his wee son Prince Edward tae five-year-auld Mary the wee queen o' Scots, Sir John? The English king had his eye on the Scottish throne o' course, but good Scots had no stomach for that scheme so the evil man ordered a murderous rough wooing for Scotland. Many good Scotsmen were put tae the sword afore the tiny lass was got safely across the sea tae France but then defenceless Scottish folk were left tae face a vicious vengeance. Honest women were raped and old men killed by so-called English gentlemen—'

'Mistress Sturrock, I would never condone—' he interrupted indignantly but she silenced him with a glare.

'Gentlemen like *yoursel'*, Sir John! When I saw ye had a roving eye upon bonny Christina Gilmore I had tae put a stop to that so I conjured up a murderous vengeful father. My only aim was tae deter ye and protect an innocent lassie from harm.'

He stopped pacing the floor and glowered. 'Not so innocent perhaps! When first we met in the street she cradled her tiny newborn baby in her arms and there is no talk of a lawful husband!'

Phemie looked blank and then enlightenment dawned. 'Och, land's sake, ye daft gowk!' she exclaimed. 'That would be her sister's bairn born weeks afore its time. Christina carried the frail wean across the street from the cottage tae the palace for better care. You'll no' find a more virtuous maiden in a' Fife than bonny Christina Gilmore!'

The warm room swam before John Haxton's eyes, and when his vision cleared he was left so shaken he could barely stand. He sank on to the chair and stared in horror at Phemie Sturrock. 'Woman, what have you done?' he said wretchedly. 'I love Christina with all my heart and would never harm a single hair on her head. If she would only consent to be my wife I would be the happiest man in England — but I've accused her of wolfish ways, insulted her honest father and doubted her virtue all because of your evil make-believe. Is it any wonder she loathes me now?'

'Maybe that's just as weel!' Phemie declared stubbornly. 'It goes against the grain o' society wi' you and her. You're of noble stock and she's but a farmer's daughter.'

He sighed. 'There are many degrees of nobility, Mistress Sturrock. True, my kin have held title and deeds of our lands since Doomsday but Haxtons are low in the pecking order. My father and I plough many a furrow behind the oxen. I am just a farmer's son by birth.'

'But no' by inclination!' she countered.

He frowned. 'I left with my father's blessing to serve in Queen Elizabeth's court and see a little o' the outside world. Perhaps in my secret heart I hoped to find a special lady to share my life, but all I found was life at court is shallow and tedious and political intrigue devious and dangerous. Weeks ago I had decided to heed my parents' plea and return to the land right gladly when my work in Falkland is done.'

'But what about Christina?' Phemie demanded anxiously. She was beginning to fear that her well-meaning meddling had ruined the poor lassie's chances o' a grand love match.

He slumped wearily in the chair. 'The damage is done. Now she will not believe a word I say.'

'You're a handsome lad, Sir John, a fine catch for some lucky lady. Why break your heart over a country maiden when ye can have your pick o' ladies?' Phemie asked daringly.

He smiled wanly. 'My mother will tell ye I'm made in my father's pernickety mould and will settle for none but my own true love. When I ask my mother how shall I know her, she laughs and says my heart will tell me. So I flirted with fickle women whose attraction did not withstand the test of time – till at last I met Christina.'

He lifted his head accusingly and met Phemie's eyes. 'My heart was telling me that I had found my lady but like a fool I listened to your lies. I set out to tame a wolf cub and in the process lost a gentle soul I could love forever. I was fed false information from the start, Mistress Sturrock, and therein lies the tragedy!'

She wrung her hands and wailed. 'I meant no harm!'

'Maybe not, but you tied a knot wi' your tongue that can never be loosened.' He rose from the chair and crossed to the oaken stairway, aiming for the sanctuary of his room.

Distraught, she called after him. 'I'll mak' amends, Sir John, I promise ye!'

But he went on mounting the stairs without sparing a glance in her direction. She heard the creak of hinges and the drop of the sneck as his door closed.

Phemie wiped away tears. He had no faith in her promises now – if indeed he'd even bothered to listen. And who could blame the poor soul? she thought.

February's snows maintained the month's reputation of *February fill the dykes* but March came in like the lamb. Softer air brought a thaw that turned burns to roaring torrents and roadways and wynds to treacherous stretches of glutinous mud.

There was great activity within Lochleven Castle however. Fine weather meant the annual spring 'redd-up' could get under way early and boatmen were kept busy ferrying legions of scavengers, chambermaids and washerwomen to and fro across the water.

Hugh Ross pulled away from the mainland one mild March morning, boat laden to the gunwales with washerwomen and their paraphernalia of wooden buckets, brooms and quantities of coarse black soap.

'It's high time thon place was cleansed,' one woman remarked. 'The stink frae the middens as ye walk in the gate would mak' ye spew.'

'Aye, it's worse this year wi' a' the soldiers guarding the poor young queen. She's accused o' murder now and mair closely guarded, while guilty men in power walk free. Nae wonder they darsna let her oot!' another said.

'Wheest!' someone warned, and they all eyed Hugh warily.

He pulled moodily at the oars. So he was suspected of being one o' the laird's creatures, was he? Nothing could be further frae the truth!

The women disembarked and crossed the trampled grassy strip, disappearing through the open gate into the courtyard. The air was thick with the reek of burning and hazy with smoke from fires reducing rotting rubbish to ashes. The castle shoreline was dotted here and there with servants either casting filthy contents of buckets into the loch or drawing fresh water from it.

The heavily laden boat had gathered a wave or two on the way across and Hugh paused to bail water from the scuppers. He was preparing to leave to pick up the next load when he spied two washerwomen scurrying towards him. Both breathed hard and were bent almost double, lugging a large bundle of bedding between them. He lent a hand to stow the burden on board and took up the oars after they were seated.

'There'll be a fine drying wind on the bleaching greens the day,' he remarked.

They nodded silently, which was odd.

These two are awfy uncommunicative! he thought. He found the silence unusual for washerwomen, who were the biggest blethers under the sun. He rested on the oars a moment to study his passengers. He knew most women called to work at the castle, but he didn't recognize these two. One was so hunched he could not see her face properly for the shawl.

'Where are ye from, mistress?' he said conversationally and bent forward to take a closer look.

The woman hastily raised a hand and tugged the shawl to hide her face.

Hugh's heart gave a convulsive leap. He had never seen hands so white, fingers so long and shapely, nails so well tended.

'That's never a washerwoman's hand! Lady, who are ye?' he challenged softly.

She sighed resignedly, straightened her shoulders and pulled the shawl aside to reveal eyes that glowed with a mischievous excitement and delicate features framed by red-gold hair. Hugh's breath failed him. He had rowed the bonny young queen and her husband the Lord Darnley across the loch to dine at the castle on their honeymoon, in happier days. Now Hugh knew he looked into the beautiful nut-brown eyes of Mary Stuart, Queen of Scots.

'Your Grace!' he breathed.

The queen sighed and eyed her hands ruefully. 'I thought the disguise perfect! I forgot about the hands.'

'Has George Douglas engineered this escape?' Hugh demanded.

'George? Oh no, he quarrelled with Sir William and was ordered off the island days ago.' Mary smiled modestly. 'This plan is mine. Friends and servants rallied round when I suggested it. Gates were left unlocked and my guards besieged by armies bearing brooms and buckets of water. Marie Courcelles and I donned washerwomen's gear, gathered an armful of bedding and walked out. It was much too good a chance to miss!' she ended gleefully.

The queen showed not a trace of fear but Hugh had a bad feeling about a plan devised upon the spur of a moment without careful preparations put in place. He was sure the escape was doomed to failure and was downright dangerous. He glanced up at the massive square tower and high walls looming over them, still much too close for comfort. At least there were no signs of an alarm – yet.

Mary followed his gaze. 'Why so gloomy?'

'I fear for ye, Your Grace,' he told her honestly. 'It's only by outside help ye can be saved and I can see no force o' horsemen waiting on the other side.'

'People will rise against the rebels when they know I am free.'

He shook his head slowly. 'It's true you have many loyal supporters in this district, but they darsna take the risk of battle on their own account. I consider the danger is too great without horsemen ashore to carry ye swiftly to a safer place. I'm sorry, but I will not take you over.'

'You want to see me kept a wretched prisoner?' she cried angrily.

'No. I want to see ye kept safe, Your Grace – till the time be ripe for rescue.'

Mary bowed her head and sat in disconsolate silence. Maybe she wept tears of frustration, he could not tell. She had hidden her face with the coarse grey shawl and the elderly maid held her hand comfortingly.

'For myself I do not care overmuch!' the queen said wearily at last. 'But I would not want my people to suffer if you think my plan reckless.' She eased the shawl aside and looked at him dejectedly. 'I'm at your mercy, *Monsieur Batelier*. You have only to shout for the guard but I pray you will not.'

'I'll no' tell a soul. The gates are open and ye were not missed. Make haste and go back!' he urged her.

He helped the queen and her maid clamber ashore and watched

them disappear through the gate, still lugging their burden. Hugh sat listening on tenterhooks for some considerable time but all was quiet. Taking up the oars, he rowed out across the water, a drying wind rippling the surface. He felt sad.

Mary's bold attempt at escape had failed. Still, Hugh thought more cheerfully, the queen had a grateful smile for him as she left the boat – and that was a smile he would treasure a while.

Marjorie was stirring the porridge when the first warning twinge of pain seized her. She clutched her belly in alarm. The baby! She wasna sure o' her dates and had no idea whether it was early or late but there had been other signs earlier that morning that it might be on the way. She eased herself on to the settle.

She was alone in the kitchen with the two lassies. Christina and Maggie were still not on friendly terms and the atmosphere was hostile. Maggie was making a surly attempt to prepare the griddle for a batch of bannocks while Christina sewed tiny flannel semmits in preparation for the baby's arrival.

Christina glanced up and was on her feet in an instant. 'What's wrong, Ma – is it the bairn?'

'Aye, I think so.' Marjorie felt weak and scared. It was all of ten years since Francis was born and his had been a long difficult birth. She wasn't sure if she had the stamina to face another struggle like thon. 'Send Maggie running for the howdie, please Chrissie,' she begged. She knew she would feel less panicky with the midwife in residence. This was no task for unmarried lassies.

Maggie's eyes were round with horror. 'Have ye no' heard the news, Mistress Gilmore? The howdie broke a leg hurrying down the hill tae Aggie Campbell's lying-in. It's a bad break and she'll no' walk for weeks.'

This was disastrous news and Marjorie's heart nearly failed her. 'Run quickly and beg the neighbours tae come, Maggie, or you lassies will hae tae help me when my time comes!' she cried wildly.

Maggie burst into hysterical tears. 'I dinna ken who to call on, Mistress Gilmore. I couldna stand tae watch a birthing, I'd sicken!'

Christina grabbed her by the shoulders and shook her. 'Haud your wheest! Jamie's at the stables; go and fetch him!'

That silenced her. She gaped. 'Jamie? But—'

Christina shoved her towards the doorway. 'Go!'

Maggie ran, wailing.

Marjorie was just as horrified. 'Men are excluded, Chrissie; it's women's work. Ye canna ask Jamie tae tend me!'

Christina hugged her mother reassuringly. 'Of course not. Jamie will ride to Falkland and fetch Dorcas. It's early yet and he could have her here by nightfall. Annabel told me Dorcas is often called in to help the Leith howdies. She'll ken what to do.'

'No, Chrissie, not her! Please dinna let Jamie bring Dorcas,' Marjorie wept.

Christina knew that her mother had taken a scunner at Dorcas for some reason and was obviously working herself into a state that did not bode well for herself or the baby.

Christina's heart sank for she had implicit faith in Dorcas's skill. A calm capable presence at the birth would be reassuring but she could hardly ignore her mother's wishes. The alternative was a neighbourly gathering of superstitious matrons probably similar to those present at Ninian's untimely birth. Christina shuddered at the thought. She certainly did not want a repetition of that distressing situation.

What should she do for the best? she wondered frantically. Go ahead and let Jamie ride for Dorcas and upset her mother further, or call in the neighbours?

Eleven

Springtime 1568

Jamie arrived in the room breathlessly. 'Ma, Maggie told me—'

He stopped short. His mother was in tears and Christina looked sadly frustrated. It was clear they were in the midst of a heated argument.

'Where's Maggie?' Christina demanded.

'Away home,' he answered.

'Is she bringing her ma to me?' Marjorie cried eagerly.

'Not her! She swears her ma won't venture within miles o' a lying-in.' Jamie glanced curiously at his sister. 'Why send for me, Chrissie?'

Christina was on the verge of tears. 'I want you to ride to Falkland and ask Dorcas to come, Jamie. She has helped the Leith howdie wi' many births but Ma refuses to have her. Ma's taken a scunner to the gentle soul, heaven only knows why!'

Marjorie wailed. 'Dinna bring the spinster, Jamie. Please dinna bring her!'

He crossed the room and took her hand. 'Why not, Ma dear? What has Dorcas done to offend ye – except excel at healing?'

His mother glowered indignantly. 'Healing has nothing tae do wi' it! It's what Maggie said.'

'What did Maggie say?'

Marjorie hesitated a moment and decided a timely warning wouldna go amiss. 'She says the spinster is on the prowl tae grab a gormless young bachelor wi' a fine farm at his back.'

He could not help laughing. 'And you think the description fits me like a glove?'

'Maybe no' exactly, Son, but you're unused tae wily women.'

'Och, Ma! It was Dorcas herself that put the idea of courting Maggie into my head! Dorcas favours me with nothing but friendship.'

Marjorie clutched his arm wildly. 'Don't ye see the woman has put a spell on ye, Jamie? She makes ye light-hearted. You never laugh wi' Maggie!'

'That's true.' Jamie agreed pensively.

Christina seized the advantage. 'Courting is serious, Ma, friendship is light-hearted.'

Marjorie had not thought of that aspect. If that were true then the spinster posed less of a threat. She was forced to reconsider her options. The neighbours were well meaning but she would not trust any o' the women to cope in a crisis and it could not be denied Dorcas had more than ordinary skill. The healing of Jamie's badly gashed arm was testimony to that, so . . .

She sighed resignedly. 'Aye – well – maybe I should just settle for the lady's maid.'

Christina acted fast before her mother could change her mind. 'Go, Jamie! Ride like the wind for Falkland and bring Dorcas—' And pray God ye'll be in time! she thought to herself as her mother groaned.

Jamie was already out the door and running for the stables like a man possessed.

The mare Muckle Meg was chosen for the crucial ride. The horse was not the fastest in the stable but she was willing and steady on treacherous tracks. Lachie would have accompanied him, but Jamie shook his head.

'No, Lachie. If I canna bring Dorcas in time you must ride for neighbouring women to come. Men are excluded by custom and this is no' task for Chrissie.'

Wil swiftly saddled the mare, his expression grim. 'I care not for custom. If my wife needs my help I will give it!'

Francis stood in the shadows. The boy had barely moved since Maggie rushed in bawling.

So the dreaded day has arrived! Francis thought. He sensed there was a problem already and sweated with fear. He wished he could think of a legitimate excuse to escape from events in the farmhouse, if only for a few hours. Catechism might do, but the parson did not expect him till the morrow. Besides – to escape was cowardly.

At least Jamie was riding to Falkland to bring Dorcas. She was calm and kind and would ken how tae birth a baby. She would not flap, flutter and run around cackling like some women – Maggie for instance.

Francis had liked Maggie better when her pursuit of Jamie was a family joke. Even now the fun they'd had at the washer-lassie's expense made Francis smile and he was pleasantly surprised to find he was coping better than expected with a highly fraught situation. He squared his shoulders.

Francis stepped out of the shadows and ranged himself beside Lachie and his father to speed Jamie off to Falkland. 'What can I do tae help, Pa?' he said. He was pleased with the tone of voice. To his ears it sounded quite deep and manly.

Jamie settled Muckle Meg to a fast canter that would not tax her strength as they covered the miles. The going was better than he had expected. Spring sunshine and a drying wind firmed the ground and despite the urgency of the mission Jamie's heart grew lighter.

It would be good to see Dorcas again. Her capable presence in the house caring for his mother would be a huge weight off everyone's mind. He had to admit heart and mind had felt dull and heavy since she left.

Squinting at the sun, Jamie reckoned they had made good time and were already more than halfway. He could afford to rest the willing mare and let her drink from the burn. Cupping hands in the clear water he drank thirstily too and sat on the riverbank for a few quiet moments of rest. Muckle Meg cropped fresh grassy shoots nearby.

He had rarely felt so calm although the riverbank could hardly be termed peaceful. The burn tumbled noisily on its way to join the River Leven. Water splashed and frothed around boulders and flowed into a deep dark pool where brown trout softly ringed the surface for mayflies.

Suddenly a laverock rose from a secret nest in the grassland and fluttered heavenwards singing. Jamie followed the brown bird's progress upwards, every pure note lifting his spirit higher. He sat pondering his mother's remarks that morning, no doubt spoken in the heat of a fraught moment.

It was true Dorcas gladdened his heart. He did not believe in spells and potions but could not dismiss the belief of those that did. At least if Dorcas *had* put a spell upon him it was a powerfully happy one! Jamie smiled and stood up, eager to press on.

The mare was greedily cropping fresh spring grass. He clapped her glossy neck and laughed. 'Too much fresh feast makes sair belly, my lass!'

Refreshed, they set off at the gallop, the mare's ears flat against her head and Jamie whooping for joy.

He rode more decorously into Falkland Palace stable yard an hour later and Lady Annabel's manservant Hector came out to greet him. The two had met before during the incident of the cart tumbled in the bog and that sunken recovery had created a firm bond between the two men.

Hector watched Jamie dismount. 'Ye've ridden hard, my lad. What's amiss?'

Jamie explained briefly and Hector nodded brisk approval.

'It is wise tae summon Dorcas. She's been called to many a lying-in and the women thankful for it.' He patted the mare's sweating flank. 'But this bonny lassie should rest a while. I'll have fresh horses ready for the return.'

'Will Lady Annabel agree to let Dorcas go?' Jamie asked anxiously.

'Och aye!' Hector grinned. 'Her Ladyship will agree tae onything on this earth if it's tae aid the Gilmores.'

Following Hector's directions Jamie reached the door to Lady Annabel's apartment and found the two women busy. Annabel was marking patterns at a table strewn with materials of various colours and quality while Dorcas sat sewing in good light at a sunny window. They looked up as he entered.

'I thought for a moment it was Lachie till ye doffed the bonnet, Jamie,' Annabel remarked. 'What brings ye – is it news of Christina? We miss her sorely!'

He explained the situation and the women were immediately concerned.

'Oh, poor Mistress Gilmore, what a stramash!' Annabel cried. 'Have ye come for Dorcas?'

'Aye, if ye can spare her, my lady?'

'Of course! Her fame as howdie is legend in Leith.'

Dorcas laughed. 'Leith legends are often no' suitable for gentle ears, my lady!'

Annabel shooed her out of the room. 'Away and gather what's needful while I take Jamie to see his sister. I expect Janet will be in the palace tending her wee baby.'

She led Jamie along the corridor and ushered him into a peaceful scene of domestic bliss.

Janet had finished feeding the baby and was dandling him on her knee, laughing at his antics. Ninian had prospered over the winter and although still small for seven months was lively and healthy. Janet was delighted to see her brother but pleasure was tinged with anxiety.

'What brings ye, Jamie – is it Ma? Lachie brought Lady Annabel back and Christina stayed home so I knew it must be near Ma's time.'

'Aye, the birth's imminent and Chrissie sent me to fetch Dorcas.'

'That's a weight off my mind. Dorcas has the skill,' Janet nodded.

She held the baby out proudly for his inspection. 'What think ye o' your nephew − is he no' a braw lad?'

'He's a credit to ye, Janet!' He took the baby in his arms.

Jamie liked babies and Ninian was just as intrigued by the man. Apart from his father's frequent visits Ninian's household had consisted of women. The baby fingered Jamie's chin curiously and encountered bristles, a novel experience. Continuing the exploration, he tweaked his uncle's nose.

The adults laughed and his proud mother smiled. 'My wee laddie is to come home to the cottage this very day, Jamie, now the weather is spring-like!'

Indeed, Janet's cup of happiness would be full but for the ordeal her mother faced that day. Marjorie was past the age for safe child-bearing and Janet could not help but fear the worst.

Dorcas appeared in the doorway dressed for the journey carrying a canvas saddlebag. She paused for a moment to study Jamie and the child. They made a bonny picture she would treasure. 'Ready?' she said briskly.

Jamie nodded. An imp of mischief seized him and he passed the baby into Annabel's unwilling arms. At Goudiebank Her Ladyship had declared her strong distaste for infants and maybe it was time to redress the balance.

He kissed his sister. 'I'll send Lachie to ye when we know the outcome, Janet. I pray he'll bring good tidings.' He bowed to the lady and took Dorcas's arm, hurrying her away.

Annabel was left holding the baby. She nearly panicked but could hardly drop the little creature. She eased it into a more upright position. When she was a sad and lonely little motherless girl Hector had whittled a dolly for her out of solid wood and Dorcas had dressed it beautifully. At first Annabel had adored the painted dolly, making believe it was the baby brother or sister she would never have. But very soon she found her dolly was only a hard wooden skeleton with no life in its blank eyes and painted hair. Its lifeless-ness scared and repelled her and she refused to play with the wooden baby any more. Dorcas noticed the little girl's distress and the dolly had quietly disappeared, but not before the damage had been done. Annabel shuddered at the very thought of babies.

But this baby in her arms was soft and warm. She looked down cautiously into its face and discovered the baby was examining her curiously with intelligent blue eyes. It had the promise of a curl upon its downy head and the fairest skin and bluest eyes she had ever seen. Tentatively, she stroked its cheek with a finger.

Ninian chuckled his appreciation.

A sad motherless little girl still lurking within Annabel Erskine marvelled – this was a real baby just like the brothers and sisters she had always yearned for!

Daringly, she bounced the wee bundle in her arms playfully up and down. Ninian greeted the gesture with gurgles of mirth and Annabel laughed. She gathered the soft little body tenderly to her breast. Holding this lively little one in her arms, childish memories of skeletal wood and blank painted eyes faded away.

Dribbles ran down Ninian's chin on to her gown and his shawl felt decidedly damp against her arm but Annabel was not bothered. He was only human, after all.

His mother intervened. 'Och, your bonny gown – I'm right sorry, my lady!'

Annabel laughed. 'Och, Janet, dinna fash! I'm glad to find your wee lad in such rude health.' She kissed the baby's cheek and cheerfully handed him over.

Waiting had seemed interminable to those left behind at Goudiebank. As afternoon wore slowly into evening Marjorie began to panic. She was all for sending Lachie galloping to round up a bevy of neighbours.

'Bide a wee while yet, Ma!' Christina begged. Her mother did not appear to be in too much discomfort but Christina prayed that Dorcas would come soon. She persuaded Marjorie to climb the stairs to the upper room where everything was prepared for the birth, rather than hobbling around the kitchen fussing over cooking pots and groaning heavily when a pain gripped her.

'What's keeping Jamie and the lady's maid?' Marjorie grumbled, resting comfortably in bed. 'Your father and brothers are needing their meal.'

'Dinna fash. I'll see to it,' Christina said patiently.

'There's fish skink and mutton stew for supper, Chrissie. Mind and serve fish soup tae the lady's maid in the best bowl and stew tae them all on the bread trenchers I baked yestere'en. There's a long night ahead o' us!' Marjorie predicted ominously.

The travellers arrived in the farmyard as a new crescent moon shone palely in the evening sky. A good omen, Jamie hoped.

Once the horses were stabled Christina served Marjorie's hearty meal to her hungry father and brothers but Dorcas ate sparingly, anxious to spend time upstairs with her patient. She knew it was essential Mistress Gilmore felt relaxed in her presence and Dorcas was well aware that her arrival at the birth was neither planned nor welcome. It is a case o' any port in a storm for the poor woman, Dorcas thought compassionately as she left the table and climbed the stairs.

Hearing footsteps, Marjorie braced herself. She had shown the woman no warmth when she was a guest in this house and Marjorie was prepared for cool treatment when the slipper was on the other foot. But to her relief Dorcas entered with a cheerful greeting and cast a smiling glance around the spotless room.

'I find ye better prepared than most, Mistress Gilmore!'

'It's kind o' ye to come so quick and so far, Dorcas,' Marjorie ventured. 'Christina sings your praise as howdie. There's none nearby I could trust in a crisis.'

'Do ye fear one?' Dorcas sat down beside her.

'I'd nae bother wi' the older ones but nearly lost my life wi' Francis. The wean was born weak and lame like his cripple mother and I've aye blamed myself for the laddie's misfortune.'

Dorcas smiled. 'The fault wasna yours, Mistress Gilmore. Blame it upon coincidence and unskilled howdies that did not know their business. Besides, your Francis is lively, fleet o' foot and brighter by far than most laddies his age.'

Marjorie nodded proudly. 'He is that, bless him! He keeps farm accounts for Wil and the laird promises that Francis will be taken on as household comptroller when he finishes school.'

Dorcas was impressed. 'What an honour for the lad – and not an idle promise either! It's well known Sir William's a man o' his word.'

The atmosphere in the room was now warm and friendly. Dorcas believed Marjorie's confinement was proceeding normally but one could never be sure till the last stages. She prayed the birth would go well. Dorcas herself was a foundling and she had taken the Gilmore family to her heart. It felt almost as if this household was where she truly belonged – but that was only fond fantasy of course.

The men folk were kept busy by drawing water from the burn to make sure water barrels in the scullery were full. When distant bells tolled for the silence of the night the men were ready to drop with exhaustion and Dorcas ordered them off to bed. Christina remained in the kitchen tending the fire. Cauldrons of hot water swung in readiness on the swee. She dozed fitfully in her father's chair, ready to run to Dorcas's assistance when needed.

But Wil Gilmore did not sleep.

Wil paced the floor in the room he had shared with his wife and as time wore on could stand the suspense no longer. He lifted the candlestick and went out into the corridor, tapping softly on the door at the far end.

Dorcas answered. She was seriously worried but hid her anxiety with a smile. Marjorie was tiring so rapidly with the labour Dorcas feared her strength would fail.

'I must be with my wife,' Wil said tersely. 'It is not the custom, but I canna stay away.'

'Who heeds custom when need calls? Come in!' Thankfully Dorcas opened the door wide. This could be the boost her flagging patient needed.

'Wil!' Marjorie turned her head and stared in disbelief. 'What are ye doing here?'

He laughed and sat at the bedside, taking her hand. 'Where else would I be?'

'It'll be the talk o' the touns when word gets around. Och, Wil, why risk a scandal?'

He kissed her cheek. 'Because I love ye, my sweeting. What else matters?'

There were tears in Marjorie's eyes, but she was exultant. Those were words she longed to hear and his presence proof of their sincerity. Why had she doubted him? She gripped his hand with renewed strength. 'We'll see this through together, Wil love!' she vowed, gritting her teeth.

Wil and Marjorie Gilmore's third daughter was born with comparative ease a few hours later. Dorcas wrapped the baby warmly and handed her to the parents. She was a bonny healthy baby but Dorcas carefully refrained from high praise. It was considered most unlucky tae praise the child and tempt cruel fate.

Exhausted but deliriously happy, Marjorie cuddled their perfect daughter.

Wil smiled. 'Three lads, three lasses. It is just as I hoped, my darling.'

His wife nodded. 'Wil, I'd like us tae call this wee one Yvonne, if ye agree.'

He paused. 'It was my French mother's name. It would be a great honour for me.'

'Aye, my dearest, I know,' Marjorie said and kissed him tenderly.

Lachie set off light-heartedly for Falkland next morning, carrying the good news to Janet. He also sought Lady Annabel's permission for Dorcas to supervise the newborn wean and his mother's rest and recovery till the end of the month.

He urged Kelpie to a joyful gallop. Yvonne – now that's a French name to raise Scottish eyebrows, he thought merrily. It was a bonny name though and it seemed the baby's arrival had reconciled his parents after their recent quarrel and unpleasant huffs. Lachie applauded his father's decision to defy tradition and attend the birth. No doubt Kinross matrons would bristle angrily at male intrusion into a female domain but what greater proof of a husband's devotion could there be?

In his eagerness to cover the distance Lachie was riding at reckless speed on the narrow track and a laden packman skipped smartly out of the way shaking a fist. Lachie yelled an apology and slowed to a more modest canter but could not wipe the smile from his face. He was the bearer of happy tidings for his sister and had a valid excuse to spend some time with his lady-love.

That morning, Janet Guthrie was hovering between happiness because her tiny son was home at last and fear for her mother. Had she survived – did the baby live? It was torture not knowing.

Ninian was happily installed in the cottage and slept peacefully in a cradle generously gifted from Falkland Palace. Aunt Bertha was seeing to breakfast and doing her best to stop Ninian's doting sisters slyly poking their little brother to wake him.

Unable to settle, Janet took rag rugs out into the street to beat out the dust. She was determined everything in the cottage would be kept spotless now the precious baby was installed.

You couldna be too careful, she knew. There were chills and infections ready to pounce at any moment or – Heaven forbid – fresh outbreaks of plague as the weather warmed. Mind you, she thought more cheerfully, the kind Falkland chambermaid's casual hygiene had sometimes raised her eyebrows and yet Ninian had thrived. Janet set about beating the rugs as if the Devil himself possessed them.

Pausing momentarily with the dust flying, she was surprised to see a familiar figure approach the cottage. She sighed. Euphemia Sturrock was one of Arthur's more pernickety customers, demanding linen of superior quality.

'Good morning, Mistress Sturrock, was it the weaver you wanted?' Janet called.

'No' today, thank ye. I was seeking a private word wi' yoursel', Mistress Guthrie,' Phemie said.

Janet was apprehensive. 'Will ye step inside?'

'Thank ye, the street will do fine,' Phemie said. She glanced around furtively and whispered. 'It is a delicate matter concerning Christina.'

'Has my sister been harmed?' Janet cried in alarm.

Nervously, Phemie hushed her. 'Wheest, ye'll rouse the whole street! Dinna fash, dearie, Christina's safe at home wi' your ma and pa and has come to no harm – er – at least, not intentionally. I didna mean tae harm her. I only had the poor lassie's welfare at heart.'

'I dinna follow your meaning, Mistress Sturrock. What harm did ye do?' Janet asked, mystified.

'I dealt Christina's marriage prospects a disastrous blow,' Phemie confessed. Sheepishly, she went on to outline the half-truths and subterfuge that had led to the shattering of John Haxton's dreams and the end of a most promising romance. Phemie ended abjectly: '—so I feel I'm duty bound tae make amends, Mistress Guthrie. Your sister could have married into nobility – or at least the landed gentry, if I hadna interfered. I've had Sir John Haxton lodged in my house a good while and I'll swear there's no vice in the young man even though he's English. I had ma doubts about his dealings at first but since twelfth night he's stalked deer and hunted wolves wi' Joshua, good as gold.'

Phemie looked earnestly at Janet. 'He claims tae be a farmer's son sent north to gain experience hunting predators and I believe him. Why else give houseroom tae a wolfhound that devours mair meat than most men? And you read his pa's letter, Mistress Guthrie, you saw the positive proof.'

Oh aye! Janet thought caustically, she'd seen ample proof o' the man's perfidy! But she had sworn to guard the spy's secret and she would keep her word. 'What do you expect frae me?' she asked curiously.

'Tell Christina the harm I did. It's no' too late tae mend this affair, just assure her that the man loves her truly and leave the lassie tae decide,' Phemie begged eagerly.

'Never fear, Mistress Sturrock, I'll let the matter rest wi' my sister,' Janet said.

'Bless ye, my dear! That lifts the guilt frae ma conscience.' Phemie beamed, wrung Janet's hand gratefully and set off homewards along the street.

Janet watched her go. Aye, of course she would let the matter rest! she thought cynically. Janet had no intention of mentioning a single word of this conversation to Christina.

Lachie spent a few hours at the weaver's cottage, warmly welcomed as the bearer of glad tidings. Janet was overjoyed to hear that their mother was resting after an easy birth and they now had a bonny newborn sister.

'And wee Ninian has an Aunty Yvonne tae keep him in order.' Lachie laughed.

His small nieces considered the relationship between babies a huge joke and so apparently did Ninian, bouncing merrily on his proud uncle's knee.

The visit left Lachie in happy mood as he made his way eagerly along the street from the weaver's cottage to Falkland Palace. Euphoria lasted till he bounded upstairs to the living quarters and came face to face with George Douglas.

The young nobleman had obviously just left Annabel Erskine's apartment and Lachie's buoyant spirits fell like lead. 'I heard ye'd left Lochleven, sir,' he said blankly. 'But I didna think tae find ye biding here.'

The young man smiled. 'I don't intend to bide. I needed a word wi' Lady Annabel.'

'Aye, of course. You would,' Lachie said bitterly.

George Douglas studied him thoughtfully. They knew one another of course. The two men were of similar age and had been brought up in Lochleven; one raised with privilege in the castle the other hard worked on the farm.

'Annabel says you're committed to our cause, Lachie,' George remarked.

'Aye, sir, so I am.'

'Let's pray it ends well, eh?' He grinned and bade Lachie a cheerful good day.

Disheartened, Lachie stared after him. Judging by his rival's exalted mood marriage plans were going well, Lachie thought gloomily. There was no contest in this joust between two young men for the lady's heart. George Douglas already held Lady Annabel's favour.

Annabel greeted Lachie eagerly, anxious for news of his mother and baby. She was delighted when told all was well. 'What a relief, Lachie! Yvonne is a bonny name and ye must be proud!' She eyed him curiously. 'So why the frown?'

'I met George Douglas leaving your room. His visit does not bode well for ye, lady. They say he quarrelled with his brother the laird and angered his half-brother the Regent.'

She was not perturbed. 'Aye, George is up in arms against his family.'

'Surely that's a worry?'

She shrugged. 'It can be used to our advantage. George bides with our friend Lord Seton at Niddry. He only rode to Falkland to warn me thon wretched wizard the lord o' Merkystoun has forecast an escape attempt and the queen's guard is doubled on the strength o' it.'

'Och, I heard that rumour too!' Lachie scoffed. 'The escape was only play-acting. The laird went wi' the queen and her ladies on a boat trip around Castle Island in fine weather and her ladies persuaded him the queen had escaped. There was a great to do and hue and cry and a good few sair heids at the castle before it transpired the queen played hide-and-seek.'

Annabel laughed. 'Aye, Her Grace enjoys a joke. It breaks monotony.'

She readily granted Dorcas's continued leave of absence rather to Lachie's surprise. He noted unfinished garments strewn on the trestle.

'I thought you'd miss her?' he remarked.

'So I do, but I have more urgent matters in hand.'

'Aye, George Douglas for one!' he said.

She gave him a speculative glance. 'But you will help us won't ye, Lachie?'

He nodded resignedly. 'For your sake, lady!'

Christina had noticed a happy change for the better in the farmstead after Yvonne's birth. She and Dorcas were kept fully occupied attending to the baby's needs and the rules Dorcas laid down for her mother's lying-in. Marjorie was to have complete bed rest till the end of the month when danger of childbed fever and other common complications should be past.

Marjorie grumbled at enforced inactivity but was secretly delighted to leave the hard work to others. She lay contentedly abed in the afternoons admiring her perfect wee daughter. Spring sunshine poured into the room and Dorcas and Christina kept her amused with neighbourhood gossip while sewing small garments for the new arrival. Talk flowed easily, punctuated with laughter.

A cheerful mood also pervaded fields and pastures dotted with newborn lambs. Farmhands and cottars worked the infields, singing and whistling to encourage teams of eight lumbering oxen yoked to heavy ploughs. Springtime was a crucial season for sowing barley, oats, peas and beans and the precious acreage of wheat for the laird's white bread, always with an anxious eye on a doubtful sky.

However, Wil Gilmore and his sons smiled with renewed optimism these days. A beloved wife and mother had survived childbirth and there was new young life in the family. What could possibly go wrong?

Maggie the washer-lassie was a notable exception to this joyful state of affairs.

As Christina remarked to Jamie, Maggie was just a dreep o' misery these days, her face so long it was tripping her. '—and she'll no' even spare a kind word for me when I do her work for her,' Christina ended resentfully.

Jamie frowned. He had noticed that Maggie appeared infrequently since his mother's lying-in and even then stayed only long enough to establish her claim upon him. It so happened she had turned up that morning. He found her standing near the burn moodily watching Christina and Dorcas rinsing bed sheets in the spate. They were barefooted with skirts kilted above the knee and their laughter could be heard above the water's tumbling rush.

'Why the long face, Maggie?' he asked with a smile.

'Word going the rounds about your pa will wipe the grin off *your* face!' she predicted sourly. 'They're saying i' the village that he defied the solemn laws o' nature by attending the birth and it will bring a sair misfortune tae the Gilmores.'

He laughed. 'Och, Maggie, dinna heed superstitious blethers!'

'An innocent lassie canna be too careful, Jamie!' she said. 'They blame the spinster for allowing your pa in tae view the birth.' She glowered at the pair cavorting in the burn.

'What nonsense! My mother's strength failed and she and the bairn could have died. It was only my father's presence that revived her and saved them, Dorcas says.'

Maggie shrugged. 'So the woman claims, but the talk this has caused will ruin ye, Jamie. Send the lady's maid back tae Falkland where she belongs or my pa will not be risking a fine dowry on the Gilmores,' she warned.

To add weight to the ultimatum Maggie tossed her head regally and flounced off homewards.

Jamie frowned. That was no mean threat! Money was tight in farming these days and Maggie's dowry would be a godsend.

Christina and Dorcas faced a great deal of extra work with Maggie deliberately pulling no weight. They cared willingly for mother and baby and kept the men folk fed but although Dorcas remained cheerful and undaunted, Christina's heart was troubled and worry drained her resolve.

Hugh Ross had resumed his courtship – at least, he visited Christina often and they talked with easy warmth, but never alone and never of the future. Sometimes he would fall silent for minutes on end. He made no mention of a dowry. Did that disappointment still rankle? she wondered.

'Is something troubling ye, Hugh?' she asked tentatively.

He roused from a reverie with a start. 'Och, only the weight o' my work. The castle's routine is badly disrupted wi' Lady Agnes due tae give birth any day and bonny George's sudden decision tae leave for France in a wee while. The Auld Lady's distraught and the whole family saddened by his decision to choose exile frae Scotland. They asked Queen Mary to write and beg George to change his mind. It's no secret George Douglas holds the queen in high regard.'

Wil Gilmore noted Hugh's renewed interest and took steps to encourage it with a quiet word to Christina. 'I finished your saddle and accustomed Lochinvar to the use o' it, Chrissie. Why not see if it suits ye? You could maybe ride the colt to the pier and give Hugh a sight o' our hopes for a fine dowry at Falkirk,' Wil suggested nonchalantly.

Christina laughed. 'I see through your foxy scheme, *Monsieur le Renard!*'

But she ran happily enough and changed into riding gear. When she returned and mounted Lochinvar Wil thought he had never seen his daughter look so fine. She was seated on a magnificent young stallion in a saddle fit for a queen.

Christina gathered the reins; she was an expert horsewoman and the impatient power held under her control was exhilarating as she urged Lochinvar forward.

They reached Loch Leven pier at a fast canter and pulled up in a scatter of gravel. She could see Hugh's boat on the loch, midway to the pier with a load of passengers. He turned his head and she waved gaily, sensing his surprise. Breeze ruffled white feathers in her bonnet, sunlight warmed her golden hair and the colt gleamed black as coal. They must make a bonny picture! she thought complacently. Would it be enough to encourage her wary suitor to offer for her hand?

Lochinvar tossed his head impatiently and raked the turf with a hoof. Idle waiting was not an option for him and Christina laughed. 'If it's a gallop ye need, ye shall have it, my lad!'

She wheeled the stallion around and set off decorously at first but when the Falkland track stretched ahead, wide and empty, her mood changed. There was sunlight in her eyes, wind in her hair and exultation in her heart to match the drumbeat of the gallop. Reckless excitement possessed her and she gave Lochinvar his head. Falkland beckoned and she could not resist the temptation to see once more the man who had held her hand on the snowy loch side and who she could follow tae the ends o' the earth and love to the end o' her days . . .

But – had she gone mad? she thought abruptly and hauled on the reins. Had she lost all sense of wisdom and decorum, carried away by the reckless careering thunder o' the gallop—?

Annabel had warned Christina against wily seduction by noble wolves and she must always remember that despite John Haxton's fatal attraction he despised and humiliated her and insulted all that she held dear.

The stallion reared and fought against the check before skidding to a snorting halt. Christina sat with head bowed for several minutes fighting the madness of infatuation before wearily turning the horse around and trotting homeward to the peace and quiet of Lochleven – and Hugh Ross.

Twelve

Hugh Ross waited at the pier. He lifted Christina down from the saddle. 'Where have ye been? You galloped off as if the Devil had the horse by the tail.'

She laughed and patted Lochinvar. 'This bonny young lad hasn't learned to stand idle. I gave him his head on the Falkland track.'

'It's a braw stallion. I never saw a better,' Hugh said admiringly.

She drew a deep breath. 'Pa will sell him at Falkirk Tryst, Hugh. I could have a handsome dowry.'

There, it was said. Now the decision was his.

He eyed the stallion silently for a long moment. 'My uncle is a canny man. He warns me never to count chickens till the eggs be hatched, Chrissie.'

'Are you saying you don't trust my father?' she said angrily.

In answer he caught her in his arms and kissed her. 'I'm asking – will ye marry me, Christina?'

The proposal was so unexpected she was stunned. 'Hugh, I canna – at least, not yet—'

He released her triumphantly. 'Just as I thought. *You* dinna trust him either!'

'I would trust my father with my life!'

He heaved a sigh. 'My dear, you bait a hook with promises and throw me back in the river when I bite. It makes no sense.'

Sadly, she was forced to agree. 'We're not bairns any more, Hugh; unforeseen disaster has matured us. I hardly recognize the woman I've become and when I look at you I see a man hiding secrets. Do you wonder I hesitate?'

'There's safety in ignorance, Chrissie,' he said dourly. 'I dinna ken what the future holds.'

'Are ye in danger, Hugh? Please tell me!' she begged anxiously.

But he only laughed lightly. 'Och, the only danger is sinking my uncle's boat and douking noble passengers i' the loch. Off ye go home, dear lass, and dinna fash.' He helped Christina into the saddle and stood looking up at her. 'I would fain come with ye, Chrissie, but must wait for a howdie that's coming frae Edinburgh to tend Lady Agnes at the birth.'

With that, he slapped Lochinvar's rump and sent the stallion off at startled speed.

'Mind and take good care o' that braw beast!' Hugh yelled after her.

Wil Gilmore met his daughter at the stable door. He had been awaiting her return impatiently. 'Did ye see Hugh? What did he say when he set eyes on the stallion?'

'He swore he'd never seen a better and asked me to marry him.'

Her father punched the air in delight. 'I knew it! What did ye answer?'

She patted the noble stallion fondly. 'We were both of the same mind: dinna count chickens till the eggs hatch.'

His expression darkened. 'You do not trust me to deliver!'

She laughed and hugged him. 'Dear Papa, I would trust you with my life and I told him so.'

'Then why do you not say – *oui?*'

She shrugged. 'I wish I knew!'

Marjorie Gilmore had benefited from days of unaccustomed ease. The baby thrived as mild April passed in a mix of shower and sunshine to speed the growth of newly sown crops. Marjorie lay abed contentedly contemplating the jobs she would tackle with renewed vigour once the period of lying-in was over.

She had revised her bad opinion of Dorcas and now she and the lady's maid were staunch friends and colleagues in all medical matters. They exchanged notes on the composition of breath fresheners, gargles, tooth powders and purges, as well as herbal remedies for scabs, itches, boils and carbuncles. Dorcas also had a handy fund of ways to remove stains from wool, linen, velvet and silk. Marjorie could hardly wait to commit new material to her book of receipts. They had also shared laughter that is the glue of friendship but lately Marjorie had noticed that Dorcas's laughter was in short supply.

'What troubles ye, my dear? Is it worry for Lady Annabel left to her own devices?' she spiered tentatively.

Dorcas sat quietly at the bedside stitching a binder for the baby and glanced up in surprise. She had tried to hide the melancholy mood but obviously the attempt had failed. She smiled reassurance. 'Och no! Lady Annabel can look after herself perfectly well when needs must and will welcome the freedom to do as she pleases.'

Dorcas hesitated a moment. 'If – if I seem troubled, Mistress Gilmore, it is because Jamie and Maggie have quarrelled. Maggie treats me coldly and I fear I've given offence. I know not how.'

Marjorie's brow cleared. 'Och, I can set your mind at rest, dear Dorcas! Maggie notices Jamie is light-hearted wi' you and deals dourly wi' her. I admit I was perturbed by my son's behaviour too at first till I decided friendship is light-hearted and courting more serious. You should tell that tae jealous wee Maggie!'

Dorcas laughed and laid the sewing aside. 'I'll do better than that, Mistress Gilmore. I'll find Jamie and tell him. His word will carry more weight than mine to end the lovers' tiff.'

Jamie was searching the hillside with the dogs, looking for an errant ewe escaped from the fold. To his surprise he noticed Dorcas climbing towards him and sat down on a nearby rock waiting, the dogs flopped at his feet.

'So ye fancy a breath o' hill air?' he called when she came within earshot.

'More like a stitch in the side; I'm not a mountain goat!' She laughed.

There was no laverock warbling in the upper air today but his heart soared as he gave her his hand to scramble uphill to his perch.

'Water nymph is more your style,' he teased when she was safely alongside. 'I watched spellbound as ye sported wi' my sister in the burn. Your gown was kilted to show neat ankles and a shapely leg.'

Dorcas blushed ruby red. 'I'm ashamed! It was a lapse o' modesty.'

He laughed. 'Lassie, ye canna wash bed sheets without showing a leg!'

'You should not look! It angers poor Maggie.'

'Och, I pay no heed to Maggie's tantrums.'

'Then you should! She's your sweetheart.'

He paused for a minute. 'No, Dorcas, she is not!' he declared quietly. 'Maggie's but a flower of fancy you planted in my head that never took root in my heart.'

She stared in shocked bewilderment. 'What are ye saying?'

He sighed. 'Can't you see I could never love Maggie? Wee Maggie only has ambitions to be mistress o' Goudiebank and would suffer me as husband to do it.' He took her hand. '*You* are the light o' my life, dear Dorcas. Even my canny mother notices my heart is light when you are near, because I love you so.'

Horrified, she pulled the hand away. 'No, Jamie, you're mistaken! Your mother believes friendship is light-hearted and love is much more serious.'

'So it is,' he agreed. 'But love founded on friendship is a powerful force I canna resist.'

He went down on one knee. 'Will you marry me, Dorcas? Will you be my friend, my lover and my wife?'

'No!' she cried in panic. 'No, Jamie! Please don't ask me to marry you!'

He stood up abruptly. 'Why not, dear lass? Dinna deny that you're drawn tae me as powerfully as I am drawn tae you for I see love's light in your eyes and feel its heat whenever we touch.'

'I fight the attraction and so must you! You are courting Maggie!'

'Och, Maggie's just a distraction thrown in my way,' he said impatiently. '*You* are the special lady I looked for and dreamed of finding one day. Oh, my darling Dorcas, why won't ye marry me?'

'Be sensible, dear lad!' she said sorrowfully. 'Of course I love you dearly – but you are a bonny young man in your prime and I'm a spinster nine years older. I will not have you made a laughing stock for marrying an old maid!'

'Dinna be daft, Dorcas! Ridicule can't hurt us!'

Older and wiser, Dorcas sighed sadly. 'Oh but it can, my dear! Ridicule can rip reputations to shreds in a few weel-chosen words. No, Jamie, my mind is made up. When your mother is well enough I'll leave. I will not marry and bring shame upon ye.'

'You could never do that, my love!' he declared staunchly.

She met his eyes bleakly. 'Ah – but you do not know my past history, dear heart!'

'Do ye think I care?'

He made a move to kiss her but she pushed him away.

'No, it is impossible! You must not—'

Tearfully she turned and scrambled recklessly downhill. Jamie called her name again and again forlornly but she was soon lost to view behind gorse bushes planted to stabilize the marsh. He groaned. The future seemed bleak indeed. Maggie would herald Dorcas's departure as victory and his mother would put more pressure upon him to marry the washer-lassie.

In his wretched heartbroken state there was no saying what Jamie Gilmore would do now that his love Dorcas had rejected him.

★   ★   ★

Lady Annabel Erskine's thoughts were buzzing with exciting schemes as April drew to a close. She had managed remarkably well without Dorcas in attendance. Although bereft of dear Dorcas's companionship Annabel had welcomed freedom of movement at this critical juncture in her affairs. It was indeed fortunate that the lady's maid was safely out of the way, Annabel thought gratefully.

Faithful Lachie Gilmore – more disgruntled with every trip – brought a fresh crop of letters weekly from George Douglas, who was lodging with friends near Lochleven village at present. The correspondence unveiled plans intended for Annabel's eyes only and she was careful to commit every page to the flames.

She was kneeling by the fire watching the latest letter reduce to ashes when the maidservant announced a visitor. Annabel rose with a smile, expecting Lachie with more news, but this time it was not the trusty courier.

'Papa!' she exclaimed in astonishment.

Sir Allan Erskine hugged his daughter. 'Roses in your cheeks and bonnier than ever!' he declared with pride. 'I was wise to send ye to Falkland though you've been sadly missed. My household's dark and dreich without ye.'

'Have – have ye come to take me home, Papa?' she demanded apprehensively.

He noted the reluctance thoughtfully. 'That's what I intended, dear lass. I'm told that George Douglas is out o' favour with both the Regent Moray and the laird and I feared you were caught up in the feud. However, it seems you will be safer in Falkland after all. Before I left Leith I heard there's an outbreak of plague in Edinburgh.'

'Oh, no!' She shuddered. That was every citizen's nightmare.

'The Edinburgh burghers acted quickly and may have nipped it i' the bud,' he said reassuringly. 'The sick are isolated outside the gates in hasty hovels erected on the Burgh Muir.'

'Poor souls!' Annabel said compassionately. 'Will you bide at Falkland now, Papa?'

'No, alas, my dear. I've a shipment due and must be back in Leith by nightfall. I came only to make sure all was well.'

Annabel hesitated. Her father had no idea she passed the time sewing for the captive queen. She felt guilty. He deserved to know the truth. 'Papa, we've been sewing gear for Queen Mary's comfort all these months. She had no clothing fit tae wear when brought suddenly to the loch. I'm sorry I deceived ye.'

Her father laughed. 'Did ye think I didna ken what ye were up to, you wee minx? But I reasoned you'd be safer sewing in Falkland than rabble-rousing in Edinburgh for the queen's release.' His expression changed to concern. 'But ye must take great care, dear lass!'

'Of plague?'

'Nay, of plots.' He paused a moment, frowning. 'Tell me about the young man on the piebald horse. Hector keeps watch for me and swears the lad is loyal to you but maybe not so loyal for the queen.'

'You mean Lachie Gilmore?' She smiled. 'Och, Lachie's an honest lad and serves nobly as my courier, Papa. The Gilmores are Sir William's farm tenants and my dearest friends.'

Sir Allan was not reassured though he made no comment. He distrusted the Gilmore family's heavy obligation to the queen's jailer and noted that his wily daughter had barely skimmed the surface of her dealings with the man on the piebald horse.

'Where's Dorcas?' he asked suddenly, looking around.

'She's at the Gilmores' farm attending Mistress Gilmore's lying-in. Lachie's mother gave birth tae a healthy wee lassie and Dorcas acted as howdie. Dinna fash, Papa, she'll be back in Falkland soon after May Day.'

The news added to her father's disquiet. Allan Erskine had counted upon wise Dorcas keeping a tight rein upon his impetuous daughter. However, he had another guardian in mind and knew better than raise fiery Annabel's stubborn hackles with protests and lectures.

He settled down to spend precious time with his much-loved only child. An interesting hour or two passed, bringing Annabel up to date with cargoes from the Low Countries and brisk encounters with pirates swarming in the Firth of Forth.

It was a wrench to end the short visit but Allan Erskine had another matter to settle before heading for the barque waiting moored at Anstruther to carry him across the Forth.

Hector had his master's horse waiting in readiness in the stables.

'Did ye see the Englishman?' Sir Allan demanded.

'Aye, sir. He's a canny man but agreed tae wait for ye on the road.'

'Good lad!' Sir Allan Erskine smiled at his trusted servant and friend. 'Keep vigilant, Hector!'

He grinned. 'Am I not always?'

John Haxton was accustomed to wait and watch. That was the nature of his work as a spy and he was expert at fading into a background.

His horse was hobbled and grazing peacefully well out of sight. John sat with his back to a gnarled old pine on a hillside overlooking the road, a site chosen because his sad grey attire – as approved by the Reformed Kirk – blended perfectly with tree bark. Grey cap tipped forward to shade his face, he was confident he was well-nigh invisible to the casual eye but was intrigued to find that the Scotsman approaching on the road had detected his presence quite far off. This was a watchful man!

It reinforced the respect John had established previously for the Scottish royalist, after the secret meeting one dark night in an Edinburgh tavern.

John rose and walked to the verge. 'Well met, my friend!'

Allan Erskine dismounted and the two shook hands warmly.

'You have news for me?' John asked curiously. 'Your man sounded urgent at my door. It's lucky Mistress Sturrock was snoring on the settle and did not hear.'

The Scotsman shook his head. 'Alas! All I have is a nose for trouble. It has sent me across the Forth to ask a favour of ye.'

He raised his eyebrows mockingly. 'You would trust an English spy for favours?'

Sir Allan smiled grimly. 'I pride myself I'm a fair judge o' men and I liked the cut of your jib when we met in Edinburgh. Besides, who am I to carp? I follow the same secret trade for my ain Scottish queen and country!'

'What is the favour?' John demanded warily.

The Scotsman hesitated. He was about to lay cards upon the table that took a serious gamble. 'My daughter is Lady Annabel Erskine, lodged in Falkland Palace sewing for Queen Mary. I've reason to believe that those on the mainland serving Queen Mary will soon face grave danger and retribution. I fear for my daughter's life.'

John's heart missed a beat. Christina! he thought anxiously. 'Sir, I only observe,' he warned. 'I've no authority to draw sword to rescue victims.'

'Force wouldna be necessary. Your lug is close to the ground and would detect the first tremors o' trouble. All you need do is warn Hector, my man at Falkland Palace. He has instructions to immediately spirit my daughter and her maid across the Forth to safety.'

John frowned. 'Lady Annabel has another loyal helper called Christina Gilmore. Where will Christina find shelter?'

Sir Allan paused, frowning at the coincidence. 'Did ye say Gilmore? That's a common enough Fife name but my man tells me a lad called Lachlan Gilmore is a frequent visitor to Falkland Palace. He rides a showy piebald horse that canna be missed and I suspect he carries dangerous, incriminating letters from George Douglas to my daughter.'

Light dawned upon John Haxton. He remembered the canny farmer at Kinross Inn who had later proved to be Christina's father. Did that fly Fifer Wil Gilmore spin John a likely yarn designed to throw an English spy off his son's scent? Of course he did! 'Lachlan Gilmore will be Christina Gilmore's brother!' he exclaimed.

'If that is so, God help her, for I cannot!' Sir Allan declared grimly. 'That family will pay a heavy price, should Sir William find out what's blowing i' the wind.'

The Scotsman prepared to go on his way. The road remained empty but the two men had no wish to be found together. He remounted and smiled down at John Haxton. 'Keep your een open and lug close to the ground, Englishman!'

John grinned. 'Dinna fash, Scotsman!'

He watched the older man gallop off towards the coast. There must be desperate times ahead if a Scotsman must entrust a precious daughter's life to an English spy! he thought seriously. He prayed fervently that any unforeseen events would not incriminate Christina, whom he had believed to be safe at home with her parents. Now it appeared her brother was acting secretly as courier for the renegade George Douglas and that put the whole Gilmore family at serious risk.

Christina must be warned at the first hint of danger, John decided anxiously, even if he himself could be powerless to help.

Wee Francis Gilmore was very familiar with ancient history. He knew that in days gone by heathen fires blazed on hilltops on the first day of May to welcome summer and encourage fertility and growth. These beacons were known as Beltane fires and lively May Day dancing, frolics and dubious revelry had followed on village greens.

But May Day 1568 passed dull and dreich at Goudiebank with not so much as a hint of pagan fun and jollity. Francis wakened on the second day of the merry month feeling decidedly depressed.

The black mood had been growing darker for days past.

Francis had been overjoyed when Yvonne's birth went well for both mother and baby. The boy had no experience of newborn infants but knew that newborn calves, lambs and pups were soon gambolling nimbly. Kittens, blind and mewing at birth, grew fluffy and playful in no time at all. His expectations for the new baby were high.

'Can I hold her, Ma?' Francis had asked eagerly a few days after Yvonne's birth.

Marjorie was touched to find the laddie so fond. 'Aye, if you're very careful, lovie.'

He took the shawl-wrapped bundle tenderly in his arms and looked down expectantly into the baby's face. Francis had dreamed of this magical moment. He was confident his sister would recognize her big brother, mentor and friend instantly.

Shocked, he found the baby's gaze unfocused and uncaring. After a moment or two its tiny face puckered and it gave a piercing wail that scared the life out of him. Francis stared in horror at the red-faced, ugly wee changeling.

'What did ye do, Son? Did ye nip her?' Marjorie asked in dismay.

'I never touched her. She doesna like me, Ma!' On the verge of tears the lad had handed Yvonne back to the comfort of her mother's breast.

After that cruel disappointment life at Goudiebank seemed far from happy.

Francis was always susceptible to other people's moods and soon detected something had gone wrong between Jamie and Dorcas. Formerly, their happy companionship lit the house like sunlight but now they avoided one another and rarely spoke. Dorcas made it known she would leave the moment Ma was fit to take up the reins and Francis felt bereft. He would miss her terribly.

To make matters worse, Christina was distracted and sad and Lachie had turned dour and sullen after an unexpected visit from bonny George Douglas. The young nobleman had turned up in the stables one morning and talked long in private with their father. Wil Gilmore remained grimly tight-lipped about the visit afterwards.

May heralded the start of summer and should be a hopeful time, even though the parson condemned it as wanton and virtuous maidens took care not to choose May to marry.

Francis found the gloom clouding everything and everyone unbearable and was desperate to escape, if only for a few carefree hours.

At breakfast on May the second, farmhands reported that yesterday George Douglas had visited Castle Island briefly to bid farewell to his mother Old Lady Douglas before leaving for exile in France.

The Douglas family and Queen Mary were said to be distraught and wee Willy Douglas planned dancing and May time frolics and a masque in the inner courtyard that day to cheer the queen and her ladies. There was hellfire and brimstone predicted for the lot o' them if the Kirk ever found out, the men added darkly.

Even despite the threat o' hellfire this festivity was an opportunity not to be missed, Francis decided.

He made sure those within the house believed he was working in the fields, while those in the fields were confident he was either in the house or on the hillside minding sheep. That done, Francis sneaked off with a clear conscience for the pier.

'Where do ye think ye're off tae?' Hugh Ross scowled when he discovered the boy skulking amongst the morning load of passengers.

'Willy Douglas said I could join the fun on the island,' Francis declared stoutly. Which was not exactly true but legitimate in Francis's opinion since the young Douglas owed him payment for many past fibs and favours.

Hugh gave him a searching look but reluctantly manned the oars and headed out across the loch.

Francis had visited Castle Island several times with Jamie on barges delivering livestock and various items of farm produce to the castle storerooms. He was familiar with the outer courtyard entered through an open gateway leading from the loch side. This extensive outer area housed soldiers' and servants' quarters, storehouses, kitchens and workshops and was always a hive of activity. The inhabitants worked, gossiped and scurried to and fro within the high walls encircling the entire castle complex. Only a narrow beaten track remained around the island's perimeter, bounded by the loch's chilly depths.

The square tower dominating the heavily fortified inner courtyard was separate from the public area, its massive walls proclaiming the castle's real purpose as fortress and state prison. Wee Willy Douglas lived in the main tower with the Douglas family and Francis knew that the Queen of Scots was held prisoner in the small tower set in one corner of the inner courtyard. The planned entertainment must be taking place within the impregnable inner sanctum that lay beyond high walls and a locked doorway. Willy was nowhere to be seen and Francis could find no way in.

He was standing disconsolately outside the locked door when a heavy hand fell on his shoulder. An armed halberdier towered over him. 'Move along, laddie. We stand for nae mischief here.'

Francis eyed the wicked halberd in the guard's grip nervously. It was a fearsome weapon, union between axe and spear mounted on a shaft tall as a man. Francis stood his ground bravely. 'Please, sir, I'm wee Willy Douglas's friend come tae join the celebrations.'

The man relaxed. 'Ye'll no' pass through this door, son, for the laird keeps the key,' he said kindly. 'But I can let ye through the guards' postern on to the wall-walk. You could reach the inner yard from there.' He led the wee lame boy to a narrow aperture in the rampart.

Francis thanked the man profusely.

'Och, laddie, it'd be a shame tae miss the show,' the soldier grinned. 'It's a celebration for warmer weather and the birth o' Lady Agnes's bairn and there's to be a football contest in the outer courtyard after supper. Halberdiers versus musketeers wi' halberdiers tipped tae win, o' course. Ye can give us a cheer!'

Finding his way easily round the wall-walk to ground level inside, Francis encountered Willy Douglas crossing the inner courtyard. The older lad was barely recognizable in long red cloak, fanciful head-gear and luxuriantly applied charcoal moustache and beard.

He glared fiercely at Francis. 'What the devil are *you* doin' here?'

'Och, there's nae luck aboot my house, Willy. I've come tae join your fun.'

Willy Douglas studied him narrowly for a full minute. It was a disconcerting look, Francis thought uneasily – cold, calculating and unfriendly. Allied with the unfamiliar garb and devilish black chin it sent cold shivers down Francis's spine.

'Och, very well.' Willy shrugged. 'I suppose I could find ears, tail and sackcloth to make ye Balaam's donkey. I'm the Lord o' Misrule and everyone must follow me and do all the daft acts I command.'

'Even the queen?' Francis asked, intrigued.

'Especially the queen!' Willy Douglas said dryly.

Annabel Erskine had slept fitfully till the early hours of May the second.

Rising in the dark, she dressed in riding habit and black riding cloak and stole silently by candlelight along the palace's dark corridors to the stables. Once inside, the need for silence was not so essential. Hector slept soundly in the servants' quarters.

Annabel chose Muckle Meg for the ride to Lochleven. It was fortunate the Gilmores had not yet returned to Falkland to retrieve the mare, she thought, since the horse knew the route well. Annabel

saddled Muckle Meg expertly with the side-saddle, unlocked the
stable door and led the mare quietly past the janitor snoring in
the gatehouse.

The village street was dark and deserted as she mounted and rode
silently along the grassy verge. Outside in open countryside, she urged
the horse to a canter and set off for the loch.

Faithful George would be waiting by the pier as planned. Was he
feeling as tense and excited as she was? Annabel wondered. The sky
seemed brighter and soon it would be dawn on a memorable day.
Her heartbeat skipped to the rhythm of the hooves. If all went well
the course of many lives must change today, but if the plan failed
– she dare not contemplate the consequences!

The morning was mild and pleasant but Wil Gilmore's thoughts
were far from tranquil. He had his favourite Muckle Meg back in
the stable but with the mare had come trouble in the guise of Lady
Annabel Erskine and George Douglas.

Annabel was facing him now, dark eyes flashing, arguing in rapid
French. 'But you promised, *Monsieur!*'

'And I keep my promise, *Madame*. Take all the horses you need –
but not the stallion.'

'*Mon Dieu!* Why not?' she cried in exasperation. 'It is the finest
and fastest in the whole stable by your own admission.'

'You cannot have Lochinvar. It is Christina's dowry,' he said
stubbornly.

'Then let Christina decide!'

Wil met the lady's determined eye and sighed. This was the most
personal and cruel of all the difficult decisions that must be made
that morning but he agreed that Christina should make it. He called
the stable boy and sent the lad to fetch his daughter from the house.

Christina came running, sensing urgency, and was astonished to
find Annabel and George Douglas closeted with her father, 'What's
to do, my lady – are ye to marry Mister George?' she asked. Poor
Lachie will be broken-hearted! she thought.

The young couple looked amused. George Douglas laughed
outright.

'Marry Annabel? Heavens no! I've great affection for my fiery
cousin but my bonny queen Marie Stuart holds my heart.'

Annabel lowered her voice to not much more than a furtive
whisper. 'Listen, Chrissie, George has a plan in place to free the queen
today. If her escape across the loch succeeds, loyal support is waiting

ashore to usher the queen to a safe haven. Your father offers us all the horses we need from Sir William's stables – except one. Queen Mary must have the fastest and the best.'

'And that is Lochinvar, my promise for a better future!' Christina said.

Annabel clutched her arm desperately. 'Oh, my dearest friend, your sacrifice could save Her Grace's life!'

Christina met her father's eyes. Sir William's horses were to be used in the queen's escape and that would unleash the full force of the laird's fury upon her father. He must be well aware of the terrible danger he and his family faced but he was not deterred. Christina smiled quite merrily. 'Of course Queen Mary must have my brave Lochinvar – and she'll ride tae safety on a wonderful saddle my father made that's truly fit for a queen!'

Francis Gilmore was tired but happy as festivities on the island drew to a close. The entertainment Willy Douglas devised to amuse the queen had been the greatest fun. Francis's sides were still sore laughing and Her Grace had retired to her rooms in the Glassin Tower, claiming exhaustion. Willy Douglas's reign as Lord of Misrule had been wickedly hilarious. He had opened the henhouse gate causing pandemonium and ordered the queen and her ladies to catch the indignant cockerel and his squawking flock and chase them back inside the pen. He had scuppered boats beached ashore by pulling out the bungs and goaded Samson the billy goat to butt Drysdale, the leader of the queen's guard, into the midden. The furious musketeer had gathered remnants of his dignity out of the mud and withdrawn to the outer courtyard to muster his team for the football contest.

As evening drew near, comparative peace was restored in the inner court.

Sir William Douglas crossed the courtyard, following his daily routine to foil any risk of poisoning or foul play and served the Queen's supper to her in the Glassin tower. The laird then checked that the lock on the courtyard doorway was secure and retired to the main castle to enjoy his own meal with the family. Wee Willy Douglas, face washed and soberly dressed, followed the laird up the outer stairway to the second floor, a clean napkin folded neatly over one arm ready to wipe his benefactor's greasy fingers at the finish of the meal.

That afternoon Francis had played his part as stubborn donkey to everyone's amusement. His reward was a bread trencher filled with roast trimmings from the fat goose George Douglas had brought to the island yesterday as a farewell gift before leaving for France.

Francis sat on the lower step of the castle stairway to devour the treat. The early summer evening was golden and peaceful, the air hazy with smoke from cooking fires. The inner courtyard lay quiet after the gaiety of the festivities with only a few servants passing to and fro sweeping and tidying and attending to evening chores.

In the outer courtyard the ball game between rival soldiers had begun and loud yells, cheering, jeers and laughter echoed across the calm waters of the loch.

Francis wiped his mouth and hands on sackcloth remnants of the donkey costume still belted round his waist. Gravy had soaked the bread and a stream of goose grease had dribbled down his chin. He had never tasted a fatter goose, not even when Ma celebrated Christmas before the Kirk forbade it.

Willy Douglas appeared suddenly at the top of the stairway. He clutched a stained napkin in one hand. Pausing, Willy stared towards the Glassin tower and raised his free hand, fist clenched in a triumphant gesture before coming bounding downwards. There had been enough mischief for one day and Francis was tired. He yawned. 'I want to go home now, Willy.'

The older lad made no answer, hauling Francis roughly to his feet. 'Haud yer wheest and follow me!' He dragged the startled boy to the gatehouse arch and stood in its shadow.

'Willy, dinna—' Francis began, suddenly terrified.

'Save yer breath tae cool yer porridge!' Willy growled curtly, gaze fixed intently across the courtyard.

Francis looked but could see nothing out of the ordinary. There were women with brooms sweeping the flagstones and gossiping, others coming from the well with buckets swinging from yokes across the shoulders. A man trundled a barrow load of logs from the wood store, another rounded up goats for milking and a housewife opened a window and flung out bones for dogs to snap and snarl. Two maid-servants came from the lower doorway of the Glassin tower carrying slop buckets, one stooped and old, the other more quick and spry. They made their way to the midden under the castle stairway close by the gatehouse. Willy's grip on Francis's arm tightened painfully.

The women emptied slops on to the midden and stepped into deep shadow beside the boys.

'Do you have the keys?' one whispered.

Willy tapped the folded napkin. 'Aye, I have them. Sir William's a man o' habit. He lays the keys on the table beside him till he's eaten wi' the family and drunk a tassie or two. George made sure the goose was fat and the laird feasted well before calling for basin and napkin tae wipe his hands. It was easy tae drop the napkin over the keys and lift them unnoticed. I made sure Sir William's tassie was well charged wi' French wine George brought. The laird will have hazy memory o' the meal by now!'

The servant woman smiled. 'Well done, my leetle orphan!'

Francis felt suddenly faint. He had heard the queen use that very same endearment to Willy that afternoon, in an accent with a hint of foreign charm. Looking more closely, his suspicions were confirmed. Queen Mary wore an old grey shawl and servant's brown worsted kirtle and stooped like an old woman to disguise her height, but Francis knew that this was no masquerade. Unwittingly, he was involved in Willy's attempt to free the queen. They now stood on the brink of success or failure and his heart gave a sickening lurch. Either way could only mean serious trouble for Francis.

He had to admire Willy's daring. It was clear the celebration was deliberately planned with her escape in view and innocent mischief now had sinister purpose. Boats lay disabled on the shore to foil pursuit. Halberdiers and musketeers fought out fierce rivalries on the playing field, cheered on by wall-walk guards caught off guard. The laird dozed in his chair in the dining hall, blissfully unaware that even at that moment his orphaned protégé was fitting the stolen key in the lock to set the royal prisoner free.

Willy closed and locked the door behind them and the little group stood holding their breath in the shelter of the castle wall.

There was a festive air in the outer courtyard with some dancing and feasting taking place nearby. The ball game was in progress at the far end with warlike ferocity. Nobody gave the boys and two servant women a second glance.

Beyond the open gateway leading to the loch, Francis saw Hugh Ross waiting at the jetty. Unhurriedly, they walked out through the gate and stood for a moment with the wide loch stretching before them. A few washerwomen paddled at the water's edge rinsing linen and another followed them through the gate with a bundle of dirty washing. To Francis and Willy's horror, it was Maggie.

The washer-lassie frowned and pointed accusingly at Francis. 'What's *he* doin' here, Willy Douglas? His ma will half kill him if—' she broke off and her jaw dropped as she recognized the queen, half-hidden behind the shawl.

'Oh, God save us. It's Her Grace!' she whispered faintly.

Willy seized her arm. 'Haud yer tongue or you'll start the hue and cry!' He shoved Francis roughly into Maggie's arms. 'Here! Look to this innocent lad. He had no part in this.'

Francis tried to struggle free, but the terrified washer-lassie held him fast.

They watched Hugh and Willy help the queen and her maid into the boat. Mary lay down out of sight in the scuppers, the maid crouched in the stern and Willy sat watchfully at the bow. Hugh pulled on the oars and the boat surged forward on to the loch, away from the island.

Francis and Maggie stood frozen on the shore.

Maggie groaned softly. 'Ahh, Hugh, lad, what have ye done!' She had a bad feeling about the escape. All those involved, of high or low estate, risked losing life and limb in the aftermath of this night's work. Desolately, Maggie hugged the wee lame Gilmore laddie close to her breast for comfort.

Thirteen

George Douglas waited alone on the shore. He watched the small boat embark upon its dangerous journey from Castle Island across a mile of sunlit water and hardly dared breathe. Other loyal supporters of Queen Mary hid behind bushes near the shore keeping watch to westwards. Annabel Erskine watched with them, ears strained as she listened for a sudden cry and thunder of hooves that meant discovery but the busy Kinross road remained empty.

Why so quiet? Annabel wondered. Had word of the escape leaked out and crafty enemies waited to catch them in the act? The very thought chilled her. She was glad of thick folds of the black travelling cloak to hide the shivering.

The boat was at its most vulnerable now, crossing calm water in full view of the castle and well within musket and cannon range. Hugh Ross knew the danger yet dared not increase his leisurely stroke lest it attract attention. In his fraught imagination the castle's dark windows held suspicious eyes turned upon the loch. The sinking sun lay low in the west making a golden pathway his boat must follow to the shore.

The queen crouched between the thwarts at his feet with bowed head and clasped hands. Maybe she prayed, he thought. She would remember the last failed escape attempt in March but he had more faith in success today. This attempt had been meticulously planned with strong backing awaiting the queen on the far side – if the boat could only gain the far shore in safety.

A sudden chorus of shouts echoed from Castle Island and the terrified chambermaid screamed.

'God have mercy, they've seen us! Heaven help ye now, Your Grace!'

Mary sat up and stared apprehensively towards the castle.

Perched in the bow, wee Willy Douglas laughed. 'Och, dinna fash. That's just a battle cry frae the football contest. Halberdiers and musketeers canna stand sight o' one another and it's open warfare on the field.'

The queen relaxed and thankfully resumed her prayers. Distant sounds of strife faded to a low grumble.

Hugh breathed again. They had passed the point of no return now and must go on whatever happened. Willy Douglas leaned over the side and dropped the laird's heavy key into the water with a resounding plop.

'We'll no' need *that* ony mair!' the lad said smugly.

But no sooner was the deed done, they faced another alarm.

'Hold fast, Hugh!' Willy cried suddenly. 'There's a stranger on the shore.'

Hugh glanced over his shoulder and groaned. 'Oh michty! It's my uncle come frae the boatyard. He's noticed something amiss.'

'He'll no' betray us, will he?'

'He's a canny man – but there's no telling what he'll do.'

Hugh continued rowing with a heavy heart. His uncle's boatyard lay on Douglas land, its very existence dependent upon the laird's custom and favour. He knew Ebenezer Ross feared Sir William Douglas's displeasure above all else.

George Douglas was so intent upon the boat he had not noticed the intruder till Ebenezer spoke.

'Good day to ye, Master George!'

George spun round, startled. He knew the boatbuilder of course, but had no idea where the man's loyalty lay.

Ebenezer found the young man's manner odd. He eyed him curiously. 'What's a' the stir today, Master George?' he asked. 'I saw Lord Seton and a band o' nobles riding full gallop on the Kinross road. It seemed an unco strange gathering and a wee bit out o' the usual.'

George had a plausible explanation ready. 'Falkirk assizes are held at the start o' May, Mister Ross. I believe the lords were summoned to give evidence at the trial o' cattle thieves. No concern of yours, so I expect ye'll be on your way,' he said, praying the awkward man would take the hint.

The boat was nearing land. Mary scrambled up eagerly to sit on one of the thwarts to see the shore she left ten and a half long weary months ago.

The sudden movement caught Ebenezer Ross's attention as he turned to go. He paused to take a closer look. He thought he knew all the local serving women but he did not recognize this one. He frowned in annoyance. The contract wi' the laird put more siller in his pouch wi' a full boatload. Hugh knew fine that two women in an empty boat didna pay for his porridge.

Uneasily, Ebenezer eyed a travelling cloak Master George carried slung over one arm. It was of superior quality, velvet lined with sable, fastened with jewelled clasps. The colour was a rich purple such as only royalty wore . . .

He broke out in a cold sweat as its implications hit him. I'll wager it's the Queen o' Scots in that boat, he thought, horrified. He grabbed bonny George's arm. 'I ken what you're up to now, my lad! You and your cronies are plotting tae free the queen. Sir William Douglas will not expect treachery from his ain brother!'

George whirled round, hand on the dagger hilt. 'Maybe so, but my allegiance is no concern o' yours. Stand back and save your breath if ye value use o' your tongue!'

Wisely, Ebenezer retreated sullenly to a safe distance to watch proceedings.

Hugh brought the boat close to shore, drifting in gently to nudge the stone pier with a soft scrape of wood. Wee Willy Douglas hopped ashore to hitch ropes to mooring rings while George Douglas stood by on the pier.

Mary lifted her gaze gratefully heavenwards then glanced anxiously towards the castle. All was quiet. She breathed a sigh of relief and grasped her rescuer's hands, before scrambling on to the rough stone.

'Welcome back to your kingdom, Your Grace!' George cried exultantly.

Smiling broadly he whisked away the old shawl shrouding the queen's head and shoulders and flung it to the chambermaid, re-placing grey worsted with royal velvet. He knew she would remember this favourite travelling cloak worn on many royal progresses around Scotland in happier times. Patriots from Holyrood Palace had removed it stealthily before rebel lords laid thieving hands upon her wardrobe.

The cloak transformed Mary instantly from washerwoman to queen. The young man stood back proudly to admire his handiwork. Well-worn leather buskins donated by a devoted washerwoman were still visible beneath but the queen looked down at her unusual footwear and laughed. She owed freedom to the humble gear of faithful servants and a timely reminder of the debt did not seem out of place.

With that thought in mind Mary Stuart's laughter faded and she glanced across the loch for one last look at her island prison. The fate of those left behind troubled her greatly.

Her dear friend and lady-in-waiting Mary Seton took the queen's place should a guard on the wall-walk decide to check occupants of the Glassin tower. She prayed that this last faithful unmarried member of her four dear Maries would not be treated harshly when the deception came to light.

She knew the escape would prove disastrous for Sir William Douglas and hoped he would not be made to suffer on her account. The laird and his ladies had treated their royal prisoner with courtesy from the start and although he made sure she was closely guarded, she bore him no ill will. They shared a tenuous link of kinship and mutual fear of the dour Regent Moray who was now virtual ruler of all Scotland.

George Douglas grew impatient at the delay. 'Dear lady, please dinna dither. We're in full view from the castle,' he warned.

Castle Island remained tranquil but any moment an eagle-eyed sentry on the wall-walk might notice unusual activity on the far shore.

George was confident the Gilmores would have the pick of his brother's stable hidden in the spinney and he hustled the queen and her maid along the path towards the trees.

Hugh and wee Willy Douglas followed, but Ebenezer Ross barred the way. 'Weel, nephew, so you're awa' wi' bonny George and devil tak' the consequences!'

'I can hardly bide in the district now,' Hugh said.

'Aye, ye've burned your boat an' no mistake!' Ebenezer agreed grimly. 'Sir William will have a price on your heid but I'm damned if I'll share the blame. The laird must be told. Stand aside and let me at the boat!'

Hugh stood fast. 'Have pity, Uncle! Mary may be queen, but tae my mind she's also a young lassie up against crafty men wi' a history o' ruthless murder and scant respect for monarchs. Give her this chance!'

'Oh aye? And what chance will I get when the laird hears I looked through my fingers while his prize prisoner slipped awa'? Am I tae face ruin because it was *my* boat and *my* daft nephew that did it?'

'All I ask is time to get away, then ye may do as ye will,' Hugh said.

Wee Willy Douglas intervened. 'Aye, even if ye warn the laird now, sir, it'll be dark afore he can muster a pursuit. Besides, I took good care to scupper every boat on the island.'

'The devil ye did, ye artful wee scunner!' an outraged Ebenezer bellowed.

To the casual eye the second day of May seemed a normal working day at Goudiebank but Christina Gilmore knew better. Ever since George Douglas and Lady Annabel's visit that morning she had been on edge. All day furtive comings and goings had emptied the stables of the laird's best horses. Small groups of men descended upon the stalls, chose the fastest and galloped off to an undisclosed rendezvous.

Her father stood by protecting the stallion Lochinvar from envious eyes. Lochinvar was pledged to the queen.

Wil supposed it was an honour but he still grieved for his daughter. Outwardly Christina seemed resigned but he knew fine that the sacrifice must weigh heavily upon her heart.

An uneasy peace settled upon the farm as the day wore on. Many stalls in the stable were now empty. Only elderly Muckle Meg, Lachie's faithful Kelpie and several garrons, ponies and packhorses remained from Wil's carefully bred bloodstock. Lochinvar and a few others, the very best of Sir William's depleted stable, kicked impatiently at the wooden partitions. No doubt the intelligent animals sensed excitement and the promise of a gallop.

Despite Wil's decision to keep Dorcas and Marjorie in ignorance of today's events, the two women had already noticed unusual sights and sounds. Marjorie was up and dressed in the afternoons now and was rocking Yvonne's cradle with a foot while sitting with Dorcas by the window for a breath of fresh air.

'What's a' the stir?' she wondered, looking out. 'That's another troupe o' strangers riding hammer and tongs in our wynd, Dorcas!'

Dorcas looked, and frowned. 'I dinna ken, Mistress Gilmore. Christina was loath to talk at dinner but she did let slip that George Douglas was in the district. I worry about Lady Annabel with bonny George on the loose. She's easily led astray.'

Marjorie tightened her lips. 'Aye. Wil wouldna meet my eye this morning either. Some mischief is kept frae us, Dorcas, I feel it in my bones!'

Dorcas set the mending aside and stood up. 'If it'll set your mind at rest, dear, I'll go and spier at Jamie for an answer. Jamie won't lie to me!'

'No, my dear, I don't expect he will,' Marjorie said kindly.

She too had noticed a cooling of the joyful friendship that had brought light and laughter to this house. It had saddened Marjorie more than she'd expected.

Jamie Gilmore was relegated to the hillside to keep watch upon Castle Island when Dorcas tracked him down.

He saw her coming and his bruised heart gave its familiar painful lift. He resolutely quelled its thudding and was calm when she arrived. 'It's a bonny day for a dander,' he remarked.

'Much too chilly to sit idly on an open hillside though,' she observed shrewdly. 'Your mother senses trouble afoot. What's to do, Jamie?'

'The sheep—'

'Och, the sheep are behind ye safely grazing. Why keep watch upon the loch?'

'Maybe tae count geese,' he growled, hardening his heart. 'Why don't ye go back to Falkland? You're no' needed here.'

Dorcas winced. To think love should come to this! 'I should bide a few more days for your mother's comfort,' she said.

He shrugged. 'Och, the family can care for my mother and the bairn. Waste no time. Just go!'

He turned away and gazed unseeing at sheep on the summit. It was the most heartbreaking moment of his life, but he prayed it would spare the woman he loved from the laird's revenge – which he knew would be far reaching.

When he turned his attention back to the loch some minutes later Dorcas was making her way downhill. He choked back tears that blurred his sight. Now he must pray that her tender heart had taken such grave offence she would leave Goudiebank and ride safely out of harm's way to Falkland.

Christina slipped quietly out of the farmhouse and arrived in the stable as her father and brothers were preparing the horses to leave for the loch side.

'I will ride Lochinvar,' she declared.

Her father was dismayed. 'No, my dear. It's too dangerous.'

'Do you think I care? I'll no' rest till I see the queen safely in the saddle.'

Wil shook his head. 'We dinna ken if George's plan will work. Maybe it's daft to hope fun and games can lower the laird's guard.'

She looked her father squarely in the eyes. 'But you think it's worth a gamble?'

Her father looked away. Any mention of gambling shamed him
– as well she knew! 'Och, very well, Christina. You'll ride Lochinvar
and I'll bide to keep watch over your mother and the innocent
bairn. I haven't told her of the danger yet.'

'I wouldna care to be nearby when ye do, Pa,' Lachie remarked
with feeling.

Waiting in hiding with the horses was tedious. Christina and her
brothers sat in the shelter of the spinney with restive horses tethered to trees. Time dragged slowly by. It must be past supper time
and Christina was hungry. She had only managed a bowl of broth
and a bite of bread at dinner time while parrying Dorcas's pene-
trating questions. She smiled ruefully. Trust clever Dorcas to take
heed of unusual activity!

'I can see the boat coming!' Jamie said.

Christina sat up. 'Can ye see the queen?'

'Aye, and her maid and wee Willy Douglas. Hugh has brought
them safe across the loch without a cheep o' protest frae the castle.
God be thanked!'

Christina stared in consternation. 'You mean Hugh's at the oars?
But I thought they'd bring a stranger from outside Fife tae row.
Hugh's kin owe allegiance to the laird and Sir William will count
his part as wicked treachery.'

'I do pity ye, Chrissie,' Jamie said awkwardly. 'But Hugh offered
his services willingly to George Douglas a good while past. The
man's royalist at heart and kens the loch like the palm o' his hand.'

'I knew he was troubled!' she cried. 'He proposed marriage but
offered no hope for a future. Now I ken why!'

'Come, Chrissie,' Lachie said kindly, helping her to her feet. 'Time
to go.'

George Douglas arrived with the queen and joined the Gilmores
as they led the horses to open ground. The chambermaid followed
her royal mistress with Hugh Ross and wee Willy Douglas not far
behind. A jubilant group of Mary's supporters rushed from various
hiding places with Lady Annabel Erskine well to the fore. Her sudden
appearance caused an alarming lurch to Lachie's vulnerable heart.

'So ye've thrown in your lot wi' bonny George!' he challenged.

She gave him a sideways glance. 'Wi' Mary Stuart, to be exact,
Lachie.'

'Huh! A royal excuse tae elope wi' your noble lover.'

She flushed angrily. 'You think that's my intention?'

'I ken fine it is, my lady!'

Her dark eyes were bright with angry tears. 'When will ye take the damned blinkers frae your blind een, Lachie Gilmore?' she cried and scuttled off to join George and make her curtsey to the queen.

Christina kept out of the way as Lochinvar was brought forward to Queen Mary. It was an emotional moment. The queen greeted the fine young stallion with an exclamation of delight, petting him and whispering in his ear, perhaps with a quiet word of encouragement. Christina felt comforted.

She sensed Lochinvar's royal mistress would treat him kindly. Mary was reputed to be a fine horsewoman with a passion for horses and wee lapdogs. In fact, in the early days before the bonny queen fell from grace every detail of Mary Stuart's dress and toilet was common knowledge. Hair, flawless complexion, elegance of bonnet and gown were remarked upon and eagerly copied by those blessed wi' enough siller to do so. It was also reported that at first Mary spoke and wrote English haltingly, preferring to communicate in French with English associates. Christina was pleasantly surprised to hear the queen speak merrily to loyal supporters in fluent Lowland Scots, albeit with a douce French accent.

But no time could be lost blethering. The protesting chambermaid was kissed, hugged and sent off weeping to the safety of relatives living in Kinross.

Hugh sought out Christina to bid her goodbye.

'Must you go?' she asked him.

He smiled. 'I darsna stay after this day's work, my lass!'

'Then God speed ye, Hugh,' she said tearfully.

'Aye. But I'll be back one day, God willing. My heart's left here by the loch.'

With a smile and a fond kiss, he left her.

He had no sooner gone than wee Willy Douglas sidled up, looking somewhat sheepish.

'Er – Christina, about wee Francis—'

'Francis?' She frowned. 'What about him?'

'He's – um – out there on Castle Island.'

'Wha–at?' She grabbed the lad and shook him till his teeth rattled. 'What in Heaven's name is Francis doing at the castle? Last I heard he was herding sheep!'

'Ow, Chrissie, stop it!' Willy howled. 'It wasna my fault. The wee scunner turned up and begged tae join the May Day revels, that's all.'

She released him despairingly. 'And now Francis is up to his lugs in the plot!'

Aggrieved, Willy rubbed his bruises. 'No he's no'! He was none the wiser and just took part in the capers along wi' other bairns. I left him safe in Maggie's care.'

'Maggie?' Christina cried wildly. 'Maggie couldna care for an abandoned pup if ye paid her!'

'Aye well, she'll care for Francis for nothin' just tae keep him quiet. She was scared oot o' her wits when I left them,' he said sulkily. He turned and ran but shouted truculently over his shoulder. 'I thought the Gilmores should ken – now I wish I hadna bothered!'

In the meantime, George Douglas had helped Mary into the saddle. After many restless months pacing the limits of Lochleven's small garden, the queen was in her element. She gathered the reins and laughed as Lochinvar snorted, sidled and tossed his black mane. Curling strands of Mary Stuart's long auburn hair came free from coils and clasps, blowing in the wind and brushing her cheeks as she urged the stallion forward.

So the Queen of Scots left the loch side. Only George Douglas and wee Willy Douglas escorted her, mounted upon the fastest horses Sir William's stable had to offer, but Lochinvar's hooves sent divots flying from the loch side track, outstripping them both.

No cheers marked her departure from those left behind. A curlew rose alarmed from the grass with burbling cries of 'whaup, whaup!' and they all froze. The slightest unusual sound set nerves on edge. Although the castle on its far island remained quiet they all knew it was still too soon to claim success.

Hugh Ross prepared to follow with the other riders to the agreed rallying point, but first he cast an anxious glance towards the shoreline. Ebenezer sat brooding at the end of the pier and the boat still bobbed idly at the moorings. Hugh breathed a sigh of relief and urged his horse onwards with a lighter heart.

The three Gilmores watched the cavalcade ride off. Lachie's spirits ebbed as Annabel prepared to ride with them. He held his breath as she hesitated, holding the restive horse on a tight rein for several indecisive moments. He met her gaze but foolish pride would not let him beg her to stay. At last, with a defiant toss of the head she dug a heel into the horse's flank and set off recklessly after the rest. Dumb with misery, Lachie watched his lady-love ride out of his life. To make matters worse, for a moment as their eyes met he could have sworn that she was aware of the danger and begging to bide.

The Gilmore brothers and sister set off wearily to trail home to the farm, drained of energy after several tense hours. All Sir William's best horses had gone and now they faced the consequences. It was a sobering thought. Christina broke a heavy silence to tell her brothers about Francis's plight.

'We'd no notion what he was up to!' she said. 'He told us he was off to work in the outfield and tend the oxen.'

'The sly wee devil!' Jamie declared indignantly. 'He led us tae believe he was helping womenfolk around the house.'

Christina stopped and looked anxiously across the loch. Shadows were creeping in. It would soon be dark. 'What's to be done now – how can we fetch the laddie home?'

Jamie sighed and shook his head. 'We canna, Chrissie. To cross to the island now would rouse suspicion and compromise the queen's escape.'

'Oh, what a fankle!' she cried in anguish. 'But at least Willy left Maggie to care for the bairn!'

'And ye'd trust wee Maggie, would ye?' Lachie said dubiously.

She subsided unhappily. The three trudged on in silence, lost in their own troubled thoughts.

'At least Janet and her man and bairns are safe in Falkland,' Jamie said.

Lachie kept quiet. He knew Janet was worried and scared. On Lachie's last visit his sister had confided she'd unwittingly read a letter intended for an English spy. She'd kept knowledge of the man and the letter's content to herself, but was that wise, she'd wondered, or would some harm come of it?

Lachie had reassured Janet at the time, but now he was not so sure.

Approaching a bend in the road they heard the sound of approaching hooves and drew into the side to let the rider pass. To their surprise round the corner came Muckle Meg at a smart trot. The rider was Dorcas.

Jamie stepped recklessly into her path. She reined in and sat looking down at him.

'So you're off to Falkland?' he said dourly.

'I am not! Your father told us the truth of what was planned today – which is more than you did, Jamie Gilmore. You banished me most unkindly!'

'For your ain good. There'll be hell tae pay at Goudiebank when the laird hears his horses were stolen.'

Her severe expression softened. 'Aye well, I'd worked that out for mysel', thank ye. Your pa gave me leave to ride to find Lady Annabel at the loch side and talk some sense into her.'

'Too late!' Lachie said moodily. 'Annabel joined the queen's entourage and grabbed her chance tae elope wi' bonny George Douglas.'

'Och, Lachie, who fed ye such blethers?' Dorcas scoffed. 'Annabel certainly will not marry George; they have fought like cat and dog ever since they were wee bairns! No, George Douglas's heart is set upon the queen. He loves Mary devotedly and would marry her tomorrow if she'd have him, but Sir William rules he's ower mean a match for monarchy. That's why the brothers quarrelled. Didn't ye know?'

'No, Dorcas, I didna!'

His thoughts were anguished. Now he realized why she had hesitated. She was sweer to leave and he was too steeped in jealousy to beg her to bide.

He groaned. What a daft fool he'd been! Worse still, his jealous dithering had driven Annabel off into unimaginable danger. Queen Mary's escape did not guarantee peace in the land. On the contrary, the nobles ruling Scotland would not surrender power without a fight to the death. There would be civil war between the two factions with Annabel caught in the thick o' it.

Fortunately he knew what to do now to make amends. 'I'll ride after the lady and bring her back, She can't have gone far!' He turned and ran like the hare for Kelpie, still left standing in the stall.

'Lachie, wait!' Jamie yelled after him with a premonition of disaster. Predictably, his brother paid no attention.

Dorcas leaned down from Muckle Meg's back and offered Jamie a hand. 'Quick! Ride wi' me. We'll maybe catch him before he leaves. I'm praying George Douglas will have the sense to send Annabel home. This venture's for men!'

He hesitated. 'I canna leave Chrissie here on her own.'

'Och, Jamie, I'll be fine,' she assured him. 'Away ye go and stop the hothead before he causes more strife!'

He vaulted on to the horse's back and took the reins without more ado. Dorcas wound her arms around his waist and laid her cheek against his back. He wheeled Muckle Meg around and set off at a fast trot.

Christina stood in the roadway to watch them go. They looked so comfortable together she felt saddened. She did not know what had caused their bitter quarrel, but it filled her with grief.

Shadows lengthened and the evening grew dark and dreich as she went on her way. Wraiths of mist rising from the loch sent chilly drifts inland to cool the air. Walking on her own in the inhospitable dusk added to her loneliness now that Hugh had gone. How dismal the future seemed!

Christina discounted the secret love she dare not acknowledge even to herself. Her thoughts shied from the memory of a man who had held her hand and broken her heart.

Shivering, she pulled the plaid around her ears and did not hear the beat of approaching hooves on the track behind her. The horseman rounded the corner at full gallop and was almost upon her before she was aware of the danger. She scrambled aside and ended deep in the ditch. The rider cursed, struggling with the startled horse. While he calmed his rearing, plunging steed, Christina sat up dazedly. A large dog she recognized was licking her face. 'Boris – stop it!' she said weakly.

Badly shaken, John Haxton dismounted and let the quivering horse stand to recover. His heart still pounded from the shock of rounding a corner to find Christina in his path. To his relief she seemed none the worse as he gave her a hand to climb out of the ditch.

'You believe in living dangerously, my love!' he remarked, picking muddy leaves from her hair.

'I am *not* your love!' she declared, just as shaken.

'Oh yes, you are!' He kissed her hand, muddy though it was. She dragged it away.

'Will ye stop your daft nonsense? It's a wonder ye can look me in the ee after the grief ye caused me!'

'Now wait a second,' he said seriously. 'There's much to be resolved afore we proceed further. Are ye promised to that drunken oaf your father favours?'

She was startled. 'Hugh? No, I'm not promised to anyone. My future's uncertain.'

'Hurrah!' John Haxton cheered. He had been tormented by a fear that she had married and gone beyond reach.

She shook her head despairingly. 'I suspected you were moon-struck. Now I know it for sure!'

Jubilantly, he decided Fate had presented him with the ideal opportunity to unravel Phemie Sturrock's tangled web. He was not sure if the hurt had gone too deep for redemption but he loved Christina Gilmore and she must know the truth.

Standing in the roadway facing a barrier of suspicion, John revealed the diet of half-truths and fibs his well-meaning landlady had fed him over the months.

Christina listened in silence clutching the plaid close to her chin. He could not tell what she was thinking but when he finished he took a canny step closer.

'I can understand what drove Mistress Sturrock to do it, Christina,' he said seriously. 'She lived through an English invasion as a child and has scant regard for English morals. When I met you and fell in love, she acted quickly to scare me off. She believed a jealous, murderous Highland father might do it. She was wrong. I would die for your sake, if it came to that.'

'Deeing is easy enough, Sir John,' she said coldly. 'But you were very ready to believe my sister's baby was my own child of sin. How can I forgive ye for that?'

He groaned. 'How can I ever forgive myself? My mind was poisoned with lies. I set out to redeem a wild wolf's whelp despite a jealous father whetting a claymore in his Highland lair.'

She was silent for a long moment while he held his breath, then to his astonishment she began to laugh. He was forced to steady her while she mopped her eyes weakly on a corner of the plaid.

'Oh michty, you were brave!' she gasped. 'I acted the snarling wolf cub tae perfection too. You scorned my old plaidie and insulted my gentle papa whose only fault is bad judgement at the gaming table, and I glowered like a wildcat in a whin bush and went for your throat.'

He grinned. 'Aye, and fighting spirit only made me love ye more!'

He ached to kiss her but sensed that was a liberty only to be taken with consent.

Christina suddenly realized how close they stood and how dizzily her senses were reeling. She retreated hastily. 'Aye well. Fine sentiments are easy spoken and sooner forgot,' she said lightly. She frowned. 'What are ye doing here? I can hardly believe it's on my account since you were nearly the death of me.'

'It's true my visit wasn't planned though I've been summoning

courage to come and end our misunderstanding,' he admitted. 'Hector
the Falkland groom came knocking at my door this morning to tell
me Annabel Erskine was missing. He said she must have left Falkland
in the silence of last night, riding a horse from your father's stable
and possibly intending to meet up with George Douglas. In a rash
moment I had promised Annabel's father to keep an eye upon his
wayward daughter so I rode to Lochleven hoping to find her at
your farm. At the same time I hoped to see you, of course, and to
warn your family to steer clear of any intrigue the young lady has
in mind.'

She felt colour leave her cheeks. How could she tell him he was
already too late? He would learn about the queen's escape soon
enough but till Mary was well on her way to safety it was better
to leave him in ignorance.

'You won't find Annabel at the farm. She's gone,' she said.

'Gone? Where to?'

'She didna say. She rode off wi' George Douglas.'

'Damnation!' he swore, thoroughly annoyed. 'I did hear rumours
that bonny George was paying court to her at Falkland Palace. Don't
tell me they've eloped?'

'That's what my brother believed,' Christina said truthfully.

'Her father should be told. I must leave for Leith at once.'

He took her hand. 'At least you'll be safe at home, my love. Plead
my cause with your honest papa. Tell him I'll come back to ask for
your hand in marriage and I will not be deterred by skean dhu or
fisticuffs, but please—' He pulled her close and looked down into
her eyes. 'Make him promise to keep clear of plots and intrigues till
I come for you, my darling.'

With a quick, chaste kiss on her cheek he mounted the horse,
wheeled it around and galloped off with a yell, a wave of the bonnet
and excited baying from the wolfhound that sent roosting rooks
rising from the woodland, cawing in rowdy alarm.

Christina stood motionless, hand on the cheek where his lips had
touched. For a glorious moment she had lived an impossible dream
– or was it nightmare? Would her lover dare come back to claim
her when the truth was out?

Down by the loch side, Ebenezer Ross rose and stretched limbs
stiffened by a long wait in the cold. A thicker mist crept on to the
inland road from the loch and it was growing dark. He could see
pinpoints of yellow light from the castle and the smoke and flare of

cooking fires in the outer courtyard. The island lay peacefully quiet but no' for long, he thought dourly.

Ebenezer stepped into the boat and unhitched the ropes. He seated himself on the thwart, settled oars in the rowlocks and headed out purposefully through chilly drifts of mist towards the castle.

Fourteen

In the month of May 1568

Shaking with fear, Francis watched the queen and her maid set off in Hugh's boat with wee Willy perched in the bow in a desperate attempt to escape across the loch. The supper of roast goose consumed earlier churned and grumbled apprehensively in Francis's innards.

Maggie the washer-lassie was hugging him to her breast like a long-lost cousin, which added to the horror of the situation. Usually he was lucky to get a civil word.

He struggled free. 'Maggie, what'll we do? I'm no' supposed tae be here. My ma will be wild!'

'That's your hard luck!' she said, casting a scared glance at the women rinsing washing at the loch side. Nobody had noticed anything out o' the ordinary so far, but they soon would if she and the loon stood gawping.

Thinking fast, Maggie retrieved the bundle of washing she'd abandoned and grabbed Francis by the slack of his breeks, propelling him over the grass and into the loch.

'Hey Maggie, whit are ye doing? The water's freezin'!' he howled.

'Wheest!' she hissed crossly. 'Freezin's preferable tae hellfire if the laird catches ye. Tak' the other end o' this sheet and dowse it i' the water. Quick noo!'

Up to the knees in icy water, Francis obeyed.

The other washerwomen straightened up to watch.

'Ye've a fine wee helper the day, Maggie!' one called.

'Aye, start 'em young and make better men of 'em!' Maggie answered dourly.

The women cackled and went back to work. Soaked and miserable, a subdued Francis helped the washer-lassie rinse and wring the rest of the bundle. She hustled the shivering lad back to the outer courtyard and pushed him close to the grateful warmth of the wash-house fire while she hung bed sheets to dry.

'How'll we get hame, Maggie?' Francis asked forlornly. It would soon be dark and he was in enough trouble as it was.

'Not wi' Hugh Ross, that's for sure,' she said grimly.

A brawling hullabaloo arose from the football field accompanied by raucous yells of encouragement from onlookers.

'Could we maybe go an' watch the contest till somebody comes?' he asked hopefully.

She saw no harm in that. She felt safer mingling with a crowd. 'Aye, maybe we could, but for Heaven's sake haud your wheest and dinna let on ye're bosom friends wi' thon daft wee devil Willy Douglas!' she warned.

The game had reached a crucial stage when they arrived. Scores were even and there were equal numbers of players from either side lying groaning in the outfield. The remainder still battling on the pitch were mostly walking wounded.

Maggie and Francis secured a vantage point at the front and Francis recognized his helpful friend the halberdier on the pitch. The exhausted man had the ball at his feet with several opponents bearing down upon him. It was madly exciting.

'Come awa' the halberdiers!' Francis yelled at the top of his voice.

The boy's high-pitched treble rang out across the field before Maggie could clamp a hand over his mouth.

His champion rallied, fended off defenders with his fists and gave the ball a thumping kick. It sailed through the air past the musketeer guarding the goal to a howl of glee from supporters. The halberdier, now voted champion o' the contest, beamed in Francis's direction and some partisans in the crowd patted the lad on the back.

Maggie hauled him into a quiet corner and shook him. 'I warned ye no' tae draw attention, ye daft wee gowk!'

'A'body was yelling, Maggie. Nobody paid any heed!'

'Aye well, ye'd better pray they didna,' she declared ominously.

'I want to go hame,' he gulped.

'Och, stop girning!' she said impatiently. 'The fun's over and there's servants to transport back across the loch some way. Fishing boats are aye sitting ready outside the gate. One o' the fishermen will row us over.'

'No, they'll no',' Francis said. 'Willy Douglas scuppered every one.'

'The foxy wee whelp!' Maggie howled and sat huddled in the corner in gloomy silence for several minutes.

'Och well, a' we can do is wait.' She sighed. 'There'll be hell tae pay on this island when they find the queen's gone. Questions will be asked so dinna let on ye ken wee Willy. Keep your tongue behind your teeth and we'll maybe get away yet.'

Time passed, it grew dark, flaring oil lamps lit courtyard walls
and smoke from cooking fires drifted in the breeze. A gaggle of
serving women gathered grumbling by the gate looking for a boat
and impatient to be home.

'Here's a boatie coming now!' somebody cried.

Maggie shot to her feet and grabbed Francis. 'Quick! It'll be
Hugh come back for us feigning innocence.'

'That's brave!' Francis remarked.

'Foolhardy, ye mean!' she said. 'Let's get oot o' here!'

She hustled the lame lad through the gate towards the women
waiting by the jetty.

'Och, it's no' Hugh Ross, it's his auld uncle,' a woman shouted
in surprise as the boat came closer. Maggie gave a strangled gasp
and Francis stopped breathing for an instant. The substitution did
not bode well.

Ebenezer Ross moored the boat and leapt ashore elbowing clam-
ouring women aside. 'Oot o' my way! I need tae speak urgently wi'
the laird!'

Maggie grabbed Francis and hastily mingled with the crowd. Her
worst fears were soon realized. The sudden stramash down by the
jetty alerted the guard and several soldiers appeared to investigate.
Ebenezer ran towards them, shouting.

'The queen's escaped, lads! Master George and wee Willy Douglas
led ye all by the nose. The May Day revels were a feint tae get Mary
across the loch and awa'.'

The astounding news was greeted with screams from the women
and howls of rage from the guard and pandemonium ensued.
Ebenezer was hustled off to inform the laird while the excited
women streamed into the courtyard to spread the news. Maggie and
Francis remained in their midst.

'This could be a stroke o' luck for us,' she hissed in his ear. 'We'll
get back wi' the auld man when he goes.'

The courtyard was soon in uproar, householders rushing to and
fro in panic as the horn sounded a call to arms. Word spread that
Sir William was in such a state when the news was broken to him
that he'd tried tae fall upon his dagger and was only prevented frae
the mortal sin o' self-destruction in the nick o' time.

Maggie and Francis wandered through scenes of wild confusion
made all the more eerie by darkness and the flickering flame of
torches. They could hear soldiers in the inner courtyard yelling
commands and women weeping and wailing. Maggie drew her shawl

closer and shivered. Soldiers of the guard rushed for the boats and raised a furious outcry of curses when sinking craft reached water and the extent of Willy's sabotage became clear.

Francis found the excitement thrilling and soon lost all sense of fear. He knew he was due a skelping when he reached home but considered the adventure worth it. He paused for a moment to retrieve a roasted chicken leg abandoned beside a cooking fire before scavenging dogs found it.

'Hey!' a hand fell on his shoulder. Francis whirled round guiltily to find himself face to face with the friendly halberdier now armed with pikestaff and helmet and looking very far from friendly.

The soldier scowled. 'I ken who you are; you're the wee lame runt that claims friendship wi' wee Willy Douglas. You tricked yer way past me into the inner court, my lad. You're one o' the conspirators!'

'No I'm no'!' Francis protested in horror. 'I only came over tae join the revels. Ask Maggie the washer-lassie. She'll vouch for me.'

He looked around confidently for Maggie but at the first hint of trouble the washer-lassie had vanished hastily into the darkness.

News of the queen's escape had sped across to the mainland when bells tolled for the silence of the night but Mary and her supporters had long since gone, riding fast through Fife and crossing the river Forth at North Queensferry. Once on the other side, the cavalcade headed for Lord George Seton's castle at Niddry, a few miles west of Edinburgh. Lachie Gilmore and Annabel rode with them. Tired but jubilant, the royalist party had reached their planned destination by midnight.

Earlier on, Lachie and Kelpie had made good progress after leaving Goudiebank and caught up with the queen and her rescuers not far from Kinross. If Annabel Erskine was pleased to see him she hid it well.

'I thought ye were minded to stay at home, Mister Gilmore,' she'd remarked coldly.

'And I thought ye had a loving protector in bonny George – till Dorcas told me otherwise!' he retorted. 'I came to persuade ye to turn back.'

'And miss this glorious event? Never! You go home if ye must but I'll follow the queen.' With that, she had urged the horse to a defiant gallop.

The sound of cheering had echoed in Lachie's ears as country folk recognized Mary and rushed out to greet her. There may be celebration today but there will be retribution to follow, he'd thought apprehensively. Lachie's head had advised him to go home, but his heart had refused to let his lady-love ride into danger. He'd urged Kelpie after her at the gallop.

By dawn next morning Niddry tenants had awakened to news of Mary's arrival at the castle. The queen rose early and rushed out to greet local folk gathered at the gates to welcome her. In her delighted haste Mary did not wait for her ladies to dress her red-gold hair and it hung down her back and cloaked her shoulders like any carefree young maid of a lower degree. She met her loyal subjects with tears and opened her arms as if to embrace them on this, her first morning of freedom. The women wept at sight of their bonny young queen and the men flung bonnets in the air and cheered her till they grew hoarse.

At Lochleven Castle Sir William Douglas had recovered his wits by daybreak and set his men to work repairing the boats. Soon the loch swarmed with activity and the island was in uproar. The laird ordered the garrison to stand by in case of attack from the queen's followers and set off for the mainland with a select band of musketeers.

When the laird and his men arrived at Goudiebank, Wil and Jamie Gilmore were in the stable counting the cost of yesterday's endeavours. Lachie had gone storming off yesterday in pursuit of Lady Annabel and had not returned and spirits were low when Sir William strode into the empty stable, Drysdale at his heels. The soldier had Francis by the scruff of the neck and tossed the boy down at Wil's feet. 'I believe this hare-brained brat is yours.'

The family had spent a sleepless night worrying over the lad's fate. Wil felt faint with relief as Francis scuttled to safety behind him.

Sir William glared furiously around the vacant stalls. 'So my brother's treachery reached further than I thought! I'd trusted Gilmores at least to stay leal tae their lord! Aye well, what's ill done is done – but will not be forgot!' He scowled. 'It's my misfortune that the Regent has gone tae Glasgow – whether to escape Edinburgh plague or confer wi' allies I know not, but he'll hear the truth o' this escape only frae me. The queen has found the weak link that broke her chains and used her winsome ways to turn my young brother's head. But I swear that in ten long months under my roof I found no vice in her.'

Glancing round the stable in disgust he spied Muckle Meg. 'My men will make do wi' your farm garrons and packhorses for the journey, Gilmore. I'll tak' the mare.'

Wil's heart missed its beat. Dear Muckle Meg had been part of their lives for years. He had raised her from a filly and loved the horse dearly but he dare not deny the laird. Broken-hearted, Wil saddled Muckle Meg for the last time.

'By the by,' Sir William said offhandedly, 'I ordered my soldiers tae forage in your kitchen for provisions.'

Wil and Jamie stared in consternation. 'But, sir – our womenfolk are left alone and unprotected!'

The laird shrugged and mounted the mare. 'Then your womenfolk will just have tae suffer gladly.' He gathered the reins and glowered at the vacant stalls. 'Now Gilmores ken how dreich it feels tae face an empty stable!'

Marjorie Gilmore had opted to come downstairs. No more lying idly abed, she'd told Dorcas firmly. Her place was wi' her man facing whatever misfortune befell the family now. She sat by the fire nursing the baby when the door crashed open and the soldiers burst in. Marjorie covered her breast and screamed. Dorcas and Christina rushed to her aid.

'How dare ye break in without leave?' Christina cried.

'The laird gave us leave. Farm provisions are his for the taking.' They brushed her aside and began to raid food stores already depleted by a severe winter. Marjorie's bannocks and prized cheese went into their packs followed by smoked hams, dried fish, salted beef and precious stores of salt and honey. The thirsty men slurped bowls of goat's milk and made merry on elderberry wine, tipsily emptying what they could not drink on to a mess of broken bannocks trampled to mush on the floor.

Soon the kitchen resembled a midden and the shelves were bare. In a final spiteful act a soldier lifted his boot and tipped the stew pot swinging on the swee into the fire. A hiss of steam and the acrid stench of burning meat filled the room as sizzling gravy dowsed the flames. The loss of the family's dinner was the final straw that tumbled the haystack. Christina yelled indignantly. 'That was a wanton act!'

The man laughed and reached for her. 'I'll seal a wanton act wi' a wanton kiss, lassie!'

Dorcas snatched a poker from the hearth and stood between them. 'We dinna grudge the laird produce from his own fields but no man claims unwelcome kisses in this house!'

Sobered, the soldier eyed the poker and glowered sullenly. 'I ken who you are, woman! You're the Falkland lady's maid that sewed for the queen at the castle. Now you're allied wi' the ruined Gilmores and heaven help ye!'

At that moment they heard the garrons and packhorses arrive in the yard. The men left the ravaged kitchen and set about loading their plunder.

Sir William's troop of musketeers mounted the last of Wil Gilmore's garrons and departed. The laird rode lugubriously at the head of the column. He did not relish his task of acquainting the Regent Moray with details of the queen's escape. It would take all his store of courage to face that harsh man's fury.

Jamie arrived at the farmhouse carrying Francis piggyback. The boy was unharmed but utterly exhausted after a terrifying night of interrogation in the castle guardroom. Marjorie's relief at having her laddie home safe and sound was so overwhelming she failed to administer the skelped backside the rascal richly deserved. He was sent to bed to recover and contemplate his narrow escape.

Jamie and Dorcas set about cleaning the kitchen and salvaging whatever was edible. Christina found her brother in remarkably good spirits considering the horrid mess.

'Och, there's plenty trout i' the burn. We'll no' starve,' he said merrily.

Dorcas declared her intention to bide till Lachie and Lady Annabel returned and Jamie's heart soared. He and Dorcas worked shoulder to shoulder and there was laughter in Marjorie's disordered kitchen that made light of chaos. Christina shared a secret smile with her mother and left them together.

She made her way to the stables. What she found there almost broke her heart.

Wil Gilmore stood dry-eyed in Muckle Meg's empty stall. The stable was deathly quiet, not even a mouse stirred the straw. Christina hardly dared intrude upon his sorrow, but she put her arm around his shoulders.

'She was not the fastest, Christina,' he said huskily in French, 'but she was the bravest and most faithful and I loved her. I pray the laird treats her well.' He roused himself with an effort. 'But I think only of myself, my dear. You lost your Lochinvar and all hope of a good dowry. Do you regret it?'

'Of course I do. But I could never marry Hugh Ross.'

Her father sighed. '*Mais oui.* The laird will not easily forgive what Hugh has done.'

'I pity Hugh, Papa, but I do not love him. The Englishman I walked with on that cold Twelfth Night is the only man for me,' she admitted.

Wil was astounded. 'That scoundrel! Are you mad?'

'Papa, please listen!' she begged. 'John Haxton is a good and honourable gentleman. We were trapped in a web of deceit woven by Mistress Phemie Sturrock.'

He scowled. '*Vraiment,* that Falkland woman is a famous busy-body! What mischief has she done now?'

'Well-meaning mischief with far-reaching affects, Papa!'

Standing in the silent stable Christina told her father of the strange twists and turns of her own unique love story. He listened in silence but remained doubtful.

He frowned grudgingly. 'I have a better opinion of your Englishman now, Christina, but I do not believe he came to Falkland to hunt wolves.'

She looked him boldly in the eye. 'I dinna care whether John is an English spy or not, Papa. We love one another and he is coming soon to ask for my hand in marriage.'

'And will you marry him gladly if I give my blessing?'

The dream suddenly dimmed and she hesitated. 'John Haxton is a gentleman of high estate, Papa. I can hardly marry him lacking a dowry. His parents will despise the match, the Gilmores will be shamed and I could not stand for that.'

Wil shook his head sadly. 'Who would think one reckless gamble at Falkirk Tryst could end in such disaster?'

Christina kissed him. 'Dinna blame yourself, dear Papa, the family's future is uncertain anyway now the queen has escaped. That may weigh heavily against me with the Englishman. He may not come to claim me but I am resigned to that.' She smiled. 'A spinster daughter can still find contentment, Papa, caring for parents she loves.'

Jamie and Dorcas fetched water from the burn to mop the kitchen flagstones. She knelt to wash hands and face in the stream while Jamie watched.

'How bonny you are!'

She laughed. 'I'll no' be won by flattery, Jamie Gilmore!'

'How can I win ye, Dorcas? Tell me!' he demanded seriously.

She rose and looked at him sadly. 'If I tell you I was a newborn foundling abandoned at a convent door, will ye still want me? Who's to know what I am and where I came frae?'

'I can tell ye where. An angel dropped ye by accident frae the heavenly cherubim, just by the convent door.'

'Och, Jamie, be sensible!' she spluttered, laughing. 'Mind you, my arrival at St Triduana's does seem heaven-sent. The good sisters of St Anthony raised me, taught me to read and write and gave me work in the hospice. We tended the monastery gardens, grew medicinal herbs and cared for the sick and blind that visited the saint's shrine.'

'I kent you were an angel! That explains your marvellous skill, my love,' Jamie said.

She shivered. 'Aye, but there's a more sinister tale to tell! I was thirteen and preparing to take novice vows when Knox's Reformers attacked the convent. They smashed sacred windows, defaced holy statues, burned prayer books and looted and reduced the chapel to ruins. The brave sisters fought and died bravely to stop the desecration, but to my shame I ran away.'

Overcome, Dorcas buried her face in her hands. Jamie held her in his arms.

'Sweetheart, you were just a frightened wee lassie; there was no shame in running.'

A little comforted, she wiped her eyes. 'Aye well, Jamie, maybe so. At any rate I fled till I reached the outskirts of Leith. Next day, Lady Annabel's kind mother found me lying exhausted and took me in and hid me from enemies that searched for me. She was my benefactress and friend thereafter and before she died so young, I promised her faithfully that I would care for little Annabel who was barely three years old.'

'An onerous task!' he remarked.

'Which I have failed! Annabel has gone heaven knows where!'

'Dinna fret, my darling! Lachie will find her.'

Dorcas sighed. 'Aye. I believe my little lady has found a stronger hand than mine to guide her. She doesna need me now.'

'But *I* need ye, Dorcas!' he said softly. 'Why won't ye marry me?'

'Dear lad, the Reformers knew me as Sister Martha but for my safety Lady Erskine named me Dorcas. It is the only name I've known for many years but if we went to the Session Clerk for signing o' the banns questions will be asked. The Kirk Session has a long memory, Jamie. How dare I marry? They will never forget the sisters that guarded St Triduana's holy shrine so valiantly.'

'We'll find a way around this, my sweetheart,' he said reassuringly. 'After all, the parson does not deny the sacrament to illiterate folk who sign only wi' a cross. Then the Gilmore name will be yours for a lifetime when you marry me.'

Dorcas was not given to tears but she was tearful now. 'Oh, my dear lad, how I long to spend a lifetime loving you!'

'Then so ye shall!'

Jamie gave a triumphant whoop that set dogs barking. He lifted Dorcas off her feet in a wild bear's hug and kissed her soundly.

'Mind you, Dorcas,' he said more soberly several ecstatic minutes later. 'The Gilmore name lies under dark clouds the now!'

She smiled. 'Dear heart, any farmer will tell ye that dark clouds can have a silver lining.'

Lachie and Annabel rode companionably from east coast to west coast across the narrow waist of Scotland. They travelled with a small group of loyal followers, servants and packhorses, in the wake of the queen's growing army of supporters. Mary's destination was Dumbarton Castle set on craggy volcanic rock across the river Clyde, an ideal royal haven to rally support from both north and south.

The queen's army had grown to impressive proportions by the time they approached Glasgow and her cavalcade halted at Cathcart Castle to review the situation. The soldiers were encamped in thousands upon an elevated position surrounding the loyal Hamilton stronghold that overlooked the fields and diverse dwellings comprising the single small parish of Glasgow town.

Mary had hoped to avoid confrontation before reaching Dumbarton, and it was an audacious move on her advisers' part to venture so close to the Regent's Glasgow base. However, Dumbarton was not far and optimism remained high when sunrise next morning revealed a much smaller enemy force camped in waiting upon a hillside across the valley.

The way ahead to the coast past Langside village was effectively blocked but the queen's commanders were not unduly perturbed. By all accounts Mary's troops vastly outnumbered the Regent's smaller force. Lachie and Annabel joined a group of onlookers gathered on the castle knowe to view the menacing situation.

'Will ye fight if it comes to the bit, Lachie?' Annabel wondered anxiously.

'No,' he said.

Contrary as ever, she was immediately up in arms though secretly relieved. 'You wouldna fight for Mary? I never thought ye a coward, Lachie Gilmore!'

'I'm no' daft, dear lady. On the battlefield a man on a showy horse is a target for every pikestaff and musket. The queen has her lords and bonny George to fend for her. I will fight tae the death only for you.'

That silenced her for several thoughtful minutes.

'Lachie,' she ventured tentatively. 'When this is over and the queen restored to the throne, would ye consider working in Leith for my pa? He has no son and lacks a good right-hand man.'

The suggestion appealed to Lachie but he was sweer to give an answer. The future was too unclear at present for life-changing decisions. As if to confirm his fears, horns suddenly blared a call to arms and Annabel clutched his arm.

'Michty, the battle's begun!'

'So it has,' he said grimly.

This confrontation would not be a sight for gentle eyes but before he could advise a return to the castle an excited host of cooks and chambermaids had spilled from the kitchens on to the knowe, jostling for position to view the fight. Annabel spied the queen on horseback surveying the scene with her courtiers around her and resisted all Lachie's efforts to persuade her to leave.

'If Mary sees fit tae bide, then so will I!' she declared stubbornly and Lachie was forced to admit defeat. He turned his attention to events in the valley below.

Mary's large army obviously held the advantage on higher ground. The Earl of Argyll had been placed in command of tactics since his own northern Gaelic-speaking Highlanders had very few words of Lowland Scots, cavalry kept tight rein upon restive horses and a massed army of Hamiltons and Highlanders waited behind them, itching to settle old scores still festering with the Regent Moray.

Pale morning sunlight glinted upon drawn swords, battleaxes, pikes, muskets and burnished armour. Clan standards fluttered in the breeze and there was some impatient rattling of broadswords on shields. Jeering insults and war cries echoed from the ranks.

Lachie was no military tactician but he could see it made sense to wait for the enemy to try a risky uphill attack against a superior force. The hope was that the Regent's men would lose nerve, turn tail and flee back to Glasgow with not a sword unsheathed.

But to Lachie's astonishment the Earl of Argyll suddenly ordered his men to advance and the queen's cavalry to start thundering downhill into the valley below. The eager Hamiltons went streaming after them to be caught in the bottleneck of Lang Loan and the restrictive confines of the village of Langside.

Of course the opposing army at once gleefully took full advantage of the tactical blunder. Storming down from Langside hill the Regent's men efficiently repulsed the cavalry and fell upon the Hamilton force trapped in the village. The Earl of Argyll's Highland hordes could have saved the day, but at that crucial moment the Earl collapsed and was borne swiftly off on a litter, leaving his clansmen confused and leaderless with various clan factions scrapping amongst themselves. In the short space of less than an hour it was evident that the queen had lost the battle.

Mary was all for riding down into the melee to rally her troops, but faithful Lord Herries caught her bridle and pulled the stallion Lochinvar up short.

'No, Your Grace, for God's sake dinna! Argyll's Highlanders speak only Gaelic and will not understand your Scots tongue. There's no shame in living to fight another day.'

Distraught, the queen stared down at appalling scenes of carnage and saw the wisdom of advice foreign to her natural fighting instinct. Tearfully, Mary swung the horse's head around and galloped back towards the castle.

There the queen was met with frantic scenes of panic. Women screamed and wept and men ran in fear for their lives. Annabel clung to Lachie. Her courage failed as the queen rode past them fleeing at the gallop with a group of loyal lords grouped around her. Lachie recognized John Maxwell, Lord Herries, one of a few powerful landowners in south-west Scotland, an area that still remained loyal to the queen. At least Mary would be assured of sanctuary, if only she could ride south-west.

'Lachie, what'll we do? Where'll we go?' Annabel wept.

He glanced west to Dumbarton, but that could only be reached across dangerous enemy territory and a crossing of the river Clyde. No time for that, he thought. Looking eastward to the road home to Fife his heart sank. The track swarmed with the Regent's victorious troops battling with beaten remnants of the queen's army. To escape north with Argyll's Highlanders was too dangerous to even contemplate. It would seem all routes were denied them, bar one. He put an arm around Annabel and hustled her towards the stables.

'We'll ride south and follow the queen,' he decided.

*   *   *

News of the disastrous defeat of the queen's army at Langside reached Goudiebank soon after the event. It was rumoured that well over a hundred of her supporters were killed and many more taken prisoner, including Lord Seton and, it was whispered, Hugh Ross the Loch Leven boatman. The Regent Moray's men were riding south in hot pursuit of Mary.

Marjorie Gilmore thought her poor heart would break when they told her. She wailed inconsolably. 'Lachie, Lachie, my bonny laddie!'

'We dinna ken Lachie was there, Ma dear,' Jamie said.

But Marjorie refused to be comforted. 'Aye, he was! He went chasing after Lady Annabel and she was awa' wi' the queen.'

Christina feared for her brother too but her distress was tempered with concern for Dorcas. They both loved Annabel dearly but Dorcas had tended the motherless lass since early childhood and Annabel meant much more to Dorcas than a lovable, mischievous charge. The lady's maid stood pale and silent and Christina gave her a quick hug.

'She'll be well cared for if Lachie's her champion, Dorcas,' she whispered and prayed the words didna lack conviction.

Uneasy days passed in the turbulent month of May. There was news of arrests and imprisonment but no word of Lachie and Annabel. No word either of Sir John Haxton as days dragged into weeks and Christina's hopes gradually faded. She smiled to hide heartbreak but wept secretly in the night, for she had loved him well. She forgave the Englishman for shying away when her involvement in Queen Mary's escape became known, but his behaviour hurt all the same. Was it her destiny always to be rejected by unwilling suitors? she wondered sadly.

Plans for Jamie and Dorcas's marriage in June were now well advanced and Maggie the washer-lassie avoided Goudiebank and the Gilmores like the plague, having been spurned and insulted to her way of thinking. The men worked every daylight hour to convert the old stone barn and steading attached to the farmhouse into a dwelling fit for the happy couple and the sound of hammering and sawing at least brought some promise of happier times. But the Gilmores still waited with growing apprehension for Sir William Douglas's return. The laird's stables remained empty and his resentment no doubt still smouldered and grew. Wil Gilmore put a cheerful face upon the future but secretly feared the worst.

★   ★   ★

Sir William arrived at their door on foot and alone a few days later. The weather was dull and showery and he shook rainy droplets off his cape. The family assembled hurriedly and congregated anxiously in the kitchen. Marjorie seated their lord and master ceremonially in Wil's carved armchair. She could see that the laird looked thrawn and weary so she hastily filled a goblet with wine saved from his men's looting and pushed it nervously towards him on the trestle.

They waited breathlessly while he took a restoring sip and wiped his mouth before beginning judgement.

'By now ye'll be well acquaint wi' news of the queen's defeat so I'll not labour the point. Old scores betwixt Douglases and Hamiltons and many treacherous clan feuds were settled at Langside.' His expression darkened. 'As for me, I was put to shame and ridiculed for Mary's escape and my young brother condemned and outlawed. The queen lived under my roof for many months and I had opportunity to observe her gentle wiles and canna bring mysel' to blame George for devotion – but enough o' that!'

The laird took another brisk sip of wine and eyed the family dourly. 'The Regent Moray has ordered cruel retribution for those that engineered this escape, so what's to be done wi' the Gilmores?' he demanded.

Nobody spoke. There was heavy silence in the kitchen broken only by burning logs settling to dying ashes in the grate.

Fifteen

Full circle in the month of June 1568

Francis Gilmore sat cross-legged on the rag rug by the hearth to hear the laird's verdict. His father was sure they'd lose the farm and the family looked scared out of their wits but the boy felt only a growing sense of injustice. Gilmores had farmed this land for centuries, aye, maybe scratching a living from the soil long before ever a castle rose upon the island. Sir William Douglas had no right to order Gilmores off their ancestral land, no matter what punishment the cruel Regent had in mind! Francis glowered at the laird. 'Sir, ye promised!'

His family stared in horror.

Sir William scowled. 'What in heaven's name did I promise, boy?'

'You promised I'd be comptroller o' your household when I'm grown because I'm skilled wi' accounts – and my Ma swears you're a man o' your word.'

Marjorie suppressed a groan. It was true that in sinful pride she'd encouraged the clever laddie's dream, but Sir William looked as if he'd searched for a mouse in a meal poke and found an adder. They were for it now!

Nobody moved a muscle. Petrified, the family hardly dared breathe but to their astonishment the laird laughed.

'Mind you listen tae your ma, my lad, she's a wise woman! Never fear, there will be a special place kept for ye in my household.'

'Thank ye kindly, sir.'

Francis subsided into satisfied silence.

Sir William took a final draught of wine and wiped his lips. 'As for you Wil Gilmore, I charge ye to fill my stable wi' fine horses at your ain expense. That will be you and your heirs' lasting debt for my displeasure.'

Sentence delivered, the laird rose and left, pausing for a moment in the doorway. 'By the by, Wil Gilmore, your sturdy mare is back in her stall tae start your stud.'

With that, he turned and left the stunned family.

'Muckle Meg's home? God be thanked!' Wil cried, tears in his eyes.

Marjorie ruffled her youngest son's hair fondly. 'Aye, Wil, thanks tae the Almighty's mercy and our loon's impudence we've escaped lightly.'

'Not so lightly, Ma!' sighed practical Jamie. 'A good stud stallion costs ten pounds or mair. Gilmores will struggle tae settle the debt for many years tae come.'

But nothing could quench his father's optimism now that Muckle Meg rested in the stall. Wil smiled. 'Not if a man has an eye for a bargain, *mon fils!*'

Or the thirst for a gamble! Christina thought wryly.

She was downcast anyway and in sadly pessimistic mood for there was no sign of her lost lover, no visit to seek her hand in marriage, no loving letter or affirmation of his love now that her family was so deeply and publicly implicated in Queen Mary's escape.

No word either of Lachie and Lady Annabel or a bonny black stallion that had once carried Christina's hopes and dreams and now – God willing! – carried a royal lady to some safe refuge. All – all had fled with the defeated queen and the scattered royal retinue. However, Christina kept silent. She would not dowse her father's optimism with melancholy thoughts.

After the queen's defeat at Langside, Lachie often doubted the wisdom of his decision to ride south, though he had not told Annabel so. They had ridden through unfamiliar wild terrain and rugged hills with pursuit not far behind. They dared not stop and Lachie had deemed it wise to travel at night like owls although that made finding the way more difficult. If they were fortunate they found shelter by day in a shepherd's sheiling on the breast of a brae or were offered a bowl of brose in a kindly crofter's heather-thatched hovel. Most days they went hungry and drank from the burn, sleeping fitfully outdoors wrapped in travelling cloaks in whatever hiding place they could find.

If Annabel had been inclined to weep and wail the hazardous journey would be a nightmare, but the hardy lady seemed to relish hardship. She braved moorland tracks in darkness with only stars to guide them and entered dark lonely glens threading through black border hills without a qualm. She did not share Lachie's annoyance on reaching the banks of a sizeable river to find the wooden bridge destroyed. Instead, she covered delicate ears against his curses and teased him. 'Och, dinna be so gloomy! I expect the queen passed this way and her escort felled the bridge so that none could follow.'

'Aye, and that means us!' Lachie growled.

'We'll find another way,' the lady declared confidently.

Riding downstream put extra hours on the night journey and horses and riders were weary and chilled after fording the river at daybreak. Lachie found a sunny sheltered spot on a nearby hillside to rest and eat grey bannocks crofters at Culdoach had kindly donated. Local folk had told him Lord Maxwell's castle at Terregles was not far off and it was certain the queen and her escort would bide there in that stronghold. They assured Lachie that the pursuit had slowed. The Regent's men were entering areas loyal to the queen and made slow progress, harried by loyalists. The news boosted Lachie's spirits. He planned to ride boldly for Terregles in daylight and have Annabel safe within castle walls by nightfall.

Meanwhile, she lay dozing in the sun with Lachie propped on an elbow beside her. They had breakfasted upon stale bannock washed down with water from the burn while the horses cropped spring grass nearby. It was very nearly an idyllic scene, Lachie thought dreamily. Annabel yawned, stretched and sat up. 'A soldier's life will be like this at times. Why wasn't I born a lad?'

'Heaven forbid! I like ye better as you are.'

'But if I were a soldier I would be your comrade in arms, Lachie. That's not possible wi' an honourable squire and a virtuous maiden, is it?' she teased wickedly.

'Aye – well—' He gulped.

She gave his flushed cheeks a mischievous glance and changed the subject. 'What will the queen do now, think ye?'

On safer ground, Lachie shrugged.

'She may decide to stand fast in the Borders where she has strong support or take ship to France. I believe she has relatives and revenues there to help raise an army.'

Annabel nodded. 'Either way makes sense.'

It was a bonny morning on the hillside. Leaves were fresh virgin green on sauchen trees weeping by the water and blossom was budding on the may. He was surrounded by beauty but his thoughts were bleak.

'If the queen goes to France, will ye go with her?' he asked abruptly.

'Aye, of course I will. I'll follow wherever she leads. Will you?'

Sadly, he shook his head. 'No, Annabel, not even for your sweet sake. I couldna turn my back on my country and my folk.'

Neither had words to express the heartbreak of parting and heavy silence fell between man and maid.

Presently, Lachie Gilmore sighed, assumed a cheerful smile and held out a hand to help Annabel rise from their grassy bower. 'Come, my lady, time we went upon our way.'

Christina and her mother sat companionably alone by the hearth, sewing.

Christina was working upon Dorcas's wedding gown. By tradition the bride must not wear this important dress before the wedding day. Even to don the unfinished garment for a fitting was considered unlucky, an odd superstition that resulted in many ill-fitting gowns and tearfully disappointed brides. Dorcas loved Jamie devotedly and would cheerfully wed him in sackcloth if that were so ordained, but Christina was determined her dear friend should have nothing less than perfection.

Fortunately Christina had a good eye for fit and Marjorie had bequeathed four ells of bonny material from a kist harking back to early days of her own marriage. French silk had been Wil's betrothal gift to Marjorie who modestly considered this much too grand and chilly for the season and settled for kersey wool.

The silk was a smoky blue-grey far removed from the sad grey approved by the Kirk and shimmered seductively as Christina sewed. However, she was confident the church interior would be ill lit and crowded on the wedding day and modest opulence would pass unnoticed. The minister's sight wasna all that perfect anyhow, she thought. The man peered gey close to the Good Book and often stumbled in the readings.

Marjorie sat at the other side of the hearth rocking Yvonne's cradle with a foot while altering Francis's Sunday doublet. The laddie was growing fast and as strength and muscle increased the limp was much improved. Francis would be a bonny young man to turn lassies' heads one day, she thought fondly.

That brought handsome Lachie to mind and a silent tear to her eye. As weary days passed with no news of her son and the lady Annabel the more Marjorie mourned. But she knew her son too well and was resigned to the situation. Be it good or ill Lachie would follow where love and loyalty led. All a mother could do was worry and pray.

A loud rapping at the door broke the peace and startled both mother and daughter. Christina laid the half-finished gown back in the kist and hurried to answer the imperious summons. She found a stranger on the step.

'I would speak wi' the woman Dorcas!' the elderly man demanded.

Christina found his manner rude and did not budge. 'May I ask why?'

'You may ask, lassie, but my business is wi' Dorcas,' he grunted, aggrieved. 'Tell her Sir Allan Erskine would talk wi' her urgently.'

Lady Annabel's father — and in a fair state of choler by the look o' him! Christina thought in alarm. She stood aside. 'Come in, sir. I'll call Dorcas.'

Dorcas was in the henhouse collecting eggs when Christina brought word of the visitor. The news sent Dorcas running to the farmhouse in a state of panic. Sir Allan's arrival did not augur well. She was filled with dread as she bobbed an agitated curtsey to her master in the kitchen.

Dorcas had known Sir Allan as a kindly man but today he was changed almost beyond recognition, gaunt and hollow-eyed with worry, and she trembled under his fearsome glare.

'I sent my daughter to Falkland for safety and charged ye to care for her diligently, Dorcas,' he cried harshly. 'Yet unbeknown to me you abandon my precious lass to ply your trade as howdie here in this house. Naturally enough Annabel seized her chance to venture off wi' George Douglas who is well known as Queen Mary's champion. Now Edinburgh resounds tae rumours o' the Regent's vengeance upon Her Grace's supporters. The Almighty alone kens the danger my dear lass faces since the defeat o' the queen's forces at Langside. My heart fails me to dwell on't!'

Dorcas was driven to tears. 'Lady Annabel owes the Gilmores a debt o' kindness and hospitality, sir. When word of Mistress Gilmore's difficult labour came to Falkland my lady urged me to go to Goudiebank and help with the birth. I saw no harm since I knew not what Lady Annabel had planned and I am heartfelt sorry for the unknowing part I played.'

'Sorry is easy said and the damage is ill tae mend, Dorcas!' he said dourly.

Shamed, she buried her face in her hands.

Marjorie had sat cowed and silent while the gentleman raged but with Dorcas subdued she felt obliged to speak. 'Sir, you should ken that Dorcas saved my life and the wean's, and my son Lachlan rode after Lady Annabel wi' all speed vowing to bring your daughter home safe. Lachie's a resourceful lad with high regard for the young lady. He'll keep a staunch guard upon her till the vow be kept.'

Sir Allan waved her aside impatiently. 'I've little faith i' Gilmore vows, Mistress Gilmore! A friend came to me from Fife saying that Annabel crept frae Falkland in the night to keep tryst wi' George Douglas at the Gilmore farmstead.'

Christina gasped involuntarily. 'John Haxton told ye!'

Sir Allan spun round incredulously. 'You ken the man?'

Too late, she wished she'd kept her tongue behind her teeth. 'I − I ken Sir John from working in Falkland Palace, sir,' she faltered. 'But we met on the farm track at Goudiebank when he came seeking Lady Annabel. I told him she'd gone wi' George Douglas and he rode straightway for Leith tae tell ye.'

Vivid memories stirred of their meeting on that historic day. He had called her his love and promised he'd be back to claim her hand in marriage. But he did not come and had sent her no reason why. With sinking heart she remembered his ominous warning − *keep clear of intrigues* − and how she darsent compromise the queen's escape that day to tell him that the Gilmores were already heavily involved.

Allan Erskine eyed the apprehensive lass speculatively. On the face o' it Christina Gilmore seemed an ordinary farm lassie, if bonnier than most − and then light dawned. This was the lass that had sewed for the queen with Annabel and Dorcas. But how much had she gleaned about John Haxton's mission as an English spy and his own secret activities to further Queen Mary's cause? he wondered anxiously. Dangerous knowledge indeed for all concerned!

He forced a casual smile. 'Aye of course! My English friend spent a few months o' leisure time hunting in Falkland so I asked him on the quiet tae keep an eye on Annabel's welfare. John made haste tae Leith when you told him she'd gone off wi' Bonny George. He had intended returning to Fife next morning till word o' Queen Mary's escape changed his mind. There was nae dilly-dallying then. He rode for the border wi' his great grey wolfhound bounding alongside as if the de'il himsel' was on their tail.'

Christina had heard talk of heartbreak in Fife recently but she had not realized the condition was so devastating till the man she loved callously abandoned her.

She could understand his misgivings of course. Scotland was in turmoil verging on civil war and the Gilmore family dangerously compromised as followers of Queen Mary. Who could blame John Haxton for rejecting the woman whose love came at too high a price?

But oh, the hurt was sair!

Dry-eyed, she met the older man's thoughtful stare. 'It − it was wise o' John tae leave when he did, Sir Allan. Falkland Palace is a fickle lodging now and I am down on my knees daily praying my Lady Annabel is safe.'

He sank down heavily on Wil Gilmore's carved chair. 'Michty me!' he exclaimed bitterly. 'A Gilmore lad pledges Annabel's safety and a Gilmore lass gabbles prayers for her! Tae set the cap on exasperation I hear that Dorcas is promised to another o' that ilk. Am I never tae be rid o' this pestilential brood?'

Insult to the family she loved was more than Dorcas would stand for. 'Gilmore is a worthy name in the Kingdom o' Fife and my man Jamie Gilmore more respected than most!' she protested indignantly. 'You ken *my* history as nameless foundling reared in a nunnery, Sir Allan. It could be the Kirk Session will forbid me and my beloved tae marry – but if the kirk doesna give its blessing at least I had hoped for yours!'

He sighed and put a hand to his head, which was beginning to throb. Ah, but he was tired out! Even the driving force of anger was spent.

He was not blind to his dear daughter's shortcomings. Annabel could be recklessly wily and wayward if she had a scheme in mind. Honest Dorcas's account was most likely the truth. To be sure, the evidence was here before his eyes in the sprightly older mother and healthy babe asleep in its cradle. He accepted that he had accused Dorcas unjustly and was sorry. Besides, she was more to him than household servant. She was his late beloved wife's devoted carer and confidante and a dedicated nurse and lady's maid to their motherless daughter. Surely faithful Dorcas deserved a measure of happiness?

'Aye weel, Dorcas,' he decided awkwardly. 'Should a Gilmore lassie's prayers be answered and a Gilmore lad brings my precious daughter home, perchance you and your Gilmore swain will earn a blessing.'

As predicted Queen Mary and her escort had reached comparative safety in Lord Maxwell's castle at Terregles. The queen's flight southwest from the battlefield at Langside with the enemy in close pursuit had been a nightmare none would forget. It involved ninety miles of hard riding across inhospitable terrain with few opportunities to rest and no female attendant for Mary's comfort. The castle was a welcome haven near the coast in which to consider the future.

Lachie and Annabel arrived at Terregles to find the queen already cloistered in discussion with her advisers. Lady Annabel was commandeered to swell a small group of Maxwell ladies attending Mary in the council chamber.

Lachie was excluded but invited to take supper in the great hall. The diners could hear sounds of fierce argument coming from behind closed doors and it was an uneasy meal. Afterwards, while servants cleared the table and lit candles, Lachie wandered restlessly to a windowed alcove and gazed out into the peaceful gloaming.

The coast lay not far off to the west and would be the chosen route to France, he thought. However, entrenched within stout castle walls in friendly territory the possibility of standing fast while rallying popular support was inviting. Lachie wondered anxiously which option Mary would choose.

He had no doubt Annabel would follow the queen and faced the daunting prospect of losing his lady-love. A burning desire to see Annabel safe back home in Leith was not purely selfish. Lachie feared there must be danger and hardship ahead for Queen Mary's loyal followers.

'Ahh – Lachie!'

He swung round. Engrossed in sober reflection he had not heard the door of the council chamber open. Annabel stood behind him tragically.

'Oh, Lachie!' she sobbed and burst into tears.

It was a devastating sight. He had never seen her cry. 'My lady – what's ado?'

'The queen is to leave for – England.'

'But that's madness!'

'That's what Lord Herries told her!' Annabel wept. 'He warned her not to place her trust in Elizabeth and her foxy adviser William Cecil. He told her that her own father wouldna set foot across the English border to treat wi' King Henry for fear of treachery. The lords stormed and pleaded, went down on their knees and wept at her feet, but the queen would have her own way. She commanded Lord Herries tae send a courier to her cousin Queen Elizabeth seeking sanctuary and permission to enter her country.'

Lachie groaned. 'It's weel known in the land that Scottish lords have survived for years on English pensions and the Regent Moray and William Cecil are bosom friends!'

She wiped her eyes. 'Aye, but Mary insists Elizabeth condemns the Scottish rebels. She believes kinship ties are strong and Queen Elizabeth was her only comfort and champion during long months as prisoner on Loch Leven. Mary's confident she'll be back in

Scotland by August at the head o' an English army to win her throne. Her advisers try every argument they can devise tae change her mind but the queen winna budge!'

His heart sank. 'Will you go to England?'

'Aye, of course! Her Grace had no ladies to attend her on the flight from Langside and her bonny hair was shorn by her squire for fear she'd be recognized; oh Lachie, it's so sad!'

Fresh tears trickled down her cheeks, which gave Lachie legitimate excuse to take his lady in his arms and hold her close to his heart – maybe for the first and last time.

Word spread quickly after the Queen of Scots set sail across the Solway Firth on Sunday sixteenth of May. She sailed with little ceremony attended by six ladies and an escort of fourteen loyal supporters in a small fishing craft. The news reached Goudiebank four days later and brought consternation.

'Surely Queen Mary wouldna turn to England?' Marjorie cried in disbelief.

'It seems she did, Ma,' Christina said 'The messenger rode from Dumfries bringing word to Kinross. The man said he watched the queen come down the path from Dundrennan Abbey to the Solway near by the Abbey burn. The intention was tae catch the high tide that afternoon. He says she was meanly dressed but in high spirits, embracing those left behind. He saw her climb on to a rock attended by a small escort and loup quite nimbly aboard the wee ship. Last he saw, its sails were fully set and it was making slow progress tacking against the stiff wind. The queen was committed tae the English shore by then and couldna turn back to Scotland or make for France even if she'd wanted to.'

Marjorie groaned. 'Lachie wouldna follow Queen Mary, would he?'

'Only if Annabel did,' Christina said. She knew from experience that love is a powerful force, hard to resist.

Her mother decided to take comfort from the words. 'Och, the lassie wouldna be so daft.' Marjorie nodded complacently.

Christina left her with Dorcas, whose presence had a happy knack of calming troubled minds. Too restless to join them in preparing the midday meal, Christina walked outdoors.

It would soon be the end of May and still no news of John, no letter of explanation, just endless silence more chilling than the written word.

An aimless dander across the meadow led her to the loch side where reed beds and water had been part of a happy childhood, paddling in the shallows with Hugh and her brothers.

The loch was calm today, unlike her thoughts.

'Are ye dreaming of me, Chris?'

She spun round, startled. 'Hugh!' she cried and kissed him joyfully. 'We've been so worried. Last we heard you were taken at Langside!'

'So I was! Flung into the castle dungeons wi' a motley crew o' grooms, farriers, labourers, carpenters and cooks. We were deemed too mean a breed o' humanity to warrant much food or attention.'

He bore the marks of his ordeal and had lost the healthy outdoor look.

'How did ye get away?' she asked sympathetically.

'The jailers unlocked the doors, whipped us soundly, cuffed our ears and kicked us oot into the rain. Fortunately the Regent decided tae treat us lesser mortals as misguided sinners for the kirk tae deal with.'

'Has Sir William put a price on your head?'

'Nah, his brother George Douglas shoulders all the blame for corrupting simple country folk. Canny Sir William flitted north wi' his family tae Lady Agnes's kin till the stink o' the queen's escape blows over. The Earl o' Morton comes and goes tae the island but that's nae bother. He's a hard man to please but good boatmen are scarce.'

'I'm glad for ye,' she said sincerely and reached for his hand. Once in the innocence of youth she had believed herself in love with Hugh, till she loved and lost John Haxton.

Water lapped and rippled at the loch's edge as a placid family of mallards dabbled close by in the reeds. Hugh lifted his head and looked at her steadily. 'Nothing's changed for us, Chrissie. My situation's mair precarious than before.'

His grip on her hand tightened, the palm calloused with many seasons spent tugging at the oars. She could have wept for him then. He'd had the chance of a better life and her kin had snatched it away.

He let her hand go and stepped back. Only a tussock of marshy grass lay between them but to Christina the gulf seemed wide.

'I'm sorry, Hugh. Can we still be friends?' she asked tentatively.

He looked away across the loch, eyes narrowed against the water's glare. 'Always friends, my dearie, but I had dreams of so much more . . .'

★   ★   ★

Christina occupied the days with preparations for Dorcas and Jamie's nuptials as May month ended. The gown was finished and a master-piece of modest simplicity that Christina prayed would fit the bride.

But the couple still remained on tenterhooks lest the Reformed Kirk forbade the union. Dorcas hesitated to submit a name to the Session Clerk. Would the kirk realize she was the sole survivor of the martyred nuns of St Triduana?

'Any name plucked out o' a bonnet will do, my darling, who's to ken?' Jamie argued reasonably, but . . .

'I'll no' start married life wi' a lie!' Dorcas insisted stubbornly.

It was an ongoing argument and Christina sighed as she listened once again. Her busy needle was at work on delicate embroidery at the hem of an otherwise unremarkable petticoat to be worn under the wedding gown.

Her mother eyed the adornment doubtfully. 'Michty me, Chrissie, if the minister gets a keek at all that finery he'll order the poor lassie out o' the kirk into sackcloth and ashes!'

They turned with amused laughter as the outer door swung open.

'I'm pleased to find you so cheery,' Lachie remarked truculently in the doorway.

After an absence of many dangerous weeks he would have felt more cherished to find his dear ones in a state of woe. However, an ecstatic welcome soon reassured the prodigal. Lachie was hugged, kissed and installed in a place of honour in his father's carved chair.

Marjorie wept copiously. 'My bonny laddie's home safe, God be thanked!'

There was an awkward pause. Nobody ventured the question uppermost in every mind till Christina spoke apprehensively. 'Lachie dear – where's Lady Annabel?'

They all held a breath. Dorcas feared the worst and clutched Christina's arm.

'Annabel?' Lachie said casually. 'Och, she lingered in the stable wi' Pa, airing her French.'

Christina's relief was so overwhelming she turned without a word and ran for the stable.

She found her father and Annabel leaning elbows on the stall rail. Kelpie the piebald was back in the stall, weary and muddy but otherwise none the worse. Lady Annabel was tousled and travel stained but in excellent spirits.

'Oh, my lady, ye look so fine!' Christina cried joyfully.

Annabel laughed and hugged her. 'Wi' hair like a bird's nest? Och, Chrissie!'

'We feared ye had followed the queen to England!' Christina said.

Annabel sighed. 'I went with her to the Solway and ready to board the boat, but I had forgotten that Her Grace is aye mindful of faithful servants. There was one special one that had brought her safely from Langside to the Solway shore and was closest tae her heart. She dismounted and kissed the bonny stallion Lochinvar and charged me to return him to the lass that sacrificed much to give him. I swore that I would do it, Chrissie, but my poor heart was fit tae break when I watched Queen Mary sail for England!'

'Lochinvar is here?' Christina gasped. It seemed wonderful beyond belief.

Her father smiled and pointed into the shadows. 'In the end stall covered in glaur but otherwise in fine fettle, *cherie!*'

June is a fickle month for farmers. Rain and sunshine in equal measure are needed to bring on green shoots of oats, barley, peas and wheat, but sturdy growth can be blackened in one harsh night of late frost or shrivelled in a torrid heat wave.

At Goudiebank there were lambs and calves to rear and cattle to keep out of growing crops. Rabbits were a menace but welcome for the pot.

Aye, June is a fickle month – but Jamie Gilmore whistled while he worked, Dorcas sang as she rinsed bed sheets in the rushing burn and their love brought light to the farmstead while the rest of Fife suffered sorely under the Regent Moray's displeasure.

The question of Dorcas's name was settled at last. Sir Allan Erskine gave his blessing to the union on the safe return of his daughter, granting Dorcas a dowry and title of adoptive niece of the Erskine clan. The Session Clerk declared his satisfaction and the banns were read in the kirk. A June wedding could go ahead as planned.

'It's a gey dreich affair!' Marjorie grumbled on the happy day as she donned a sad brown gown and tied a freshly starched mutch over her hair.

Baby Yvonne was swaddled in sober plaid and girning and grizzling in protest. Impatiently, Marjorie handed the bairn to Francis. 'Here, Son. You take her!'

Francis accepted unwillingly. He had avoided contact with the baby since its birth and expected it to howl the roof down.

Surprisingly, the girning stopped. He glanced cautiously at the bundle in his arms.

To his surprise a bonny wee face with pink cheeks and dark-blue eyes looked up at him and as he stared in amazement the wee mouth broadened in a gappy grin.

'Ma, she smiled at me, she kens me!' he yelled.

'Of course she kens ye, lovie, you're her brother!' Marjorie said. She hid a smile. The laddie's aversion to the baby had bothered her. Maybe what Francis saw was but a wee grimace o' colic but no matter, she thought. It had worked wonders.

The family procession set off for the kirk, swelled by the arrival from Falkland of Janet, her husband, bairns and Arthur's Aunt Bertha. Hector and Lady Annabel arrived from Leith and Dorcas rode at the head on Muckle Meg. Jamie walked by her side. His bride's grey gown shimmered in afternoon sunlight and the plaidie draped around her shoulders was dyed in God-given colours of heather, lichen and moss. Bare headed, she was a picture of modest innocence and Jamie's heart sang.

The minister found no fault despite a suspicious scrutiny. The marriage contract was agreed and signed without ceremony and the man began a long harangue on the solemn duties o' marriage wi' a face that would curdle milk, as Marjorie remarked afterwards.

Back at the farmhouse Dorcas donned a white lace cap signifying her married status and the whole family relaxed before the evening feast. Marjorie was in her element with grandchildren around her. Janet's wee lasses played chuckie stones on the floor and Wil dandled their grandson Ninian on his lap. Wee Ninian was now a bonny bouncing baby of ten months and a credit to Janet's tender care. Marjorie surveyed her family with pride and vowed to be down on her knees counting her blessings, soon as she had a moment to hersel'.

Dorcas drew Annabel aside. 'Dear lady, how will ye manage without me?'

'Famously, Dorcas!' The lady grinned mischievously. 'I've discovered I can fend for myself wi' more freedom and long-suffering Hector will be my guardian when I travel to visit the farm.'

She did not divulge an intention to lure Lachie Gilmore away from farming to be her pa's right-hand man in the port of Leith. That intriguing prospect could wait.

Age-old custom must be observed to bring good fortune to the happy couple and after the wedding feast was reduced to gnawed bones and scattered crumbs the family crowded noisily out of the kitchen with bride and groom in tow to their new dwelling next door.

At the open doorway of the converted barn, Christina broke a cake of sweet shortbread over Dorcas's head.

'Are ye sure a dunt on the heid's lucky?' the bride laughed, rubbing her brows.

'Aye, it is!' the family chorused, scrabbling for broken pieces.

Keeping to tradition, Dorcas grabbed a broom and swept the step clean to show off housewifely skills.

Jamie had had enough of tradition. He lifted his bride, broom and all, and carried her over the threshold. 'Goodnight and God bless ye, every one,' he called and kicked the door shut.

A quiet lull of many days followed. Christina rode the stallion every day. She had an agonizing decision to make and took care to avoid riding on the loch-side road to Falkland that held bitter-sweet memories.

Returning from a canter on lonely hillside tracks she found her father alone in the stable. Wil helped her dismount and ran an expert hand over Lochinvar's withers.

'He's in fine mature shape. You can expect a good dowry at Falkirk, *cherie*.'

'It seems I've no need o' a dowry now, Papa. I have a better plan. I will give you Lochinvar. He is yours to do wi' as you will.'

Wil was staggered by the enormity of the sacrifice and deeply saddened by the heartbreak that prompted it. He wiped away a tear. 'Bless your generous heart, my dear Daughter!' he said huskily.

Empty stalls were ill to fill in these hard, uncertain times.

Christina felt more content with the decision made. She would never marry now that John had gone out of her life. A future as an old maid lay ahead of her but she consoled herself with the knowledge that at least the man she loved had acted prudently to save life and reputation.

Scotland seethed with partisan unrest and there were tales of minor battles, arrests and executions. The Gilmores had escaped mishap so far but the family faced persecution should the harvest fail to satisfy the island castle's needs. Rain had worried Jamie at the start but June looked set to end in a spell of fine weather, to everyone's relief.

Dorcas shooed Christina out of the house for a breath of fresh air after a fine morning spent indoors, diligently patching men's working breeks.

So drab duty has its reward! Christina thought, her spirits lifting as she rode Lochinvar upwards along deserted hill tracks only sheep and shepherds knew. On the summit of the hill high above Goudiebank she paused to let the breeze tangle her hair and sun warm her skin. The stallion was content to stand after the long climb, ears pricked alertly and nostrils flaring.

At this height she had a fine view of surrounding countryside and the ribbon of the Edinburgh road winding far below. Shading her eyes, Christina noticed a rider far off along the road. As she watched idly she suddenly caught a breath. Could the dark shape bounding at the horseman's side possibly be a wolfhound—?

In her agitation Christina lost sight of horse and rider and rubbed her eyes. Was it a vision born of wistful daydreams? But if it should chance to be the man she loved down there, dare she hope that John Haxton came riding at last to claim her hand or had his English masters sent him north to investigate rumours of a rising for the queen in Perth?

Resentment flared so powerfully she could almost weep. For weeks on end she'd had no word from him, no message, no hope! Could she forgive such casual cruelty?

Christina wheeled Lochinvar around and began a reckless down-hill career towards the road. The path was not much more than a sheep track and the sure-footed stallion slid and slithered on loose scree that threatened to topple horse and rider.

Against all odds they reached lower ground unscathed and Christina urged the stallion forward with a wild yell, bursting on to the roadway not many yards ahead of a rider travelling at the gallop. The meeting resulted in a panic-stricken confusion of whinnying, rearing horses, struggling riders and snarling wolfhound.

When comparative calm was restored John Haxton shakily wiped a sweating brow. 'Must ye make a habit o' dicing with death, my beloved?'

'Are ye riding to Perth?' she challenged with lifted chin.

He raised his brows. 'St John's toun? I'm told it's bonny, Christina, but no. I've come to ask your father's blessing on our union; I told you I would.'

Her heart lifted like a laverock soaring into the blue, but the hurt of lonely, hopeless days and weeks was ill to mend. 'Oh, aye, you made glib promises sure enough!' she cried bitterly. 'Then sent no reason for leaving in an unco hurry. I was left without hope o' ever seeing you again, so what was I tae think? Naturally I surmised you'd changed your mind about loving me when you heard the Gilmores had conspired to free Queen Mary.'

He shook his head and sighed in weary disbelief. 'Christina Gilmore, will ye kindly stop glaring at me like a cornered wolf-cub! I swear I will love ye till the day I die, my darling, but when news of the queen's escape reached Leith I was duty bound to report to Nicholas Throckmorton in London. I risked capture by the Regent's forces as an English secret agent so dare not return to Fife lest I endanger you and my Falkland contacts.'

He looked at her in anguish. 'But I *did* write to you, my dearest love! Do ye really believe I would leave you sorrowful, without a word? When I reached Sir Nicholas's home I wrote a letter. Every word came to ye straight from the heart, the first love letter I ever wrote and a masterpiece o' passion, though I say it myself. I beseeched you to wait patiently for me even if there must perforce be weary weeks o' parting first. I swore on every oath I could summon to mind that I would be back to marry you.'

She shook her head in bewilderment. 'But no love letter came to Goudiebank for me. If it had I would hae kissed the precious document and cherished every loving word.'

The horse grew restive, snorting and sidling on the track. He calmed it with a word and groaned aloud. 'Just as I feared! There were rumours of covert searches for coded documents and summary arrests at Carlisle after Queen Mary entered England seeking sanctuary. I entrusted your letter to an official courier travelling north to Perth. I suspect the man was apprehended and the mail he carried scanned and confiscated.'

The explanation had the solemn ring of truth, Christina thought. She mourned a lost love letter that would have earned a place next to her heart but nae matter! The man she loved was here in person. She could imagine no greater joy than to have him so near, braw and gallant on a prancing charger – but even as she looked, dark thoughts clouded the joy.

A travelling cloak and doublet of fine Bristol cloth and a white cockade in the velvet cap trumpeted to all he met that here was a man o' substance.

And what was she?

Christina despaired. Homespun russet worsted proclaimed her lowly state; daughter of an impoverished farming family struggling through hard times.

'It was ill o' me tae doubt ye, Sir John. I beg pardon, sir,' she said, inclining her head.

He raised his brows. 'Why so formal of a sudden, my love? Now what ails ye, seated on your high horse?'

'The high horse is not mine, sir. The stallion was my dowry and when you did not come I lost faith and gave him away. I cannot marry lacking a dowry.'

'What?' John roared incredulously. Even the restive horses laid back their ears and the sensitive wolfhound whimpered. 'Do you think I care a snap o' the fingers for a dowry, if I have you?'

She lifted her stubborn chin. 'But I care! Folk will whisper I married above my station for gain and not for love. Even your ma and pa will wonder and I couldna bear that shame!'

He smiled, highly amused. 'Chrissie dearest, when I told my parents I have found my own true love in Scotland and will forsake life in London for a home on my father's estate with my bonny lass, my mother danced a jig o' joy around the room wi' my long-suffering father. There was no talk of a dowry when I left. She was busy sewing bed hangings for our marriage bed.'

She was on the verge of tears. The dowry was a matter of fierce pride. 'Even the meanest milkmaid brings a dish or platter to the marriage, and I have nothing. I will not step over your threshold like a beggar wi' empty hands. I love ye with all my heart, but you cannot marry a pauper.'

He sighed and shook his exasperated head. 'Chrissie, Chrissie, how do I defeat formidable pride? Have I tamed a wolf whelp only to be faced with a lioness?'

'So you are reluctant tae marry now I've shown my claws,' she said despondently.

'Not a bit o' it, sweetheart!' He laughed and reached for Lochinvar's bridle. 'We'll ride to your father and beg him to make sense o' this daft argument. I formed a high opinion o' that good man's cunning when we met once in a Kinross hostelry.'

'Oh aye? Over a tassie o' strong ale nae doubt!' yelled Christina, clinging on for dear life as the stallion lunged forward.

'Of course, what else?' John whooped, elevating the gallop into a wild stampede.

★   ★   ★

Wil Gilmore was working peaceably alone in the stable when the breathless pair on two sweating horses came clattering noisily through the archway into the stable yard. Wil strolled over and eyed the young nobleman quizzically.

'So you did come after all, *Monsieur!*'

'Aye, sir, a pack o' wild wolves would not keep me away from Christina, but negotiations with London took time.' He slid from the saddle and helped her down.

'So – what happens now?' Wil asked with interest.

Christina broke in quickly. 'Papa, Sir John kens I will not marry him. I have no asset to bring tae the union nor will I break a solemn pledge. You shall have Lochinvar to breed new stock for your empty stable, never fear.'

Wil turned to the young man. 'Are you still of a mind to marry this stubborn lass?'

He laughed. 'Sir, a selfless display of honest pride only makes me love her more!'

Wil gave a satisfied nod. '*C'est bien!* In that case I give my blessing willingly to the marriage.'

'*Mais non, Papa,* I told you! It's not possible. It will not happen!' Christina cried.

Her father turned to her with a patient smile. 'Listen to me, dear Daughter. I have news for you. Lochinvar's work is already done. Muckle Meg is in foal and our young stallion is the sire.'

'Papa, this is wonderful!' she exclaimed warmly, delighted for him. She knew how deeply the loss of his beloved horses had affected him. If all went well, this was a new start to the stud.

He laughed, dark eyes gleaming. 'Ah, Christina, what a foal I shall have come next springtime God willing – a foal wi' Meg's steady heart and Lochinvar's spirit!' He leaned forward and kissed her cheek. 'But Lochinvar is not mine, *cherie*. He was never mine to keep, always yours. Even the queen knew it, God bless her. She understood how much you had sacrificed and so she kissed his faithful head and sent him home to you. Ah, Christina, how could I keep him from ye, after that?'

'Papa – I – I don't know what to say!' she whispered brokenly.

He smiled. 'Then say nothing, my Daughter. There are certain words the man ye love waits eagerly to hear from ye, *cherie*.'

Tactfully, Wil led the horses to the far end of the stable and left the young couple together. He walked slowly, battling with conflicting emotions of sadness and joy. Perhaps he had known deep in his heart that this beloved daughter was too bright a star to shine in their humble farmstead. She would travel far away when she married the man she loved but in this good man's care her talents could flourish. That thought gladdened Wil's heart as he returned his daughter's precious stallion to its stall.

'Never mine to keep,' he sighed, and rested a gentle hand wistfully for a moment on the gleaming black hide.

The horse turned its head and looked at him, just as if somehow, it understood.

Meanwhile John Haxton was down on one bended knee regardless of soiled flagstones, holding Christina's hand. 'Again I ask ye, sweetheart, will ye marry me?'

Christina cast a canny glance towards her father, out of earshot in the shadows. This moment was too precious to share.

John waited with bated breath to hear what his dear contrary lioness would say.

She spluttered with laughter. 'Och, my beloved noble gowk, there is no need tae kneel. Lochinvar will be yours now – and so will I, my darling!'

He leapt to his feet with wisps of straw adorning his finery and grabbed her in his arms, whirling her boisterously round in an excess of delight.

'Haud still! Haud still!' Christina cried, laughing fit to choke.

And so he did, to concentrate on kissing.

Christina laid her cheek blissfully against her nobleman's breast and listened to the quickened thudding of his heart. Dreamily she recalled the parson's sermon a wee while ago. The fierce man had set a fearsome slant upon the theme that Sunday morning, thundering frae the pulpit and thumping splinters frae the woodwork threatening hellfire and damnation for neglect o' faith and duty. But the spoken words had stuck in her mind, apt for this moment of commitment.

She raised her head and smiled at the man she loved so constantly.

'I'll never leave ye or return frae following after ye, John Haxton, my jo. Whither ye go I will go, where ye lodge, there will I lodge, and your people shall be my people.'

'Amen to that!' John added fervently sealing the promise with a solemn kiss, mindful of a watchful father standing smiling in the shadow.

Epilogue

Lady Christina Haxton's busy needle paused. She lifted her head reflectively from a repair to her husband's doublet.

Exactly twenty years wed to this day!

She wondered if John had remembered the significant anniversary. He had made no mention of it when they rose at cockcrow that morning but Yorkshire farmers are notoriously taciturn wi' market in mind.

It was Knaresborough market on the morrow and her husband's mind was set on the selection of young breeding ewes for sale at market or perhaps in exchange for the valuable Ryeland ram John had his eye upon.

There was aye a scramble for Haxtonford ewes at market for Sir John Haxton's vast flocks dotting the estate's rolling uplands were among the finest in the Dales. By now Christina was well versed in the vagaries of the woollen trade, having watched her clever husband drag his father's ailing Haxtonford estate out of near bankruptcy to prosperity. It was achieved over the past twenty years by the gradual influx of lustrous curly fleeces shorn from sheep brought from Cotswold hills to flourish famously in Yorkshire dales.

Wise, clever man! she thought smiling tenderly. Earlier years spent at court or travelling the country as an English agent had not been wasted upon John Haxton. He had noted that wool was a commodity the country could not do without. It was estimated that half the wealth of England was riding on the backs o' sheep.

Seated sewing in the spacious solar above kitchens and servants' quarters in a newly built wing attached to the ancient farmhouse, Christina glanced out through mullioned window panes. Below in the yard a team composed of her husband, their two manly sons William and Nathaniel and a merry host of men and women farm workers loaded packhorses with bales of fleeces. These would soon begin the journey to warehouses situated in the busy market town over five miles away. Shrewd wool merchants from Leeds, Wakefield and Halifax, towns central to the thriving West Yorkshire cloth industry, would be waiting to cast a gimlet eye over fleeces, looking for superior quality.

Christina was confident they'd find it in Haxtonford bales. The length and strength of the staple was without peer, longer filaments strong and resilient for heavy cloaks, the shorter soft and fine for shirts. If John should be successful in his bid for the Ryeland ram that would bring further improvement to the staple. Ryeland wool was reputed to be exceptionally fine and a thread fine as silk could be drawn from it.

Golden fleece, indeed! she thought.

But there was a dark threat menacing the land at this very moment.

A four-year Spanish embargo on wool exports had very nearly bankrupted southern coastal towns already taxed to the hilt to defend England's shores but northern producers had fared better, switching to trade with Flanders and Lombardy and the estate still prospered.

Ah, but the Spanish threat! Christina thought with a chill of dread.

All over England forces were mustered to repel the Spanish attack and invasion of Britain planned by King Philip of Spain. News had already reached York that a vast armada of one hundred and thirty Spanish galleons had assembled in the channel. It was a terrifying prospect.

Catholic France and Spain were united for once, waging Holy War against Protestants with unprecedented cruelty.

Tragically, the execution on February the seventh last year of Mary Queen of Scots, who chose to die as a martyr for the Catholic faith, provided Philip with an excuse to unleash religious fury upon Queen Elizabeth and her Protestant realm. The Virgin Queen had once rejected Philip's offer of marriage in no uncertain terms and the humiliation still rankled with the vain, unstable man.

Christina shed a silent tear for poor Queen Mary. Alas, the Queen of Scots' fond dream of returning triumphant to Scotland at the head of a vengeful English army never came to pass. Instead she had endured nineteen wearisome years of loss of freedom, malicious rumour and character assassination, forever the daughter of discord and unresolved debate.

In the aftermath of the queen's execution Christina had spent sleepless nights worrying about her own folk caught up in the storm of Scottish protest at the injustice done to their queen. There was brave talk of war with England, Scots being quick to exact revenge upon those that harm one of their ain, but so far Dorcas's letters had been reassuring.

Aye well, maybe it's an ill wind that doesna blow somebody a wee bit o' good, Christina thought; it seemed the Spanish menace had concentrated minds the length and breadth of the land upon defence of the island. She sighed. The twentieth anniversary of their happy marriage seemed ill-starred by events. No wonder it had slipped John's mind.

The original ceremony with only family members present all those years ago had been quiet enough, to be sure! So quiet it had felt furtive, overshadowed by the Regent Moray's evictions of those sympathetic to Queen Mary, the destruction of property and whole-sale burning of crops. By good fortune the Gilmores and Goudiebank had been spared retribution for aiding the queen's escape. The farm's produce was vital to sustain the household on Castle Island. The devious Earl of Morton, head of the Douglas clan, had taken a notion to bide there more securely, in the absence of Sir William, still wisely skulking in the far north.

There were no wellwishers at the kirk door that day. Local folk shunned Christina Gilmore for marrying an Englishman – and a rich ane, tae boot!

Ah, but a honeymoon spent progressing cannily southwards over the borderlands to the Yorkshire Dales had been a taste o' Heaven! Nights of love spent under the stars, dangerous days avoiding roving border patrols. She had ridden beloved Lochinvar, seated in a saddle fit for a queen, warmly greeted with tears of joy and delight by Sir Edmund and Lady Margaret Haxton, John's much-loved ma and pa.

But all was not sweetness and light for Christina at first.

Knaresborough had suffered murder, pillage and destruction at the hands of marauding Scots in previous centuries and Scots were not popular. It had taken time, heartache and the steadfast love of her husband to overcome antipathy and suspicion. Gradually, hard-headed Yorkshire men and women were won over by her charms. Sir John's bonny Scottish lass could hardly be blamed for her unfortunate accident o' birth.

How quickly the first ten years of marriage had flown by! she recalled. Busy years with John working all the hours God gave to rescue an ailing estate, Christina giving birth to their growing family, two bonny lads followed by adorable twin lasses. Her eyes filled with sorrowful tears. Ten years ago a scarlatina epidemic raged through the district claiming many young lives. The two boys aged nine and seven were able to withstand the illness, but the twins were only three and lacked the stamina to survive. The loss was devastating, leaving Christina ill with grief.

It was at that sad juncture that John decided to mark the tenth year of marriage with a visit to Scotland.

They went by sea, bound for Leith with a cargo of wool bales on one of John's merchant ships. It was an inspired sail northwards along the coast that restored colour to his wife's wan cheeks and delighted his two young sons.

Lady Annabel was waiting impatiently to greet them at Leith's crowded docks.

Christina felt the years slip away as she hugged her old friend. 'Oh, my lady, it's so good tae see ye!' she cried emotionally.

Annabel laughed. 'My lady yoursel', Chrissie Haxton! It will be plain Annabel noo, I'm thinking.'

There was a carriage waiting outside in the street. Christina and Annabel walked arm in arm, John and the boys following with the baggage.

'I had expected to see Lachie on the quay,' Christina remarked. Her brother had been persuaded to leave farming for commerce some years ago and Annabel had kept her promise to make Lachie her ageing father's right-hand man. Lachie and Annabel were poor correspondents. Letters were very few and far between and Christina felt out of touch with their affairs.

Annabel hesitated. 'My dear, I'm afraid your brother's not here any more.'

'Where is he?' she demanded, startled.

'Lachie bides in Italy attending to our trade in fine silks. He married Egizia, who I gather is a pleasant home-loving woman that suits him fine. They have a growing family of wee Italian bairns.'

Christina was silent for a moment. She detected chilly under-currents. 'What happened? I aye hoped you and Lachie would marry. He worshipped the ground you trod, Annabel.'

'Aye well, Lachie did ask me to marry him and I very nearly said yes,' she sighed. 'But it transpired that if we married he would expect to take over my position as merchant trader in my father's business. He wanted me to bide at home twiddling my thumbs an' giving birth to bairns. I told him I would never leave my work at the ware-house. Why should I? I'm respected by mariners and skippers alike and drive a hard bargain wi' merchants. I can deliver a spicy piece o' my mind when it's needed. I'm the equal o' any man, Chrissie, but your brother couldna stomach the thought. He wanted me up

on a pedestal when my feet have aye been firm on the ground. So
Lachie asked my father's leave to handle the silk trade abroad and
we parted as friends. I haven't seen him since.'

'And ye havena married, either!' Christina observed, eyeing
Annabel's ringless fingers.

She shook her head. 'No, I'm married tae my work. I'm Papa's
right-hand man now he's old and feeble.' She grinned the old impish
grin Christina remembered fondly. Annabel's dark eyes gleamed. 'But
I'm no' lacking a bairn, Chris. Wi' our dear Dorcas's history in mind
I adopted a tiny newborn babe, a foundling lass abandoned at the
kirk door. So I'm proud mother o' the bonniest brightest five-year-
old lass in the toun o' Leith and I'm confident you'll agree when
ye meet sweet Natalie Erskine later.'

The family spent three happy days in Leith before boarding the
pinnace to sail across the Forth. Christina could hardly contain her
impatience as they rode the hired horses through Fife towards familiar
sights and sounds of her childhood. There was a mist upon the loch
and a few boats out, none rowed by Hugh Ross today, however.
Some years ago Dorcas wrote with wry amusement that Maggie
the washer-lassie and Hugh had married. Hugh had gained a partnership in his uncle Ebenezer's boatyard with the aid of Maggie's
dowry and was no longer a boatman. He had grown staid and portly,
Dorcas reported, while Maggie ruled the roost inside a bonny cottage
with her docile husband and a clutch o' bairns.

Christina smiled to herself. She could guess who wore the breeks
in that household.

But oh, when they reached Goudiebank, she would never forget
the joy of finding her loved ones assembled there, ten years older
and marked by hard times faced with fortitude. Yet the homely
welcome that greeted the homecoming was as warm and spirited
as ever.

Her mother, elderly now and predictably in floods o' tears, hugged
her daughter emotionally. 'Ah, Chrissie, how we've missed ye, lass!
Letters are grand wi' all your news, but that's no' quite the same as
seeing your bonny face.'

Wil Gilmore sat in his old carved chair. Apart from pure white
hair he seemed little changed, but with the eyes of love Christina
noted her father had lost much of his lively fire.

She kissed him. 'I look forward to seeing the product of Muckle
Meg and Lochinvar's union, Pa.'

'Erasmus is a fine stallion, *cherie*.' He sighed. '*Malheureusement,* the horse has inherited the slow pace o' Muckle Meg and the wilder attributes o' Lochinvar. Many the bite and kick I've endured frae the contrary beast and its progeny's no much better.'

'And ye thought to breed a wonder horse, poor Pa.' She hugged him and tried not to smile. Life, as always, proves unpredictable.

Turning to the fine-looking young man standing in the background she puzzled over the stranger for a minute before recognition dawned. 'Francis, my wee brother, how you've grown!'

He grinned. 'Thank heaven for it, Chrissie. I'm twenty-one!'

He had a sombre, clerical look, she thought. 'Are ye comptroller o' Sir William's household accounts, as the man promised?'

'No, I'm no', though Sir William has sneaked back into favour wi' the powers that be since the Regent Moray was killed. He comes back on the island now and then.'

Marjorie piped up proudly. 'Francis is to be a preacher, Christina. He's studying theology and several mair ologies besides at St Andrews. He hopes tae be ordained quite soon. He reads the lessons in the Kinross kirk, the parson being old and dottled and Francis hopes tae step into his shoes.'

Christina laughed and kissed her brother. 'So those weeks spent wi' wee Willy Douglas on the catechism did bear fruit. Mind and turn a blind ee tae Yule logs and snowball fights!'

'Aye, Chrissie, so I will – and maybe embroidered petticoats as weel.'

There too stood Dorcas and Jamie. Christina turned to them with special pleasure. Words could not express her joy to see them again, though a tearful hug and heartfelt kiss might do it.

Her brother was grey-haired now, spare and wiry, his face lined and weather-beaten with many years of hard work on fields and hillside. A man grown old before his time, his sister thought sadly. But Jamie had loyal Dorcas by his side, calm, caring and capable as ever and in time, God willing, Jamie could hand over the reins o' responsibility to the three fine sons Dorcas had borne him.

'And are ye howdie for all Kinross noo?' Christina asked Dorcas quizzically.

'Oh aye, my dear, and the cream o' Fife as weel!' she answered serenely.

How crowded with folk and memories the old farmhouse kitchen seemed that day! Yvonne, the wee sister Christina had last seen as a babe in arms was a shy wee ten-year-old lass with their father's black hair and dark, clever eyes.

Matronly sister Janet, her weaver husband and their bairns had travelled from Falkland for the reunion. Janet was noticeably hesitant on meeting John again, Christina observed. No doubt her sister found it hard to forget she and John had once shared the deadly secret of his identity as an English spy. Janet had aye been lukewarm about the match!

But wee Ninian, born weeks afore his time, was a delight. A strong, wiry wee lad who promised to be a clever engineer, his proud father told her. Already his son had seen useful improvements to be made to the working o' the loom, although Arthur did not hold out much hope o' the laddie as a first-class weaver.

Och, it was such pleasure to recall that joyful reunion ten years ago, Christina thought wistfully today, the twentieth wedding anniversary. Pleasure, tinged with sadness! Two precious members of that family group had gone. Wil Gilmore first, found lying peacefully in the stable beside his beloved horses and Marjorie, soon after her husband. The old lady penned a final receipt for rose-hip tonic in the precious journal's last page and gently closed its covers Then Marjorie laid down the quill with a sigh and closed her eyes in peaceful, eternal rest.

And now, what can be expected of this significant anniversary? Christina wondered. Very little, she thought tearfully. Her beloved man had forgotten the date. Who could blame him with so much care resting on his shoulders – but oh, the love had grown so strong with the passing of twenty years and her heart was sair.

The clatter of childish feet on the stairs roused Christina from her reverie. She turned to face the doorway with a smile. This child had done much to ease the sorrow of loss.

'Mamma!'

The little four-year-old lass arrived at full pelt and hurled herself on to her mother's lap. Bethany Haxton never walked when running would serve.

'Careful!' Christina whisked John's doublet out of danger just in time. 'Your boots are covered in glaur and heaven knows what else.'

'Prob'ly it's heaven knows what else,' said the child cheerfully. 'We came back through the cow pasture after we visited Grandpa in the graveyard.'

Slower footsteps on the stair heralded the entrance of an old lady, the Dowager Lady Haxton, leaning on a maidservant's arm. The maid gently removed the old lady's cloak and bonnet and seated her in the chair opposite Christina.

'Thank you, Bessie dear,' Christina said.

Bessie bobbed a curtsey. 'I'm right pleased to give ye a break from caring, ma'am. My Lady was good as gold. I'm no' sure if the same can be said for Miss Bethany.' She frowned at the little scamp nestled on her mother's knee.

'It was only a very small frog, Bessie,' the little girl protested.

The long-suffering woman scowled. 'Maybe so, but that beastie's place was i' the pond, not down mah neck.'

The old lady stirred. 'Is it time to go home?'

Christina sighed. Her gude-mother had slowly lost her wits after Sir Edmund died. The old dear was sweet and docile, the question an oft-repeated mantra needing no reply. John's mother required constant supervision lest in her muddled state she wandered off searching restlessly for the home that was no home now that her beloved man had gone.

The maidservant whispered to Christina. 'By your leave, I'll infuse a posset o' chamomile an' honey for the poor soul, my lady. That will soothe her.'

'Thank ye, Bessie. What would I do without ye?' Christina said.

The woman left smiling, head held high.

John Haxton took the stairs to the upper room two at a time, work-clothes stained and dusty, sweat still on his brow from heaving bales.

Christina laughed. Her husband's presence lit the room and her heart lurched. 'John, you big bairn, you're no better than Bethany, coming in at the gallop!'

He kissed his three womenfolk. 'The bales are loaded and our lads have permission to start for the town. There's a storm brewing by the look o' the sky and the strength o' the wind.' He grinned. 'Even so, our sons were remarkably eager to leave, only pausing to wash and put on their best gear. Could it be our lads have fancy set on two bonny maidens?'

'They are men enough for it,' Christine said laughingly, then added with sudden dread. 'And men enough to fight the Spaniards, John! What if the armada reaches our shores and my dear menfolk are called tae arms?'

'Sweetheart, I heard that eight fireships besmeared with pitch and resin, packed to the scuppers with brimstone and combustibles, were sent blazing amongst Spanish galleons anchored off Calais. Galleons are cumbersome brutes, I always thought, built more like castles than navigable craft, the wood quick to flare and burn. If flames do not disperse the Spaniards' ships then our navy and this looming storm will do it.'

He looked at his anxious wife tenderly. 'Don't be afraid, my love. Not today, of all days!'

'Papa!' Bethany said, sitting up alertly. 'What are you hiding behind your back? Is it a gift?'

'Not for you, wolf cub, for your dear mother, although perhaps she may let you and grandma take your share.' He produced a small wicker basket from behind his back, handing it to Christina with a flourish.

Wondering, she looked inside. 'Ripe plums!' she cried.

The years fell away. Once more she was a young lass dressed beyond her station standing in Royal Falkland's garden beneath a wondrous plum tree. She recalled that she had turned her head to smile cannily at an Englishman she regarded with wary suspicion. And from that moment she was his lass forever, although at first she did not know it. 'Oh, John, you remembered!' Christina said tearfully.

John Haxton laughed. 'Twenty years wed this day, my love. Of course I remembered. Had I time to visit York I'd have bought ye a golden jewel set with rubies, but that was before I saw the old plum tree i' the orchard laden with fruit.'

'And that brought a memory of moments more precious to us both than gold,' she said softly.

'Aye, so it did, sweetheart,' he nodded tenderly.

John met Christina's loving look. It was a marvel how sweetly in tune they were, now there was no Phemie Sturrock around to meddle, he thought.